"The many plot twists and turns will keep readers flipping through the pages at lightning speed. This novel has it all: love, laughter, murder, and hope."

- Booklist starred review

This intriguing Sliding Doors-style story makes the reader think about how a single decision can change our entire future. Both suspenseful and emotional, *The Things We Lost* will keep you turning pages right until the end.

-Kathleen Barber, bestselling author of *Truth Be Told*

In *The Things We Lost*, debut author, Maggie Giles has crafted a page-turning contemporary allegory about the domino effect of our choices and our desires. Book clubs are sure to devour this one, as Maddie Butler's "Then" and "Now" intertwine and interrupt with unexpected twists and reveals that will have readers contemplating the "What If?" in their own lives as well!

-Amy Impellizzeri, award-winning author of *Lemongrass Hope*

"THE THINGS WE LOST is an emotional story with an intriguing "what if" premise that will make readers wonder about their own path not taken..."

-Alison Hammer, author of *Little Pieces of Me*

Fans of *Gone Girl* and *Oona out of Order* will enjoy this tale of switched realities where a heroine is thrown back to her mid-twenties. *The Things We Lost* is a fast read, with clever writing and a complex plot that will have you pondering your own choices in life, and remembering to be grateful for the gift of those we love.

-Lainey Cameron, award-winning author and host of The Best of Women's Fiction podcast

I'm guilty of getting lost in "what ifs" from time to time, so this story immediately caught my attention. And Maggie Giles's debut did not disappoint. *The Things We Lost* is a thoughtful look at the choices we make and how one decision can snowball out of control. It's the perfect clear-off-the-calendar read! Maggie Giles is a delightful new voice and I'm looking forward to seeing what comes next from this talented author.

-Orly Konig, author of Carousel Beach and founder of the Women's Fiction Writers Association

MAGGIE GILES

Text copyright © 2021 by **Maggie Giles**

All rights reserved. For information regarding reproduction in total or in part, contact Rising Action Publishing Co. at risingactionpublishingco.com

Cover illustration © Ashley Santoro Designs ashleysantoro.com
Proofread by Beth Attwood

ISBNs:
USD Print ISBN 978-1-990253-44-7

BISAC: FIC044000   **FICTION** / Women

For Celeste,
without you I would not be writing

The Things We Lost

One

NOW

The hot water stings my hands as I dip them back in the sink and grab the remaining frying pan. The cut on my thumb still hasn't healed from nearly two weeks ago. If only my anxiety would allow me to stop picking at it.

My mind drifts to him while the sponge swirls back and forth against the stainless steel. It's been something I've caught myself doing of late: thinking about him. The way his hands explored the sensitive spot behind my ear, the birthmark on my thigh, the soft skin of my breasts, every part of me.

I shiver at the thought but don't allow it to escape. I imagine he's home now, watching the hockey game, tired after a long run or a strenuous workout. I picture the way his muscular arms stretch behind his head as he leans back on the couch, hoping his team will score the next goal. I'd told him to give up on the Leafs long ago, but he's a loyal fan.

At the commercial break, he'll go for a beer, and his nails will scratch at the label throughout the next period because his anxiety starts to get the best of him. It's these little quirks I remember most, which remind me of our days together populated with fits of laughter, stolen kisses, and simple longing.

His firm torso comes to mind before I can stop it. He has grown fit and confident over the years when many let their fitness goals fall to the wayside; he takes pride in the man he is and what he can offer a woman. My fingers tingle when I remember tracing his perfect muscles and how they always manage to creep carefully towards what lay below.

"Momma?"

I jump at the sound of Haley's voice, the pan falling from my hand and splashing back into the soapy water. I grip the edge of the sink and steady my breathing, embarrassed that my youngest daughter caught me daydreaming. I put the girls to bed ten minutes ago.

"Yes, Little Lamb?" I turn with a forced smile, worried the tone of my voice gave away my guilt. Loneliness isn't a good enough excuse to get distracted by him again.

Haley gazes up at me with large brown eyes; she has this awful puppy-dog stare that makes me bend to her every desire. Her lips hold a steady pout, and I know what will follow before she speaks.

"Will Daddy be home to read to us tonight?"

Guilt tightens my throat, but I push it away. "Not tonight, Little Lamb. But he promised to make it up to you tomorrow." I hate lying, but I hate seeing the disappointment even more on the girls' faces when their father misses bedtime stories—again. Tomorrow when they ask him why he missed their story time, Nathan can deal with it.

Haley beams at the prospect of a day with her daddy.

"Back to bed," I say, hopeful of avoiding any follow-up about my absent husband.

Haley looks away and kicks at the kitchen tile, her typical action when she wants to say more. I don't let her.

"Go make sure Ava is in bed too. I'll be up in a minute once I'm done with the dishes."

Haley nods and scampers back the way she came.

When I am alone again, I take an unsteady breath and reach for the fallen pan. With a final rinse, I force my eyes away from the sink and place the last pan in the drying rack, then pull the plug, listening to the suck of the drain as the bubbles start to swirl away.

Letting myself be distracted by him was a mistake. I have to let him go.

I climb the stairs towards my girls' bedroom and enter to find Haley leaning over her sister's bed. When Haley sees me, she hurries across the room, throws herself into bed, and wraps her arms around her PAW Patrol Everest plushie with her loved-off ear and torn pom-pom hat. She wears an innocent smile like she'd been waiting there the whole time.

I go to her side, give her a gentle kiss on the forehead, and pull the covers to her chin. "Sweet dreams, Little Lamb."

Haley coos a response as her eyes flutter shut. She'd always been fast to sleep, even as a baby.

My eldest daughter, Ava, sits on her single bed across the room, scanning her chapter book. It's a few years beyond her reading level, but she has always been bright. I love when she squints at the words she doesn't know.

"Time for bed, Kitten." I cross the room to sit on the edge of her bed.

"One more chapter, Momma. Puh-leeze?" Ava gazes at me with large, light green eyes. Nathan's eyes. The reminder wakes a long-dormant flutter in my chest.

My husband's eyes used to be my favourite thing. I loved the way they popped against his umber skin. I still remember the first time my gaze landed on him; he was so distinguished, so handsome, I'd been unable to look away. When was the last time we actually looked at each other? Connected as a couple? Months. Maybe years. Nowadays, we're too busy avoiding one another so we don't have to engage in conversation.

"Not tonight." I reach for the book and set it on the nightstand.

Ava huffs. I stifle my amused smile and bend to kiss her.

"Good night, girls." I move to the door and flick off the light. Haley's nightlight illuminates a small portion of the room. I pull the door partly closed.

Alone again.

My heartbeat quickens with every tiptoed step to my bedroom. I have to break things off tonight. Knots twist my stomach as I reach for my phone and select his name.

I sink onto the bed listening to the phone ring, my leg shaking. Confrontation has never been my strong point, but we both need closure.

It feels like an eternity before Jayson answers.

"Maddie, are you okay?"

His concern is a knife to my resolve, making me falter, and I consider hanging up. It's been two weeks since we last spoke, though the daydreams make it feel like it hasn't been so long.

I shake my head to clear my thoughts. This has been hard, but it's for the best. This is the only way our love story can end.

He gave me an ultimatum when I left his condo two weeks ago: him or Nathan. It's a choice I wasn't willing to face at the time, but Jayson was good to me when I needed it. I can't let him wallow in my silence; he deserves better than that—than me. "I had to call. To say sorry for the way I left things."

"Maddie, don't."

I picture him pacing the room, eyebrows curved in concentration, his forehead creases deepening by the moment.

"But you were right," I say, my tone slow and sad. "I over-reacted."

He releases a long breath. "It wasn't my place to make demands."

"It doesn't change the fact that I have to tell him the truth and face the consequences."

There's a long pause.

"Mads…"

I close my eyes at the sound of his nickname for me. Jayson wasn't someone I'd just met; he was my first real boyfriend. When we ran into each other at a bar a few months ago, all the memories of being with him when we were younger came flooding back. He had the same boyish grin now that he did years ago. Love seemed so simple in my first year of university. Would life be different if I had stayed with Jayson? Would we have two daughters and still be in love? Sometimes the loneliness made that daydream easy to believe.

I draw a slow breath. "You know I'm right. You told me yourself."

After everything that's happened–the pain of lying to Nathan about the affair and the thought of only seeing my girls part-time—it was all coming to a crashing halt, a realiza-tion that I could lose everything.

Now with the addition of the threats to expose my double life, I'm reminded why I can't walk away from my family. Not now. Not ever. I don't want to.

Had it not been for last month's writers' conference—Muse and the Marketplace—Jayson and I may have never rekindled our first-year affair. My choices were foolish.

This is the life I chose. It's time to live it, no matter the consequences.

"I'm sorry." My voice is weak with the hurt I've caused—his, mine, Nathan's.

It's several seconds before he responds. "You know you can always call if you need me."

I listen to his breathing. "I know."

"Goodbye, Maddie."

"Goodbye."

Hitting end on the call is slamming a door on another life. Letting go of that part of me makes an empty pit form in my stomach. I try not to think of the way his hand slipped into mine so innocently as we walked the streets of Toronto only a few weeks ago or how his lips felt as they trailed across my cheek and down my neck. The way his attentive gaze never left mine, never judged me. Or how his voice was filled with excitement when he answered my calls.

But I won't allow myself to cry over that life any longer. I've picked my family and must look forward. My unending loneliness doesn't compare with Ava's avid curiosity and bright mind or Haley's pure heart. I'll do anything for them, even if it means giving up my happiness. Even if it means forgetting everything Jayson and I had.

I once loved Nathan above all. He'd been my rock, a supportive husband, a loving father, and once my very best friend. He'd seen my highs and my lows and had been there through it all. We'd let the past five years of distance define us, but we could love each other again.

We have to.

I fiddle with my wedding band and the old engagement ring that needs a shine.

Together we made a mockery of our lives; maybe it's too

late for forgiveness. I steady my breathing, reach for the phone, and dial his office.

"Nathan Page." His formal greeting sounds distracted, uninterested—his typical business tone.

"Hi," I say, but my raspy throat and quiet sniffles give me away.

"Maddie?" Nathan's voice changes from business to concern. "Why are you crying?"

"It's fine. I promise. Will you be home soon?"

"I have a few more things to work on, so a half-hour, maybe. Shouldn't be long after that."

"Okay. Dinner will be ready."

"Sounds good." He hesitates. "Are you sure you're all right?"

"Of course. I'll see you soon."

"You will."

"And Nathan." I want to get it out before I lose the nerve. It's been too long since either of us has spoken these words, and while I made an unforgivable mistake, my feelings for Nathan are still there. "I love you."

There's a pause, long enough to make me doubt. Then the short laugh that used to come whenever Nathan would form his adorable half-smile sounds over the phone. "I love you too."

Relief washes over me.

I end the call before noticing Ava standing in the doorway. My voice must have been enough to get her out of bed.

"Momma, are you crying?"

I smile through the tears and wipe them away with the back of my hand. "No, Kitten. I'm okay." I hop to my feet and motion Ava away. "Just making sure Daddy was coming home soon. You should be sleeping."

"Sorry, Momma."

I follow Ava back to their room and tuck her into bed again. "Sweet dreams."

"Night, night." Ava yawns and clutches the blankets close.

I glance over at Haley. That girl sleeps so soundly.

I go to the kitchen to plate our dinner. This evening it will be just Nathan and me sharing a meal for the first time in years. And, hopefully, taking steps to rekindle our lost love.

With the food keeping warm in the oven, I sit on the couch with a glass of wine then check my watch. It's going to be a late dinner. I grab the book I'd discarded earlier in the day and pick up where I left off, a light feeling in my chest.

As the pages turn, the clock slowly ticks by. It's been an hour and no word from Nathan. I try calling his office, but the call goes straight to voicemail. The same happens when I call his cell phone. I'll wait another ten minutes. If he'd left the office, he wouldn't be long.

I complete another chapter and give in to my grumbling stomach. I fetch my dinner and take it to the set dining room table. I light the candles like I'd planned and proceed to eat alone. He's busy. I need to respect his time. Sadness bubbles up inside me, reminding me that Nathan doesn't respect *my* time.

When the second hour passes, I try calling his cell again; the slow ringing is torturous as it beeps through to voicemail. I reach for the bottle of wine I opened after finishing the first one nearly half an hour ago.

Giving up on the evening I hoped for, I stand on wobbly legs, moving slowly as my head spins. I blow out the candles, carry my plate to the kitchen, and drop it in the sink. I reach for the dinner I'd left for him, though it has long cooled, and throw it in the sink next to mine. Nathan will see my disappointment in the spoiled food when he finally makes it home.

I try his cell once more, but when his voicemail picks up again, I take the bottle of wine upstairs. I strip and crawl into bed, my body shaking from alcohol and tears. The loneliness is eating me from the inside out. Where could he be? Does he honestly not care to come home when he knows I'm waiting? Nathan has been checked out of our marriage for years, longer than I have. First came the girls, then work. I barely make it into the number three slot. I wish I could remember the last time I'd felt his affection, his love. His absence makes me question everything.

When did my life go wrong? It's more than a writers' conference in Boston and my terrible mistake. My life hasn't been right for ages.

I clutch tightly to the covers and wonder how life could have been different if I had never met Nathan.

Two

THEN

The screams of the excited crowds in Fenway Park could be heard from the streets. Another win for the Red Sox. Despite the excitement in the air, I sat alone in the hotel bar after the formal dinner at the writer's conference had concluded. My feet throbbed from a long day of standing, followed by my keynote speech, and my nerves were only now beginning to settle.

I massaged my cramping hand. The ache from signing hundreds of novels for fans radiated from my palm through my fingers. Their praise was difficult to accept, given I felt like a fake and undeserving of their love. How could they love me when my husband couldn't?

All of the other attendees I knew had retired to their rooms, and although the bar was packed, I felt alone, something that was all too common lately. Even the wine didn't help. I'd barely drank in the years I'd been with Nathan, a huge change from my party days. It used to be a running joke that Nathan "tamed" me. I'd never found it very funny.

I reached for my phone, silent since the last message from Nathan several hours ago, and considered calling home to check-in. It would be nice to hear my daughters' voices and wish them good night. Would it be worth the awkward conversation with Nathan though to speak to them? His distracted mind had become a lonely partner. I couldn't remember the last time he asked about my day, let alone pretended to care about it. Sometimes I tried to decipher where it went wrong and when our bed went cold. I often thought back to Haley's birth. My postpartum depression lasted for the year that followed. Nathan had been supportive for some time, but soon my depression weighed on him, as all my feelings seemed to now. My mom had come to stay with us when Nathan could no longer be away from work, and since then, our distance defined us. Five years later, our love seemed like a myth.

I forced the thoughts from my mind and flipped through photos on my phone, admiring my beautiful girls, hoping that seeing their faces would be enough of a fix. I'd be back home with them in another two days. My photos were clumsy and far from professional, featuring quirky angles and sometimes blurry shots. Still, Ava and Haley's vibrant smiles broke through every imperfection, making every one of my photos a treasure. The sight of them made my chest tighten with loneliness and an urge to hug the two people who loved me the most.

Usually, pictures of my daughters cheered me up, but tonight, they reminded me how far I was from them. I scrolled through my contact list, stopping at Dee's name. She's the person I'd normally reach out to—my most consistent rock, the one person who knew me better than I knew myself most days. But I couldn't. Not about this. Not with anything negative about perfect Nathan. I couldn't tell anyone about that. Everybody loved Nathan. Dee would never believe he was anything but a loving husband.

Dee could never understand that home had become an unwelcome place, busy with young children and a distracted lawyer. Because that's all Nathan was these days, a lawyer, not a husband. At least he was the doting dad he always was: he still took the girls on weekend outings for ice cream or to see the Blue Jays play from the company box.

Most times that only hurt more. He held affection, just not for me. I couldn't remember the last time we'd had sex or the last time I'd gone to bed happy.

Even though my loneliness was unbearable, I had to credit Nathan for once being my biggest supporter. He'd been there through the struggles of my career, the countless rejections, and the times I felt like a fraud. He had lifted me up and given me the confidence to be the author I was. Was feeling alone worth forgetting about all the good that came before, even if it seemed like a distant memory now?

"Maddie?"

The familiar voice made me jump in my seat, causing my phone to slip from my hold and crash to the floor.

Jayson?

He chuckled as he reached down and picked it up. "Sorry, I didn't mean to scare you."

"You d-didn't," I stammered. I looked up at the man who had been my first boyfriend.

He passed me the phone, and my lips tingled as I thought of our first kiss, stolen in secret behind the ball diamond. The way his fingers trailed down my arms and grasped my hips, drawing me against him.

I had to glance away to shake the memory from my mind.

Jayson looked different than I remembered, though his smile was the same. The wrinkles around his eyes were more prominent, and his jet-black hair was peppered with gray. He would be forty-two now; nearly fifteen years had passed since we last saw each other.

It had been the night of Dee's party, circus-themed and overdone. I had attended with Nathan, and on my way to the bathroom, Jayson cornered me, begged me to take him back, claiming we had a future. He was drunk and tried to kiss me. I pushed him away in frustration but was taken aback by the sadness in his eyes. He didn't speak; he only turned and left. The last thing I saw was the back of his flannel disappearing into the crowd. That was the party where everything went wrong.

"What are you doing here?" I asked, fiddling with the stem of my wineglass, avoiding eye contact. I forced the memories aside.

"Editor." He pointed at his chest. "Remember?"

"Right. I forgot you were working towards that." I should have known. It was something he developed an interest in when I was determined to write my first novel. He wanted to support me however he could. He always saw us working together in love and in life.

"Eons ago." He laughed. He motioned to the barstool next to me. "Do you mind?"

"No, it's fine." While the company was welcome, seeing him again sent a swirl of mixed emotions through my mind— attraction, regret, desire, denial. Memories of lives past and paths chosen; some were long forgotten with time, others hidden away in guilt.

I pushed away the thoughts, refusing to let them in. Of course Jayson was attending the conference, as it drew hundreds of writers, editors, and agents from around the globe.

Despite the mixed emotions I was feeling, running into

him was a welcomed surprise in my loneliness. His friendly smile reminded me of cheesy movie nights and board games that spurred endless laughter. The rough way our relationship ended had been softened by time.

We met through my close friend and his sister, Arabella, in my first year of university and were together for three years. Jayson was six years my senior, but he always gave me the attention I desired. It was easy to turn visits to Arabella's house into date nights with her brother. We were planning our future, talking about marriage, kids. Then things changed. Other guys offered attention, indulgences, and limitless fun. While Jayson was worried about his career, I thought about my next party and if I could get away with skipping class because of a bad hangover. Ultimately, I ended our relationship, more interested in living my present life than thinking about our future. We were in the wrong place, wrong time.

"I hoped I would see you," Jayson said, sipping his beer. "I've been following your success. Three bestsellers."

"Thanks." I was surprised he'd kept tabs on me after all this time. Sure, I had an avid social media following and posted on a steady schedule as my publisher wanted, but I couldn't help but wonder if he'd sought me out or if my book had simply fallen across his desk. With a sheepish smile, I said, "I wish I could say the same."

Jayson chuckled. "Authors are a bit easier to track than editors. Especially ones like you."

"I guess." I looked back to my glass of wine, nearly empty, and realized the thought of finding him hadn't crossed my mind.

"So, if you're married, did you not take his last name?" He said it playfully, but his eyes fixated on the ring wrapped around my finger, and disappointment edged his voice.

"I did take his name," I said, fiddling with the band. I'd always wanted to share the same last name as my children. "But I have two daughters, and I thought being Madison Butler to the public would help shelter our lives a bit." I'd always told myself publishing under my maiden name had been for separation's sake; business from personal. Maybe that part of me wanted something separate from Nathan, from being Mrs. Page.

"Nice, two girls. Like you always wanted." Jayson looked down at the beer in his hand. "It's crazy how things work out. I always thought you and I would be together one day. It made sense to me."

"Life is crazy," I agreed.

Our conversation lulled, and I gently nudged my empty glass away. "I think it's time I head to bed. I'll be expected to be in top form at the workshop in the morning." I'd had enough wine and knew better than to stay out too late with a busy day ahead.

Jayson laughed and agreed. "I'll get this."

He tossed a bill down on the counter and ushered me out of the bar. Together we walked to the elevator and climbed in. I was on the fifth floor, but the ride up felt like it took ages. The confines of the walls made me flush around the neck. All I could smell was Jayson's potent woody cologne and, along with the wine, it was making my head spin.

When the doors slid open, I released the breath I had been holding with relief. I called over my shoulder, "Have a good night!"

Except Jayson followed, letting the elevator doors close behind him. My stomach flip-flopped. What was he thinking? Had I been more flirtatious than I intended?

"Let me walk you to your room." He waved down the

hallway. "What kind of gentleman would I be if I abandoned you now?"

"It's okay. It's not very far."

Jayson didn't listen, only stepping ahead and leading the way as if he knew where he was going. This had to stop, as I feared I'd extend our visit and invite him in.

"I'm this one," I said as he passed by my hotel room. "Thanks for walking me, and it was great to see you."

He opened his arms and I hesitated before leaning in to hug him. Immediately I relaxed in his hold. The familiarity of his limbs wrapping around me made the memories of our love come crashing back. It's like the time he held me after my grandfather passed and doted on me for the weeks that followed. Or when I'd been stuck in the hospital to get my appendix removed. He was there waiting at the start of visiting hours, and the nurses had to usher him out when it was time to go.

The hug was different too. He was fitter now, less soft around the belly. Although his body gave my mind an excuse to wander, I almost missed the plushness of his supple stomach; once, a hug from Jayson was the most calming and comforting thing.

"I'll probably see you around," Jayson said after we separated. His face was flushed. I could still feel the warmth from his embrace. The distance between us was short, making it hard to focus beyond my memories, his athletic torso, and his intoxicating scent.

He fished out his phone from his pocket, fumbling as he did.

"But why don't you give me your number? We can have a drink again. Also, I'd love to introduce you to a few of my coworkers. Most don't believe me when I say I used to date Madison Butler."

I hesitated before taking his phone. Was giving my new phone number to an old boyfriend a crime? Would Nathan care? I pushed the questions away. It's innocent—a request for a drink, a networking opportunity.

"Sure, why not."

Our fingers brushed as I grasped his phone. The touch was electric, sending a shiver through me and almost making me drop the device. Drawing a sharp breath, I punched in my number and handed it back to him, careful to avoid touching him again.

"Don't be a stranger." I winced the second the words left my lips. For someone who gets paid to write, I was a walking cliché.

"I won't be." Jayson grinned as he pushed the phone back into his pocket. Then he turned to head towards the elevator. He hesitated before getting too far and looked back at me. "I'm still in Toronto, you know. Not Lawrence Park anymore, but downtown. We could meet up back home if you feel up to it."

I couldn't help the slow grin that crossed my face. It was the first genuine one I'd had on this entire trip and, apart from my daughters, the first feeling of affection I'd had in months.

It would be good to catch up with an old friend. There was nothing wrong with seeing Jayson again. Everyone needed friends; Dee had been trying to pin me down for a girls' night for how long—weeks? But I never had time; most days, I woke up earlier than the sun to squeeze in some writing time before waking up the girls and getting them ready for school, and by the time I went through the whole thing in reverse at the end of the day I was worn out and ready for bed.

Nathan had urged me to make more time for myself.

"You've been looking pretty run-down, babe." The thought of those words made my blood boil.

Well, yeah. What did he expect?

It would be nice if I had a little help at home during the week. It would be nice if Nathan were home more than the seven hours at night when he flopped into bed next to me.

Pushing the irritation towards my husband aside, I nodded at Jayson. "I'd like that."

"Great. Good night, Maddie." Jayson headed back towards the elevator, and I watched him until he turned the corner out of sight, the steady smile still on my face.

Three

NOW

Darkness surrounds me.

Though I lie still, my heart raps an anxious beat in my chest as if trying to escape its confines. *Where am I?*

This bed feels different, softer. The covers are heavy and too warm. Unfamiliar snores break the silence.

Something is wrong.

Keeping my breathing quiet, I glance to my side, terrified to find out who lies next to me, but only the outline of a body is visible in the darkness.

Hands shaking, I lift the covers and slide out of bed, careful not to disturb whoever is beside me. After ten years of marriage, I know that breathing does not belong to Nathan. Sweat prickles on my brow. I'm hot—too hot. I know I went to bed alone. *What happened last night?*

The digital clock across the room reads 6:30 a.m. in neon red. The clock is the only familiar thing in this unfamiliar room. Feeling my way through the darkness of my bedroom, on a route I've taken thousands of times blindly, I find the bathroom. I'm in my own home with another person in my bed.

Yet, I swear Nathan crawled into bed next to me last night. There was wine, about that much I'm sure. There's a foggy memory of the bed moving and Nathan speaking. At least I thought it was him.

I place a palm against my warm forehead. How much did I drink?

I reach for the bathroom light, illuminating the small room. My first glance makes me pause. This is definitely the master bathroom in my North Toronto house, but the wall-paper is different, and the crack in the sink where I dropped the hairdryer last year has somehow disappeared. The window shutters are drawn and white—identical to the shutters here when I first owned the place, not the expensive wooden ones I recently replaced them with. I rub my eyes, attempting to clear my vision. Could this be some wine-induced dream?

As my shaking hands pull away, I can't believe what I'm seeing. My middle finger is no longer crooked from when I broke it three years ago. My wedding ring has vanished, and the skin on my hands is smooth and soft; all former wrinkles are gone. My nails are coated with chipped black polish, a colour I haven't worn in years. I lift my shirt to examine my abdomen, surveying my body. My stomach is tight, free of the flesh that clung after two pregnancies. My hands travel further, investigating my buttocks and breasts; the latter are as firm and perky as they were before breastfeeding. This is wrong. Everything feels like I'm in another person's body. This isn't the body I've come to know over the past few years.

Rushing forward, I risk a glance in the mirror. My breath catches. Who is that staring back at me? I mean, sure, it's me.

My brown hair and dark eyes are the same, but I look ten years younger.

I try to swallow the tightness in my throat and bring a shaking hand to touch my soft skin. My heart slams against my rib cage. There's no way to process what I'm seeing. There are no wrinkles around my eyes and my lips are smooth. The scar on my forehead I got from a car accident six years ago is gone. I squeeze my eyes shut tight, hopeful that when I open them, I'll realize I'm hallucinating.

When I'm met with the same sight, I turn and throw the bathroom door open. The light casts a yellow glow across the bedroom, revealing my sleeping bed partner. I immediately recognize the curve of his jaw and the messy black hair. My heart thuds faster. This is not my husband, but Jayson. My throat constricts. Did I drunkenly call him last night and take back everything I said? Did Nathan never come home? Did he see him here and leave?

I start to shake and make for the hallway, desperate to get away from this horrible nightmare. When I see the door to my daughters' room cracked open, I move quickly and push my way through. Once inside, I stop. Nausea builds inside me. Their twin beds no longer rest side by side. The *Frozen* wallpaper is gone. Ava's tiny form does not slumber, sprawled across her mattress. There is no gentle purr of her breath. Haley is also nowhere to be found; her tanned arms are not wrapped around her Everest toy. Now, a plain double bed rests in the centre, and a generic landscape painting hangs on the wall.

I throw open the closet, hoping to see their toys and clothes to prove I'm only losing my mind. Instead, it is void of my girls' things and filled with storage boxes, which I promptly rip apart, finding only documents and old clothing.

The room is filled with silence; it's a typical, plain, spare bedroom.

I dash to the guest bathroom, kneeling over the pristine toilet and spewing the remainder of last night's dinner into the basin. I sit back for a moment, shaken by the disorienting changes. I refuse to accept it. It's impossible. My girls cannot be gone.

I descend the stairs to the main floor, desperate to find any trace of them in the house. Something to tell me this is all some cruel joke, a bad dream, a horrible prank.

This is the same house I've lived in for over thirteen years, but it doesn't seem to have seen the fights between Nathan and me or the babies growing up. My wedding photos have vanished. Not a single picture of the kids occupies the walls. Once the stairwell was full of them, but now the white paint is completely undisturbed.

The kitchen is different, back to the way it was before I decided on that disastrous renovation. The vaulted ceilings are in place and the natural wood beams remain. The sitting room rug no longer bears the stain of red wine from our fourth wedding anniversary.

It's like I've somehow gone back in time.

I shake the idea from my head. That's impossible.

There are pictures of Jayson and me, either alone, with friends, or with family, on the mantel in the sitting room. They show vacations, parties, gatherings, and events I cannot remember or am unsure even occurred. It's as if someone erased all records of my previous life and replaced it with a fictional creation featuring my university boyfriend and recent lover.

"Maddie?" Jayson's voice comes from upstairs, making me freeze. Instead of causing a stir of excitement, it fills me with dread. "Maddie? Are you all right?" His footsteps sound on the upper level then descend the stairs. His tone, though raspy from sleep, is full of worry.

"I—I'm fine," I manage to say, though my shaking hands won't steady. I rub my eyes, trying to remember how I got here, but ten years of conflicting memories cloud my mind. Perhaps I am dreaming. I pinch my arm hard. The scene remains the same. My last clear memory is the thoughtless question I asked myself before sleep took me—how my life could have been different if I'd never met Nathan. It seems impossible that thought has come true. It *is* impossible. This isn't real.

"Maddie?" Jayson's warm hand touches my arm.

I jerk away from his touch, feeling trapped, confused. My chest tightens. It's hard to breathe.

"Hey." His voice is soft as he reaches out for me again.

I risk a glance at him, and I'm met with concerned brown eyes, thin lips, the familiar mole on his chiselled chin, and a steady smile. I allow him to take me in his arms and pull me towards him in a strong embrace, though the action causes my body to shake. His hand finds the back of my head and holds me against his chest, like a father protecting his child.

"What's going on?" Jayson whispers into my hair. The affection makes my skin crawl. I can't think of anything but my girls.

"Nothing." There's a threat that I might hurl again. I have nothing close to a logical explanation. "A bad dream, I guess." No, this is a nightmare. A world without my daughters. It can't be true.

Jayson pulls away. "Do you want to talk about it?" His feet shift, and his eyes dart to the clock. It's quarter past seven. He clearly hopes I don't want to. He probably has to go to work soon. Do I?

"No, it's fine." I force a smile, though my body rages with

chaos inside. I need him to go away; I need to figure out what's happening. "It's over anyway, right?"

"Right." Jayson's hand runs through his already-messy hair. "Let's go back to bed."

I shake my head. "I need a minute."

A yawn escapes his lips, encouraging him to heed his suggestion.

"Don't be too long." He gently squeezes my arm, then makes for the stairs. When he's gone, I lower myself onto the couch and run my hands over the soft upholstery, dark blue from my university days. It's aged but so comfortable. This is the first piece of furniture I bought for the house. I thought I had it refurbished years ago.

Again, I squeeze my eyes shut and try to scan my memory for an explanation. All I can remember from the previous night is tucking my girls into bed. Nathan was working late—typical—but I had made my choice. I vowed to make it right. To clear my conscience of the choices I'd made, choose my family above all else, and pray we could move on together. How did I end up here with Jayson?

My eyes fall on the computer across the room. I flick it on, tapping the desk as I impatiently wait for it to load. It's an old iMac, one I remember wanting for my twenty-fifth birthday. Nathan didn't buy it for me, splurging on a trip instead. But somehow, it's in my house. I hope I can find the answers I'm looking for.

Pictures of my daughters used to be my desktop background; now it's a photo of Jayson and me, dressed in tropical attire on a white sand beach. Some vacation I don't remember. Or do I? Images of seafood dinners with sandy beaches and sunset backdrops and dancers in skimpy sundresses pop into my head as if I actually had been there.

According to the date in the top corner of the screen, it's

three months before my twenty-sixth birthday, four and a half years after I should have met Nathan. That can't be right.

No files on the computer feel familiar. Or do they? I can't tell.

There are no photos of my daughters, a few of my family, and less of the friends I think I remember. Who are these people surrounding me? Focusing on one, I recognize the strange couple with us. A name comes to mind—Kerry—and a memory with it, a book club where we're laughing and sharing a bottle of red wine. We're good friends, but she moved out of town and I haven't seen her in ages.

I exit the photo shaking my head. How can I have a memory that I know I didn't experience? The confusion and conflicting recollections make my head spin. Could they be real or as fabricated as these photos seem? It's as if someone took my face and plastered it onto another body to mess with me. Is this an extremely elaborate joke? No other explanation makes sense.

Beside the computer is a cell phone, though a much older version than the iPhone I have. The date matches the one on the computer, yet I refuse to believe what I'm seeing. The stupid thing needs to be reprogrammed. I scroll through, finding no familiar photos and several missing phone numbers. Luckily, I know my husband's cell by heart.

As I dial his number, I hope this is some twisted punishment for my foolish actions. But the line comes up as a dead end. It's unregistered. It's not Nathan's.

I glance at the time—it's nearly eight. Nathan often worked early and returned late. It wouldn't be unusual for him to be in the office. I dial the number and extension he'd had for years. The ring through is quick, and I'm met with an unfamiliar baritone voice.

"Bruce Ross."

"Uh, I'm sorry," I sputter, thrown by the answer. "I must have dialled the wrong extension. I'm looking for Nathan Page."

"Hold on."

The joyful hold music fills my ear but rather than cheer me, the delay only makes my anxious heart beat faster as I wonder what's taking so long. It feels like an eternity before the deep voice returns.

"I'm sorry, ma'am. There is no Nathan Page in this office."

Dread sends chills down my spine.

"Ma'am?" he questions when I don't respond.

Unsure how to answer him, I disconnect the call.

At half-past eight, Jayson descends the stairs again. This time he's dressed, his hair is slicked back, and he carries a leather briefcase.

"Are you trying to work?" His eyes hold the same concern from earlier.

I suck in a sharp breath. "I'm trying to find some pictures."

"Which ones?"

"From my birthday last year," I say, thinking on my toes.

Jayson grins. "You won't find anything from that night." He moves across the room and plants a gentle kiss on my temple, one that makes me stiffen. At first, the reaction surprises me. Only a couple weeks ago I'd considered throwing my entire life away for this man. And now his touch causes that same nausea from before to boil up inside me, like my subconscious knows something is wrong. "You were so wasted you broke your camera. After that, you forbade anyone from documenting the night." He chuckles.

Another memory surfaces. The barstool was cold under my short, pink party dress. I recall grasping at a camera with a jammed lens. I'd dropped it while I was dancing.

I shake my head to clear it, my skin prickling with unease. "That's too bad."

Jayson shrugs. "I'm surprised you forgot. You were pretty upset the next morning about it." He shakes his head. "I'll see you tonight—oh, and happy anniversary. Four years since we got back together, man, I feel like it's been forever."

I laugh nervously, unsure what to say. He seems uninterested in the idea of an anniversary. Shouldn't he be excited? But I know the thought is foolish. When he touched me, I jumped away from him, and I don't know whether to believe this is real or fake. The last thing I need to worry about is if Jayson is excited about an anniversary I can't remember having.

He's gone without another word, and I watch from the window as he walks to the silver Beemer waiting in the driveway. The same car he drove when we started dating. The first place we had sex and the last, until recently, of course.

He turns and looks back at me before climbing into the front seat. He speeds off down the road. A quick decision has me on the phone again, dialling a number by heart. It rings only twice before she picks up.

"Hello?"

A wave of relief washes over me at my best friend's voice. She answered. She can tell me what's going on.

"Dee, it's Maddie."

She doesn't reply, and the feeling of dread begins to build again. I'm sensing, like everything else, something is wrong.

"Dee? Are you still there?"

"Maddie, why are you calling me?" Her tone is cold, hollow. My throat tightens. Dee's never been so curt with me.

"Something weird happened this morning. I'm freaking out and need to talk to someone."

"Then why are you calling me?" This time her voice

changes, anger evident in her short, breathy words. "You made it pretty clear last month you weren't interested in talking."

"What? I never would've—"

"Maddie, you hung up on me!"

"But I—"

"Then you refused all my calls. Not subtle. I got the idea."

That can't be right. Dee and I have been best friends since we were ten.

"But to be honest, I'm glad you called because I've been waiting to do the same thing to you." The phone clicks before I have a chance to respond.

I stare at the phone, shocked by the confrontation. What did I do to upset her? I can't imagine turning my back on Dee or pushing her away when she needed me.

Amongst the confusion, my mind goes back to my girls. I grab my coat and dash out the door. It's nearly 9:00 a.m.— they should be at school. No teacher would deny a worried mother access to her kids.

My worry makes the short drive to Havergal Private School excruciatingly long. Haley should be in her kindergarten class with Ms. Topp and Ava her second-grade class with Mrs. Braxton. I pull into the driveway of the school and a startling realization settles on me. The extension they put on two years ago is missing. The building looks ancient, almost identical to the day Nathan and I looked into possible private schools for Ava. The timeless feel of Havergal had struck us, and they'd assured us a renovation was in the future. But now, so many years later, the old windows still remain, and the weathered shingles are peeling back. How is this possible?

I throw open the car door and hurry up the front steps to the office. I ring the doorbell and am greeted by an unfamiliar young woman dressed in a posh pantsuit, who offers me a smile that looks sarcastic.

"May I help you?" Her voice is sickeningly sweet. Her eyes dance down to my outfit, and I immediately feel foolish. I pull my coat tighter around my body, hoping to hide the aged pyjamas from sight. I must look crazy, but I can't think about that now.

"I'm looking for Haley and Ava Page." I overenunciate their names to be sure she hears me correctly. "I'm their mother."

Her expression falters as if she doubts my words. Still, she turns and leads me to her desk. When she sits at her computer, she asks, "Which grades?"

"Kindergarten with Ms. Topp and second grade with Mrs. Braxton."

Her fingers hesitate over the keyboard. "I'm sorry, Mrs. Page, but Mrs. Braxton is teaching fourth grade, and I'm afraid we don't have a teacher by the name of Ms. Topp."

I swallow hard. "Can you please check for them?"

She grits her teeth. "I'm sorry, Mrs. Page. We can't release any student information."

A deafening sound rushes in my ears, and I try to keep my breathing calm.

"Please. My eldest, Ava, won the achievement award for her grade last year. She's right here on the wall." I point to where her plaque is hung.

I follow my instruction, glancing towards the portrait of my proud little girl, only to see that while the photo and plaque are still in the correct spot, neither Ava's name nor her photo is there. My skin prickles, and dizziness sets in. The year pictured under the award is all wrong. It's ten years earlier than it should be. A lump forms in my throat. It's not possible.

The secretary stands when she sees my expression. "I'll fetch the principal. She'll know what to do."

But I don't need her to fetch anyone. It all begins to sink in —my young age, the phone date, Nathan's nonexistent phone number, Dee's resentment, and now my missing daughters.

My steady pounding heart feels like it stops.

Four

NOW

Before anyone can return, I hurry out the door and back to my car, pushing the impending tears away. I grip the steering wheel, unsure what to think. How could my life simply reset and everything I had, everything I wanted to fight for, vanish without a trace? Worse, where are they now?

I've only a moment to consider my circumstances and let the weight of my choices push me down before my phone springs to life with an old club tune from my university days.

To my surprise, Arabella's name flashes across the screen. Jayson's younger sister and my least favourite person.

I ignore the call; however, she only calls again and again. On the fourth attempt, I pick up, knowing Arabella is relentless. Maybe she can help clear up this mystery.

"Maddie, where are you?" her shrill voice comes through the receiver. The sound of her makes me shudder with memories of our university days and the accident we both deny. We haven't been close since our final year of undergrad. Beyond seeing her a week ago when I asked for the extortion money, her life is a mystery to me. "You were supposed to be home. I'm here, but you're not."

"What are you talking about?" I pinch the bridge of my nose as the frustration wells up inside me. Nothing is making sense.

"We have a wedding meeting, Maddie." Her irritation is clear. "We're going to be late."

"Wedding? What wedding?"

Arabella groaned with displeasure. "My wedding. The one you, my best friend, are Maid of Honour for. C'mon, Maddie. Enough with the games. I don't care where you are. Get home now. We need to go."

My head spins. Wedding, Maid of Honour, best friend. How did this happen?

"I'm not feeling great," I lie. "I'm at the walk-in clinic."

"I don't care," Arabella snaps. "Madison Butler, go to the doctor later. I can't have my Maid of Honour missing this meeting."

I cringe as she uses my full name, realizing that I am no longer Mrs. Maddie Page—no longer Nathan's wife.

"I'll see you soon."

Arabella ends the phone call without a goodbye.

I rush home, focused on the road and hopeful that Arabella can share some more facts about my bizarre life changes. There's a limo waiting on the street outside my house; I cannot see the driver through the tinted windows.

Inside my home, I'm met with my first truly familiar view. It's Arabella, her bleached hair tied back in a teased, painful-looking ponytail and wearing a short, pink dress in four-inch heels that match. Her makeup is perfect and she has books, bags, and other wedding paraphernalia piled on the floor in front of her. A real-life Barbie doll, as Dee and I used to joke.

She plants her hands on her hips and raises an eyebrow as

she glances up and down at my ensemble. "This won't do at all." She waves to the stairs. "Off with you. Some actual clothes would be nice. I did you a favour and picked an outfit for you. It's on your bed."

"I told you I wasn't feeling well." Given my state of mind, I don't think I needed to fake illness at this point. I am sick. Sick with the changes, sick with confusion, sick with the idea that my babies never existed.

"And I told you I don't care." She cocks her hip, hands still planted. "The girls are meeting us at DT for brunch, so you'd better hurry."

"DT Bistro?"

"Obviously." She rolls her eyes.

I open my mouth to retort but snap it shut, realizing the comment would sound ridiculous. That place closed five years after we graduated from university.

A pout takes over Arabella's smile. "Didn't Jay tell you?"

"He must have forgotten." I turn to the stairs, but before I reach the top, I hesitate and look back at her. "Hey, I was wondering something."

Arabella glances up. "What?"

"I called Dee today—"

"You did what?" Arabella's interest switches to rage. "You swore you stopped talking to that slut after what she did."

"I know I did," I said, playing along. "I had a weird dream last night and gave her a call this morning. It was stupid anyway. She hung up on me."

"Bitch." Arabella sneers. "Sounds like her. Stealing boyfriends, fucking brothers, and ruining people's lives. She did you a favour hanging up."

I frown, unsure what Arabella is referring to.

"Did you hear she's bisexual now?" Arabella rolls her eyes. "Like, did she not get enough action when she was straight? She's going to go after girls now too? I guess none of us are safe."

I bow my head, unsure what to say. That doesn't sound like Dee at all. In fact, that sounds similar to how Arabella used to exaggerate in our university days. Why would I pick the less credible side?

I don't have time to react, as Arabella's expression shifts again; this time, with narrow eyes and tight lips, she says, "Don't call her again."

"I won't. It was stupid." I concede to her will. I already look crazy enough.

"Yeah, it was." Her stern look vanishes, and a smile returns. Her voice becomes light and airy once more. "Now off with you. Get ready. We don't want to keep the girls waiting."

I nod and scamper upstairs. When I descend in the tight blue dress Arabella left out for me, she's waiting at the door, holding out a pair of black pumps. They look painfully hard to walk in.

"I might wear something more sensible." Hoping to reach for the flats I spy by the closet.

"Not at my meeting, you won't." She pushes the pumps towards me. "Now, let's go. Vincent is waiting."

She drags me out the door and towards the waiting limo.

The driver, who Arabella greets as Vincent, is a middle-aged man with a shock of white hair and sunken cheeks, hurries from the driver's side to open the door for Arabella. Then he looks at me as Arabella calls me in.

Vincent closes the door behind me, and I gaze around the large car. I can't remember ever riding in this limo, but I experience déjà vu as I take in the blue lighting. The fine leather seats feel familiar under my palms. My chest constricts as the anxiety rushes in. I can trace the details without looking and know this isn't my first ride in this limo.

The car jerks forward, and Arabella rambles on about her bridesmaids and the girls we are meeting. The names are unfamiliar, and I find myself drifting as I glance out the window watching the busy Toronto city pass by. Everything looks different; construction that hasn't happened, parks that need restoration. The daily newspaper tucked into the door of the limo reminds me the date is ten years earlier than I remember. My life has vanished without a trace.

The wedding meeting is where I begin to accept this isn't some bad dream. This is my new reality. Arabella and her friends order several drinks—martinis, cosmos, and expensive champagne—and proceed to gossip about their families, friends, and other people in our tight-knit Lawrence Park community. Each speaks as if they know me well. Being with Jayson seems to have completely changed who I am. Or was.

How could I be in a relationship with Jayson again? Four years ago in my old life, Dee had planned to set Nathan and me up. It was a way for me to get over Jayson, move on from my tryst with an undesirable, and start growing up. I'd been reluctant at first, but the moment I set eyes on Nathan, I was hooked.

"Why are you so quiet, Maddie?" Arabella asks, pulling me from my calculations and memories of my life. Her expression is pinched with annoyance, and her so-called friends—our friends, I guess—wear looks that match. "We kind of need your help."

I have to get through this meeting, convince everyone I'm not as crazy as I feel, then figure out what the hell is going on and where I went wrong.

I force another fake smile, trying not to think about how

my face is starting to hurt. "Of course. I'm sorry. My attention is all yours."

Arabella returns the grin, and the conversation continues. "Kimi suggested bottle service at Cobra for the bachelorette, but I desperately want your opinion."

I lean closer to Arabella, glancing over the notes she'd been marking down. Cobra has been closed for years. We'd frequented it in our university days but outgrew the dark lighting and loud music.

"Cobra?" I ask, trying to ignore the angry look Kimi shoots me from across the table. "I'm not sure."

"That's why I asked. You always take us to the hottest parties." Arabella beams at me.

I frown. I'm a total fraud. What was open ten years ago? I realize our once favourite club would still be open.

"Maison Mercer," I say with confidence. Every night spent on their rooftop terrace was epic. "Bottle service, obviously. But getting to drink under the stars is always a plus."

"White dresses?" Arabella prompts.

Wasn't the bride supposed to be the only one in white? A memory of a university party comes to mind, one of Dee's ragers that Arabella promptly re-themed and decorated into a classy cocktail party. Dee hated every second of it and blamed me for forcing Arabella on her. She always used to joke that I was the bridge between two very different worlds when it came to their friendship, but I'd only wanted them to get along. As always, Dee was a good sport and went along with Arabella's changes, but it was no surprise she refused to let Arabella help plan any party after that.

"You should wear white," I say. "Accent it with a gold belt, and the rest of us can get gold dresses to match."

Arabella considers this for a moment before producing a genuine smile. "Yes, it'll look perfect. My golden girl posse."

"What you've always dreamed of," I say, to my surprise. What has happened to the old me? The conflicting feelings that I'm Arabella's best friend when I know how our lives ended up makes me dizzy with regret and confusion.

"Thanks, Maddie." She places her hand on mine, then turns back to her other bridesmaids and continues discussing the plans.

I lean back in my seat, pulling my hand away from her touch. Weirdly, I seem to know all these things about Arabella. Like I am in my own episode of *The Twilight Zone*.

My morning should have begun with me helping Ava and Haley pick out their outfits before taking them to school. I should have kissed both their foreheads and hugged them tightly, inhaling their soft, flowery shampoo, and watched them skip off to see their friends.

Instead, I wear a dress too short to bend over in, and I'm spending my day gossiping with girls I have no interest in. I want nothing more than to wake up from this nightmare and hold my girls close.

Arabella finally frees us after nearly three hours of discussion. My vision blurs, and my body feels light. The champagne has gone to my head. Arabella hooks my arm with a giggle as we stumble out of DT Bistro. Her cheeks blaze red, and her eyes are glassy. The classic Barbie is gone, replaced with a staggering mess of a girl. So much for Arabella always being the picture of grace.

"Bye, ladies!" Arabella grips my arm, swings around, and waves at her departing friends.

"Where to?" I don't want her coming home with me. More

than anything, I want to be alone, get out of this dress, and try to figure out how I got here.

"Anywhere! My driver's not here," she slurs, a dopey smile in place. "I told him we'd be longer than this." She giggles. "I thought I would keep you for hours." She already has.

"So, we're cabbing?" My place is at least half an hour uptown if the traffic behaves.

Arabella waves a hand forward. "Let's walk a bit." She pulls her phone from her purse, still gripping my arm in the process. "I'll call Vincent and get him to meet us as soon as possible."

I try to keep us steady, but we sway from side to side. I hope our walk will be short-lived, as my feet are killing me from the painful heels Arabella insisted I wear.

I remain silent while she makes her demands to the driver, then hangs up and tucks her phone away. After which, she wraps both arms around mine and rests her head on my shoulder as we make our way down the street.

"Thank you," she mumbles from where her head rests. Her eyes close as we walk.

"I always make sure you get home, Arrie." The words come out so naturally it surprises me. I have no memory past university of ever stumbling home with Arabella in tow. Our friendship had waned when she rejected my younger brother, Declan, in our final year. Jayson and I were over, and Declan had been long infatuated with Arabella. She never discouraged his attention, but when he finally had the courage to ask her out, she humiliated him in front of the entire party. I knew then we couldn't be friends. Why we were so close now was beyond me. Maybe Declan hadn't dared to ask her out this time around, or something stopped him.

"That's not what I was talking about," Arabella says,

distress rising in her voice. "I mean for everything you've done. Fixing my relationship with Jack, denying Dee, and, of course, how you helped Gina."

I trip, taking Arabella to the ground with me.

"Hey!" Arabella cries as we crash onto the grassy patch of someone's front yard.

I scramble to my feet and pull Arabella to hers. She's quick to whine while trying to brush away the dirt and grass from her dress. I can only focus on what she said.

"How did I help Gina?" I blurt. The mention of her name makes my chest contract with guilt and my breathing shorten. The memory of her accident still burns in my mind, though I've tried to forget it.

Gina was a university friend—at least in the life that vanished. She and I dated the same guy—Brian. It had been nothing short of tragic when her totalled car was found on the side of the road, her dead body inside. It had been ruled an accident due to impaired driving, but a part of me knew there was more to the story. No one ever spoke up; there was never any proof of foul play. It was something I'd spent my adult life trying to forget.

Arabella narrows her eyes. "You are acting weird, Maddie. You know that, right?" Her expression fades, and she grips my arm again. "I'm talking about all that stuff with her psycho ex and the night of Dee's birthday party."

I remembered it well. That night we all witnessed Brian's aggression and his disregard for Gina. Nathan and I had been dating a few weeks already, and I didn't want to involve him in my history with a former fling, so we'd avoided the whole situation. I didn't want Nathan to know about the cocaine Brian and I had done together, or the times we were high that ended in violent fights. He brought out the worst in me. Or maybe we'd brought the worst out of each other.

To this day, I wish I could take it back. I was so enticed by the allure of drugs and fun I let my guard down and gave in to my inhibitions. When I look back on it now, there was never an emotional connection with Brian, only sex, drugs, and alcohol. And regret.

To this day, I wish I'd had the courage to step in and stop Brian from abusing Gina emotionally and physically. But I fear a part of me was happy he'd moved his attention from me and I'd gotten off easy. Gina wasn't so lucky.

"Oh, right." I pretend to understand the reference, although my insides twist with a desperate need to know more. How had that night been different? Did I confront Brian like I wish I had? Did I take Gina away from the fight?

The limo pulls up next to us and Arabella groans with relief. "Finally!" She pushes away from me and staggers towards the door.

"So, where's Gina now?" I ask once we're seated and the car jerks forward.

Arabella pours us another glass of champagne, not that we need it.

"She went home to Costa Rica." Arabella's gossipy smile falls in place. "But I heard Gina and her man are having problems. No surprise since she has such awful taste in men." Arabella gives me a small smirk. "At least you got your sense back when you gave Jayson another chance."

I force a tight smile.

Arabella leans back in her seat. "Anyway, we should expect Gina's return in the next day or two. Apparently, her man was caught with another woman. Oh, the scandal." She cackles at the misfortune and tips back her glass. That's the Arabella I remember.

While Arabella is sipping champagne and checking her phone, I focus on one fact: Gina is alive. And Arabella implies it's because of me. Because I am here, right now, Gina is alive. A sick feeling almost makes me double over. If I find a way back to my real life, the one I am desperate for, she will be dead.

"I hope she's okay." I finish my drink, hoping it will settle my nerves. It doesn't.

Arabella shrugs. "She's fine. She has to come back for my wedding anyway." Her gaze finds the window; she's bored with the conversation, but my curiosity won't settle.

"What happened that night?" The only memories I have are of my former reality. "Didn't she storm off in a drunken huff?"

Arabella regards me with a perplexed expression. "Maddie, you know perfectly well that Gina barely drank when everything happened with Brian. But, whatever, he's paying for it now. Attempted murder will do that."

I cough as I choke on my champagne, and Arabella regards me with confusion. I keep my mouth shut as I try to work through the discomfort at the mention of his name and the thought of his cruel smile. I'd seen him only a few weeks ago in my former life when he'd approached me at the bookstore and threatened to expose my affair. Before that, I hadn't seen him since Gina's funeral, a day I wish I could forget.

I had hoped I was done with him after the pay-off, but now he's coming front and centre again. It's as if I will never escape him or the guilt. At least he's in prison and can't hurt me in this life.

Not wishing to discuss Brian further, I change the topic. "Right. So, Dee's been pretty awful to you, then."

I expect anger at the mention of my former best friend but instead am faced with Arabella's same bored expression as she refills her champagne glass.

"I guess," she says. "But I hate her more for how awful she's been to you."

That doesn't sound like Dee—the friend who brought me wine and chocolate any time something bad was going on in my life. She's Ava's godmother and happily took shifts with the babies when Nathan and I needed a break. The friend I talked to every single day since elementary school—the sister I chose.

Arabella places a hand on my knee. "I'm glad you and Jayson were able to get past everything." She smiles in a way that seems genuine. "I was so angry at him for what he did to you. You are the best thing that ever happened to my stupid big brother, and I'm glad he knows it now."

"Of course." I guess that Dee slept with Jayson, from Arabella's implication and accusing tone, and a part of me wonders if she did in my former life as well. Still, it doesn't add up. Had she done it recently enough that I just found out? How does Gina tie into it all?

"You are too good for him," Arabella says. "At least in my case, I had the fame and fortune to go along with Jack's stupidity." She laughs at her joke and swallows the rest of her champagne.

My mind gives me an image of Jack, at a restaurant down-town, unabashedly flirting with the server bringing drinks. He's classically handsome, but his aloof grin makes him appear arrogant. So Arabella's fiancé is a cheater too. For a moment, I am disgusted by the idea of Arabella forgiving him for his actions. How could this self-assured woman stay with a man who betrayed her? But I remind myself I am just as guilty. I'd hoped for forgiveness, so is it so wrong that Arabella forgave him? I imagine him apologizing profusely, knowing he's done wrong. On his knees, staring up at her with tears in his eyes. But as I picture it, the image vanishes.

Something inside tells me he isn't the type of man who begs for forgiveness.

Before I can consider it further, Arabella grabs my hand and tilts her head back. "Thank God for you, Maddie. I don't think I could do this without you."

I glance away from her, unwilling to answer, as all I can think about is how I can't agree. Before this morning, I had daughters that I loved, a best friend, and a great career, all without her.

Five

NOW

When the limo comes to a stop, I help Arabella out and then exit myself. We aren't outside my house but at Arabella's Rosedale mansion she shares with Jack. The man is a mystery to me beyond news articles and social media. Though it feels like I've never met him, given my close relationship with Arabella, we must have interacted more than once. If only I could remember.

At least their story seems the same and unaffected by my choices.

Vincent speaks, but instead of directing his words towards Arabella, he stares at me. "Mr. Davenport will be done by five. I will pick him up from the office and go with him to fetch Ms. Knoll for their dinner, which will be followed by tonight's charity event. The instructions are on her dresser. Mrs. Torres will know what to do."

He looks down his nose at Arabella, who still grins ear to ear with her stupid, drunken smile. His pinched expression shifts back to me. "Make sure she gets some rest." He turns on his heel and moves to the front of the car. Pretty snotty for a chauffeur.

I help Arabella through the front door of her massive home and direct her up the stairs. I find my way easily enough, following the steps I'd taken only weeks ago when I was still in my thirties. A few staff members glance our way, and most hold disdainful looks for Arabella. She isn't as well-loved as she thinks. Despite my issues with her, I pity her. Our whole lives, Arabella was always the centre of attention. The pretty girl, the one who got what she wanted whenever she wanted it. And now, she acts like she has a picture-perfect life and believes she is the envy of those around her. But in reality, she's a drunk faking her way through life.

Arabella heads to the washroom as soon as we reach her room, and a few minutes later, she returns to flop onto the bed and snuggle into the fluffy comforter. "I love bed," she murmurs.

"Get some rest." I glance at the clock. It's half-past two. "You'll have to be up in an hour to get ready."

"Mmm." Arabella hums her response. Her eyes close, and she looks quite small and innocent, wedged between the large pillows. It gives me pause, remembering when she stood up for me in fifth grade, isolating herself from the other kids to make sure I wouldn't feel alone. Or the time I cried on her shoulder after my high-school crush Brad was making out with Stacey at the grade twelve dance. Once we'd been so close, and she'd been a best friend. How had such a sweet-looking girl become so manipulative? Where did our relation-ship go wrong? Though I'd asked myself that question many times before. As we got older, our priorities changed. We wanted different things. Arabella and I were never meant to remain friends, so why had we now?

I leave without another word. Standing in the hallway outside the main bedroom, I feel out of place and unwelcome in such a large home. My panic bubbles to the surface with no distraction to force it aside. I move to leave when an older woman approaches me. She wears a black pantsuit and imparts an air of importance with her lifted chin and flat-ironed hair.

"Hello, Maddie. The office is set up as usual for your use." She waves a hand down the hallway to an opened door at the end. "I'll have Beth prepare some food to soak up the champagne."

"Thank you." I return her smile and head for the office, though I'm not sure why. Did I often bring home a drunken Arabella and use their office?

The room is square with a large mahogany desk and a sleek desktop computer. Bookshelves are lining the back wall, and both Arabella's and Jack's degrees are posted above the desk, impressively framed. Hers is in psychology, and his is in business. In my old life, Dee told me Arabella gave up working when she started dating Jack. It wasn't a real surprise when I heard. Arabella had never taken school seriously. When we graduated high school, she'd always planned on being a trophy wife. She encouraged us to do the same. *"Pretty girls don't work. They wife."* She was the only one who took the idea seriously.

I glance to Jack's degree. He was a few years older than us, from what I remember, and gained notoriety when he was on *The Bachelorette* as a contestant. He'd made it to the final six before he'd been sent home, or so I'd read. I was never one for reality TV. From there, he took over his father's business as a hotel tycoon—anything to keep his wealth skyrocketing.

A memory surfaces of Arabella pulling me into a darkened club where Jack was making an appearance. She'd been desperate to meet him since she obsessed over his good looks on the show. His return to Toronto was the perfect opportunity for her to make her move.

Obviously, she'd been successful.

My phone rings, pulling me from my thoughts. Jayson's name flashes across the screen.

"Hey." My tone is flat. My gut still twists with unease and unfamiliarity. Though, in hindsight, it might be from the boozy lunch.

"Hey, babe." His voice is cheery on the other end, and for a moment, he makes me forget I'm alone in this confusing reality. There is a comfort in speaking to him, though it is short-lived. "You sound better. Did you have a good lunch?"

"More like a liquid lunch." I take a seat at the desk and flick on the computer, hoping it will reveal more about my life.

Jayson laughs. "That sounds like Arrie. Have you gotten any work done?"

"On the bachelorette, yeah, I think so. Though after the fourth bottle of champagne we may have been somewhat distracted."

"Hopefully someone took notes." Jayson chuckles. We're silent for a few seconds. I wonder what he's thinking, why he called, what he wants. Though I'm sure my reactions to this morning are as confusing to him as this life is to me.

"How's your day going?" I ask, trying to break the awkward tension.

"Better now. I was worried about you this morning."

"Yeah, I know. I'm sorry." *I'm still worried.*

"Do you want to talk about it?" he asks. "I'll bring Chinese home tonight. We don't even need to cook."

"That would be nice. But I don't need to talk about it. I freaked out a bit after that weird dream. I'm a lot better now."

A lie, but what else can I say? I need to know more before I start stirring the crazy pot again.

He's quiet on the other end for too long. Something else is up.

"Jayson, tell me."

"Arrie told me you talked to Dee this morning." His tone is flat.

Is that what Arabella did when she went to the bathroom? Of course she'd call Jayson and report my strange behaviour. Did she tell him about my "visit to the doctors" in my pyjamas as well?

"Yeah, it was a brief conversation."

"Why did you call her?" Jayson presses.

"I had a weird dream. Instinct, I guess." I hesitate before adding what I think he wants to hear. "It was a mistake."

His tone lightens. "Okay, next time if you need to talk, call Arrie or me. We're the ones who love you most."

"Of course, I know that."

"Okay, babe." Jayson pauses. "I should get back to work, and hopefully you can get some work done before Arrie demands your attention again. Call me if you need anything."

"I will."

"Love you."

I hesitate before adding the obligatory "You too." It feels so strained after finally saying it to Nathan again last night. At least, I think it was last night.

I place my phone down and notice the clock—the kids would be coming home from school. My throat tightens at the thought of Ava's smile as she would rush inside after school, anxious to open her homework so she could finish and move on to her book. Haley would drag her feet, begging for a snack and hoping to chat my ear off so I didn't ask if the teacher had given her any work to do. She hated homework, preferring to run off to her room and play with her dollhouse or send Everest on another crazy adventure. I almost catch myself wishing I could call Nathan so he could comfort me like he did the night before my first book tour.

I glance at the computer and push away the heart-wrenching memories. The desktop is empty save for a few applications, but I find a folder with my name. In my twenties, I worked as a freelance writer and, from the notes in the folder, that hasn't changed.

When the computer gives little insight into Arabella and Jack's life and how I may have helped as she suggested, I pop open a web browser and search for Jack Davenport. There's a lot online about Arabella's future husband and his business ventures as well as several pictures from his time on *The Bachelorette.*

He's a wealthy young man who graduated from McGill University and inherited his father's hotels and fortune. Though, according to *Business One* magazine, he'd done a great job of expanding the business by opening prestigious resorts all around the world.

Searching his name along with Arabella's brings up what I'm looking for. She's listed on the Best Dressed lists and featured in magazines for her fashion and design. As I cycle further back in the news, I find the scandals. Drug abuse and affairs. According to *Hello!* Magazine, Arabella did a one-month stint in rehab for cocaine following the rumours of her fiancé's infidelity. One story says he cheated with a waitress from Texas, and another claims a fitness trainer in Paris. They may both be true.

The next article indicates that after she was released, Jack issued a public apology, and they appear happier than ever. There doesn't seem to be many recent scandals connected with them, and most articles focus on Arabella's iconic fashion choices and Jack's booming business.

Arabella implied I fixed her relationship with Jack somehow, though the gossip blogs don't reveal a thing.

I stare at the screen for several seconds. At some point in the last few years of my life, everything changed. My course altered and I never met Nathan or stayed close to Dee. I lost the life I had built. I lost my daughters.

Next, I access Facebook. The platform has gone through so much remodelling in the past ten years that the old graphics and different shades of blue are jarring, but luckily our university alumni group still exists. I search Gina's name. Her profile says she was married last year, and together they moved to Costa Rica to build houses for charity. Pictures featuring her next to a dark-haired, buff man in front of half-built houses, saving sea turtles, or dancing with children, brag to her friends about her successful endeavours. She seems pretty stable despite what Arabella said otherwise.

Her husband is someone I don't recognize. His smile seems genuine. Perhaps he is from Costa Rica and gives her an escape from the life she had here.

Gina's Facebook page reveals nothing of substance, so I push further. I know I have to look Brian up. He's the next likely source for any information.

My throat constricts as I slowly type his name into the search bar. When nothing comes up, relief washes over me. I don't want to see his picture, and I'm fearful of the memories seeing it might trigger. Instead, I search for Nathan though it, too, is another dead end. He always did hate social media, so it's no surprise I can't find him.

Back at Gina's Facebook page, I open private messages and start typing.

Heard you were heading back to town. Would love to catch up. Shoot me a message when you can!

As I close the browser, my heartbeat falters. I don't know what I will learn from her. I don't know what to expect. But if there is any hope of finding out the truth, she seems like the best place to start.

Six

THEN

The flight home from the writers' conference was long and lonely. I tried to sleep through the bumpy turbulence and chatty passenger beside me, but nothing seemed to silence the dizzying thoughts in my head. Seeing Jayson again brought back memories I wished had stayed forgotten. But now they sat in the front of my mind, forcing me to consider where my life went wrong.

Was it the decision to support my brother and leave Arabella behind, and with her the entire life I'd built? Or maybe it was the choice to push Brian aside and pursue Nathan, forcing Brian into Gina's arms, which resulted in the confusing facts about her death, the unanswered mystery that was a drunk driving accident when we all knew better.

In a way, we could all be implicated in her murder.

Whatever the reason, I couldn't stop thinking about all of it.

My distracted thoughts ran rampant as the plane landed and I made my way through customs and eventually to the parking garage. I'd never forgiven myself for Gina's demise and I worried it tainted my entire life. From the way I pushed my feelings about Jayson aside and chose to be with Nathan or the friendships I picked.

I wanted my girls as far away from my history as possible. I'd hoped to leave Toronto entirely, though Nathan never agreed to that. The most I got were weekend trips to the ski hills in Collingwood or a friend's cottage on Lake Muskoka. When the weekend ended, we returned to the city where all the demons still haunted me.

Eventually, I'd managed to suppress the memories and pretend it never happened by telling myself that there was nothing I could have done. Gina couldn't be saved, and those past relationships were better buried.

The past was better left forgotten. Better for my girls, better for my relationship and better for me. Too many questions led to more open-ended answers. We'd all built lives around the guilt of Gina's passing; wasn't it better to leave well enough alone?

Now I longed to know more. Questions swirled around my head as I pulled the car into my driveway. I stepped out of the car and a cool wind whipped my hair, sending a chilling shiver down my spine. Maybe it was too late to bury my secrets again. Jayson brought those memories to the surface and now they may never disappear.

The house was quiet as the girls were already in school and Nathan at the office. There was a note on the counter welcoming me home and two drawings, one from each of the girls. The daily newspaper rested beside the pictures. I made a cup of coffee and reached for the paper.

I was only through a few pages when a photo caught my eye. It was Jack Davenport posing with his fashionista wife in front of their newest hotel.

I'd never met Jack, only knowing of his relationship with

Arabella through the news and social media. They'd had a lavish wedding ten years ago that had been documented by the tabloids. It seemed their life consisted of fancy trips, outlandish rumours, and endearing rekindling ever since. Arabella had flourished, or at least the media made it seem like she had. Even during her low points like cheating scandals and rehab, her life seemed pretty amazing. I couldn't help but resent her. She'd nearly broken Declan beyond repair and yet got everything she'd ever dreamed. If we'd remained friends, would I have ended up as one of her socialite girlfriends?

But we couldn't have remained friends. The night Arabella broke Declan's heart was impossible to forget. Jayson and I had been long over, and I made foolish decisions with friends, boys, and school. My undergrad was nearly complete and I was passing by a hair. The honours I'd received in previous years had been lost to too many parties. University was for fun, not to learn, at least that was what Arabella always said. Screw school. We came from rich families, we'd marry rich men, and we'd live our perfect trophy wife lives. The U of T Queens, Arabella had crowned us. And for a time, it was what I wanted most.

Meeting Brian put a hitch in the plan. He wasn't what Arabella would deem worthy, but he was a great lay and had a seemingly endless supply of cocaine, which he gave to me for free. For months, we did lines and had sex everywhere imaginable—the more public the place, the better.

My friends worried about me, and it manifested in different ways. Arabella scolded me for choosing someone beneath my standing where Dee thought the drug use was going too far. But I was mesmerized, sucked in by Brian's rugged life, his disregard for authority, his troubled past, and his great drugs.

When the buzz wore off and I met Nathan, I knew there was no future with Brian and cut him off. As I got clean, Arabella dove deep with Lance, a banker's son and a known cokehead. Unlike me, her habit continued past university until she met Jack and was forced into rehab. By then, our friendship was long over.

Declan had always worried about Arabella and her drug use, constantly following her around and cleaning up her messes. She encouraged him by batting her eyes and giving him drunken kisses in a tease but nothing more. My poor naive brother didn't know any better. He thought she liked him.

I drew a sharp breath as I remembered the party when Declan tried to pull Arabella off of Lance. The way the smug bastard only smirked before reaching for his eight ball and forming a line on the table. The way Arabella's anger turned on Declan, spewing insults about his dorky glasses, his lower status, and how he'd never be with her.

When I saw Declan's heart crushed before me, the rage boiled up inside. After everything that had happened in school the past few years, and Arabella's selfish behaviour, that was the final straw. Our friendship ended as soon as my palm struck Arabella's cheek.

After that, we never spoke again—until Gina died.

My phone rang, pulling me away from the newspaper article. I was glad to see it was Dee's name and not Nathan's flashing across the screen.

"Hey," I answered.

"Welcome home!" Dee called out in a singsong voice. "How was the flight?"

"It was—"

"Actually, no," she cut me off. "Don't tell me. Come meet me. Usual spot. Coffee in an hour." The call ended before I could agree or protest. Typical Dee—only giving me an hour to get ready and meet her.

Still, I smiled. At least someone was genuinely excited to have me home.

Seven

NOW

I t's another two days before I see Gina, and each day is stranger than the previous one. I've managed to determine that, along with Dee, I stopped communicating with most of my closest friends and some I'd never made connections with at all. This is evident from the contacts in my phone and my Facebook friends. As badly as I want to know the reasons behind these changes in friendship, I'm worried about how asking will make me look. Who wakes up one morning and doesn't know their entire life?

Gina and I meet at Starbucks on Lawrence, a ten-minute walk from my house, though I've never loved the big franchise. Ordering a regular coffee feels odd for a place with so many variations. Gina is late, which is different than the woman I remember. She'd always been one to arrive early.

The last thing I remember about Gina was how wild-eyed and flushed she had been when I tried to stop her from leaving. She'd turned at the door and, in a voice that still haunts me, said it was my fault she was treated so bad, and I was the one to blame. She stormed out of Dee's party, and a week later she was being lowered into the earth, the lacquered mahogany casket spotted with drops from the pouring rain. Her family had spared no expense on their youngest child's funeral.

Our friends and I crowded around the graveside, faces wet with tears as we watched what was left of Gina disappear. Brian had lurked off to the side. Guilty, but off scot-free.

When she finally walks in, I almost don't recognize her. In university, she was a husky girl. Now she's thinner and wearing a flowery sundress. This would have been so unlike her four years ago. Despite the disappearance of her chubby cheeks, her tanned skin remains the same. Her round brown eyes are the way I remember them, and though her hair has grown long past her shoulders it's still as dark as the night sky. She's the same Gina. But she's very much alive, four years after her funeral.

Gina grins when she sees me but orders a drink before walking over. I stand to meet her.

"Hola, Maddie." She smiles and pulls me into a tight hug. Her hair smells of fresh roses, sweet and sickening. "Oh, it is so good to see you."

"Welcome back," I say as we pull away and return to the table. Her accent is stronger than I remember, but being back home immersed in her culture likely accentuated it.

"The return of La Princesa." She wiggles her shoulders as she says her old self-coined nickname in a singsong tone. "It's good to be back." Then she blinks her large eyes. "How are you?"

I shrug, unsure what to say. Is there a way to explain that my life is in turmoil? That I should be in my thirties with a family, not my twenties planning a socialite's bachelorette or that the woman in front of me should be dead? I don't know what to say to any of this, so I smile and say, "Great."

Despite my enthusiasm, Gina doesn't buy it. "Ah no, Maddie. I know something is up."

"Yeah, I guess." I look away from her, unsure how to bring up our shared past.

"It's about Brian, right?"

I don't answer right away, and Gina continues.

"Don't let the fact that Brain has a parole hearing freak you out. That bastard isn't about to get off for what he did." She grabs my hand. "Have the police asked you for another statement? I said I would give one."

"No. Besides, what could I say to help?"

"Maddie, it was our testimony that landed him in prison in the first place." Gina pulls away from me. "You were the only witness. You took me to the hospital. Even if there was other evidence against him, he's in prison because of us."

I swallow the lump that formed in my throat as the ideas swirl in my head. I witnessed the accident that killed Gina in our former life. I am the reason she is still alive. Something changed that prevented Brian from doing whatever he did. Feeling dizzy, I place my face in my hands and squeeze my eyes shut in hopes the world will still.

"Hey." Gina's voice is gentle, like a mother speaking to her wailing child. "It's okay, Maddie. I'm tired of all of it. I'm ready to give my statement and then, if I have to, get a restraining order."

I risk a glance into her eyes. They're filled with concern, glistening with tears.

"I'm sorry. I guess I'm surprised he's getting out so soon."

"He didn't succeed in killing me," Gina says, now looking at the table rather than at me. "You made sure of that."

Then she touches my arm, and a familiar feeling fills me. There's a flash of memory.

A darkened sky, her arm wrapped around my shoulders as we hurry away from the parked car. A glance behind me reassures me that he'd been struck hard and was still lying on the ground.

Gina is weeping, her body shaking, racked with sobs. "Why?" she keeps muttering. "Why?" I try to talk to her down, calm her sobs, and assure her that she'll be okay. But my words fall on deaf ears as we continue down the street. I have one goal in mind. Get to the hospital. Call the police. But my phone is missing.

When she releases my arm, I flash back to the present and nod. My throat is too dry to speak. Did I just see part of that night, a memory of this life, or something from the past? Or maybe I am dreaming all of this. I can't be sure.

"I've never forgotten that night," Gina says. "I can't forget it. He was awful to us both, you know."

I only nod again. I might not remember the exact events of that night, but I do remember Brian. *Awful* doesn't begin to describe him.

"Have you seen him since?" I ask when neither of us speaks.

Gina shakes her head. "Not since the day of the trial."

I shiver at the mention of the trial, and another memory comes to light. Brian getting too close, swearing he'd make us pay for what we'd done. Vowing we wouldn't be comfortable for long. His lifeless eyes void of emotion, his laugh hollow, haunting. If not him, someone would avenge him, some time, somehow.

We're quiet again, avoiding each other's gazes, and I wonder if she's thinking the same as me. Is she remembering the trial, considering the threat of revenge? Her expression doesn't give away her inner thoughts. She looks neither scared nor confident. Instead, she looks tired, as she said, and emotionless.

"I guess you've been gone since then," I say. Facebook told me of her adventures abroad, helping others. Had she been distracting herself from the memories?

"Yeah," she says. "I had to get out. Do something for me, you know? I always thought helping others would make me feel better after everything. And it did. I wouldn't have come back if I didn't have to."

"Because of your husband?" I ask; at least that was what Arabella implied.

Gina cocks her head towards me. "What has Arabella been telling everyone?"

"That he was as bad as Brian."

She cracks a smile. "Dios mío, Arabella was always one for exaggeration."

"It's not true?"

"No," Gina says. "But we are very different people. We met by fluke when I had a particularly stubborn sea turtle to help. He was my saviour then, but when I told him why I was coming home, he flew off the handle. Pretty much forbade me to come back. He couldn't protect me here and doesn't think I can protect myself. He only wanted to control me. He never really loved me. So, I left him there."

Now I smile. That sounds like the Gina I know, hard headed once she put her mind to something.

"Plus, after everything you did, I wasn't going to make you face Brian alone." She looks away from me. Her expression is rigid. "Arabella said you've been talking to Dee again."

"Just once."

"Be careful around her. After what she did with Brian—" Gina pauses. "I hope you're sure you can trust her."

I nod, at a loss for words.

She stands, and I follow. "Sorry to cut this short, Maddie, but I have to go meet my lawyer."

"I'll walk out with you."

Once we are outside, she gives me a hug. "Keep in touch, sí? I'll let you know what happens with Brian."

"Thanks, Gina. I'm glad you're home." And glad she's alive.

"See you."

I watch her leave down the street, then I grab my phone and dial Jayson.

"Hey, babe," he answers. "How's Gina?"

"Jayson, did you know about Brian Cordes's parole hearing?"

Silence.

"Jayson?"

"I'm sorry, Mads, I didn't want to freak you out."

"Why would I be freaked out?" I'm unable to hide the tremor in my voice. I may not entirely know what happened, but I certainly remember Brian's aggression. Worse, I remember how he looked at the funeral, standing off to the side in the pouring rain—the way he then grabbed me and threatened me.

"I know what he said before he went away," Jayson says. "But it doesn't matter. Brian is going to have a hard time getting out of this one. They won't just let him off."

"What happened?" I demand before I can stop myself.

Again, I'm met with silence. This time I wait for him to speak.

"Maddie, it's been a rough couple of days," Jayson says. "I think you should go home and relax. I'll head out early today to be with you, okay?"

It's clear I'm not about to get any more answers from him.

"Fine."

"I'll see you soon." The phone call ends before I can say anything else. I can't go home feeling like this. There's only one person in the city who I can always count on for straight answers, and even though I doubt she'll talk to me, I have to try.

Eight

I wait outside Dee's Davisville high-rise condo building for nearly twenty minutes before I dare to go inside and buzz her unit number. No one answers, and security is away from the front desk, but luckily someone comes through the door while I wait and I'm quick to grab the elevator to her floor.

I knock twice before I hear footsteps in the suite, and when the door opens, I'm met by a twenty-six-year-old Dee complete with bright purple hair and round cheeks, exactly how I remember her. Nostalgia whirls up inside me. University nights when we drank bottles of wine in our pyjamas and watched cheesy rom-coms and that stupid human sexuality course she insisted we both take as an elective. I'd never get the textbook photos of STIs out of my head.

Dee's confused expression shifts to anger as she tries to shut the door. My hand flies out to stop her.

"Dee, wait."

"Why should I?" she snaps, her narrow gaze fixed on me. "It's all my fault, after all. And let me guess, Brian getting parole, that's my fault too, right?"

"Dee, please, I need to talk to you."

"I don't care. Last month I needed to talk to you and you shut me out. I'm not interested." She pushes harder on the door, but I resist. Her five-foot-four frame is easy to fight against.

"C'mon, Dee. I don't know what happened between us."

The pressure on the door lets up. Her gaze hasn't softened, but she tilts her head with interest. "How can you say that?"

Seeing young Dee makes all the word vomit I'd been holding back spew to the surface. I know I sound crazy, but I need to tell someone to lift the constricting pressure off my chest.

"Four nights ago, I was thirty-six and living a completely different life," I explain. "Then I woke up in my house, with a new boyfriend, no kids, and everything changed. I have no idea what the hell is going on."

A weight lifts from my shoulders, hopeful my former best friend will be receptive.

Her expression doesn't change. "What are you talking about? You sound crazy."

I do, and I wonder if maybe I am. Maybe the life I thought I had never existed. I'd looked into finding a therapist to talk to, someone to analyze what had happened to me. Though I doubt anyone could explain this phenomenon.

"Maybe I am, but I don't know when we stopped being friends or why I'm dating Jayson. This isn't how it's supposed to be."

She stares at me for what feels like a long time before she steps back and opens the door. "Fine. Come in."

Relief makes my shoulders drop. I step into her condo, and it is exactly how I remember it. The back wall is home to a large bookshelf, cluttered and filled with various books and pointless collectables. Figurines from *The Simpsons* are arranged like they are acting out a scene. A miniature replica of the *USS Enterprise* is encased in plastic. The entire Harry Potter series, Lord of the Rings, His Dark Materials, and Narnia, all in hardcover. There are two lightsabers crossed on the wall like swords—Luke Skywalker's green one and Obi-Wan Kenobi's blue. She has a replica of Harry Potter's wand on a stand on her desk that I remember picking up with her from the exhibit at the Ontario Science Centre. I wonder if I was still a part of that in this life.

Dee makes room for me on the old leather couch in her TV room and sits in the creaky rocking chair across from me. Her stiff posture doesn't ease; she crosses her arms over her chest. She doesn't trust me.

The way she stares me down makes my heart ache. This is the godmother to my girls, the one who loved them and cared for them when Nathan and I were away. She was Aunty Dee to Ava and DeeDee to Haley. She was the one I would call whenever something went wrong. Especially after drunken nights that resulted in stupid fights with Nathan. Her voice would be groggy as I pulled her from sleep with my phone call, but no resentment or annoyance present. She would be at my house in minutes whenever I needed her. I kept her secret for a year before she was ready to come out to her parents and I was her first call after her mother's passing. We spent the night crying and remembering, making the morning seem a little brighter.

I miss her support almost as much as I miss the way my girls' tiny hands would close around my fingers or their arms would try to wrap around my waist.

"Go ahead," Dee says, not trying to mask her resentment. This strange change in our friendship is something I can't grasp.

I drop my gaze from her accusing eyes. "I have daughters, or I did only a few nights ago. Beautiful girls, ones that you loved beyond words. I know it sounds crazy. But I have a whole life different from this one. A life with no Jayson, no Arabella. A life with you still in it."

I glance upwards but her expression remains rigid. I know it all sounds too insane to be true.

"Their names are Ava and Haley." I choke on a sob, and I try to force back my tears. "You waited at the hospital through both their births. Ava, my eldest, is brilliant like my brother and wise beyond her years, and Haley's ability to grasp empathy amazes me every day."

I suck in a sharp breath. "In this life, you were their godmother. We never stopped being friends. You were at every birthday, a part of every memory. Our friendship was unbreakable. And now, life couldn't be more different."

Dee continues to regard me with disdain. She doesn't believe me.

"And the biggest surprise for me beyond our lost friend-ship is that I don't think I've ever met Nathan."

Now Dee's stern expression breaks. "Nathan Page?"

I allow a small smile to form on my lips. She'd set us up in my other life; I had no doubt she still knew him now. They'd met the summer before university at camp. Nathan had been a counsellor and Dee a brand-new counsellor-in-training. He was three years older and had been her mentor; they became fast friends. It wasn't until he graduated from Dalhousie University out east and returned to Toronto that I met him. Yet she'd regaled me with how amazing he was for years before then.

"I have no idea what happened to him."

"You decided you were too pissed to come to my party," Dee scoffs. "So, Nathan thought you stood him up."

A quick calculation tells me I dated Brian four months longer than I should have, probably thanks to my stubbornness.

Dee continues. "It was a shame too, because he is a much better man than Jayson."

"Well, you proved that, didn't you?" My hand flies up to cover my mouth, but it's too late. I have no idea where that resentment came from. I confided in her only to push her away.

Dee's narrow expression returns. "So much for not remembering." She pushes herself from the chair. "I should have known you were coming here to spew bullshit as usual. I think you should go now."

"No, Dee, wait." I stand too but don't move towards her door. I honestly don't know what I expected from her when I told her about my old life, but I still need answers. "What about Brian?"

"What about him?"

"What happened to land him in prison?"

Dee plants her hands on her hips. "You happened." Then she waves towards her door. "Now go."

I follow her command but hesitate before I leave. "I'm sorry for what transpired between us. I always wanted to stay close."

"Don't be." Dee shrugs. "I got to see who you really were." She shuts the door before I can respond and leaves me standing alone in the hallway.

I choke back the tears of mourning for our lost relationship. We were the best of friends, even into adulthood. Once I trusted Dee with almost everything and now it seems I had forfeited it all.

Nine

THEN

I stirred my coffee aimlessly as I waited for Dee to arrive; she was always late. We'd been meeting at this exact spot every Sunday at two for almost three years now. It was our weekly best friend time and my break from Nathan and the children.

When she finally blundered through the door she looked like her usual tornado self. Her shirt was poorly buttoned, and her purse hung off her shoulder, almost spilling its contents across the café floor.

"Sorry!" she called from the door, making the few patrons in the quaint place glance in her direction. "You wouldn't believe the shit show of a morning I've had." Dee plopped down across from me and gathered her green hair into a tight bun. Her blond roots were showing, something that usually bothered her, but she was too flustered apparently to care.

I gestured to the empty cup in front of her and the coffeepot beside it. The waitress knew our orders. We were regulars by now.

"Explain," I said. "Something to do with Maria, perhaps?"

I motioned to the misbuttoned shirt as I referred to Dee's on-again, off-again girlfriend.

Dee glanced down then rolled her eyes, unbuttoning then rebuttoning her shirt. "No, I'm done with her. Old news." She waved her off like she was so passé. "But there's this new guy, Wayne." She wiggled her eyebrows with a suggestion.

"And Wayne is…"

"The IT guy at work."

I snorted a laugh. "Because work flings have worked out for you in the past."

"There's always a first time." Dee shrugged with a wicked grin. "Plus, this one may be worth it. He's got abs like a Ruffles chip; you just want to lick those salty ridges." Classic Dee.

I didn't feign a smile.

"Ugh." Dee dropped her hands to the table. "What's wrong with you, girl?"

I reached for my coffee. "Nothing, I'm fine."

"That's the fakest thing I've ever heard." Dee reached across the table and grasped my arm. "Now spill."

My throat constricted. I was unsure if I should tell Dee the truth and make my problems hers. After all, Dee was the reason I'd met Nathan in the first place.

"It's Nathan," I finally said. "I don't know what to do."

Dee's face went stony. Immediate anger filled her eyes. Always the defensive lioness. "What did the bastard do to you?"

"No, no, Dee." I waved my hands. "He didn't do anything to me."

Her expression softened. "Then what?"

"I—" Should I tell her about seeing Jayson at the conference last week? About texting with him and meeting for drinks? I wasn't sure she'd understand. "I guess I'm not happy anymore." As I said it, a weight lifted off my chest at finally expressing the truth and making my feelings a reality. "I think I've been unhappy for ages, and I've kept denying it. I keep wondering if I made the wrong choice."

Sadness—no, pity—filled Dee's eyes. "But you love Nathan and the girls."

"Of course I do. But what if love isn't enough? I can only tell myself that I'm happy and in love so many times before the reality and the exhaustion beat it down."

"It sure sounds like something happened, Mads." Dee pulled away, scrutinizing me from across the table.

Something had happened. I found the affection I thought I wanted in Jayson. He always answered my texts right away. He asked about my day and was interested in my problems. Nathan barely responded anymore, let alone asked how I was. He was always working; cases were too important to be distracted by idle chitchat. My life was easy, he'd told me. I'd chosen writing as a career, and I could work whatever hours I wanted. The law was more serious.

"It isn't one thing; it's everything. He's always focused on work or thinking about work. When he's home, he's attached to some device or another. His life is literally work, work, work. It's like he forgets he has a wife."

"You've always known he takes his work very seriously," Dee said.

"It seems like more than that." I sighed. "Some days it seems like me and the girls, we're an inconvenience, an imperfection, a case he can't win." *Less the girls, more me.*

"Maddie…" Dee's pity-filled gaze found me again. She may be my best friend, but she'd been close with Nathan since she was eighteen.

"Forget I said anything." It was a mistake to bring it up. The look on Dee's face said everything. Quick on the defensive but ultimately not convinced I had a case. She didn't believe Nathan could be dismissive. That wasn't the Nathan she knew. The last thing I wanted to do now was tell Dee about my secret communication with Jayson. She wouldn't understand. She'd only see the fault and make me feel guilty for seeking happiness where I shouldn't.

"Maddie…" Dee began again.

"No, really." I forced a smile. "I'm probably overreacting. Forget it, please." I reached across for the coffeepot and replenished my mug. "So, tell me more about well-endowed Wayne."

She regarded me with concern for a moment longer. "You're sure?"

"I'm sure."

"Okay, good, because I'm dying to tell you about this." Dee grinned and started going on about her office romp with the "big-dick IT guy." I kept my face neutral and listened.

I tried to take my mind off my own problems, but all I could think about was how happy Nathan and I had been. I thought back to when we met, and when we had Ava, then Haley. Back when it was easy, and life was about us and no one else. If only I could figure out why it went wrong when one fight turned into too many. When the love and companionship I craved stopped. Then maybe, just maybe, it could be fixed.

Ten

NOW

Jayson's accusing stare meets me the moment I step through the front door. He stands in the foyer, arms crossed, as if he's been standing there waiting for me the whole time.

"You didn't come straight home?" he asks, or rather, demands.

I drop my purse on the floor, annoyed but unwilling to give him the real reason behind my tardiness. "I'm sorry. My head is spinning. I decided to walk. You know, to help clear it. I should have called. I thought I would only be a few minutes late."

His expression softens. "I understand. How's Gina?"

"Seems fine, given everything." I shrug, not wanting to discuss the coffee date or Brian's upcoming trial.

"She was always a strong one," Jayson says with admiration in his tone. How well do they know each other? Gina had been such a small part of our relationship in my former life, but given the changes, I'm not surprised it is different now.

I nod in agreement but say nothing more on the topic.

Jayson continues to regard me, fidgeting like there's something I don't know.

With a sigh, I ask, "What is it?"

"Your mom called."

I raise an eyebrow. "And?"

"She's coming home. She wants to do lunch on Sunday."

"Sounds good." I gather my purse and head for the stairs, wanting nothing more than to change out of my clothes into sweats and lie down for a minute.

"You nervous about that?" Jayson calls after me.

I stop and look back at him, confused by the question. "No, why would I be?"

My mom has travelled loads since she split with her second husband during my final year of university. I can never remember where she is or who she spends her time with. Ever since Dad died, she could never settle. It caused a rift in our relationship that we can't seem to repair.

Jayson looks at the floor. "You were pretty mad at her when she left on this last trip, and you haven't answered her calls." He pauses. "It's been over a month."

"I needed some time." I brush off his questions. Whatever my mother did can't be more selfish than when she blew off babysitting my girls because she hopped a flight to LA for a Jay-Z concert with the fling of the month. Or the time she failed to show up at my university graduation because Holt Renfrew had an epic sale—they always have sales. "I'm sure the space has been good for her too."

Again I turn for the stairs, but Jayson catches me in his arms and turns me towards him. "Everything okay?"

"Yeah, why?"

"Not to sound like a jerk," he says, unable to mask his smile, "but we were having a great sex run, and I feel like everything went cold a few days back. After your bad dream."

"Oh." I try not to twist in his hold, though I wish he'd let me free. I've rejected all his advances over the last few days. It's beyond having trouble with my abrupt life change. I should be happy to be in Jayson's arms without the guilt I felt in my other life. But being forced into this decision without choice isn't what I wanted. I'd been ready to give him up, and now he's all I have.

I squirm out of his hold but keep a steady smile in place. "I've been bloated and stressed about the wedding planning. It's almost my time of the month."

His expression fades to disappointment. "Oh, yeah, of course. Forget I said anything." He runs a hand through his hair, his posture now stiff and cold. "I'm going to run down the street to grab something for dinner tonight. See you in a bit." He leaves without a touch of affection.

I peek out the window and watch him walk down the street. It's only then that I feel relief.

I move to the sitting room and allow my slow breathing to continue. Not only is my mind not right, but my body also rejects Jayson's advances. Everything about this choice feels wrong and dirty, but I'm beginning to feel like there's no way out.

I push the thought from my mind, having two other things I want to focus on. First, I reach for my laptop and Google Brian. Other than university alumni information, nothing comes up about his arrest or his crimes. It's as if the information was never reported, and the records are blocked. *Weird.*

I set my laptop aside and reach for my phone. I dial my younger brother, Declan, to let him know about lunch with Mom on Sunday, but all I get is voicemail.

I try Declan again first thing in the morning as he didn't answer my texts or calls. This time the phone rings four times before he picks up.

"What do you want, Maddie?"

"Hi, Dec," I say, though my voice was unable to mask my confusion at his greeting. "Everything all right?"

"Not sure why you care." His voice is flat, indifferent.

For a moment, I pause and worry makes my stomach sink. Have I done something in this life to ruin my relationship with Declan too? I swallow the lump in my throat and press forward, hoping it's just a bad morning.

"You know Mom is coming home?" I ask. "On Saturday. Do you think you could make lunch on Sunday?"

"Doubt it."

"C'mon, Dec. You can bring Naomi."

"Who?" The surprise in his tone throws me.

"Uh—I thought you said you were seeing someone." The pit in my stomach expands, and I force myself to sit so as not to double over. Declan had been dating his wife, Naomi, since they were twenty-four, and now I begin to realize that, like me, he'd never met his future partner in this life.

"Not like I would tell you or that you'd care." His flat tone returns. "I'm not seeing anyone." There's a commotion on the other side of the phone, someone calling his name. It sounds female. "Listen, Maddie. I have to go."

"But Dec, Sunday—" It's too late; the phone clicks and the dial tone returns.

I stare at the phone in my hand for a long moment. Declan and I were once so close. This has to be my fault, like everything else. Whatever choices I made, they'd wrongly affected my brother. Only a few weeks ago, I'd picked him and Naomi up from the airport, and they'd shared their exciting news about the pregnancy. I choke back the sobs that threaten to surface. Ruining my life was one thing, but ruining his life, I'd never forgive myself for that.

I go to shower, tired from all the confusing changes. Is Jayson this toxic to the rest of my life, or did something bigger happen?

As the warm water splashes down my body and my tired mind tries to rest, I know that I brought all of this on myself despite my willingness to blame others.

Eleven

THEN

O nly an hour into my work, my phone buzzed with the text I'd been waiting for. Declan's plane had landed, and he needed a ride. Closing my laptop, I pushed my work aside and grabbed my coat before heading for the car.

Outside, my phone pinged again, this time from a different number. Jayson.

Hope you're making it through the day. Have a free minute for a drink later? Call me when you can.

I stared at the text for a moment before tucking my phone away. We'd been talking nonstop for two weeks—constant messages, the occasional drink, totally harmless stuff. Each time I tried to avoid his messages, something would trigger my need for comfort, and his number would pop up first. I told myself it was because Nathan couldn't understand, but maybe it was because I didn't want to make him understand.

I tried to ignore the message for the entire drive to the airport. Traffic was minimal for the middle of the day, and the drive was quicker than expected. I left my phone in the car as I parked and went to meet Declan in Terminal One.

Passengers filed out of the doors, some pulling their wheelie bags, parents carrying small children, young women gossiping and looking freshly tanned. But I couldn't see my brother amongst the many travellers. I continued to glance around, looking for his tall stature and red hair, but with little luck. As the crowds began to disperse, I instantly regretted leaving my phone in the car. What if I was in the wrong terminal? What if he'd already made it through customs and was waiting somewhere else?

I turned to head back to the parking lot to get my phone when I collided with a broad chest.

"Whoa, little sis."

I glanced up at my younger brother grinning down at me. His usually shaven face was tanned and covered with a bushy, untamed beard. He wore a ball cap over his unruly, long hair.

"Little?" I scoffed. "I've got sixteen months on you."

He patted my head gently. "I meant in size."

I wrapped my arms around his waist and gave him a tight squeeze. It had been a year since he and his wife had left for South Africa on a work excursion. Video calls and emails didn't cut it.

"I'm glad you're back."

"Me too."

I pulled away, reaching for his suitcase, which he snatched out of reach. "Uh-uh, sis. I've got this."

"Where's Naomi?"

"Getting some coffee." Declan grinned. "It's been ages since I've had a good Timmy's Double Double."

I pursed my lips. "Declan, that's gross. You need to cut out the white stuff. It kills, you know. We aren't young anymore."

Declan waved off my concerns as we headed towards the

nearest Tim Hortons booth. "I'm barely thirty-five. I think I'll survive."

I rolled my eyes while we waited for Naomi to finish at the counter. When Declan's wife turned to meet us, I was awestruck at how beautiful the southern sun had made her already tanned skin. Then I noticed it—the round bump showing on Naomi's usually tight stomach.

Speechless, I looked from Declan to Naomi and back again.

"Surprise." Declan grinned. He reached for the coffee from Naomi and gave her a quick peck on the lips.

"What?" I said. "When? How?"

Naomi laughed. It was light and angelic, like everything about her. "I think we've shocked your sister, babe."

Declan winked at his wife. "She'll be all right once her mouth catches up to her brain."

"Congratulations," I sputtered. "I'm sorry. Congratulations." I reached for my sister-in-law and pulled her into a quick hug, feeling her protruding belly bump. When I pulled back, I glanced down. "May I?"

Naomi smiled, reaching for my hand. "Of course."

I placed my flat palm on Naomi's round belly. The feeling was so familiar to my own pregnancies, and it made my heart flutter with excitement for Declan, joy for Naomi, and possibly for me. Could another baby be the answer? Even as I thought it, I knew Nathan would never agree.

"How was the flight?" I asked.

"Just fine," Declan said. "You know Naomi, always the cautious one. She insisted on being cleared by the doctor before we came home." He beamed at his wife. "She is nineteen weeks and very healthy."

Naomi placed her hand on her belly. "We wanted the baby to be born here, surrounded by family."

"Mom is going to freak out." I reached for Naomi's bag, taking it from her shoulder despite her protest, and led them towards the parking lot.

On our way back from Pearson Airport, Declan insisted we stop in at a local restaurant he'd worked at in university. Despite coming from a wealthy family, he'd always wanted to make his own money and spend it on travel. While we partied our days away through school, Declan worked late nights, saved tips, and spent a year after university seeing the world.

He was greeted warmly by several of the waitstaff, and the head chef sent out a special dish on the house. The entire time, he and Naomi smiled.

"How's Nathan?" Declan asked. "I can't wait to see the girls."

"They can't wait to see you." I cast a sideways glance at Naomi, who was picking at the chicken wrap on her plate. The way she pulled it apart but never actually ate it told me the pregnancy was making her more nauseous than she let on. "And Nathan is good. Busy, of course." My stomach knotted at the mention of the husband I'd barely seen in several days. My phone suddenly felt heavy in my pocket. I'd never answered Jayson's message.

Naomi's eyes brightened. "That sounds like Nathan. I've certainly missed him. It feels like ages since we all had dinner together."

"It has been more than a year." I forced a smile.

"We should arrange something," Naomi said.

"Of course." Though I knew it would be nearly impossible. Nathan barely had time for the kids, let alone a night out with Declan and Naomi.

"I'll ask him now." Naomi pulled out her phone before I could protest and moved her fingers across the screen with rapid-fire movements. Within seconds there was a chime, and her screen lit up. He'd answered.

"He says he can't wait." Naomi beamed, sliding her phone across the table so I could see the message. Sure enough, his enthusiasm bled through the screen, complete with exclamation points and emojis oozing excitement for a possible get-together. He even asked about her flight. I could barely get an acknowledgment out of him, let alone an engaging conversation. My chest tightened, and knowing my worried face would betray my emotions, I excused myself from the table.

I clutched my phone in the bathroom, staring down at the text thread between Nathan and me. He hadn't responded to my last message yet had read it given the fact he answered Naomi in seconds. My heart ached as I remembered the way we used to engage in conversation. The times when we couldn't stop texting one another. When the morning began with a good morning message and ended with good nights and x's and o's, now I was lucky to get a one-word response, if any at all. He'd grown tired of me. Naomi, or anyone, was more exciting to engage with. I was a burden, a chore, too uninteresting to be given a moment's time.

Without another thought, I clicked over to Jayson's message and answered.

Sure. Name the time and place. I'll be there.

It was barely a minute before Jayson answered.

SpeakEasy on Adelaide. 6 PM.

I hadn't been to the downtown bar before, but it would be easy enough to find. Luckily, the girls would be picked up from school by their weekday nanny, and she'd stay until Nathan or I came home. Nathan would work until at least eight, giving me enough time to go downtown and return home before he arrived. Worst case, I could say I'd been at the gym. That had been the original plan anyway. Besides, Nathan wouldn't miss me; he probably wouldn't notice.

See you then.

I tucked away my phone, put my smile back in place, and returned to sit with my brother and sister-in-law, feigning utter happiness.

Twelve

NOW

A huge sale at Holt Renfrew always draws a crowd, and Arabella insisted I be a part of it. I met her outside the Yorkdale location, ready to shop till we dropped.

My "bestie" greets me with open arms and glossy lips—a tight squeeze and a sloppy kiss on my cheek. Arabella's eyes are glassy, and I swear her breath smells of booze. I don't mention it and let her drag me into the store and over to the first designer.

Two hours and way too much money later, I have a new dress, shoes, and hat, as well as the two tops Arabella told me to buy and the ass-hugging jeans that were half off but still way overpriced. Shopping is followed by tall mimosas at Arabella's favourite lunch place, conveniently located inside the store—Holts Café.

"So, what's been up with you lately?" Arabella asks after our first drink arrives. "I'm not an idiot. I can tell something is different."

"Nothing, I swear. It's been a busy few weeks. Things are

hectic." Hectic is an understatement, but what more can I say? Life is crazy because I live in an alternate reality where someone who died years ago is alive and well? Yeah, that's not crazy at all.

"Tell me about it." Arabella groans and plants her hand on the table between us, then looks me square in the eyes. "Still, I can't have you forgetting about our arrangement. And that includes Dee."

Her serious tone catches me for a moment. I've only ever seen her this intense once. It was back in our final year of high school when we'd nearly been busted shoplifting at one of the local boutiques. It had been a stupid idea, but as dumb teens, we were excited by it. It wasn't until we had cops asking questions and Arabella swearing us to secrecy that it sunk in how stupid we'd been.

While I don't remember any agreement with Arabella or anything that involves Dee, her focused gaze and stiff expression tells me something awful happened.

"You shouldn't be talking to her," Arabella continues when I don't respond. She sips her mimosa. "She will ruin everything."

I suck in a sharp breath, ready for her to chastise me for visiting Dee after she'd told me not to call her. *How had she found out in the first place?* It's like Arabella has spies everywhere.

"Even just a silly phone call is against the agreement." Arabella eyes me from across the table.

I nearly let out a laugh, realizing she has no idea about my visit to Dee, and she's still focused on the two-minute phone call from days ago.

"Would she ruin everything?" I ask, hoping to prompt Arabella to share more without making her too suspicious. "We were once very close."

"So were we," Arabella says. "Until that thing with Brian and Gina."

I drop my gaze to the table. There it is again. The story of Brian and Gina. What had Dee done?

"Do you think you'll ever want to forgive her?"

Arabella's eyes narrow. "That's not possible. So, you need to stop communicating with her."

"What if I—"

Arabella puts up her hand to stop me and speaks slowly.

"Even if you don't care about our arrangement, if Dee talks, we're all screwed." Arabella leans closer to the table and lowers her voice. "Don't forget. You owe me."

Her concentrated gaze makes my mouth go dry. I'm desperate to know what I owe her for and what really happened that night, frightened by the intensity of her tone and the implied threat. Whatever happened had to be horrible.

Tight-lipped, I nod and drop my gaze to the table.

"Good, because God forbid I have to show someone that video for you to understand how serious this is." Arabella rolls her eyes then says nothing more on the topic after the waitress comes by with an appetizer of bruschetta. She shifts the conversation to our great finds at the mall, the stress of the coming wedding, and the amazing vacation Jack has planned. But all I can think about is what she said. What video is she talking about? Did Dee push Brian into hurting Gina? Brian swore his revenge on only me and Gina, as far as I could grasp from the glimpses of memory available to me. How did Dee tie into it all?

After another round of drinks, Arabella changes the topic to the upcoming bachelorette party, which is tomorrow and supposed to be a total blast. I still can't stop thinking about

Dee, Brian, and Gina. And about that night. How was it different than the one I remember? How did I save Gina?

When our food and drinks are done, Arabella asks the waitress for the bill, then questions the topic I'd been trying not to think about.

"Things with Jay are good?" Her head tilts slightly to the side.

"Yeah, I think so," I say, not sure how else to respond. "He's good to me."

"I'm glad, but don't forget our little deal," Arabella says with a sweet smile. "We wouldn't want the real truth to come out."

I frown as she squeals and jumps to her feet. I glance behind me. That's her greeting for her husband-to-be, who is approaching our table.

Jack slides his arm around Arabella's waist and turns her away from me.

"Let's go, Maddie," she calls over her shoulder. He doesn't acknowledge me, and I am left to trail behind them like an obedient puppy as they walk to the front of the café. At first, I'm annoyed by the clear disinterest in me, but I soon realize I don't care. Between the arrangement with Dee, the mysterious video, and Arabella's comment about the "real truth," my mind is spinning with confusion. At least when they ignore me, I don't have to pretend to be okay.

At the front desk, Arabella drops the cash and the bill for the waitress to handle. I'm not sure the girl got a good tip, so I leave another twenty on the counter.

Outside, I study Jack and Arabella from behind; they are talking closely about something I can't hear. He's different than I expected, relaxed with a loose collar and missing tie. His shirt is untucked, and his gelled hair is messed up and run through. Not the typical businessman I've seen in pictures. His day is likely over.

Arabella gabs on, and he glances over his shoulder at me. His dark eyes dance down my body before meeting my own. His smile unnerves me. Happy to see me, it seems, but not happy enough to say hi. A feeling of dread creeps up inside me. What can this possibly mean about our relationship?

I'm hit with a flash of memory. A quaint French café along the Rue des Rosiers. A well-dressed gentleman sits across from me though he's shrouded in a heavy fog. He says something, and I laugh.

The memory vanishes when Jack looks back at Arabella and says, "Would Maddie like to join us tonight?"

The comment makes me pause, and I feel my eyes grow wide at the start of panic. Join them doing what?

"Oh," Arabella says. "I hadn't thought of that." She leans over Jack's arm, almost stumbling as she does so. "Maddie, you and Jayson must join us for dinner tonight."

"Can't tonight. I promised I'd be home early. He has something planned."

Arabella giggles and pushes herself out of Jack's arms. "He's so brilliant. Doesn't he always do something special for you?"

Jack seems to stiffen at the comment but says nothing. He wraps his arm back around Arabella. "C'mon, Arrie. Let's get you to the car." He glances over his shoulder again. This time the look is colder. "We need to get Maddie home."

After that, I get nothing but coldness from him, as if my saying I have to be home has offended him somehow.

I grab the mail from the mailbox before entering to find our house empty. Checking my phone, I see there's a message from Jayson saying he's stepped out and will be home within the hour. He promises us a night of dinner and maybe a cozy movie. Whatever I want. A quiet night sounds good since, no doubt, tomorrow will be crazy with the bachelorette party.

Before placing the mail on the counter, I notice a tattered envelope that holds nothing more than a thin letter. When I turn it over, there is no return address, only a blue stamp that reads "Beaver Creek Institution."

My breath catches. Is this where Brian is serving time for attempted murder? Can the letter be from him? How was he able to write me? How does he know where I live?

I tear open the envelope to find a short note inside.

Madison Jayne,

The truth will come out no matter how hard you try to hide it. I know everything and you will pay for putting me in here. I've seen the life you've built. A real shame if that world were to come crashing down around you. Don't forget, you ruined my life and I can easily do the same to you.

B.

I shake as I fold the letter back up and slip it into the envelope. Then I rip it into several pieces and toss it into the trash, hoping Jayson won't see it. "B" has to be Brian. What truth is he talking about? How could he ruin my life? He'd done so once already in my old life, and I don't doubt he can do it again now.

Chilled and frightened by the ominous letter, I double-check the locks on the door and head upstairs to have a shower. In the shower, I try to think about my dinner with Jayson but can't stop the tears from falling. I lower myself to the floor and wrap my arms around my legs as I sob. The warm water splashes over my body as my tears mix in with the water falling from the tap. My own choices put me here, and I will have no one to blame but myself if Brian's threats ring true.

Thirteen

NOW

The following morning, I head downtown to see my lawyer. Sean Onyx has been close to my family since before I was born. My father's best friend and partner. My other dad. He was a former defence attorney before shifting to family law. He's straight to the point and never sarcastic but can be playful with the people closest to him. If anyone can answer questions about Brian, it will be Sean.

Onyx and Associates is a prominent law office in the centre of downtown. The company takes up three floors with Sean on the highest floor in the largest office. As the lead partner in his practice, he doesn't often take on minor cases, but he deals with most of our family affairs, including my father's will. He always has time to help us out when we need it. I love and trust him like my own family.

When I approach his assistant, she blinks at me with narrow blue eyes hidden behind her dark bangs, which are too long.

"Ms. Butler, right?" She taps a pen against her chin.

"Yeah, Maddie's fine."

"You're early." She motions to a chair on the opposite side of her desk. "Mr. Onyx is occupied." Her intercom chimes.

"It's fine, Laura. Send Madison in."

Laura presses the button. "Right away, sir." She motions to the glass-walled office behind her. "You're good to go."

"Thanks." I push through the large glass door that is one and a half times my height and into Sean's large rectangular office.

"Madison." Sean stands and rounds his desk, giving me a gentle embrace and a kiss on the forehead. I pause here, holding the familiar hug longer than usual.

"Good to see you. How's your mother?" he asks when I finally release him from my hold.

"Travelling."

"Again." There's a familiar twinkle in his eye. He wears a fine dark suit, and his hair, flecked with grey, is slicked back. "A new beau? She's stopped asking for my assistance with her marriages." After a moment and a playful smile, he adds, "Or divorces."

"You know my mom." I laugh, sitting in the large leather armchair across from his desk. He knows my relationship with Mom has always been strained. But his lighthearted approach to her choices always made me smile. No matter what, I have him to back me.

Rather than returning to his seat opposite me, he takes the other leather chair next to mine and turns towards me.

"Can I get you anything? Water? Whiskey?"

I consider accepting the whiskey before folding my hands and answering, "I'm okay."

"No." Sean taps his chin. "Definitely not okay. Anxious at the very least."

I fiddle with the hem of my sleeve, tugging at a loose

thread. The deafening silence of the office is broken only by Laura's muffled phone conversation.

Sean always sees right through me.

"What is it?"

"I wanted to ask you about Brian Cordes." I press my hands into my lap, trying to stop my leg from shaking. "I've heard rumours that he's being paroled."

Sean's posture stiffens. "He did request parole, and they granted him a hearing. That doesn't guarantee his release."

"The thing is—" I hesitate. "That time in my life is very—hazy. And I'm having trouble finding any information about his arrest."

Sean grimaces. "Madison, you know there was a publication ban on the case at the request of Ms. Rojas's attorney. The courts determined it was for her safety and yours. Mr. Cordes made his intent to hurt you both quite clear. I'm afraid you won't find anything in the media."

When he says it, a memory jumps out in my mind. One of Arabella joking about the arrest records.

"At least they've hidden the details away from the media," she said. "No one can prove the story is different than what we say." A dangerous gleam appeared in her eyes. "Besides, if anyone ever tries to bring any of that trial to light, we have ways of making things disappear." She rubbed her thumb against her fingers then cackled at her morbid joke.

I shake my head clear as my heart starts to thump harder in my chest. "What if they ask me to give a witness statement or to testify at the hearing?" The flashes of memory I seem to be experiencing aren't enough to give me details on the night. How could my statement be of any value now?

"It was made clear at his first trial that you would not be participating in any further hearings," Sean assures me. "Any request to give a statement or testify will be denied, at your request."

"How did I help in his arrest?" I ask. My desperate need for information rises in my throat as it tightens and constricts. I hope he'll tell me what he knows without questioning me.

"Madison, I only know what you told me." Sean gently touches my shoulder. "You were the only witness to his actions. You saved that girl's life."

The way my stomach twists implies there's more to the story. There's something hidden in the arrest, some secret my friends and I decided to keep. Sean won't be able to tell me about that.

"Is he at Beaver Creek?" The words barely come out as a whisper.

Sean nods, though the movement is hesitant, stiff. "He was moved there a month ago. Overcrowding and good behaviour were the reasons they gave for the move. I don't advise a visit."

"I wouldn't dream of it." This only confirms my suspicion that the note was from Brian and that he believes I ruined his life in one way or another.

Sean regards me with skepticism. "Madison, if something is bothering you, you can tell me."

"I swear, it's nothing." I scramble from my seat. "I guess I panicked when I heard about his hearing. I feel better now." I can hear the lies in my tone, but Sean respects me enough not to question me further. He stands beside me.

"If you need anything—"

"You'll be the first to know." I back up towards his office door. "Thanks again."

Outside on the busy streets, I check the time. I have only a couple of hours before Gina will be banging down my door to take me out for Arabella's bachelorette party, something I am certainly dreading.

I hop into my car and start the traffic-filled drive back to my home. With each slow intersection, the pit in my stomach grows. I long for my daughters, my husband, and my old mistakes. Not knowing what had happened to land me here has put me on edge. With each new discovery, that life seems further and further away.

The doorbell rings before I'm ready, and I have to rush down the stairs, pulling my dress over my head in the process.

Gina scrunches her nose as I open the door and takes in my frazzled state. "Maddie, you're not ready. Vámonos!"

"I'm sorry." I wave her through the door. "It's been a hell of a day. I need a minute to grab my shoes and some cash."

"For sure. I'll let Arrie know we'll be a bit late."

I dash up the stairs in search of a suitable pair of footwear and my purse, though a million thoughts dance through my mind. Seeing Gina still threw me. I never thought I'd see the day she lived beyond her twenty-second birthday. Worse, I know that with each thought I have of my girls, with each dream to go home, I also wish for her death. It's easy to forget it when we spend time apart, but now with her standing in front of me—breathing, laughing, talking—it makes me pause. How can I wish for my girls' lives when it means wishing away the life of an old friend?

My stomach flip-flops as I grab my shoes, but the purse is a dud. It's got everything *but* cash.

If I remember anything from our time together, Jayson always stashed cash in his top drawer. It's the first place I look, but it's also empty. For kicks, I search the other drawers, unsure if his habits have changed along with my life. But in the second drawer from the bottom, where he keeps his jeans, I stop. When I flip over a particularly worn pair of pants, there's something that makes my breath catch. A box. A ring box, to be more specific. And when I look inside, I see a thin gold band featuring a large diamond with smaller ones embedded around the base—an engagement ring.

I don't know how long I stare at it, but it's long enough to annoy Gina, whom I soon hear whining from the floor below.

"What's taking so long?"

I snap the box shut and shove it back where I found it, hopeful I arranged his things in a way that wouldn't show I discovered his secret. I still haven't found any cash. Guess I'm out of luck. Thank God for plastic.

"Coming," I call as I push his drawer shut. Jayson is planning to propose to me. My head spins with the idea. Can I marry him? No, I can't let my rightful life go. I need to fix this. I need to find a way home.

A shrill ring from my purse changes my focus for a minute. I grab it, seeing Jack's name flash across the screen.

Worried something may be up with Arabella, I answer.

"Hello?"

"Hey, Mads." Jack's smooth voice comes through the receiver. "Have a minute?" The way his voice dips low causes a strange sensation in my abdomen.

"Not now. About to meet your fiancée."

"Oh." His response is stiff. "Do me a favour then, don't drink too much, and call me later with the details."

"Okay, bye." I end the call with a weird feeling. Do I usually report Arabella's actions to her future husband? How sneaky and dishonest. I hurry down the stairs when I hear Gina groan again, knowing I am pushing our timing.

"Sorry." I flash her a smile. "Let's go."

She gives me a once-over and maintains a steady frown

but doesn't say anything about the way I'm dressed. "You look flustered."

Of course I'm flustered. A weird phone call, an engagement ring, an unsettling letter, and a missing life hangs in the balance right now. How can I focus on a bachelorette bash?

"Can I ask you something?" I slip on the heels I grabbed from my closet.

"Sure, what's up?"

"Has Brian written to you?"

Gina stiffens. "No, of course not. Why? Has he written to you?"

"Yeah, I think so," I say.

"Can I see it?" Gina demands. Her forcefulness makes me pause.

"I got rid of it. I didn't want Jayson to see it."

Her tense shoulders fall. "What did it say?"

"It was just a threat. Claiming I'd ruined his life and he'd do the same to me."

"Oh." Gina doesn't speak for a moment, then her expression brightens. "I'm sure it's nothing. He's behind bars, after all."

The unsettled feeling inside me says something different. "Right, yeah, of course. It must be empty. Just trying to scare me."

"Exactly," she says. "Don't let him get to you. Are you ready?"

I run a hand through my straightened hair. "Yeah, let's go. I'd hate to make Arrie wait."

"Me too," Gina agrees, gathering her purse and heading for the door. "I won't hear the end of it, and you'll get off scot-free."

I follow her to her waiting car but still feel the discomfort whirling around inside me. Why had she brushed off my concern about the letter? Maybe she's trying whatever she can to get past all of this.

"That's not true."

Gina rolls her eyes as she climbs into the driver's side. "When's the last time Arabella blamed you for anything? I'm sure it's been years."

This gives me pause, given the relationship I remember having with Arabella; I was always the problem.

"Honestly, I think the only time was when you were going to dump Jayson." Gina laughs as she pulls out of my driveway and starts down the street. "She guilt-tripped you so hard for that." Gina shoots a glance at me before looking back to the road. "As much as we love him, we also know she's the only reason you gave him another chance. He's lucky he has such a demanding sister."

"There's a lot of good in Jayson." It feels like a natural response. And I know it's true. Despite everything, Jayson has always been good to me.

"All the good ones have sex with Dee." She giggles. She immediately shoots me an apologetic look. "Sorry."

I look away from her. "Big tits and being easy has that effect." Again, the words come out of my mouth before I know what I'm saying. I don't know where the resentment comes from, but I immediately regret it. This is not how I feel about Dee, at least not in the memories I have. The idea that I have some buried resentment for her is hard to process. Dee has been my person for as long as I can remember.

Gina only laughs again, snorting and slapping the wheel. "That was wicked, Mads."

I am glad she doesn't see the horror that crosses my face. Who am I?

By the time our dinner is finished, and we pile into the waiting limo, my head is swimming, and Arabella is drunk—

a common practice, I am coming to learn. It's clear Arabella has a drinking problem; what isn't clear is why no one in her life seems to address it. Except for Jack, it looks like.

Arabella grips my hand the entire way to Maison Mercer, a massive luxe club where she has arranged bottle service and an exclusive booth for her and her closest twenty friends. It promises to be a wild night, and despite the dread in the pit of my stomach, I'm excited to revisit the club. It was a hot spot in my late twenties but closed when I'd entered my thirties.

Maison Mercer is all I remembered it to be—low lighting, glass bars, comfy booths, and a massive rooftop terrace. The dance floor is crowded with steady dance beats playing. The hottest music of the day plays, including Enrique Iglesias's "Tonight" and LMFAO's "Party Rock Anthem." I still remember how awful I was when Nathan tried to teach me the shuffle dance.

The thought of Nathan causes me to look around the club, hopeful I may lay eyes on him. We frequented this club with our friends for years before we settled down. Arabella grabs me and pulls me towards the booth, finding us a seat right next to the bottle of vodka. Gina wiggles in next to me. I glance around again. I was foolish to think he'd be here.

"Weddings all around you," Arabella says. "So how about it, Maddie? Any engagements in your future?"

I cough, choking on my drink. Does she know something? "No idea. We haven't talked about it."

Arabella grins. "Maybe you should talk about it. My brother is in his thirties, after all. You know he's thinking about it."

I stiffen at the thought but force a shrug. "Jayson's always thinking about that next step."

"He's always wanted kids," Arabella pushes.

"Yeah, me too." My hand instinctively goes to my stomach. Memories of the first flutters from when I was pregnant with Ava overtake me, forcing the breath from my lungs. I think about how she was nearly a week late, how my ankles were so swollen I could barely walk, and how Nathan, each time he laid eyes on me, would declare I was the most beautiful woman in the universe.

Next, I naturally think of Haley and how I fell ill shortly into my second trimester. The cold ravaged me and sent me on a downward spiral of depression. Nathan stayed home from work for two days, making sure I was cared for, and Ava was looked after. And when he had to return to the office, he called to check in every chance he could.

Despite where we ended up, Nathan was once my greatest hero.

Sure, I want kids. I've always wanted kids. But I want the kids I already had. I don't want a new life with a new husband and different children. I want my girls—the ones with Nathan, not Jayson.

Arabella nudges me with a playful smile. "Then you should definitely think about it."

I smile in response; she has no idea how much I am thinking about it. My thumb runs across my left ring finger, feeling the ring that used to sit there. Memories of my lost husband and absent daughters. Worse, thinking of the weight of the giant diamond ring sitting in Jayson's drawer.

Arabella's expression changes from playful to serious when she asks something new and surprising. "Would Declan come to our wedding if I invited him? I mean, I'm already inviting your mom, and you're in the bridal party after all."

I raise an eyebrow at Arabella. "I don't know. Dec has always done his own thing. Who knows where he is right now, or if he'd want to come."

"You're right." She nods. "Just thought I'd ask."

"Better to let him be."

Declan had a thing for Arabella ever since we were in high school. It hadn't gone well in my past reality, and something tells me I shouldn't encourage that infatuation again. Besides, he would never want to go to her wedding. The event will be so un-Declan.

The thumping beat shifts to Rihanna's "S&M" and Arabella lets out a loud scream.

"I love this song." She grabs my hand and pulls me to my feet, dragging me towards the sweaty bodies gathered on the dance floor. Many of the girls join us, and Arabella spins around, screaming, "I can't believe I'm marrying Jack Davenport!" Her words are met with loud cheers as all the girls dance and celebrate her upcoming wedding.

I feel lost on the dance floor, not having been to a real club in years. The last time I stepped foot in Toronto's bar scene was to meet with Jayson a few weeks ago, in another lifetime. Now, despite the distraction, celebration, and flowing alcohol around me, my mind keeps returning to a disturbing letter, a diamond ring, and Nathan and the girls.

Fourteen

THEN

I stood outside the glass building staring at Jayson's daunting bar of choice. The entire restaurant was visible with a fishbowl effect. It's not the typical secret meeting spot. SpeakEasy 21 was a sleek cocktail bar in the centre of the financial district of downtown Toronto. It had been prospering in this location for several years now and was a hip venue for upper-middle-class residents to unwind after a long day at the office. The open-concept bar had a 1920s theme with modern aluminum finishes mixed with the timeless touches of leather seating and brass edging. The ceiling above the tables had a honeycomb motif to inspire the idea of a hive. The concept is a bit discomforting, and I felt out of place wearing my tired black leggings and a long semi-sheer top. I was a mother approaching middle age, not a suited-up business mogul drinking a fancy cocktail and sporting a sleek, expensive-looking briefcase. For a moment, I worried about the stares as I entered the crowded restaurant where I didn't belong. As I moved through the room looking for Jayson, none of the patrons glanced my way. Someone like me wasn't even on their radar.

Jayson sat at the white marble bar, two drinks already in front of him. I stopped, hidden behind a bar table and the four occupants deep in discussion. A couple walked over, the man asking Jayson about the empty barstool next to him. Jayson pointed at the second drink and said something. The couple moved further down in search of someplace else to sit. I stared at the empty stool, the sweating drink on the counter. *What was I doing here?*

When his eyes found me, he smiled and waved me over. I'd been seen; there was no escaping now.

"Hey." Jayson grinned and slid an off-coloured martini across the bar. "I ordered for you. I hope that's all right?"

"That's fine." I leaned forward and sniffed the drink before taking a hesitant sip. Coconut and a hint of pineapple. Definitely vodka. Tangy. Strong but good.

"One of their specialties," Jayson said, nodding to the martini in his hand. "It's creatively named the Coconut Martini."

The smell takes me back to a family vacation to the Dominican Republic when Arabella and I were in our first year of university. Jayson and I were secretly dating, and our families were still very close. Our parents had thought the trip down would be good for us. Little did they know Arabella and I spent the nights out late with Jayson and Declan. We danced the nights away in the discotheque, drinking Bahama Mamas and Piña Coladas. It ended with us skinny dipping in the ocean and secret sex on the beach—the days when I was still impulsive and fun.

As pleasant memories came back, I couldn't shake the guilt that rose inside me. That fun, impulsive person was also the girl involved in Gina's accident. The one who refused to step in despite knowing the dangers Brian posed.

I swallowed the thought, trying to force it from my mind. Tonight wasn't supposed to be about the past. This was about now.

I forced an awkward smile. "Clever."

"First time here?" Jayson asked.

I nodded. "It's a bit fancier than my usual spots."

"It's one of my favourites." Jayson swirled his glass before sipping again.

"You fit in." I glanced around the room, noting the similarities. Though devoid of a tie, Jayson's pressed Armani suit made him look like all the other financial guys in the place. I, on the other hand, didn't resemble the classy women with their pencil skirts and pantsuits.

Jayson gave me an amused grin. "Feeling out of place?"

"Always." A weight lifted off my shoulders as I admitted it.

"Relax," Jayson said. "You used to be a regular on the hip club scene. This shouldn't make you feel that uncomfortable."

It made me squirm with heated memories of Jayson and me grinding on each other as the bass thumped through the darkened club. The sweaty bodies surrounding us, pressing us together and forcing us to move with the music. The alcohol, the drugs, the numbness. Everything was easier then. Before life became complicated with death, marriage, children, and unhappiness.

Jayson nodded towards a small stage in the far corner of the room. There, a man attired differently from the patrons fiddled with a speaker and cable. "There will be live music soon. It's always mellow. I promise you'll love it."

I didn't answer, taking another sip of my drink.

"Long day?" Jayson asked.

"Kind of. I picked Declan up from the airport today. Sorry I didn't answer sooner."

Jayson waved off my excuse. "You're allowed to be busy, Mads. You do have a life."

A life I was avoiding at present.

"How's the little bro doing?" Jayson asked. "It's been ages since I saw him." They'd been close when Jayson and I had dated. Declan made friends easily. He liked almost everyone, and the feeling tended to be mutual.

"Married and expecting. I found out today when I picked them up." As hard as things were for me and as easy as it was to compare their life to mine, I was happy for him. I had to be.

"Crazy how things change." Jayson gulped back the rest of his drink and waved down the bartender. "Another?"

I glanced at my martini; it was barely half gone.

Jayson took my silence as an affirmative and ordered another round.

"What are you working on right now?" Jayson asked as the next round of drinks arrived.

The small talk made me fidget with the napkin. Every other time we'd met, our conversations had been easy, natural, two old friends catching up. But this time, this place, made it seem weird. Before I answered, I finished my first martini in two large gulps. I reached for the new one and told Jayson about the novel I was planning.

"Time travel, hmm." Jayson mused. "Any particular reason you were inspired by the idea?"

I shrugged. "My heroine is so fascinated by her history that when she gets a chance to go back in time and live as her ancestors, she jumps at the opportunity. But, of course, time travel has its consequences. You can't place someone into the past without changing things. After all, they say the butterfly effect is a real thing. One different step can create a whole alternate reality."

By the time I finished my story, Jayson had downed his martini. He waved down the waiter for another round, ordering before I could stop him. "You sound superstitious."

"No," I protested, finally starting to relax in the crowded speakeasy. "I'm realistic. You can't go back in time and change things and expect everything to remain the same. Everything happens for a reason."

The waiter set the new drinks down, and I finished my second quickly. My head was starting to swim.

"Maybe," Jayson said in a dismissive tone. "But if that's true, I'm trying to figure out this reason."

As he made the suggestion, the lone guitarist started playing, causing much of the surrounding noise to be drowned out. It was difficult to hear, let alone talk. It was very loud for a single guitar and speaker, not the mellow tunes Jayson had promised.

As if reading my thoughts, Jayson waved down the bartender with his credit card. Then he leaned closer to me.

"Let's finish up and go."

I nodded.

We only listened to a single song before gulping back the rest of our martinis. I followed him through the crowd and out the main doors onto the busy street. He immediately caught my hand and steered me through the commuters. His touch sent a prickle up my arm, reminding me of the way he used to spin me on the dance floor when we were still young with our entire lives ahead of us. The way we'd stumbled down the street after a night of drinking, giggling and kissing as we went. Everything with Jayson had been easy, comfortable, and reliable. And a part of me wanted to feel that way all over again. Before anything went wrong and I made bad choices.

The alcohol was making me dizzy, and I kept my stare on the sidewalk as Jayson led me away from the bar. Three drinks shouldn't be enough to intoxicate me, but I guess chugging them didn't help. I also didn't know how much alcohol was in them. Plus I'd barely eaten all day. As I considered my exit strategy for the evening, Jayson stopped, and I found myself outside a condo building.

Jayson ran a hand through his hair, loosening the tight gel and making several strands tumble forward. I wanted to reach up and brush them back, to feel his soft stubble under my fingers and his lips against mine. I shook my head, trying to clear the thoughts from my mind.

Jayson shifted from foot to foot, looking at the entrance. "Would you want to come up? One last drink?"

I should refuse, but I didn't want to. Instead, I told myself I wanted to see Jayson's place and where his life had taken him. I had spoken so much about myself and my life over the past few meetings, it was his turn to divulge.

"Sure." I gently squeezed the hand that still held mine. "Sounds great."

Jayson grinned and led me into the lobby of his building. I ignored the twisting guilt in my stomach, knowing I'd rather be here than going home to Nathan.

Fifteen

NOW

S unday morning brings an unwelcome post-bachelorette hangover and the sinking realization I have to have lunch with my mother. Jayson is up well before me, having not drank the night away.

"Good morning, sleepyhead." Jayson swivels in his chair as I enter the main room. His greeting is pleasant, so I guess I wasn't as big a mess as I thought last night. The last time I remember coming home to Jayson blackout drunk was back in university. I'd been so sloppy drunk—or so he told me— that I passed out with my party dress on and McDonald's French fries scattered across the floor. The entire day following, I got nothing but a cold shoulder from Jayson. Today is different.

I give him a small nod, the headache throbbing behind my eyeballs.

Jayson chuckles. "No surprise you're not feeling so hot today." He stands and takes me in his arms. "Though I had quite a blast with you when you came home last night." The sparkle in his eye tells me all I need to know. Alcohol always makes my clothes fall off.

I groan at the thought of drunken sex with Jayson.

"Go have a shower," he says. "I'll make a fresh pot of coffee. You still have a couple of hours to get ready before you have to endure your mom."

I'm grateful for the idea of coffee and simply do as I'm told; first a shower, then everything will look better.

Whether it's the steam or the coconut shampoo, I get out of the shower feeling like a regular human again, though the headache is still present. Nothing a few painkillers won't help. And when I have my first sip of hot coffee, the day suddenly doesn't seem as awful as I thought it would be. Until I remember my mom.

"There!" Jayson grins, turning away from his computer again. "Don't you look chipper."

"I definitely feel better."

"And she speaks!" He throws his hands up in mock celebration. "Hurray!"

I giggle. Jayson always had a way of making me smile in the worst situations. Like the time I failed my final exam in my Experimental Narrative class and was confident I would fail the course. Jayson was quick to whisk me away for the weekend to get my mind off the grades. We ended up at a quaint bed-and-breakfast on the outside of town, where we spent the day in each other's arms. By the time we returned, the exam was forgotten, and thankfully, the grade wasn't bad enough to make me flunk the whole course.

"Thanks for the coffee," I say.

"Anything for my girl." He winks, then looks back at his computer screen.

Back in my bedroom, I search for something appropriate

to wear at lunch. I haven't seen Mom in forever, let alone spoken to her. She loves to criticize me and comment on my shortcomings. I was Dad's favourite. She never liked that. Today, I have to put on my best show to avoid any judgement or nagging.

Finding an outfit takes a bit too long, and soon Jayson is calling for me to come down so I won't be late. He's taking a break from his work to drive me to lunch—in case I have a drink or two to calm my nerves.

"You sure you don't want to come?" I ask when we're in the car.

Jayson flashes me a smile. "Trust me, it's better that you reconcile with your mom before I get thrown back into the equation."

"She's always liked you," I protest.

"She's always liked my family's money. How long did she stay with us last time?" His tone says it was too long, and I have a flash of a memory of Mom making herself at home with Jayson and me for nearly a month.

"Fine. You're right. Plus, I know you have work to do." He's in the middle of editing an article I have to submit by Wednesday.

Parked outside the restaurant, he leans close and kisses me. "Smile and nod, and you'll get through the meal quickly. There's nothing to worry about."

"I know." I roll my eyes. "I already have it all planned out."

"That's my girl."

I climb out of the car, and Jayson is on his way. I stand on the sidewalk, staring at the entrance, considering blowing off the whole thing. But if I do, I'll have to deal with my mother another time. It's better to get it over with.

Mom catches my eye before I have a chance to speak to

the hostess. Mom's flamboyant outfit, coupled with her dark makeup and bright red lips, makes her a familiar but disturbing sight. She wears her grey hair pulled back, with a wide-brim cap discarded and hanging from the back of her chair. She is precisely the same woman I remember. She waves me over and stands to greet me with a firm hug, a quick peck, and that familiar strong odour of rosewood and patchouli that she calls her chic perfume.

"Hello, baby girl," she coos like an adoring mother. It isn't lost on me that this is apparently the first time we've spoken since she left over a month ago. She always treated me like an object to coddle. It's an act, of course. Her true feelings will be revealed after a few hours together.

"Hi, Mom." I take my seat, keeping my response stiff but polite. The idea of this lunch is nothing but exhausting. A farce I'm forced into joining.

"No Jayson?" she asks as she hands me a menu.

"Not today. He had to work."

She pouts, clearly put off she didn't get to fawn over my beloved boyfriend, then nods her understanding and smiles. "Aren't you going to ask how my trip was?"

I guess we're done talking about me.

"I'm sure you'll tell me all about it." I glance over the expensive meal choices with a bored tone. I'm certain my mother expects me to foot the bill for today's lunch. She always mooched off people when she could. That's likely how she's been able to travel in style.

"It was marvellous," she gushes. Our conversation stops there when Mom looks up and gasps. Her eyes squint, then fill with tears as she hops to her feet, nudging the table with her eager movement.

"Oh, I can't believe it!" Her voice rises three octaves, coming out as an excited squeal.

I turn to see the cause of her excitement and find I'm on my feet too. There, in the restaurant entrance, still standing at the same six feet despite slouched shoulders, with brushed-back ginger hair and square hipster glasses, is Declan. My baby brother.

Mom scurries across the room and wraps her arms around Declan's waist. He stands several inches taller than her and offers only a stiff response.

His gaze is on me instead. Only when Mom pulls away does Declan look at her. She leads him across the restaurant to our table, where he takes the only empty seat. The one that now occurs to me might have been reserved for Jayson.

"Thank goodness you came," Mom says.

Declan runs a hand through his hair, indifference in his tone. "I was in the area."

"Where are you staying?" I ask. "You can always stay with me." He used to always ask for a room when he was between places.

His eyes shift to me with a tired expression. "I don't need your help."

"Dec—"

"No, Maddie." His voice is sterner this time. "I don't want it."

"Shh, Maddie," Mom scolds. "Don't upset your brother." Then she smiles at her son. Her pride and joy. Dad's spitting image. "Tell me, sweetie, how are you?"

I sit back, watching Declan's demeanour relax as he speaks to Mom about where he's living—with some friends outside the city in a small apartment—and where he's working—general labour for a local manufacturer. All of which is news to me. Declan was a traveller, sure, but he had a degree in archeology and travelled for research in my old life, something he and his wife, Naomi, did together. With her, he had a job at the university, where he was a professor and a researcher—distinguished and renowned. My selfishness has completely changed his world.

We order our meals, and the conversation shifts to me. Mom asks about work, about Jayson, and the house. Then finally, she asks about Arabella and Jack's upcoming marriage.

Declan's relaxed posture stiffens as he stares at his plate, uninterested. How did I manage to piss him off so much that he's indifferent to my life? I'm dying to learn more about where he's been and where he's living, but he barely spares a glance in my direction.

"I bet the dresses look gorgeous on you girls," Mom enthuses when we shift the discussion to Arabella's chosen bridesmaid gown. "Oh, I wish I could see it."

"Lucky for you, you will." I reach for my drink, feeling clever that I thought to order wine. Already the lunch and conversation feel simpler under a light buzz. "Arabella told me she was inviting you to the wedding."

Declan cocks his head towards me. "Seriously? Why would I go to that?"

"Not you, Dec," I say gently as I look towards my brother. "I didn't think you would be interested. So I told her not to worry about it."

"Of course you did." His eyes shift to focus on his phone on his lap to express extreme disinterest.

First, he's angry he's invited to something in my life, and then he's mad I got him out of it. What could have caused this much discomfort between us?

"Oh, I'm so excited," Mom squeals, either ignoring Declan's irritation or oblivious to it. "It will be the wedding of the year."

"Arabella wouldn't have it any other way." I wave over the waiter to order another glass of wine.

Declan mumbles something under his breath. I glance over at him. Mom seems not to notice.

"What did you say?"

Declan looks at me over the rims of his square glasses. "Nothing."

"I heard you." My grip on my empty wineglass tightens. "You said something."

"Saint Maddie wouldn't have it any other way either." The disgust is evident in his tone.

"What is that supposed to mean?" I snap.

"Maddie, please," Mom begs, reaching over and touching Declan's hand. He flinches, pulling away from her. "Don't pick a fight with your brother. I'm glad he came. I don't want any arguments."

Me picking a fight? Declan's the one being hostile with no explanation.

"What about the floral arrangements?" Mom asks, pushing the conversation away from Declan and me. "I remember all the lilies we had when I married your father." That dreamy look in her eyes returns. No wonder she always sides with Declan. He's the only one who brings forth fond memories with just his appearance.

When our lunch is finished and we make plans with Mom for the following Tuesday, I'm determined to get a moment to talk with Declan.

"Hey, Dec!" I call after him as I follow him from the restaurant.

"What do you want, Maddie?" He turns towards me with his hands pressed into his jacket pockets.

"To talk to you." I reach his side and wave forward. "I'll walk you to the subway."

He grits his teeth. "Fine."

"I wanted to say sorry for whatever I did to hurt you." I'm unsure how else to approach it. My brother and I are supposed to be close. There's only a year and a half between us. We were the best of friends throughout high school and university, at least as far as I can remember. How could I have screwed things up?

"It's fine," he says, though his tone is short. "Forget it."

I grab his arm to stop him and turn him towards me. "I can't forget it. You won't speak to me, and you barely look at me. I don't understand."

"It doesn't matter." Declan jerks out of my hold. "I don't want to talk about it."

"But—" My phone starts to ring.

He glances at my purse and says, "Get it. I'm leaving." He turns down the street away from me.

"Declan!"

He doesn't look back.

My phone stops ringing, and whoever called is directed to voicemail. Declan rushes down the street, hands pressed into his pockets and shoulders slumped forward. He turns towards the subway.

I watch until I can't see him anymore, all the while hoping he'll change his mind and come back. He never does. The avoidance makes my heart sink with sadness. The memories I have of my younger brother are happy, supportive. He was always the first person I called with good news, bad news, and everything in between. Now he wouldn't even look at me.

I turn back towards my house and reach into my bag, pulling out my phone. The missed call is from Jack, and there's a voicemail.

His voice is agitated. "Mads. I get that you didn't call me

last night, but you have to call me today. I want to meet at six. Come by my office." The message ends, and I hit delete. I have no desire to dish on Arabella, especially after the lunch I had. Right now, the idea of a bottle of wine and an afternoon hiding in my room is too good to pass up.

I always knew my family would drive me to drink.

Sixteen

NOW

The following day, I helped a drunken Arabella into her bed after another liquid lunch, one at which I'm glad I didn't drink much. I'd tried voicing my concern about her drinking, but she brushed it off as stress. Now, I'm sure it's more than a calming tactic.

The lunch was a chance to discuss the upcoming wedding only a couple of weeks away. Despite being Maid of Honour, I have been given very little information about it all. Arabella keeps every detail locked up tight. She's always loved her secrets.

When she's tucked into bed, I go over to her office, ready to dive into my most recent project, an upcoming post on the social scene in our city, something Arabella is a major part of. I was writing a lot for a local blog—something unchanged from my memories. Writing had always been my career of choice. My main goal was to publish a novel or multiple novels. That hasn't panned out yet.

I'm in the office only a few minutes before Jack walks in and interrupts my work. Arabella's fiancé looks different than when I last saw him. Now he resembles the man from the articles I researched the previous week: suave and distinguished. He isn't the relaxed, just-off-work guy who picked us up from the mall. Now he's all business, looking as if he's come from a serious meeting.

His expensive pin-striped suit is flawless, and it looks as if he just put it on. His styled hair is slicked back, and a large gold watch is prominent on his wrist. He reminds me of the rich gangsters from those classic films my mom used to watch. Sleazy and about to do something criminal.

My chest flutters at the sight of his angular jaw and straight nose, sending the same strange feeling through me as he had at the mall. His eyes are dark and brooding, peering right into mine as his lips part slightly.

"There you are." Jack closes the door behind him and flicks the lock. He's across the room in a few short steps, approaching me like a lion ready to pounce. "You've been avoiding me."

Before I have a chance to respond, he catches me in his arms and presses his lips against mine as his hands slide down my waist and pull me towards him. For a moment, I freeze, unsure how to react. This is wrong, but the pressure of his lips and the way his tongue seeks entry feels familiar as if I've been here before.

When my mind clears, I bite down on his lip, and he pulls away.

"Ouch." His wicked smile doesn't fade, and he continued to eye me like a boy would his favourite toy.

"A little feisty today?" His fingers grip my ass. "If you'd called, that wouldn't have been a problem." He leans in to kiss me again, but I avoid it this time, slipping out of his hold and moving across the room.

"What are you doing?" I demand, finding my voice.

His eyebrows fold together, confusion gracing his handsome face. "I was going to fuck you until you started this."

"Are you serious?" I glance at the locked door. "Arabella's in the other room."

"That hasn't bothered you before." His confused expression melts into exasperation. "What are you playing at, Maddie? You're the one who started all this after the blackmail."

Blackmail? I frown. Am I sleeping with my supposed best friend's fiancé because of something he has over me? Or her? Either way, I am such a hypocrite.

"I don't think we should do this." No, we definitely shouldn't do this; at least that's what my brain screams. My body feels different, hot with the thought of Jack's fit frame. I'm dizzy with conflicting feelings. Reject his advances, give in to them. Push him away. Pull him closer.

Jack shakes his head and moves towards me again. He doesn't care what I think.

"I've missed you." His hands grab my waist, and he bends down, nuzzling my neck, trailing kisses across my collarbone. I shudder under his touch, my body betraying my mind's logic.

"Jack." I mean to protest, but his name comes out as a low moan.

His kisses dip lower between my breasts. His hands hook onto my thighs, lifting me against him and pushing me against the wall—this time, my body takes control and returns his passionate kiss. My nails dig into his shoulders as his lips crush mine.

Stop! Stop! But my body doesn't listen to my screaming mind. It pushes back, craving Jack's touch.

A voice stops everything.

"Jack?"

I tilt my head back, breaking our contact. It's Arabella, and she's close by.

"Jack?" We hear her calling again, this time closer.

I untangle myself from his arms and straighten my skirt. I run my hands through my hair to calm it and move back to the desk.

"Go." I wave towards the door.

He moves to it but glances back before he leaves. "We're not finished here." He grins and is gone. As I fall into the desk chair, I'm reminded of the last affair I had with Jayson in another life. The guilt. The desire. The disgust. The want. Conflicting feelings are making my mind spin with confusion. My stomach twists as I reach up and touch my lips because while the guilt tells me I'm a terrible person for sleeping with my best friend's fiancé, part of me is excited by it.

Seventeen

THEN

It wasn't supposed to happen like this. One drink at
SpeakEasy was the promise, but it turned into three. Then
a nightcap to prolong the evening. But that wasn't enough.
Jayson's tender touch on my shaking hand. His soft lips
moving across my cheek to my mouth and down my neck.
The way his fingers caressed my hips and gently tugged at
my loose shirt, asking for permission, begging for approval.
The alcohol overwhelmed my senses, and I gave in to desperation. I gave in to him.

At the time, it had felt right. It was everything I'd ever
wanted. But now, the only thing that stuck in my mind was
what I stood to lose.

I pulled my shirt over my head, followed by the leggings
he'd taken off me an hour before. Jayson still lay in the messy
bed, his eyes tracing my every movement, entranced by the
way I dressed, attempting to conceal my shame.

It had been years since we'd last been this close and,
although older, he was still as attractive. His torso was as firm
and chiselled as I'd suspected from our first hug at the confer-

ence and his body hair was light. He was handsome, but he wasn't mine anymore.

"You should stay the night," he said, his voice and gaze both laced with lust.

I grabbed my phone from the dresser and turned it back on. As it reconnected, a missed voicemail popped up on the screen. I could guess who had called. It was late, after all. At least the voicemail indicated I was missed at home, though I couldn't decide if that was a good or bad thing.

"You know I can't." I tossed my phone into my small handbag and pulled my tangled hair from my face, tying it into a tight bun. It would look suspicious coming home this late, worse if I reeked like sex.

The way his gaze darkened told me his inner thoughts, a look akin to our time as a couple. "Don't be stupid. Stay."

He moved to get out of the bed.

I put my hands up, palms facing his advance. "Don't."

He ignored my warnings and crawled from beneath the covers, still naked. He strode towards me, clearly ready for another round. The man was insatiable, and it was one of the things that had always drawn me to him in the past. He was nothing like Nathan. Jayson was dangerous and hungry. Maybe that's why I was tempted back into his bed. Old habits die hard.

"Call him," Jayson said. "Tell him you're at a friend's."

I bit down on my lip as my gaze traced over every inch of Jayson's sculpted body. I didn't have any friends who would cover for me to make it a believable lie. Everyone in my life loved my "saint" of a husband.

"I can't."

Jayson's playful expression faltered, and he reached for his discarded boxers. "No, you can. But you won't."

He was right. Of course, I wouldn't. I didn't know what

this meant yet. Was it worth my entire life to be with him? To leave my husband and only see my girls half the time? Could we last? Maybe this was a fling and nothing to be taken seriously.

"I can't."

Jayson nodded, his expression defeated as he pulled on his boxers. He motioned to the bathroom. "You might want to shower before you leave."

He turned and left me standing alone in his bedroom. As cold as the suggestion had been, a shower would be a smart move. I'd lie and say I'd been at the gym. I needed to rinse off after a workout.

As the water poured down my body, I steadied my uneasy breathing. Maybe this was a good thing. It put things into focus.

Being like this with Jayson would be a whirlwind of lies. It already was … I couldn't live the rest of my life lying to everyone I loved. I couldn't even bring myself to tell Dee the truth.

Tears began to fall, mixing in with the running water. I remembered the way Jayson's hands trailed across my breasts, gripped my butt, the way his lips devoured my mouth. At the time, it was everything I wanted, and now I felt dirty, sneaky, and wrong.

I'd betrayed Nathan and our girls. I broke every vow and promise I made. And for what?

I'd let it go too far. What if it was too late to salvage my marriage and save the life I had? What if I'd already played the cards I had, and this was it for me?

All I knew now was what I didn't want. I didn't want to lie. I didn't want to lose my girls, and I didn't want to keep living unhappy.

Eighteen

NOW

After a lot of prodding, Dee agrees to meet me at Jules Café, a quaint patisserie in Davisville. It's a place we hung out while at university, and it brings back fond memories of my missing life.

She sits down across from me, her dyed hair pulled back from her face. She wears a scowl. Still, she came.

"What do you want, Maddie?" she asks, though her words suggest exhaustion rather than anger.

"I wanted to talk." I fiddle with the napkin on the table between us. "I'm doing something bad…" I trail off, unsure why I want to confess my affair in this life but could never come clean about Jayson. The idea of blackmail stuck in my mind since Jack left me alone in the office, and given the "deal" Arabella claimed we had and the video she mentioned, I'm sure she's behind it.

Dee taps the table when I don't continue right away. "Get on with it."

"I've been sleeping with Jack." I spit it out quick, like ripping off a Band-Aid.

Dee coughs, choking as she sips her water. "You're what?" Her tone isn't disgusted, as I expected, but amused.

"Sleeping with Jack," I say more slowly. "Because Arabella is blackmailing me."

Her arms cross over her chest. "And that surprises you?"

I drop the napkin, folding my anxious hands in my lap. "No—I mean, I don't think so. It's—I don't know what she could be blackmailing me with."

"Beats me." Dee rolls her eyes. "But it probably has something to do with Brian."

"Did something happen between you and Brian?" I tread carefully.

Dee's scowl breaks, and she lets out a snort of laughter. "You know what happened with Brian, even if Arabella lied about it."

"Dee, I know what I said a few weeks ago sounded strange, but I am having a hard time remembering things," I say, on the verge of begging. "I need to know."

"It's simple, Maddie," Dee says, leaning closer to the table. "You happened. Even if Arabella has convinced everyone it was my fault, we both know you're the reason that night went to hell."

I frown. "What does that mean?"

"It means your good friend Arabella must have something on you," Dee says. "Something you were willing to sacrifice our entire relationship for."

"What about Jayson?"

Dee looks away. "I don't want to talk about this."

"But I do." I tap the table between us, drawing her attention back to me. "You claim I tossed everything away because of Arabella and that you sleeping with him had nothing to do with it. I need to know the truth. What *happened* that night?"

"You left him alone at my party," Dee snaps. "You went

off to fuck Brian and expected me to pick up the pieces. I was drunk, and so was Jayson. He was miserable because you'd left him, and he didn't know why. He was looking for comfort. We both knew it was a huge mistake, but if you hadn't left, it would never have happened."

"You slept with Jayson when I was dating Brian?" The information astounds me, and my confusion seems to do the same for Dee.

"I don't know if I'd ever say you and Brian dated, but you fucked, that's for sure. Even after I hooked up with Jayson, it took you months to find out."

"But we remained friends," I say, shaking the hazy memory away. "I forgave you."

"For a bit." Dee shrugs. "Until Arabella changed the story."

Then I start to understand what she's saying, a memory spills into my view.

I pushed Jayson aside as I stormed towards Dee, swaying with each unsteady step.

"Fucking bitch!" I screamed, swinging at my best friend.

Dee ducked and avoided my hand. "Maddie, calm down."

"I won't!" My voice rose louder. "We're done, you and me. Slut." This time when I swung, I made contact with her cheek. A sickening slap was witnessed by all those surrounding the fight.

It happened quickly. Jayson grabbed Dee. Brian took my arm and pulled me from the room. Outside, he threw his arm over my shoulder.

"Fuck her," he mumbled. "I've got something that will put a smile on your face." His free palm flattened, revealing a baggy of white powder.

"Let's get the hell out of here."

"What happened with Gina that night?" I ask.

"She went after you guys," Dee says. "She'd been sleeping

with Brian too and went to confront you to get some answers. You know Brian was a hothead; he got angry."

That much I can remember.

"And he attacked her." Flashes of this night pop into my mind. Outside the car, near the side of the road. I stood there watching as Brian pushed Gina, as he hit her.

"And you stopped him," Dee finishes.

But I could have stopped him sooner. I watched him hurt her. I almost let it happen. My stomach twists with guilt. My throat constricts.

"Maddie?"

I look up and connect with Dee's eyes. For the first time in my new life, she looks concerned.

"Are you okay?"

I gasp for breath, trying to calm the guilt inside me. "No, I'm fine." What else can I say? I just realized that I had some fault in Gina's accident. That I was being hailed as a hero when, in reality, I almost didn't stop him.

Her concern vanishes. "Good."

"Why doesn't anyone know?" I ask, realizing I've been blaming Dee for something that wasn't true.

Her arms cross over her chest again. "Arabella made sure of that. She convinced everyone I was sleeping with Brian, and you were the saint who showed up and saved the day. She made sure everyone remembered our fight, though she twisted it to be about Brian, not Jayson." Then she shakes her head. "You and I have been distant for ages but never hostile. I didn't know the truth until I heard it a couple of months ago. When I confronted you about it, you sided with Arabella and cut me out."

Which is why I hung up on her the month before. "I'm sorry, Dee."

"Don't be," Dee says. "Whatever Arabella's got on you is

enough to keep you where you are, no matter how unhappy it makes you." She stands from the table, clearly not interested in finishing our conversation. "And I guess that's what you deserve. To be as miserable as Arabella and all her cronies."

She turns and leaves me alone in the booth to consider where my life changed. She isn't wrong in what she said. In choosing Arabella, I lost my best friend Dee, the family I knew, and I turned into the type of person I hate. Worse, I am starting to realize where it all went wrong—me.

I want to know more, ask Gina every detail she can remember, but I can't. The surfacing memories I'm experiencing are constricting. Brian tried to kill her; I don't need to make her relive that horror just to give me some details.

No, as scared as I am, only Brian can tell me about that night. He's two hours away, and it would be an effort to arrange a meeting with him, but I've exhausted all my other options. I have to put in a request. I have to at least try.

Nineteen

NOW

The idea that Arabella has dirt on me has been at the forefront of my mind. She and Jack are going out of town, which is my opportunity to search her old condo in York Mills. She never sold it after moving in with Jack, and if she has anything on me, it will be hidden there.

Luckily, I still have a key.

Her old condo isn't far from my house. It isn't as empty as I thought it would be, still filled with Arabella's things and looking much like it did back in university. The same furniture and decorations cover the walls. It's as if Arabella moved into Jack's house but left all of her memories behind.

On second thought, it is not so odd. This is her old life; Jack is her new one. She'd buy new things, not bring parts of her past.

I try her bedroom first, sure that any secrets will be hidden away there. Other than the unmade bed, nothing seems out of place. I open the closet to find some clothes, likely ones she never wears. I flip through the expensive fabrics, feeling the softness of the cashmere sweaters and silky dresses. They're aged, out of style, reminding me of nights out in university, from the fancy dinners to the barhopping at the hottest clubs. There is nothing beyond the old clothing in the closet, so I move to the drawers. There I find fewer items. A pair of worn jeans and some old wool socks sit in the middle, but the rest are empty. There's nothing that screams anything unusual, whether blackmail or secrets.

I duck into the attached bathroom. It's spotless save for the plush towel hanging on the back of the door.

Next, I enter the spare room, hopeful a secret might be hidden there. As soon as I step inside, something feels off. This room isn't as empty as Arabella's main bedroom, which is odd for a spare. I throw open the closet, which is packed full of clothing. Men's clothing. Collared, button-down T-shirts, zip-up sweaters, coloured jeans, and sweater vests. Something about them feels familiar, but I can't imagine Jack wearing this type of clothing. It's not his style. I try to remember if I've ever seen him in anything but a suit.

When I find nothing of value hidden amongst the strange clothing, I bend down, searching below the bed, and it's also empty.

Back in the main room, I stop, only now noticing the kitchen. My heart thumps harder in my chest. It's spotless, sure, but used. There are dishes in the sink, clean but set out to dry. Who is making use of Arabella's place? Jayson had access, as well as the rest of her family. I glance around as if someone could be hiding amongst the furniture. I suck in a sharp breath, suddenly worried whoever is living here might walk in on me.

Forcing myself to calm down and focus on the task at hand, I remember something Arabella told me once before. Sometimes she stayed here to get away from it all. Sometimes she needed to be away from the accusing eyes of Jack's staff or the pressures of her upcoming wedding.

Either way, the quicker I search, the sooner I can get out. There is a bookshelf at the far end of the room that I search through, pulling old paperback novels off and pushing them aside. There is nothing hiding here, but I grab an old photo album off the shelf, curious to see what it may hold. Most of them are from our university days: nights at her cottage, Dee's themed parties, and many photos of smiling friends and family. We were all close once. It was the fallout between Declan and Arabella that ended our friendship.

Maybe it's all about the reality of my choices. In choosing Jayson, I chose Arabella. With Nathan, I kept Dee. It's wrong that I ever felt obliged to choose between them. Guilt creeps up inside me. Even in this life, I still didn't want to have a relationship with Arabella; after all, something drove me to sleep with her fiancé. There has to be something else at play.

I sit on the long, black couch in the centre of the room, exhausted from searching and annoyed I haven't found anything.

The coffee table in front of me looks like it could hold something, so I run my hands along the edge, looking for a way to open it. Finally, I find a small latch that clicks when I touch it, and the top flips open.

Inside are a few worn blankets, a lot of dust, and I almost miss a small USB stick underneath it all.

I pick it up and examine the old piece of technology. It's bulky and likely doesn't contain much. But so far, it's my only lead.

I tuck it into my pocket and prepare to leave. As I reach the door, I freeze. There are footsteps in the hallway. I hope they're passing by, but they stop outside the door. A key slides into the lock. I glance around, trying to find somewhere to hide, but there's no time. I'm caught, red-handed, in the middle of Arabella's condo.

I hold my breath as the front door swings open to reveal the visitor. I am no longer concerned about myself. Instead, I'm focused on the person standing before me. *Declan.*

Twenty

NOW

"What are you doing here?" Declan demands with a narrow gaze.

"I should ask you that same thing. Why do you have a key?" The sinking feeling in my stomach returns. There were men's clothes in the bedroom. The place looks lived in, not abandoned. "Oh my God, you're living here?"

"No," Declan says quickly as he drops his gaze to the floor. He's never been a great liar.

My head spins. "Declan, why are you living here?"

"I needed somewhere to crash," he says. "Arabella let me."

"Why would she do that?" And why didn't she tell me?

He still doesn't look at me. "Because she's a nice person."

I almost laugh at that idea but hold back, more perplexed by the situation at hand. "Tell me the truth, Declan, or I'll call her and find out myself."

"No." Now Declan meets my gaze, and there's worry behind his eyes. "Don't do that. It will ruin everything."

"Ruin what?" I begin to feel dizzy; I'm not going to like the truth.

"Maddie, please."

I swallow, trying to clear my dry throat. "Are you sleeping with her?"

His gaze drops to the floor again.

"Oh my God, Declan. She's getting married." *Like I'm one to talk.*

"Don't you think I know that?"

"How long has this been going on?"

"Since Christmas," he mumbles.

Months. This isn't new.

"What are you doing, Dec?" I ask. "What if Jack finds you here?"

"He doesn't come here," Declan says. "He doesn't care about Arabella or her things. This place doesn't exist to him."

I frown, doubtful Jack really feels that way. Everything's an asset, even his fiancée's unused uptown condo.

"What are you hoping for?"

"Nothing from you." He finds my gaze again. "Arrie's gonna leave him. She loves me. She told me so."

I groan. "Declan, you can't believe that. She's planned this wedding down to the very last detail. She's not going to cancel it."

"You don't know anything," he says. "You don't know how she is with me. We're perfect, and we're in love. That's all that matters."

"And I'll bet she told you she has to wait for the perfect time to call off her marriage, right?" I goad him. "That she can't do it right now because it has to be done right?"

His gaze on the floor confirms my suspicions.

"She's playing you, Dec. She'll never leave him."

"You don't know that."

"I do." I lower my voice, feeling sorry for him now, seeing the sadness in his eyes, the determination in his voice. He seems sure that she loves him, but Arabella doesn't love anyone but herself. "I'm sorry. She lied to you."

"Shut up, Maddie," he growls. "I don't know what you are doing here, but I suggest you get out of here before I call Arrie and tell her."

I cross my arms, hoping I sound stronger than I feel. "I'm allowed to be here. She's my best friend."

"You certainly looked pretty guilty when I walked in here."

I storm towards him, feeling the weight of the tiny USB in my pocket. "I'll go, but don't say I didn't warn you. Arabella is a liar. She has done nothing but lie for as long as I've known her."

"It takes one to know one, doesn't it?" He sneers.

I step back from his accusations. With my finger wagging in his face, I scold him like a child. "You'll regret this."

Declan grabs the door and ushers me out. "Then let me regret it, because this doesn't involve you." He slams the door behind me, and I'm left standing in the hallway shaking with rage.

Arabella lied to me, possibly blackmailed me, and is now sleeping with my brother behind my back. I want nothing more than to hurt her. I want revenge.

Fueled by anger, I storm out of her condo building. I climb into my car and grab my phone in the process. I find Jack's name in my contacts and hover over the call button. All it would take is for me to hit send and ask where they're staying. I could be in his hotel room and taking out my anger and betrayal with Arabella on Jack. What is wrong with me?

As much as I want to hurt Arabella, I can't stoop to her level anymore. I've already done enough to damage the people I'm supposed to care about. My best revenge would be letting them go and finding the life I need. Getting back to my daughters.

I toss my phone far enough away that I can't reach it from the driver's seat and grip the steering wheel, my breathing heavy and prolonged, trying to calm my rapid heart.

When my anger slightly subsides, I make my way home determined to figure out what Arabella has on that USB.

Jayson is still at work when I arrive home, and I settle into my desk, waking up my ancient computer. Within minutes I have the USB open. It contains only a video file, which I have to download to watch. The anticipation is killer.

When it pops up, it's a poorly filmed clip. Me, front and centre, sitting in what looks like the passenger seat of a car.

"Stop it." I giggle, trying to snatch the camera.

Whoever holds it keeps it out of reach, a gentle tease.

"Brian, c'mon, stop playing."

My throat constricts as the scene plays out.

The video continues with our shameless flirting until Brian suggests we turn it into something more exciting—a dirty home movie. I dip my head low to snort what looks like a line of white powder off the car centre console, then I agree.

As I begin to remove my clothing, another voice joins the mix, calling Brian's name.

"Oh fuck," Brian hisses from behind the camera. Then it drops into darkness, but only for a minute until what sounds like a car door opening, and the camera tumbles further, hitting the asphalt.

What follows is blurry and captured at a poor angle. Brian approaches someone outside the car, grabs them, and pushes them down. There's screaming. I hear my voice, the sound of a car door, footsteps.

"Brian, stop it. Not like this."

Another scream. Crying.

"Brian, stop!"

But he doesn't. The thwacking sound of fists hitting flesh can be heard in the background of my pleas.

"Don't!" My voice is desperate now. "You're going to kill her!"

Still, he doesn't react to my pleas. He's too caught up in the violence.

"Brian!" This time I scream it.

"Stay out of this," Brian growls, giving pause to the sound of the attack.

I don't answer him. Instead, hurried footsteps cross by the camera, and there is the sound of a car door opening and slamming again. All the while, Brian continues to assault Gina.

There's a sickening crack like bones breaking, and a body falls in front of the camera.

I cover my mouth as I suppress the rising scream. My heart races and the video cuts out. This is the video that Arabella threatened me with? She has footage of me with Brian, of the crime being committed. But how?

A million questions circle through my mind. I'm guilty of something, but I don't know what.

I drag my feet as I head to the shower, hopeful the warm water will cleanse me of my guilt. Instead, the water cascades down my nude body, and the tears begin to fall as I think about the video. I was there, watching Gina get hurt, letting her get hurt. Why didn't I stop him sooner? What did I mean, *not like this?*

I sink to the bottom of the tub, wrapping my arms around my legs and sobbing as the water rains down on me. Grabbing my loofa, I scrub my skin raw, trying to wash off the guilt, the memories, the mistakes. I'm consumed by self-loathing. I feel dirty with secrets I can barely remember and mad at myself that my life has taken this turn.

As I sob, I wish I could return to where I was and come clean like I wanted to. I want to face my consequences if only to keep the life I had. I want to go back and never make the mistake of cheating in the first place.

I want nothing more than to go back, to fix it all, but that means Gina is dead and that I wasn't able to save her. How can I have such conflicting feelings?

When I finally climb out of the shower, Jayson has arrived home. His welcoming smile and genuine desire to hold me make the guilt worse. I know all my problems stem from me. I gave up fighting for my marriage. Now I was sucked into this world of Arabella's and rejected everything I thought I knew. I don't care about others. Maybe I never did. I only care about myself.

After I change into lounge clothes, I find Jayson in the TV room. He grins at me when he looks up from the show.

"Feeling better?"

"Yeah."

He opens his arms for me. I hesitate, but it's more suspicious if I don't join him on the couch as he watches the highlights of the latest golf game.

"Rough day?" He kisses my forehead.

"You have no idea."

"Want to talk about it?"

"No." I focus on the TV instead.

How can I tell my boyfriend I've discovered I was blackmailed and lied to by his sister? How can I tell him that I am questioning everything we have together and the life we built when there is an engagement ring hiding in his drawer? I can't, so I don't. All it does is make me think of the last time I lied to the man I was supposed to love. Only then it was Nathan.

Dee's right. I am miserable, and I truly deserve it. Everything's off-balance. Nothing feels right. Worse, I'm not sure I can do anything about it.

"Okay," Jayson says, simply holding me against him.

I hold back the tears that want to fall. Soon my exhaustion overtakes my grief, and I fall asleep on his chest.

Twenty~One

THEN

I t was near ten o'clock now. Nathan and the girls expected me hours ago. I sat in my car in the driveway a bit too long, trying to slow my rapid heartbeat by taking several breaths. Guilt rested like a dead weight in my stomach. After weeks of harmless flirtation with Jayson, something finally happened. It was a mistake, but one I acted on nonetheless.

With a final breath, I summoned the courage to climb out of the car and head for the front door. The anticipation of facing Nathan clawed at my throat, and I was tempted to remain outside. But waiting would only make it worse. I opened the front door quietly, worried the creak would wake the girls. Their bedtime had been an hour ago. They both had to be at school in the morning. But to my surprise, I was met with the joyful songs of their favourite Disney movie—*Frozen* —and my eldest daughter seated on the couch.

"Momma!" Ava cried when she saw me, hopping off the couch and running into my arms.

"Oh, Kitten." I pulled her into a hug. "Why are you still awake?"

"Daddy said I could wait until you were home." She grinned wide as she pulled away. "Come, watch the movie."

I straightened and glanced around. Where was Nathan hiding? "No, Kitten, I have to go find Daddy."

"He's right here." Nathan emerged from the kitchen. His usually crew-cut black hair was flat like he'd been wearing a hat all day, and stubble covered his chin. It looked like he'd avoided shaving for several nights. Though before now, I hadn't noticed. His light green eyes were focused, though curious, as if to ask me where I'd been or why I'd bothered coming home.

He crossed the hall in three swift steps and kissed my forehead. The action wasn't affection but routine. Guilt turned in my stomach, making me stiffen under his touch. "She didn't want to sleep without saying good night." Then he grinned and turned back to his daughter. "Okay, Ava. That's it. Turn off the movie. You can finish it tomorrow."

"But Daddy," Ava whined. The trolls were just beginning to sing, Ava's favourite. Though truth be told, all parts were her favourite of this film.

Nathan shook his head. "Ava, that was the deal. Now off to bed, and we'll come tuck you in."

Ava groaned but hopped off the couch and padded up the stairs to her shared bedroom.

When they were gone, Nathan turned back to me. "Where have you been?"

"Gym." The lump in my throat felt so large I was surprised Nathan didn't notice the trouble I had swallowing my guilt.

"Must have been a good workout." His tone was devoid of emotion as if he knew the real reason I was late. His eyes revealed their sadness.

"I was stressed." That much was true. "The workout helped. I'm sorry it dragged on later than I thought."

Nathan nodded then turned for the stairs. "We should make sure Ava isn't reading."

I watched him climb the stairs, noting his rigid posture and discomfort, a feeling that had been present in our relationship for over five years. When had we been happy? I couldn't remember. All I thought I needed was to feel wanted again. A bit of happiness, of joy. I thought that's what Jayson gave me when Nathan seemed only irritated by my presence.

It was a poor excuse, of course, and nothing justified my ultimate act of betrayal. This man had been my husband for ten years, and all I did was hurt him by choosing another. Jayson may offer something that Nathan hadn't in recent years, but was I willing to risk everything, to ruin my daughters' lives, for a mediocre fling with an old boyfriend?

I closed my eyes. The possibilities and consequences were overbearing, causing a weight on my shoulders I struggled to carry. I followed Nathan's steps into the girls' room.

Haley was fast asleep, her arms wrapped tightly around Everest, and a gentle breath came from her parted lips. I leaned down and kissed her forehead. She didn't stir.

I moved to Ava's side and did the same.

"I hope you're home early tomorrow, Momma," Ava said with a yawn as she curled beneath her covers and snuggled into her oversize pillow.

"I will be," I promised.

Nathan watched from the doorway as I gave my final good night, then together, we retreated from the room. We stood alone in the hallway without exchanging any words, as if he too was unsure what to say. When I braved a glance at his eyes, they were tired, defeated. It sent a shiver through me that I hoped he wouldn't notice.

He said nothing as he stepped around me towards our bedroom. I followed, the turmoil inside raging a wicked war. Only an hour before, I'd been in the arms of a man who gazed at me with longing, love, and desire, only to return home where I felt nothing but distance and disdain. Did Nathan sense my feelings? Did he know I'd been exchanging intimate messages with Jayson for weeks, only to have it result in an explicit affair?

I couldn't know for sure; I only knew that happiness had been a distant memory in recent months—a feeling I wasn't sure ever truly existed. Maybe the attention from Jayson was only a bandage on the gaping wound that was my failing marriage. Perhaps he was a cast to heal my broken heart. It was too early to tell, and I wasn't sure I wanted to risk everything to discover it. Maybe Nathan's discontent was worth the love of our family, worth not breaking up what was once a happy home.

I sat on the edge of the bed as Nathan moved silently around the room, gathering his pyjamas and entering the attached bathroom, closing the door behind him. I drew one calming breath and allowed the confusion to wash over me. Leaving Nathan had been a consideration, but each time I felt the push away from him, my girls pulled me back. The choice was draining. No matter my decision, someone would be hurt.

Nathan's return to the bedroom forced my thoughts from my mind. I stood to take over the bathroom as he climbed into bed, and once I returned, he didn't reach for me, and I didn't try either. Together we lay in the dark, nothing but silence surrounding us. I stared at the ceiling, wide awake, guilty, and unsure of what to do.

Twenty-Two

NOW

Jayson must have carried me to bed when the show finished because that's where I wake up when his alarm goes off and the sun creeps through the window.

I stretch to welcome the new morning but don't feel any better than I did last night.

Jayson pulls me against him, nuzzling my neck. "Good morning," he murmurs.

"Good morning," I reply, staying still in his hold, hoping this doesn't encourage any further interaction.

"Big day today?"

He asks me this almost every morning, but today, it means something different. This morning, I do have big plans. I'm going to try to change my life, first, by attempting to right things with Dee if it is at all possible.

"The usual. You?"

"Working." He nuzzles me again, but I continue to lie still. We cuddle like this until his snooze alarm sounds, and he's forced to get out of bed. He does it with a heavy groan and clear disinterest.

I stay in bed for another ten minutes until I can hear his movements downstairs. I get up and go down to make coffee. I grab myself and Jayson a cup and take his to where he sits in front of his computer, working.

"Thanks, babe." He smiles. "My own little angel."

For a moment, joy washes over me from his reaction. It fades, however, as my mind goes back to the idea of reconciling with Dee. I'm certain the first step to getting my life on track is reuniting with her. Unfortunately for me, this will be her decision. The last few times I've reached out to her haven't gone great.

Soon I find myself outside Dee's condo again. I don't know why I think it will go better this time around, but I am determined to try.

Dee answers her door with the same bitter expression as the last time but steps aside and lets me enter.

"This is getting old fast, Maddie," Dee says, arms crossed. "What do you want now?"

"To apologize."

"You've done that already." Her expression doesn't change.

"But I don't know if I meant it before now." I motion to her couch. "Can we sit down, and I'll explain?"

Dee purses her lips but does as I ask. When I'm sitting next to her, I start to tell her everything I've learned. How I found the video in Arabella's condo and my relationship with Brian. I tell her I was sure Arabella had lied and blackmailed me, which was why I turned against Dee. Finally, I tell her about how I found Declan in Arabella's condo. She already knew about the affair with Jack, so I don't bring that up again.

"Well?" I ask when I finish.

Dee lets out a long breath. "Shit, Maddie. You've turned into a monster."

"I know." I put my face in my hands. "Where did it all go wrong?"

Dee taps her chin. "I have one guess, and she's a bombshell blonde with a shit attitude."

Arabella, of course, but I can't blame my actions on one person. Aren't I the one at fault? They were choices I made, not ones I was forced into.

"I guess so." I meet her gaze again. "I never thought I'd be this kind of person. I've been thinking about the things I've ruined through my own choices. Our friendship is a big one." Then I shake my head. "But I'm going to make it right. I'm going to come clean to Gina." Then I stand up and look down at my former best friend. "I hope you can forgive me, Dee."

Dee stands with me and follows me to the door. "Thanks for coming by," she says. "And for apologizing."

"Of course. I hope one day we can go back to the way it was." I offer a hopeful smile.

Her expression doesn't change, but at least it's indifference, not hatred. "Maybe we can."

"Oh, Dee." I hesitate at the door. "One more thing."

She holds the door open. "What?"

"What happened with Declan?" If anyone can give me a straight story, it's her. "He won't speak to me."

"You really don't remember?" She cocks her hip.

"No, we were always so close."

Dee laughs but cuts it short. "Sorry, Maddie. You must be suppressing your memories. You and Declan haven't been okay since before graduation."

No, that isn't possible. Over four years ago? "What? Why?"

"Why do you think?"

Arabella. She's a consistent issue in my life.

"I can't remember," I tell her, hoping she'll clear the confusion for me.

Dee scratches her forehead, still holding the door open. "It was around the time you were over Jayson, but still considered being with him. You and Brian were doing drugs on the side. You'd always known Declan had feelings for Arabella, and then she completely shot him down. You and Arabella were both coked-up. You were by her side when this happened. You humiliated him, and he never forgave you. Either of you, in fact."

"It seems like he's forgiven Arabella." The bitterness in my tone is impossible to mask.

"That's easy to do when sex is involved," Dee says.

"I had no idea I'd treated him so poorly." This realization hurts most of all.

Dee shakes her head. "Yeah, you did, Maddie. You became an asshole. It happens. But it doesn't mean you can't change it. Declan could come around."

"Thanks, you know, for telling me."

"Good luck." She closes the door behind me.

I grab my phone as I wait for the elevator but hesitate before sending messages to Declan or Gina. There's one more person I need to see to get the full story of how my life went wrong before I can reach out to either of them. The thought of being face-to-face with him again makes me feel faint. Memories of our time together flood my brain. The soft yet insistent way he touched my thigh once excited me, but now the thought only draws disgust. The way his anger would flare up at the slightest insecurity and send him into a barrelling rage. He'd throw his wallet, his phone, anything. He'd gotten close to hitting me.

The last thing I want to do is look him in the eye and ask what happened. But as terrifying as the idea is, I need to know the truth. I need to speak to Brian.

Twenty-Three

NOW

I t's another day before I'm granted access to Beaver Creek Institution and allowed to meet with Brian. I suppress all the thoughts that make my skin crawl like our drug-induced sex-capades. His rage blackouts. The way he'd mumble my full name every time he got off like it was some prize he'd won. I shudder at the thought of hearing him say my name again. Beyond seeing him a few weeks ago in my old life, everything else about him is a mystery.

I wait with all the other people at the prison there to visit their loved ones. Mostly women. Some with children. How many are here to visit fathers? Brothers? Sons? Lovers?

Many don't have any bags with them. Some women have small purses, but not enough to carry much more than a wallet, possibly a phone. One woman, however, has a large, see-through bag, with only a few items visible, a change purse, some lipstick, and possibly a bottle of hand cream. Considering how security searches possessions before allowing anyone entrance, I assume she's been here several times before.

Some of the visitors wear passive expressions as if visiting an inmate is just another part of their daily routine, and it occurs to me that it likely is. The children are quiet, attentive to their mothers, but not oblivious to the guards surrounding us. Their demeanour gives way to their experience. They know how they are supposed to act here. Others look nervous, shifting from side to side, and keep their gaze locked on the tiled floor. I'm sure I resemble the latter but am determined to hide that from Brian. He always had a way to read my weaknesses. That's how he drew me in.

After the on-duty officers take my ID and usher me through the metal detector, I am shown the visitors' area. It's a large rectangular room filled with tables and benches. Here people await their husbands, lovers, brothers, fathers, or friends. I take a seat at an empty table and fold my hands in front of me. I draw a slow breath. I want to appear calm as if the memories, fresh and cloudy, don't affect me.

The door buzzes, and the inmates file in. Dressed in their prison uniforms, they all look very similar. Some have visible tattoos. Some look unhappy to be disturbed. Fathers greet their children with enormous smiles, and husbands kiss their wives. Then I see him, shuffling out with the last of the men. He looks as I remember him, but younger. Broad-shouldered with a shaved head, round brown eyes, and a short beard.

I stand as he approaches me, unsure how to greet him. His amused smile throws me, almost like he expected my visit and finds the entire thing to be a huge joke. I can't stop the shiver that crawls down my spine at the thought. He hasn't changed a bit from our university days.

"Madison Jayne," he drawls in his familiar low voice, mockery behind his words. "I didn't believe them when they told me you were coming. You're the last person I expected to see in here." He sits and reaches up, scratching his beard.

I feel almost sick at his use of my full name; my throat tightens with dryness and discomfort. I don't answer as I sit back on the bench, twisting my hands in my lap, and try to dispel the guilt, nerves, and fear. I'm not sure which emotion dominates me most right now.

"Nothing to say?" His smug smile remains in place as he crosses his arms, showing off his bulky biceps. "How unusual for you."

"You seem well." I find my voice, though awkward. What did I hope for in coming here? It seemed like such a good idea yesterday, but now, seeing him seated across from me, I'm starting to doubt it. What can he tell me that I don't already know? Can I trust anything he says?

Brian's expression shifts from amusement to annoyance. "I've been in jail for four years. How good could I be?"

I swallow hard, glancing around and keeping my voice low. "You've been moved here. Doesn't seem all that terrible."

"Compared to where I was?" Brian snorts. "This is a dream come true. But it's still jail. I avoid fights, get harassed by guards, and haven't been laid in years." His dark eyes dart to my chest, and despite wearing a sweater, I feel exposed. "But you look good, Maddie. Damn good." He licks his lips, and I can't suppress the chill that raises goosebumps on my arms. "At least the last four years have been good to you."

"What happened that night?" As I ask the question, my eyes find the table; I'm determined to get it out before I lose my nerve. "Why did you try to kill Gina?"

Brian groans. "Seriously, Mads? That's why you've come? To hash out details that we covered four years ago?"

"Yeah." I don't look at him, unsure of what was covered before he was put away. "What happened?" I need some sort of explanation—anything to make the events of my life clearer.

"Coke happened." Brian shrugs. "We loved our lines, you and me. I don't remember grabbing Gina. I only remember you hitting me with the damn tire iron." He rubs the back of his head like he's remembering the pain.

My palm tingles as I remember the feel of the cool metal in my grip, unsure if it's a real memory or a fabrication. However, I definitely remember the sound from the video of cracking bones. Had I known the tire iron was in his car, or had it just been a weapon of convenience?

He isn't angry as he recalls the memory. He laughs, amused again. "At least my pants weren't still down."

"Why is this funny to you?" I snap, unable to hold my composure any further. I need answers. I can't keep going through this life blindly.

"Because one minute I was getting laid, coked-out, and then I was lying on the pavement, my head pounding." Again, he chuckles. "Definitely not how I thought that night was gonna go."

I shake my head, eyeing him with disbelief. "You tried to kill someone; how can you find any humour in that?"

Only more laughter. "Because you wanted me to."

Time slows. Everything goes cold. Blood pounds in my ears. Brian keeps talking, but I can't hear him. All I can focus on is his words. I wanted her dead. Could he be right?

Then I remember something else from the video. Something I said ... *"Not like this..."* I shiver. No, I won't believe what he's saying.

Brian's cruel laughter breaks through my horrified haze, and he grins at me again.

"All right there?"

"That's not true!" I glare at him from across the table.

"Deny it all you want," Brian says, changing his expression to match my own. "You may have had a change of heart at the moment you saw her struggling and losing air, but before that, you wanted it. You begged for it. You hated her as much as I did, and when I was deep inside you, you asked me to get rid of her. You hated the competition. Though the joke's on you because really, there was none."

I can't calm my racing mind, worried that the words he speaks are true. When I speak again, the words come out as a pathetic whisper. "You don't have any proof. No one would believe you if you told them that."

His grin returns, and another shrug follows. "I don't need them to believe me. No matter how hard you try to deny it, you know it's true. You wanted her dead, and if you hadn't gotten in the way, she would be."

"At least I came to my senses and saved the better person." I don't know if I believe him, but his words are enough to set me off.

His joy doesn't dissipate. "Lucky for me, you've already given me all I need."

I frown. *What can he mean by that?*

He continues. "You got everything you deserve, MJ, and you're about to get a whole lot more." Brian places his hands on the table between us and leans in closer. In a low voice, he says, "you put me in here, and you're gonna get me out. Then you and that fat bitch, Gina, are gonna pay for everything you've done."

I gasp as he stands up, fearful he'll make a move against me. He doesn't, keeping an eye on the guards that line the room.

"Goodbye, MJ," he says with a smug grin. "I'll be seeing you again soon, and I can't wait. Who knows, maybe I can bring that freaky, deadly side out of you again." He circles the table and lowers his head to my level. "Just gotta find myself a good stash of blow."

I stiffen as I feel his breath against my neck. The stench is rancid, and I scrunch my nose in disgust but don't dare move. The guards watch but hold back; he isn't touching me—yet.

His voice comes as a soft hiss. "As long as you beg. And trust me, you'll be begging in my fantasies tonight as I get off to thoughts of your delicious body." His lips press against my cheek, and then he's gone.

I watch him retreat, but my heart pounds against my rib cage so hard it hurts. My lungs are deprived of air as I choke on my breath, holding back the sobs I feel at the base of my dry throat.

"Miss?" A young guard approaches me. He wears a concerned expression. "Is everything okay?"

Somehow, I stand on wobbly legs. "Fine." I steady myself against the table. "Fine. I'm just leaving." I don't look back as I force myself to leave the prison, fearful that Brian can still see me.

Sitting in my car, I try to calm my shaking body, but it's no use. I glance up with a heavy heart. The grey brick building looms in front of me, casting my car in a cold shadow. Coming to see Brian was a mistake. And as much as I plan to push it all aside, everything in my gut tells me I've only made things worse. Much, much worse.

Twenty-Four

THEN

"What's a guy gotta do to get a signed copy of your book?" The deep, familiar voice came from behind me.

I whirled around, forgetting the novel I was holding, coming face-to-face with a tall, broad-shouldered gentleman with a shaved head and round eyes. He smiled at me knowingly. His face sported a thick beard as if making up for the lack of hair on his head. Eventually, he let out a low chuckle. "I guess I've changed." He sucked in his cheeks before grinning again. "But you, Madison Jayne, you've not changed one bit."

I knew who he was before he addressed me by my full name. It was a face I'd never forget, as much as I'd hoped I would.

"Hi, Brian."

"I was hoping I wouldn't be forgettable." He stepped closer, pulling me into an uncomfortable hug. It had been years since we'd seen each other. The night of the funeral, so fourteen years, maybe? And after the last time, the cold gaze, the murder implication—a hug was not my preferred method of greeting.

"No," I said, uneasy. "Not forgettable, but it's been a while."

Brian rubbed a hand over his bare head. "Since the funeral?"

I'd tried forgetting about all of it and especially about him. He still frightened me after all this time. I swallowed the lump forming in my throat and forced a smile as I nodded. "Of course, it's been ages. How have you been?"

"All right." Brian seemed to dismiss the question, then waved at my bestseller in front of me. "I see you've done quite well for yourself. I've been keeping tabs."

"Really?" I found the concept surprising since we'd dated so briefly back in college; I barely knew him. And after I blamed him for Gina's death, why would he ever want to keep up with my life, let alone see me again?

What I could remember about our relationship was a lot of partying and sex and drinking that would sometimes turn violent. Brian had a jealous streak and a tendency to overreact. Dee introducing me to Nathan had ended our short fling. Brian hadn't been happy, but he became someone else's problem: Gina's. To this day, I wondered if I had made a different choice, then maybe she would still be alive—though perhaps I would be dead.

"Of course." Brian stepped closer to me, causing me to instinctively step back. "It's not often that someone you've been with becomes a famous author."

I forced out a stiff laugh, though the comment disgusted me. "I guess not. Though I wouldn't say famous." I turned back to the shelf I'd been perusing. "Lucky, I guess."

"I've read it." Brian's enthusiasm didn't wane. "I wouldn't say that was luck. You've got real talent." He glanced down at the cover featuring a picturesque blonde woman. "Though your main character isn't very likable."

I did laugh then. "That was the intention."

"She reminds me of a certain socialite we all used to know."

Arabella, of course. She might be an ex-friend, but she was once the main subject of my story. The girl who lived a high society lifestyle, marrying rich and flaunting every minute of it, made for a great love-to-hate character. And after everything that happened between Arabella and Declan, I saw the story as a tiny bit of revenge.

I couldn't stop my playful smirk. "It's a work of fiction."

"Of course." Brian winked. He held the book closer to me. "About my signed copy."

"I don't have a pen." Which was true.

Brian produced one and smiled with enthusiasm as I scribbled my signature on the inside front cover before handing it back to him.

"Didn't you say you'd read it already?"

Brian tucked the signed copy under his arm. "Of course. But now I have a unique copy. For my collection."

My skin prickled with unease.

"What are you doing right now?" Brian asked. "Do you have time to grab a coffee? Catch up?"

I brushed a strand of hair behind my ear, purposefully making my wedding ring visible. "I have to go pick up my daughters. Sorry."

Brian nodded, though the disappointment was evident in his expression. "Of course. Maybe some other time."

I put the book back on the shelf. "It was nice to see you."

"You too." Brian grinned. "You look great, Madison Jayne."

I forced a smile and left the bookstore, not drawing a

comfortable breath until I climbed into the car and started the engine. What had he meant by collection? He said he'd been following my career. Could he be keeping tabs on my life too?

I tried to shake the uncomfortable feeling as I pulled out of the parking lot and made my way to the girls' school. It was early still, but I couldn't get away from Brian fast enough. He had been right; the last time I saw him was at Gina's funeral. He'd been standing in the back of the crowd, dressed in a black hoodie. It was something I would never forget.

I arrived in the school parking lot. I left my car and decided to take a walk around the area until school let out. It would look weird if I were sitting alone in my car in the private school parking lot. There was a park nearby I used to write in while the girls played. It seemed like the perfect place to wait.

However, as I walked, I couldn't shake the eerie feeling. Like someone was watching my every move, like someone knew too much. It had been a while since I felt such unease. Not since my final days of college, weeks after Brian had supposedly dropped out. Seeing him again today brought back memories, bad ones, ones that I wasn't able to shake.

Twenty-Five

NOW

•

"I'll be back in three days tops," Jayson says as he kisses me goodbye the next evening. Work demanded him at the head office in Ottawa. "You'll be okay without me?"

"I've been alone before." It'll be a welcome change, but I don't tell him that.

"I know, babe." Jayson winks and turns towards his Beemer. The head office is about a four-hour drive away. They'd put him up in a hotel for the duration of the meetings. He'd call me every night.

The moment I'm alone, I breathe a heavy sigh of relief. Finally, I can stop pretending everything is okay.

Planning to have a mellow evening, I settle on the couch in sweats with a bowl of popcorn. I'm finally starting to relax when a knock at my door interrupts the Lifetime movie I found on TV. I could ignore it. My lights are off, and it could look like no one is home.

I turn back to the screen, prepared to ignore my unwelcome visitor until I hear someone calling my name.

"Maddie," a male voice calls. "Come and open the door."

His words slur together as he speaks, making his speech louder and more incoherent. I have to open the door. Something tells me he won't take my silence well. He'll stand there for hours wailing.

With a heavy sigh, I pull the door open and usher him inside.

"Maddie." This time it's said with relief. A happy smile forms on his lips, and he stumbles towards me, arms outstretched.

I catch him and steady his wobbly body against me. He reeks of whiskey and cigarettes.

"Jack." I weaken under his weight. "What are you doing here?"

He straightens up and looks right at me, though he still sways on his feet and his eyes don't focus.

"I came to see you." He slumps against the wall before falling to the floor in a fit of laughter. "You're being mean. You won't answer my calls."

"I'm not being mean. You need to take a hint." I reach down and help him to his feet, then direct him to the couch.

He falls onto the cushions with a groan. "You're being mean."

I'm not going to win any arguments with him tonight, especially a pointless one.

"It's better this way, Jack. You're starting a life with Arabella. I can't ruin that."

"But you hate that bitch," Jack says, slumping forward with his head in his hands. "You told me she was awful."

I cock my head. Maybe a drunk Jack could be a useful source of information. I lower myself to the couch beside him, careful to keep distance between us.

"What did I tell you?"

He tilts his head, so an eye is on me, though it doesn't look focused. "When this started, you told me that bitch was black-mailing you. That she was holding something over your head so you'd stay with her brother."

Jack slumps sideways onto the couch cushions. He's wasted and fading fast.

"You said you'd get your revenge by sleeping with me." A drunken grin spreads on his lips. "And lucky for me, you didn't stop there."

So that was it. Arabella blackmailed me into being with Jayson. That's why I forgave him over Dee. That's why I so easily pushed Dee aside. But what was I so afraid of when it came to that video? For a moment, I wonder if I could be implicated in Gina's attempted murder with that video evidence. Did I wish for Gina's death only to have a change of heart? Am I as at fault for her near murder in this life as I feel for her death in our old one?

I reach over and gently shake Jack to rouse him. "What else did I tell you?"

He pushes himself back into a seated position, slips an arm around my waist, and tries to pull me closer. "You told me that if I fucked you, then Arabella would get what she truly deserved." Jack places a sloppy kiss on the side of my mouth, missing his target. Then he slumps backwards. "She's a bitch, but I never got why you hated her so much."

"There's a lot of history there." Jack will never understand how Arabella and I ended up the way we did. I don't under-stand it myself. People change, and sometimes that's all it takes for years of friendship to end in hardship.

"You've won," Jack slurs. His eyes close. "I lost. We all lost. And now we're screwed ..." His words trail off, and a steady breath emerges from his open mouth. Drunk and passed out. Jack and Arabella really do deserve one another.

I watch him for only a moment more before pulling the

couch blanket over him and hitting the lights. I give up on my movie night and take a book to bed, hoping he'll be gone in the morning and thanking God Jayson is out of town.

I sleep well despite the man on my couch, and when I wake with the sun, I am quick to remove my problem. First, I dial Vincent and have the car come straight away, and then I go to the living room.

"Jack, get up." I shake him.

He groans and eventually opens one eye to look at me. "Maddie?"

"Spot on, genius," I say, my tone as dry as the Manhattans he was no doubt chugging last night. "Now get up and go home to your fiancée."

He groans again. "I'm going to be sick."

"Not on my carpet."

He rolls onto his back and groans some more. "What is this? Hell?"

I hold out a glass of water to him. "An awful hangover."

He takes the glass but doesn't stop groaning. After he gulps it down, he lets out a sigh of relief then looks at me again. This time, he smiles. "So, you couldn't resist me after all."

"Hardly." I usher him to his feet. "Some drunk guy showed up at my door last night and passed out on my couch. Kind of ruined my evening."

His smile fades. "Maddie—"

"Go, Jack. That's all you can do." It's the best thing for everyone in this situation. I only hope he can understand that.

"I don't want it to be like this." His shoulders slump forward. "I don't want this to stop."

"It has to stop. We were kidding ourselves." I push him towards the door. His movement is clumsy as he leans on me to get his shoes on.

"So, this is how we say goodbye?" Jack asks as we leave my house. "A bloody hangover and a sob speech?"

"You'll see me at the wedding and likely after."

"It will be different."

I nod. "It was always going to be."

I help him across the lawn to the waiting car. Vincent reaches out an arm, but Jack stops him.

"One for the road, then." Jack places his hands on my cheeks and presses a firm kiss on my lips before sliding into the limo. The window rolls down, and he grins at me. "Later, Maddie."

I turn towards the house but stop when I see a familiar car on the opposite side of the road. Declan's green sedan.

Declan gets out of the driver's side and crosses the street. I go back into my house, knowing he'll follow. His expression says all I need to hear.

"You've got it all wrong," I say when he shuts the door behind him. At least when it comes to last night.

"I don't think I do." Declan adjusts his glasses. A nervous habit. "Did you scold me for sleeping with Arabella when you are clearly doing the same thing with her fiancé?"

I purse my lips. "We aren't talking about this, Declan. What are you doing here anyway?"

"I came to talk to my big sister," he says. "To see if she was right about my situation with Arabella, but now I'm starting to think there's something more going on here."

"You don't know what you saw. It has nothing to do with your affair."

"I think it has everything to do with it," Declan snaps, now pacing in my front hall.

"It's a long story, Dec, that starts long before Christmas, okay?" I'm losing my patience with him. "But I'm not stupid enough to think he'll end his engagement for me. So, I told him to get out of my life and be with her. I have my own relationship to sort out. I can't be involved in theirs, and neither should you." The harsh words come out before I can stop them. He needs tough love right now, but his expression makes me weak.

His expression pinches, and he hisses, "You're lying."

I throw my hands up in frustration. "Believe what you want, but in five days, when they get married, you'll know I was right. Arabella and Jack are terrible people doing terrible things to each other. They deserve the marriage they are going to get."

"You're wrong. You'll see." Declan turns and storms out of my house. A sinking feeling in my stomach tells me I'll regret this.

Twenty-Six

NOW

After a few days, I try reaching out to Declan, but he ignores my calls. I almost consider going by the condo but don't want Arabella to know her secret has been discovered. Instead, I spend my days at her beck and call and dodging Jack's advances.

I'm lucky he doesn't stop by my house again but know I can't ignore him at the rehearsal dinner tonight.

"Ready to go?" Jayson calls from downstairs as I put the final touches on my makeup.

"Coming!" I hurry down the stairs to the door. Jayson catches me in his arms before I make it too far.

"Hey." He presses his forehead against mine—our noses touch. I force the lies and deceit aside and allow us a moment of peace.

"Hey."

"You look beautiful." He kisses me, then pulls away. "I must be the luckiest guy in the world to be with you." His joy is infectious, even if our relationship is ultimately doomed by my mistakes and choices.

The rehearsal is beautiful, but I'd expect nothing less from Arabella. It's lovely but not as glamorous as I anticipate tomorrow's wedding will be. Arabella would never subject her guests to two duplicate parties. For a rehearsal, it's overdone.

The guests are seated at round tables scattered throughout the hall. The centrepieces haven't been brought in yet, but the tables are dressed with satin tablecloths and set with gold-plated cutlery and white pearl plates. Each place setting has a crystal water glass, a wineglass, and a champagne flute. A bottle of Dom Perignon sits at the centre of each table, in place of the centrepiece, I presume. We were told not to touch it. The setup screams ostentatious, but no one will comment on it. Arabella is supposed to be a design icon.

The walls are adorned with white satin loops, and a large bow is wrapped around the head table at the front of the room. There, Arabella and Jack sit together. Their wedding party and dates sit at the two round tables beside them. They are the centre of the show. Arabella would never allow another person to take the focus of their celebration. All attention belongs to her and Jack.

We practice our entrances, me on the arm of Jack's best man. He's familiar. They call him Bird, but I never got his first name and didn't bother to ask. Gina and her groomsman enter behind us.

I take my seat next to Jayson, along with Gina, the other bridesmaids, and their dates. I can feel Jack's gaze on me the entire time, and while I avoid his eye contact, I know that I won't be able to forever.

One by one, we stand and practice our speeches. It was weird to share my speech before the big day, but Arabella makes sure that we only say what she wants to hear. She spent hours on the phone with me perfecting my "best" friend speech, guaranteed tears, as she put it.

Jack's father finishes his speech and Jack seems distracted. I fool myself into thinking I've gotten away with little attention and a simple speech.

That is until Jayson shifts in his seat beside me and stands. He taps his glass and draws all the attention towards us. Arabella beams at her older brother.

"For those of you that don't know me, I'm Jayson." He waves around the room though I figure he knows most of them already. "The beautiful bride's proud big brother." He pauses to smile at Arabella. "I want to thank you all for joining us on this special night and again tomorrow. Doesn't Arrie throw a fabulous party?"

His question is met with cheers and applause.

Jayson chuckles. "I couldn't agree more. I've been blessed with this wonderful girl as my sister and, of course, my beautiful girlfriend, Maddie, as Maid of Honour." He looks at me with a grin, and the rest of the crowd does too, sporadic clapping accompanying his remarks.

I smile, trying to hide my discomfort at being brought into his speech.

"I've been lucky enough to date this lovely woman for many years," Jayson continues, looking back at the crowd. "We were introduced by the bride herself." That isn't exactly true, but for the sake of Arabella, it is.

He finds my eyes again, and I try not to squirm in my seat.

"My sister has given me her blessing to be a part of this special day." Jayson's eyes are trained on me as he reaches into his jacket and lowers to the floor. The ring.

No. He can't be doing this now. Not here. We haven't discussed it.

"Maddie," he starts, taking my hand. "You have been the centre of my life for a long time. I know I haven't always treated you as I should but, if you let me, I'd like to spend the rest of my life doing right by you."

"Jayson—" He continues speaking before I can interrupt him more. I want to scream at him to stop and yell the truth. I need to free us both from this charade of a relationship, this lie of a life. But I don't. I keep my mouth shut—hating myself more and more with every word he speaks. Cursing myself for dragging us both further into my web of deceit.

"You and I have been through thick and thin. We have loved each other through the good and the bad, and through it all, our love has held strong." Jayson opens the box to reveal the diamond ring I found a week before. "If you would do me the honour of being my wife, I will never give you a reason to question me again." He swallows then says, "Maddie, will you marry me?"

The entire room watches. Their eyes burn into me, waiting, wondering. Will she accept? Why is she taking so long? I have to say yes. I'm trapped. Accept him, or break him. Those are my only options.

I glance towards Arabella. She wears a knowing smile and nods at me, her cheeks flushed red and eyebrows poised with excitement. Maybe this was her plan all along. She hoped that in this setting, I couldn't deny Jayson. After all, other than Dee, he was nothing but good to me. If I want to say no, I must break his heart in front of everyone.

My heart thumps in my chest. My throat is dry. I already know this isn't what I want, but I can't say no. Not now. Not like this.

So, I force a smile, look down at the man who has loved me since I was eighteen. "Yes, Jayson. I will marry you."

My acceptance is met with resounding applause and

cheers. With a broad smile plastered on his face, Jayson presses the ring onto my finger, then stands and plants a firm kiss on my lips. All the while, I keep my smile steady, faking I am the happiest girl in the world. I'm pretending that a ring has made everything in my life perfect, when in reality it has made things worse.

When the excitement dies down, Jayson returns to his seat. The meal slowly finishes, and I keep my eyes on my plate, trying not to meet anyone's gaze. However, it's nearly impossible considering the number of people who want to congratulate us on our engagement.

Finally, when I get a moment to breathe, I leave the reception hall and go to the bathroom. There I take several steady breaths and look at myself in the mirror, practicing my fake smile. I look happy but start to wonder how long I've actually been satisfied, and how long I've forced myself to think this was a life that I wanted to live. It's a joke now, considering I had happiness once and a family I loved. Daughters who amazed me every day. Yet, I picked myself over them and threw it all away the first chance I got. I was happy when I was twenty-six the first time and had everything in front of me, but I'm not happy now.

I leave the bathroom only to bump into Jack, the last person I want to deal with today. He wears a look of distress on his face and runs a nervous hand through his gelled hair.

"So, you're getting married," he says sharply. "Is that why you wanted things to end?"

I brush by him. This is not the place to have this conversation.

He doesn't let me go quietly because that's not Jack's style. Instead, he grabs my wrist and pulls me further down the hall to a secluded area where no one would see us. Then he does something drastic and presses his lips against mine.

I shove him away. "What are you doing? We are at your rehearsal dinner. Your soon-to-be wife is in the other room. This isn't worth it, and you know it."

He growls his annoyance as I try to keep him at arm's length. "This wasn't part of the deal."

I almost roll my eyes but catch myself before I do. "What deal? This whole affair has been built on a foundation of hatred and lies." I place my hand on his firm chest. "This is all we are, Jack, and this is all we'll ever be."

"This doesn't have to end just because you have someone else," Jack snaps, his irritation rising. He's not used to hearing the word *no*. Jack always gets what he wants, one way or another.

"Yes, it does," I say firmly.

"No—"

I cut him off before he can continue. "No, this is done. There is no way this can continue. This is it, and you have to accept that. I need you to accept that."

His face scrunches with anger as he runs his hand through his hair again, messing it further. He doesn't speak. He only glares at me, and I turn to leave.

"I know you don't want this to end," he says. "You've never been happy with Jayson. That's why you ran to me in the first place. And now you'll throw all this away for a life with him? A life you don't want? Damn it. I was going to take you to Cabo next month."

I take a step back away from his rising voice. If he doesn't calm down, he'll give us away.

I say the thing that I know will sting, even if I don't know its validity. "I don't want this. I don't want you. I wanted to ruin you. I wanted to ruin her for everything she's done to everyone I love. But I realize now that isn't worth it. I'm not this person, and I don't want to be."

"So what?" Jack snaps. "You'll marry her brother, and we'll all be one fucked up family. Do you think that's the life you want?"

I glance down at the diamond ring on my finger. It isn't what I want, but I don't need Jack to be the one to tell Jayson.

"What I want is of no matter to you. I will do the right thing, and I hope you do too."

Jack doesn't answer me, only regards me with a narrow gaze and pursed lips.

"Jack, I hope you can make the decision that makes you happiest. I realize your wedding day is tomorrow, and you feel like you don't have a choice, but you do. You don't have to marry her. You can leave."

I turn away without giving him a chance to respond, but he calls after me, and I stop fearing he'll make a scene.

"Why would I leave her?" he asks. "It's not like you're some special girl that made me see the light. You were a convenient fuck that was close by. I'll be sorry to lose that."

He stalks away from me before I can respond, and I watch him retreat. I allow a breath of relief to slip out, thankful that went better than I expected.

I don't go back to the reception hall; instead, I walk straight out the front doors and into the cool night air. I breathe in deep and exhale long. I glance around the expansive property and consider how my life has changed and how I could make it better.

The ring catches my eye. It is beautiful. Jayson did well, but I don't feel the same excitement I did when Nathan put his ring on my finger. I feel nothing except pity and sadness. Yet, still, I don't know what to do.

I turn back to the hall when I hear someone calling my name. Gina emerges with a look of concern on her face.

"Hey, Maddie? What's wrong?" She comes to my side and

takes my hand, running her thumb over my ring. "Felicidades."

I force a smile. "It's a beautiful ring."

"So, you're happy?" Gina gazes at me with an uneasy smile.

And I do what I've been doing for years. I lie. "So happy."

"You deserve to be happy." Gina squeezes my hand. "Come on. It's almost time to go, and Arabella will kill us if we stay out here too long."

"Are you happy?" I ask as she turns away.

Gina stops and regards me with a confused gaze. "Of course, Maddie. Why wouldn't I be?"

I step closer to her. "Do you ever wonder, what if? Like, what could have been?"

Her eyebrows furrow together. "Doesn't everyone?"

"I guess." I shrug. "But that's not what I meant. Do you ever wonder what life would have been if we'd never met Brian? If none of the bad had ever happened?"

"Sure, Maddie," she says. "But that doesn't change what has happened." She looks to where my new engagement ring weighs heavy on my finger. "Are you sure you're okay?"

I nod. "Yeah, I am, though I sometimes wonder if this life, these choices, were what was meant to be."

"Everything happens for a reason," Gina says. "Now come on, before we both get Arabella's evil eye."

I follow her into the reception hall without another word and find my seat next to my new fiancé. Jayson wraps his arm around my shoulders, his grin still in place. Our short discussion still dances in my mind. Everything happens for a reason. What could be the reason that brought me back here?

Twenty-Seven

THEN

Seeing Brian again brought too many unsettling memories crashing to the forefront of my mind, and when I returned home that day from the girls' school, I found myself online looking through old photos from university. Our final year was poorly documented after Dee's last rager and Gina's death.

I found some photos from the infamous circus party, which brought back the confusing circumstances surrounding the fight. It had been a massive night at Dee's, one to mark the beginning of exams and the approaching end of our youth. I'd known Nathan only a few short months and while we were desperately in love, neither had the confidence to say it yet, though it had almost slipped out a few times.

We weren't feeling a party that night but being close with Dee made it hard for either of us to say no. She'd been our matchmaker after all—something she held over our heads every time she would guilt us into something. I half-heartedly dressed up, and we arrived fashionably late.

To my surprise, Jayson sat on the living room couch with a

couple of friends and was surrounded by girls. He had a beer in his hand and looked up as soon as we walked in. I immediately dropped my gaze to avoid eye contact. Things had been weird with us for ages, but I could never pinpoint why. I chalked it up to hard feelings over our breakup, even if it was years ago.

"Maddie!" Dee plowed into me, throwing her arms around my neck. "You're late."

"Fashionably so," Nathan said, covering for our desire to be sitting at home in our pyjamas eating ice cream and binge-watching *The Sopranos*.

Dee pulled away and rolled her eyes in Nathan's direction.

"That's my cue to find us some drinks." Nathan grinned. He bent down and kissed my cheek before wading into the crowd towards the kitchen.

"What's Jayson doing here?" I asked when Nathan was out of sight.

Dee glanced over her shoulder, scrunched her nose, and shrugged. "I invited him."

"Why?"

"It's been years since you split. He's here to have a good time."

I glanced in his direction again as Dee hooked my arm and dragged me further into the party.

Nathan returned, and he handed me a beer, then turned to Dee.

"Just a heads-up—"

Before he could finish, there was a loud crash heard from the kitchen and screaming that followed.

"Get off of me!" Gina yelled, shoving Brian backwards.

From where we stood in the living room, leaning against the wall, we could see the whole thing. Gina's eyes were wild, her face flushed. The mini keg on the counter had been knocked over and toppled to the ground. Gina swayed unsteadily on her feet, glaring at Brian, whose face was contorted with anger.

"Calm down, you crazy bitch." He sneered.

Within moments, Dee was in the room, her overdone ring-master costume trailing behind her.

"What the fuck, guys?" Dee snapped, trying to lift the fallen keg.

I moved to help her, but Nathan caught my arm.

"Don't get involved," he murmured in my ear.

"I have to help Dee." As I said it, two others came to her rescue, lifting the keg back onto the counter and leaving her to deal with Gina and Brian.

"She can handle it." Nathan steered me away from the confrontation as I saw Dee take Gina's arm and lead her out of the kitchen. I didn't look away quick enough to avoid eye contact when Brian glanced in our direction. He held my gaze steady, cold, and emotionless until I tore my eyes away with a cold shiver, and he went the way of Gina and Dee.

I still questioned why I was ever interested in him. When the haze of all the drug use cleared, I started to see that our relationship was nothing but toxic. As happy as I was to have him be someone else's problem now, I couldn't help but worry about Gina.

"I'm going to head to the bathroom." I passed my drink off to Nathan. "I'll be a minute."

I left before he could answer me and went in search of Dee.

At the stairs leading up to the top level of the house, I hesitated, unsure where they went. Before I could find out, a hand touched my arm. I turned and came face-to-face with Jayson. He looked awful, with blood-shot eyes and dishevelled hair. His breath stank of whiskey. I guessed the beer proved to be too weak after I showed up.

"Maddie," he said, his speech slurred. "I need to talk to you."

"Now isn't a great time, Jayson," I said. "I'm trying to find Dee."

His eyes narrowed at the mention of my best friend. He took my arms roughly and leaned into me.

I shook off his hold, putting distance between us. "What are you doing?"

"Maddie." He stumbled closer to me again. "You have to take me back. We made a mistake. We have a future, you and me. This can't be the end."

I tried to push by him, finding myself cornered against the wall, but he wouldn't let up.

"I'm with someone else," I said, my voice soft to try to calm him. "Please don't do this."

But my words didn't stop him. He leaned down and pressed his lips against mine. I was quick to push him off, causing Jayson to stumble back. I braced myself for the anger that would follow but was surprised when I found only sadness behind his eyes.

"Jay." I tried to reach for him, but he turned and disappeared out the front door before I could say anything further. I stared after him for a moment, sad for the pain I had caused him. He'd been good to me, and I'd been too distracted and self-centred to appreciate him. It wasn't his fault we ended the way we did.

I glanced around when he was gone, wondering if anyone had noticed our confrontation. I was in the clear until I felt a prickle on the back of my neck like someone was staring. Another glance, and I locked eyes with Brian.

He wore an amused grin on his lips and made his way towards me.

"Madison Jayne."

I regarded him with disgust. "What do you want?"

"I thought you were done with that loser before you and I hooked up." Brian chuckled at his joke. "Now he's kissing you when your boyfriend is nowhere to be found." He did a mocking glance around. *Where was Nathan?* My stomach twisted with discomfort, wanting nothing more than to find him and escape Brian.

"You saw me push him away. Jayson is drunk and made a mistake."

Brian stepped closer. "Maybe I should do the same."

"Bri?" Gina's voice came from the top of the stairs behind me, and I sucked in a sharp breath as I turned to look up at her. She eyed me with scrutiny. "What's going on?"

"MJ and I were having a conversation." Brian smirked. "An intimate one."

Gina's eyes narrowed in my direction. "I think you're done now."

"Nah, I'm having too much fun." He reached out and grabbed my arm, trying to pull me away from Gina. "Let's go finish this somewhere more private."

I pulled my arm from his grasp and put space between myself and them. "I have to find Nathan."

"That's probably a good idea," Gina said, her tone cold. I felt Brian continue to watch me as I scampered away.

I found Nathan with a group of his friends near the fireplace. I settled in next to him and reached for the beer, but before I could get comfortable again, there was another crash, this time coming from the floor above. Abandoning my beer once more, I sprinted back to the stairs, certain Dee was witnessing the commotion.

"Leave me alone!" Gina appeared at the top of the steps, yelling towards the room at the end of the hall. She thundered down the stairs and towards the front door.

"Gina," I called, reaching out to her, but before I made contact, she whirled around.

Her eyes were wide, and pupils dilated, and they took a moment to entirely focus on me. She took a step towards me, wagging her finger in my face.

"Puta." She snarled the Spanish word for *bitch*, one she had taught me when we first met. "This is your fault. All your fault."

"What are you talking about?" My stomach twisted with her accusations.

"If it weren't for you, everything would be fine." She grabbed me and dug her nails into my arm.

I yelped in pain and shook her off. "Gina, what is wrong? What happened?"

She turned away from me, shaking her head. "All this terrible treatment, this is your fault. You made him this way."

I tried to stop her, but she was out the door before I could process what she was telling me. I followed her, calling her name, but she didn't turn to look at me as she climbed into her Jeep and sped down the road.

When I turned back to the house, I saw Brian standing in the doorway with his arms crossed. He wore his signature smirk on his face, clear he couldn't care less about the girl who stormed out.

Sucking in a sharp breath, I headed back to the house and pushed by him. "What is wrong with you?"

Brian only shrugged. "I've never lied about what I wanted, MJ. We all have to make choices. You certainly did."

He glanced over his shoulder to where I saw Nathan standing in the doorway watching us. Without another word,

I marched towards my boyfriend, grabbed his arm, and directed him away from the front hallway.

"What was that about?" Nathan asked.

"Gina stormed out." I took the drink that he was holding for me and downed the rest of it. "I'm ready to go."

"Already?" He offered an amused smile, knowing I hadn't wanted to be here at all.

"We made our appearances."

Dee had returned and was now dancing on the coffee table with two other girls, unbothered by the scene that had unfolded. Nathan and I wouldn't be missed.

"We're safe to go."

Nathan nodded and finished his beer. "Ready to find out what Tony is doing?" Nathan grinned his perfect smile as he referenced the show we were returning to.

"More than ready."

I didn't see Brian before we left, which I was thankful for.

I never forgot the way Gina looked at me or the last thing she said. The next time I saw her was when her body was being placed in the ground.

My strained relationship with Arabella was put to the test when we discovered the truth. Brian had put something in Gina's drink, which accounted for the drugs the coroner had found in her system. Drugs that Arabella's boyfriend had sold to him.

I'd wanted to come clean about the whole thing. Still, Dee was already in enough trouble with her parents having hosted the party that resulted in Gina's death. If the cops found out drugs were being sold under her roof, who knew how they'd react. Dee being the subject of that scandal wouldn't sit well with her family. For everyone, their reputations were worth everything. More than the truth about Gina's death.

Together, we covered it up. We played into the story that Gina had taken drugs, gotten upset, and stormed out of the party, choosing to drive when we knew she shouldn't.

Together, we were as much to blame as Brian was.

My skin crawled with guilt as I shut down the computer and sat back, staring at the black screen. Fourteen years ago, our friend died, and each of us played a part in causing it. I could never forget the words she spoke to me, her eyes wild. She'd haunted me for years, but I'd kept my mouth shut, forced the remorse away, and convinced myself there was nothing I could have done. I'd always known that party was only the start of my mistakes.

Twenty-Eight

NOW

A rabella twirls in her long gown, watching herself in the mirror and wearing a broad smile. "It's perfect. Everything is perfect."

Her bridesmaids are scattered about the bridal suite, putting the finishing touches on their hair and makeup. We're due to walk down the aisle soon.

I smile in response to Arabella but don't comment because all I can think of is how imperfect it all is. I was banging the groom, and the bride is still banging my brother. Yet we're none of us the wiser, except for Declan and me, of course.

Arabella is beautiful, however, with the makeup hiding any imperfections and her blond hair pinned back in braids with lush curls framing her face. The semi-sheer veil floats down her back.

The sleek white gown with the sweetheart neckline makes her look thinner than she is, hugging her waist and then spilling out over the floor. The cap sleeves are made of lace, and a large diamond hangs around her neck, placed perfectly in the centre of her breasts. Arabella could be in a bridal magazine. Her dream and her intention.

"Maddie?" she calls to me. "Don't you agree?"

"Of course," I reply. Then I step closer to her. "Why did you let Jayson propose yesterday? We've barely talked about it."

"Oh, Maddie." Arabella waves me off. "You've done nothing but talk about it. I just wanted to make sure he did something special."

"I guess I'm just surprised you let him take away some of the spotlight."

Arabella let out a soft, fake laugh. "I just wanted to make sure it was done right." She pauses, then adds pointedly, "By both of you."

Before I can press her further, Arabella turns back to the mirror with a large smile. "You look perfect too. I'm so happy we made it to this day."

"Me too." I hold a fake smile in place as I run my hands down the gold silk dress I wear. It's knee-length, formfitting, and low enough in the front to be suggestive, but not enough to be inappropriate. It's a gorgeous dress and, along with the sparkling makeup on my face, one would think this wedding is perfect. But all I can think about is the lie I am living and the truths I have discovered. Nothing about our friendship is real.

A knock at the door interrupts our festivities. Gina is quick to open it, revealing Declan. He's dressed in a suit, like a guest at the wedding, but he wears a sullen expression.

"I need to talk to you," Declan says directly to Arabella, ignoring the others in the room.

My breath catches in my throat. He can't honestly be doing this now.

Arabella obviously feels the same as she shakes her head. "Now is not the time."

"It has to be now." He gives me a hard glare.

Arabella bites down on her lip, looking unsure of what to do.

"Arrie, sweetie." Her mother comes up behind her. "Everything okay?"

"Fine, Mom," she says. "I need a minute." She gives in to her lover's wishes and shoos the bridal party out of the room. "You too, Maddie."

"No," Declan says. "I think she should stay."

Arabella's eyes widen. "Declan, you can't be serious."

"She already knows," he says. "What difference does it make?"

Arabella looks at me, her expression filled with guilt. "Maddie, I'm so sorry."

"You might want to hold on to that apology." Declan gives me a cold glare.

"Declan, stop it," I warn. "You don't know what you're doing."

"Oh, I know what I'm doing."

Arabella frowns and looks between us. "What's going on?"

Before Declan has a chance to answer, the door swings open, and Jack enters the room. His shirt is unbuttoned partway down his chest, and his cuff links are missing. He's frazzled.

"What's going on here?" He glares at Declan but doesn't meet my eyes. The last interaction we had was at the reception dinner, and before that, he slept drunkenly on my couch.

"That's what I'd like to know," Arabella demands, planting her hands on her hips.

"Please don't do this," I say to my brother, knowing the

shitstorm that's brewing. "There are hundreds of people outside waiting for this wedding to start. Now is not the time."

"There's never a good time." Declan turns away from me to face Arabella. "Maddie and Jack are sleeping together."

"What?" Arabella cries.

Jack's fists clench at his side. "Who is this asshole?"

"This is my brother." I wave towards Declan, defeat lacing my tone. "Also, the man that Arabella has been seeing for months."

Jack draws a sharp breath, his expression pinched, cheeks turning red. I've never seen him so angry before.

"Maddie!" Arabella gasps. Then she looks to Jack. "It's not true. None of it is true."

Jack glares at her. "None of it?"

"None," she says. "You with Maddie and me with Declan. It's not true, right?"

His fists release, and he steps closer to her. His voice is soft, but there's an intensity behind it. "Is that what you believe? That none of this is true?"

Arabella swallows hard. The still silence hangs heavy in the air as her gaze doesn't leave Jack's, and the reality of it all sinks in. She's been cheating on him as he's been cheating on her.

"How long?" she asks. It comes out so quiet I think I imagined it.

"It doesn't matter," Jack says. "None of it."

"How long?" Arabella screams.

Our affair bursts vividly into my memories as Arabella's angry words assault me. Images of expensive hotels, cocktail dresses, and intimate dinners sit at the forefront of my mind.

"Years," I jump in, unwilling to live a lie any longer. "Since the beginning. We travelled a lot."

Her eyes bulge as they dart between Jack and me. "You're the Texas waitress!" Arabella rages. "The fitness trainer in Paris?! Where else did you two have sex? My very own bed?"

The memory of the articles I'd read came flooding back. *I was his affair.* How many times had we slept in their marriage bed, one or ten times?

She takes three quick steps towards me and shoves me. "You're supposed to be my best friend, bitch!"

I draw a sharp breath and point to where my brother stands, his head hung low and his eyes focused on the intricate tiles of the floor. My patience snaps, and I give in to the anger that boiled up inside. "Like you're one to talk! You're lying, blackmailing, *and* sleeping with my brother? You lied to me about where he was every day."

"That hardly matters when you're engaged to my brother and sleeping with my fiancé. Must you take everything from me? If Declan wanted you to know where he was, he would have told you." Arabella lifts her arm to swing at me, but Jack intervenes, catching her wrist and forcing her backwards.

"Calm down, Arabella," he says in a stern voice. "Our entire family, not to mention our friends and the press, wait outside this house. Contain yourself unless you wish for everything to be completely ruined."

Arabella glares at her fiancé but soon snaps her lips shut with a sullen frown. She shoots one last cold glare at me. "We're done."

She storms off into the attached bathroom, her veil and dress trailing behind her.

Jack looks helplessly at me then waves to the door. "Can you wait outside?" he asks, the familiar irritation in his tone. "Appease the crowds, let them know that Arrie is having the usual meltdown."

I plant my hands on my hips. "This isn't my fault. I told you this would happen."

"Mads, I need you to go." He steps closer to me and takes hold of both my arms. "It's taking all my will not pummel your brother in front of you. This was not how this was supposed to happen."

I swallow hard. "This isn't my fault."

"I know, but you need to go."

I hesitate before nodding and calling to my brother. Declan seems unwilling to join me but eventually concedes, leading me from the house and into the waiting crowds.

Luckily none of them seem to notice the commotion. They are all still scattered about, champagne in hand and engaging in conversation. Each dressed better than the other and none the wiser of the fight at hand.

Except Marigold Knoll, of course.

Arabella's mother grabs my arm the moment I exit the house and ushers me away from the crowds of people that Declan slipped into. He isn't a guest, but that wouldn't stop him from waiting to see what happens next.

"What is going on?" Marigold hisses into my ear. She wears the same annoyed expression I often saw on Arabella's face.

"Nothing," I say, trying desperately to keep our dirty secrets hidden and calm my rapid heart rate. "Arrie is having a minor meltdown, but Jack is handling it."

"And your deadbeat brother?" Marigold continues. "What is he doing here?"

I tense at her words but push the anger aside and keep my voice steady. "He came to wish Arabella the best. His family is here after all."

She purses her lips but doesn't argue it further. "And

when will the wedding start? People are getting anxious. This is so unorthodox."

"Soon," I promise, though that may have been a lie. Arabella and Jack just discovered each other's infidelity. I doubt the marriage will survive this. A part of me hopes it won't.

"I hope so," Marigold whispers as Jayson approaches. Her stern expression melts away into a loving smile, one reserved for her oldest child. "Jayson, dear, you look so handsome. Is the groom not ready yet?"

Jayson leans down and kisses his mother's cheeks. "You know Jack, Mom. Everything must be perfect." Then he leans close to me and plants a warm kiss on my cheek. "Why, I must say I have the most beautiful woman of all today."

Marigold tuts as she moves away from us. "Wait until you see your sister."

"Is everything all right?" Jayson asks, his arm still hooked around my waist.

"Yeah." My hands shake, and I hope Jayson will chalk it up to nerves.

"Maybe a drink will help?" Jayson grabs a glass of champagne off a passing tray and hands it to me.

"Definitely." The cool bubbly liquid does help a bit. It's gone in a few gulps.

"Feel better?"

I flash a smile. "I do."

Before he can respond, the wedding planner—Paula—hurries to our side. "Maddie, the bride needs you. Jayson, the groom is requesting you."

I frown, my nerves coming right back. "Is everything okay?"

"Of course everything is okay, Mads." Jayson chuckles. "The wedding is about to start."

Maybe that isn't the case. Maybe Jack will tell the truth, and Arabella will rip into me once more.

"Of course."

He leans down and plants a quick kiss on my lips. "See you after the ceremony." I'm left to follow Paula.

I find the bride-to-be still in her bridal suite. Her dress is in perfect condition, her makeup is fixed, and she shows no sign of discomfort. She is alone.

"You wanted to see me?" I ask as Paula and I enter the room.

Arabella flashes a perfectly fake smile. "Of course, silly. I need my Maid of Honour for my wedding." Then she waves off Paula. "Go fetch the other bridesmaids and have the guests seated. We're about to start." Before Paula leaves, Arabella looks back at me and rolls her eyes. "Good help is so hard to find these days."

For a moment, I think she's gone crazy, forgetting the whole interaction from only a moment ago, that is until the door closes and her vibrant smile vanishes.

"This doesn't change anything," Arabella says. "After today, we're done. But, for now, you will do what you promised and smile as if nothing is wrong. Today is my wedding day, and you and your slutty acts will not ruin that."

"How can you do this?" I ask. "You're with my brother and still marrying Jack?"

"Declan was a mistake." She turns away. "It, along with your indiscretions, will be forgotten. After today, you will never speak to Jack again, do you understand?"

"I don't care about Jack." I also don't care about pretending to be happy at their wedding, but I'll do it for my brother's sake. He doesn't need a scandal in the tabloids about an affair or to be hunted by the paparazzi. He's naive; he always has been.

"Good," Arabella says. "Then you completely understand."

The door opens, and more women filter in. Arabella's fake smile returns, and she greets her parents and the wedding party. She seems genuinely happy to be marrying Jack, and only I know the truth.

Marigold walks by me with an approving nod. "Good."

I find my smile is starting to hurt.

———

The music starts and the processional begins as if nothing was delayed and nothing had happened.

The crowd claps and the handsomely dressed groomsmen await our arrival. I see Jayson first, as he's the tallest and wears the most genuine smile, something he's always excelled at. Next to him is the subject of my torrid affair and my biggest disgrace, Jack Davenport, who won't look me in the eye. I'm not sure which is worse, the man who loves me but I've wronged, or the man I used for my petty revenge—neither puts me high in sainthood.

The wedding plays out, as it should, with a promise to love one another and simple vows, many of which have already been broken. Then a brief kiss and several tears followed by the signing of the marriage license; my signature will be the one supporting this false marriage for all time.

The party moves into the reception hall. I sit at the table next to Arabella for several hours, pretending to enjoy myself. I stand up and give my carefully practiced speech, and she forces fake tears and kisses me firmly on the cheek. Only I can sense the coldness between us.

The music begins, and Jayson catches me in his arms. Together we dance and when the music picks up, I return to the bar in search of another glass of wine. Through it all, my smile holds steady, and my mind stays focused on the part I have to play.

All the while, I see Declan lurking in the back with a scotch in hand, but I can only think about how I feel. At some point, Arabella ruined my life and I sought to do the same to her. But as she shoves cake into her new husband's face, I know that I lost this round.

Twenty-Nine

NOW

I find my brother in a hole of a bar on the east side of town. It's been a week since the wedding, and he hasn't taken my calls. It's dark inside, despite it being midday, and it smells of stale beer and sorrow. Only a few patrons line the bar, and most are alone, hunched over some form of poison. Scotch, whiskey, beer. It doesn't seem to matter what is placed before them.

Declan sits at the far end of the bar, clutching a beer. His hair is dishevelled and knotted, and his eyes are bloodshot. His discarded glasses lie on the bar in front of him.

He doesn't look at me when I sit down. He doesn't acknowledge me when I say his name. It isn't until I touch his arm that he finally glances my way.

"What do you want?" He grips his beer and takes a long swig. "Here to rub my face in everything again?"

"That's not why I came." I let my hand fall. "I was worried about you."

"No, you aren't. Embarrassing me is what you do."

I almost point out he was the one to start the whole issue

at the wedding but thought against it. Accusing him now wouldn't change anything or help.

"Declan, please." I reach out to touch him again but hesitate. "I know it's been a long time since we've trusted one another, and I know this is overdue, but I'm sorry about everything. You didn't deserve it, any of it."

His face scrunches with disapproval. He drinks again and then waves down the bartender for another beer. Then he points to me, wondering if I want something to drink.

"No, I'm fine." It's only one in the afternoon.

Declan shrugs. "You can either drink or leave. Your choice."

I concede and order a beer, determined to nurse it while I speak to my brother.

"Are you okay?" I ask after the round arrives.

"Why would I be?" Declan grumbles. "Don't ask stupid questions. Say what you came to say, that you were right. She was never going to leave him for me. She never loved me. She was using me for the attention, and I let her." He sniffs and turns his face away from me, drinking again. "I was stupid and fell for all her lies. Again."

I want to comfort my brother. To hug him tightly and tell him that it's all my fault. Arabella is my enemy and always has been. Life changes haven't affected that; if anything, they've made it worse. I'm sure the moves she made on Declan were made against me.

"It's not your fault, Dec." I reach for his arm again, and he doesn't move away, but he doesn't look at me either. "It was a cruel thing for her to do. This is my fault, and I'm sorry you were in the crossfire of it all."

He continues to stare forward. "I told you it wasn't about you. I should have known better. I used to be smarter than this."

He shouldn't take the blame for falling in love.

"I did nothing to help you." I draw a long breath. "I want to make it right. You forgave Arabella for what happened years ago. I want us to patch that up too."

"I made a mistake." His expression shifts my way, tight and annoyed. "It's too late to fix things, Maddie. We've already come too far." When he drinks this time, he finishes the beer and sets it down hard. The bartender doesn't glance our way. In my other life, my brother stopped drinking as he got older. Alcohol often made him angry.

"Declan—" I hope he'll reconsider, but instead, he slaps a few bills on the bar as he stands, turns, and storms away.

I move to follow him, but by the time I am out the door, he's already halfway down the street. He walks with his hands plunged deep in his pockets and his shoulders hunched over. I can't change his hurt. He loved Arabella for years, and she used him and lied to him. It only makes me hate her more.

I turn away and head to my car, determined to let him sulk in peace. His heartbreak is a pain that my new life knows all too well.

———

My drive home is quick, and I find Jayson's car in the driveway. I've avoided him this past week, leaving before he came home and getting out of bed before he woke up.

Somehow our secrets managed to stay safe. Jayson has no idea about my terrible affair and knows nothing further of his sister's actions. He remains blissfully ignorant, and I'm not about to change that, at least not until I decide what I want. For now, the ring on my finger carries a weight I struggle to hold.

"Where were you?" Jayson asks when I enter the house.

"Talking to Declan." I round the corner to find Jayson sprawled on the couch with a manuscript.

He places it aside and sits up. "Glad to hear things are better with your brother."

"I wouldn't say better."

"Want to talk about it?" He pats the couch beside him, asking me to sit down.

"Not really. Declan's complicated but not worth dwelling on."

"Should we talk about something else?" His eyes drop to my ring. "Is everything okay?"

"Yeah, everything's fine." I try not to let my hands fidget.

"You seem kind of preoccupied." Jayson stands to meet me when he realizes I'm not going to join him.

"Trust me, I'm fine." I place a hand on his arm. "I'd tell you if something was up." Another lie.

His eyebrows fold together, and he stares at me in silence for several seconds before finally releasing a long breath.

"Okay." Jayson leans in and places a firm kiss on my forehead. He takes his manuscript and retreats up the stairs to our shared room.

I watch him go. He doesn't believe me, but he won't push it. He still hopes I love him enough to tell him the truth.

Thirty

NOW

The high-pitched ring of my phone jolts me out of my focus. The work I was proofreading was dull at best. Sometimes my freelance work can be tedious, but it's built up my résumé, so I can't turn it down.

I reach for my phone, expecting Jayson, but am surprised to see Arabella's name flash across the screen. It's been over a week since the wedding, and there hasn't been a word said between us. I consider ignoring it, but figure after everything that's happened, it's worth hearing her out.

"Hello." I click the speakerphone.

"Maddie." She sounds desperate, as if all the previous anger is gone. "I need your help."

"I'm not sure why you're calling after what you said at your wedding. Why would I help you after everything you've done?"

"Maddie." Her voice tightens. "I know we've both done a lot to hurt each other, but we've been friends for years. Besides, this is about your brother."

"What about him?" I ask the question cautiously, unsure if I can trust anything she says.

"He won't leave us alone." Her voice lowers. "He called me every day of our trip until Jack broke my phone. I'm getting emails and messages constantly." She hesitates. "And I'm positive I saw his car parked outside the gym. He's starting to freak me out."

"You did break his heart. I guess it's driven him a bit crazy."

"Maddie, you're not listening." She huffs out a loud breath over the phone. "If you don't fix this, I'm going to tell the cops he's stalking me."

"What? Would you do that and allow Declan to explain his obsession with you?"

"I don't want to." Arabella lowers her voice to a threatening tone. "But if he doesn't go away, I will have to."

Arabella has painted someone as crazy before to avoid any scandal. I can't let her do that to my brother.

"He's not going to listen to me," I concede. The last thing I want is for him to get more caught up in my toxic life.

"Make him." She ends the call, and I'm alone in silence.

I glance at my unfinished work and close the document. Arabella's right. I have to make him listen.

———

His car is parked where Arabella said it was: across from the gym. He isn't inside and after glancing around the street I'm not sure where he's gone. I don't see him anywhere around the gym. Could he have gone inside? I hope he isn't that pushy.

There are apartment buildings directly in front of me and

several smaller stores surround the large gym, which is made of glass. He could have gone anywhere.

The red light on the street meter where his car is parked flashes, telling me it's expired. I can't be sure how long his car sat here or if he paid the fare, but maybe it means he'll be returning soon.

The car is the same dingy sedan I saw earlier this month. This time, however, it's packed full. Nothing more could have fit in the back and the passenger's side is filled with bags. One thing is clear—my brother no longer lives in Arabella's condo. He lives out of his car.

"What are you doing here?"

I turn to see Declan emerging from the building in front of where his car is parked.

"Arabella thinks you are stalking her." I cross my arms and lean back on his car. Then I nod to the building. "Who do you know here?"

"Why? Are you tracking me?" Declan adjusts his glasses, keeping his gaze on the concrete. "Besides, it's none of your business what I do."

"Are you looking for somewhere to stay?" I press.

"What do you care?"

"C'mon, Dec. You know I own a house. I have an extra room."

His gaze narrows on me. "Why would I want to do that?"

"Why wouldn't you, is a better question. I'm your sister, Declan. We've both been screwed, and now we have to deal with it. And stalking Arabella is not the right way to do it."

"I wasn't stalking her." Declan tosses his arms up and turns away. He starts pacing along the sidewalk in front of me. "I came to see if my buddy would take me in. It's not my fault Arabella showed up at the exact moment I did."

I grab his arm, stopping his incessant movement. "Okay,

fine. I believe you. But Arabella won't." I release his arm. "She says you've been calling and emailing."

He looks away. "So what? I deserve an explanation."

"No, you don't. You were as much a part of the affair as she was. It was cheating from the start. You aren't innocent in all of this." It hurts me to tell him this, but it has to be said. He's still acting love-struck and wronged. He has to let it go.

He stares at me, his expression still tight with annoyance. "You're just as bad."

"I'm not saying I did any better. But I'm also not chasing after Jack. I'm letting him go live the life he deserves." Then I shake my head. "Did you think you'd find happiness with Arabella? Did she ever make you happy?"

"She made me feel wanted." His eyes find the concrete again. "She made me feel less alone."

His words strike my heart. "That's not true happiness, Dec. And you know it."

He doesn't look at me or speak for some time, only shuffling his feet and fidgeting with his glasses.

"I don't have anywhere to go." His eyes soften, and he offers me a weak smile.

I place my hand on his shoulder and direct him towards his car. "Follow me home. We'll get you set up in the guest room."

"Jayson won't mind?" Declan hesitates.

"No. Besides, he's away for a couple of days, and by the time he's home, I'll have explained it to him." Besides, it's *my* house.

"Thanks, Maddie."

I only nod and head for my car.

He follows the entire way home, though he knows where I live. I help him unpack his things and carry them to the unused guest room. He had enough to fill a car, but nothing was heavy. It's quick work, and soon Declan is rearranging the room to his liking. We don't discuss how long he'll stay, and I'm not rushing him into leaving.

I head downstairs and grab my phone. I shoot Dee a text, letting her know I'd asked Declan to live with me. I'd been trying to slowly thaw my former best friend with daily texts and little anecdotes in hopes she'd be receptive to my attempt at changing. So far, I'd gotten careful responses. At least she's answering.

I start early supper while Declan makes himself comfortable. Jayson won't be home for at least two days, but I'll have to tell him before then. Somehow doing it over the phone seems easier.

As if reading my thoughts, my phone lights up with an incoming call. My fiancé.

"Hello?" I flick the speaker, knowing Declan won't hear the call from the rooms above.

"Hey, Maddie." Jayson's cheery voice fills the kitchen. "How's my baby doing?"

"Good, but I have some news." Better to rip off the bandage.

"Oh?" There's intrigue in his tone. "Do tell."

"I told Declan he could move in with us for a while." I spit it out quickly. "He's unpacking in the guest room now."

My words are met with cold silence.

"Jayson?"

"I don't know if I'm okay with this." His voice lowers as it always does when I upset him. "Why didn't you ask me before you let him unpack?"

His reaction throws me. If his family needed help, he'd be quick to do the same thing. Why is mine any different?

"He's my brother. He had nowhere to go, and he needed my help. I wasn't going to let him live in his car."

"For how long?" Jayson presses. "A day, a month, the year?"

"Calm down."

His breathing has grown heavy and loud in the receiver. "I don't know why you wouldn't have thought to talk to me about this." His voice lowers further. "We're partners. We make these decisions together."

"He's family," I snap, losing my patience. Then I say the one thing I shouldn't. "Besides, it's my house."

Silence follows my statement, and I have to say his name to prompt him to speak again.

"I didn't know you felt that way." His voice is barely a whisper.

I'm not sure what to say. Though, as I take a moment to ponder a response, I'm not given a chance to speak. My phone call ends, and Jayson is gone. My gut twists with guilt. Jayson's the victim in all of this.

It's forgotten when I see an unread text message in the corner of my phone. It's from Dee.

That's great, Maddie. I'm glad to hear you two are getting along again.

I smile at it. She's opening herself to me again. With Declan back, I'm hopeful that my life isn't too far off.

"Maddie!" My brother's voice comes from the floor upstairs.

I abandon my phone on the kitchen counter. "Coming!"

I head upstairs to help my brother finish moving in and my mind briefly goes back to my angry fiancé. He'll cool down, and then I'll apologize. Right now, I'm glad Declan seems willing to forgive me.

Thirty-One

By the time my brother stumbles home drunk on Thursday, I've finished a bottle and a half of wine and am already thinking about what I'll drink when I finish my next bottle. I've also abandoned the glass. Jayson called me a few hours earlier to inform me his trip was pushed longer and he wouldn't be home until Sunday, which means I'll have the rest of the week to stew with my decision to let Declan move in and how to proceed with my fiancé. But, in all honesty, wine seems like the best option right now.

I invited Dee to join me, but she was buried in work. I'm not upset, however, as she asked for a rain check. I'm starting to feel like our real friendship is just around the corner.

At the sound of the front door and Declan's heavy footsteps, I enter the front hall and come face-to-face with my drunken brother.

"Where were you?"

He plants his hands on his hips but staggers as he does so and laughs before righting himself, clearing his throat and imitating my question. "Where were you?"

He collapses into a fit of giggles. At least this is a happy drunk Declan instead of the rage monster I've become used to.

When his laughter stops, he notices the wine bottle in my hand. "Sharesies?" He laughs again.

I glance at my bottle. "I have a better idea." I reach down and help him off the floor and onto the couch. I head to the kitchen and return with a bottle of chilled vodka and two shot glasses. This is how Declan and I drank in university, at least in the life I remember.

"Bottoms up." I hold the glass to him.

He clinks my glass and then shoots it back. He winces. "I haven't shot vodka in years."

"It always puts a smile on my face." I pour another, but Declan waves his off and leans back against the couch.

"So, where were you?"

"Pub down the road," he says. "Drinking."

"Is that all you do now?" I can't keep the judging big sister voice out of my tone.

He looks to the bottle of vodka then at me. "Let's not argue. We do it too much. Tonight, you're drinking. I'm drinking. The judgement stops there."

I reach for the vodka. He has a point. This time I pour two shots whether Declan wants it or not. He takes it, and I gently nudge mine against his.

"Okay. No judgement, little bro."

We drink and then smile. Everything feels at ease.

"Where is Jayson?" Declan asks, breaking our comfortable silence. "I thought he was only gone for a couple of days."

"Yeah, that was the plan." I shrug. "But he called. Said he wouldn't be back until Sunday. Something came up, I guess."

"Everything okay with you guys?"

I don't answer at first because I don't want to say

anything. But Declan always had a way of getting the truth out of me. I blame his big eyes and puppy-dog expression.

"I don't think so." I know it's not. I'm unhappy, lost, missing my girls. My whole life is a mess.

Declan touches my ring. "Is it Jack?"

"Jayson still doesn't know about that, and I don't want to tell him about any of it."

"Then what?" Declan's hand falls, as does his gaze. He adjusts his glasses.

"You wouldn't believe me if I told you." I laugh and pour another shot. This time I sip the cool, bitter liquid.

"Try me."

I pause. His concerned, curious expression encourages me to trust him with the strangeness of my life. Dee may have told me I sounded crazy, but she seemed to accept my need to change.

"Recently, I've started to feel like I've taken the wrong path." I knit my fingers together and avoid his gaze. "Like I made a decision that set me off the wrong way, and now I have to find my way back." I draw a breath, prepared to admit the truth. "I don't think Jayson is the person for me. Too much has happened. Too many things feel wrong."

"I get it." Declan nods. "I never imagined I'd be that guy to have an affair and to fool myself into thinking Arabella Knoll actually loved me. I knew better than that in university after our terrible fallout. I've always done things better on my own."

I touch his shoulder. "I know there is someone out there for you, Dec. Someone special. She just hasn't found you yet."

"Always the optimist, Maddie." Declan grins and takes another shot. His expression fades, and a serious one takes its place. "You know what you have to do, right?"

"Yeah." I've known for some time. "But I don't know how."

"The most we can do for anyone is be honest. Sometimes it hurts, but it's still better than a lie."

Or many lies.

"Thanks. I'll talk to Jayson when he gets home."

Declan offers a small smile, and we fall into silence.

Itching to get the topic off the table, I ask, "What are you planning? Another world trip, perhaps?" I gently nudge him.

"Who knows?" Declan says. "My life has been derailed for months. I'm not sure where to start again."

I glance around the room. "If you decide to stay in town, you're welcome to be here. I've always thought we'd make excellent roommates. If you think you can forgive me, of course."

Declan rolls his head to the side to smile at me. "Thanks, Maddie. This place feels like home. Which is saying something because I don't think I've felt that way since Dad died."

That, I understand. Our old family home didn't feel the same with Mom's back-to-back husbands.

I lean back against the couch and grab the remote.

"And Maddie?"

"Yeah, Dec?"

"I think I can forgive you."

For the first time, something in this life feels like it's back in place. My brother is by my side, and we're friends again. Maybe, with a few changes, my old life isn't as far off as I think.

Thirty-Two

THEN

The house was brightly lit, and I could hear the excitement coming from inside as Nathan and I walked up the cobblestone walkway to the black-painted front door. I rarely came to this house—the one I grew up in—as it was often vacant these days, and it brought back memories of my father. Mom had never been sympathetic to my emotions regarding Dad's untimely death, and her collection of ex-husbands always made it worse. Dad left her well off, and her second and third marriages added to that. Now she lived intimately with Stan, the former head pro at Lawrence Park Tennis Club. Mom was a walking cliché.

"Are you all right?" Nathan's voice cut through my distress, making me jump. He caught my hand.

The guilt of the previous week still weighed heavily on my conscience. I'd been dodging Jayson's calls and hadn't reached out to him in days. He was getting anxious, and I worried how far his anxiety would take him. I'd have to answer him eventually. Worse, I'd felt on edge all week, like something was off. Each time I left the house, I got the eerie feeling of being watched or followed, but when I'd look around, everything would be normal. Still, it didn't feel like I was imagining it.

"I'm fine." My voice came out higher than intended and earned a look of disbelief from Nathan. I cleared my throat. "Fine, fine. You know how Mom puts me on edge."

"Sure do." Nathan released my hand and reached up to scratch the back of his neck. "You and me both."

"Let's get this over with." I pushed open the front door but kept my gaze fixed on the old hardwood floor. I knew the front hallway like the back of my hand—oak table against the wall, decorative, not functional, covered with family photos. The large crystal chandelier that I always found pretentious, yet Mom would never part with it. And the cream-coloured carpet that lined the middle of the oak staircase, reaching up into the upper levels of the home. The bedroom where I'd grown up. One that Jayson had seen many times.

Maybe, if I kept my gaze down, the memories wouldn't surface.

"You made it!" Mom's shrill voice sounded from the entrance to the living room. She wore a flashy violet pantsuit. Her hair had been recently permed, the large ringlets framing her impeccably made-up slender face. She smacked her red lips as she leaned in to embrace Nathan, and then turned to me, cheek to cheek, making a fake kissing noise. "Oh, darling, I'm so glad you made it. We were worried something came up."

"No, Mom," I said. "Had to get the girls settled."

Mom's gaze dropped down to my plain outfit, and she pursed her lips. "Yes, it seems you spend all your time caring for your children and not for yourself."

I bit my tongue so as not to retort.

"Maddie makes sure the girls get the very best." Nathan

placed a heavy hand on my shoulder and steered me into the living room, where Declan and Naomi waited.

"Hmm, yes," Mom said as she followed us. "Much to her detriment." She offered Nathan a cool smile. "You must be a true gentleman to love her, no matter what."

I drew a calming breath and took a seat on the couch next to Declan, reminding myself we didn't have to be here long.

"Congratulations," Nathan said, shifting the conversation away from Mom's criticism. He leaned down and gave Naomi a quick hug, then offered Declan his hand. "I bet you two are excited."

"We are," Naomi confirmed, then reached for Declan's hand with a gentle squeeze. "Still a lot of things to work out, of course, but we'll get there."

"Like our own place?" Declan chuckled. He and Naomi had been staying with Mom since arriving back in Toronto last week.

"I'm going to get a drink of water." I excused myself from the group, feeling parched and looking for any escape from my family. Mom's judgemental stares, Declan's infectious joy, and Nathan's quick defence made the emotions from the last week flare up. I needed a break and was not in the right place to get one.

No one answered or followed me from the living room and, instead of going into the kitchen, I went upstairs, searching for the slightest bit of comfort. My old bedroom remained unchanged with the light mauve walls and *YM* posters from my high school days featuring New Kids on the Block, James Van Der Beek, Josh Hartnett, and the still-handsome Leo DiCaprio. The perfectly made double bed in the corner of the room seemed small compared to my king-size with Nathan, yet the floral duvet cover was inviting as I remembered falling in love between the lavender sheets.

The room felt untouched, like a time capsule awaiting my return and inviting me to open up a door to the past. It's a world where I'd made a different choice, one that would have sent me down a different path. However, it smelled of stale air and was uncomfortably warm with the spring sun shining through the closed window.

I crossed the room and slid the window open, hoping a gentle breeze would disrupt the stale stench. A gust of wind pushed its way through, catching my dark curtains and sending loose papers tumbling to the floor.

There was an envelope with my name and address scribbled across the front. I reached for it as a knock sounded at the open door. I jumped at the sound, clutching the unknown letter and turning to see who was there.

"Sorry to startle you." Naomi smiled. "When I didn't find you in the kitchen, I wanted to make sure everything was okay."

"I'm fine." The answer was becoming my stock phrase.

"That letter arrived yesterday." Naomi nodded at the letter in her hand. "Declan thought everyone would have had your new address by now."

"Yeah," I said. "Me too."

"You're sure you're all right?" Naomi tilted her head as if to analyze my reaction.

"Yeah." My tone barely convinced me. "I'll be right down."

Naomi left without another word. I lowered myself to the bed and stared at the letter in my hand. It wasn't large, the size of a typical birthday card. There was no return address, just my name—*Madison Jayne*—scrawled across the front, followed by Mom's address.

The name alone was enough to make me uncomfortable, but I slid my thumb beneath the glued edge and released the short note inside. My throat tightened as I read the few words scrawled across the page. A threat.

I shoved the piece of paper back into the envelope and stuffed it into my pocket, hiding it from sight. I couldn't react to this now and not with Nathan downstairs. I needed to be alone when I considered the implications of the note and what it was doing at my mother's house.

"Maddie!" Mom's shrill voice echoed up the stairs. "Hurry down, dear. We're going to serve lunch."

"Coming." I shut the window and left my bedroom as I'd found it—full of memories—and headed for the stairs. But with each step I took towards my waiting family below, the weight on my shoulders grew. I couldn't forget the words I'd read and their insinuation. When I got to the last step, I forced myself to smile, despite how the message burned in the back of my mind.

I know what you've been doing. Jayson's little whore.

Thirty-Three

NOW

"Where are you going?" Declan pokes his head into my room as I dig through my closet, looking for the perfect pair of shoes.

Dee invited me to a party last minute. At first, I was hesitant, but I'm going to take it as an olive branch. One I need to take if I want our friendship to blossom again.

"Dee's having a party at her parents' place. The usual rager, I guess." I pause and glance over my shoulder at him. "You, uh, want to come?" Jayson is due to return tomorrow, and we've barely spoken in days. The party will take my mind off it, at least.

Declan shrugs. His hair is messy. He's wearing sweatpants and a stained white T-shirt. It's clear he'd rather stay in, which is a relief since Dee and I are just getting back on good terms, and I don't know what to expect from this party.

"You're welcome to stay." I grab a pair of heeled boots. "You'll have the place to yourself."

His expression softens. "Yeah, I think I want to lay low right now." He offers a weak smile. "Say hi to Dee for me."

"Of course."

He leaves me alone after that and I only shout a goodbye to him before grabbing a cab to the party. Our relationship before the rift had always been easy, comfortable, and I'm glad it continued that way when he opened the doors to forgiveness.

Being back at Dee's parents' house brings a jumble of memories. Some are from my old life and others from now, but I'm not sure what's real anymore.

The house is on the far side of town and perfect for a "Dee-sized" party. Today's theme? A throwback to our university days so, along with my boots, I wear a pair of low-rise jeans and a black tube top I dug out of the back of my closet. Belly button on display. Not surprisingly, I'm not alone, finding many midriff-baring ensembles.

The inside reflects the typical party layout—a lot of people, too many kegs, and red solo cups. Britney Spears's "Toxic" pulses through the front hall as I wade through the crowd of people. I recognize some of them, and a few say hi, but none of my shared friends with Arabella are here.

I find Dee in the kitchen and am met with a warm smile.

"Maddie. I'm so glad you came." She catches my hand like she used to in school and leads me back the way I came towards the nearest keg. She produces a beer so I can join in the fun.

"Thanks for the invite. I tried to get Dec to come, but he wasn't feeling it."

"I'm glad you guys are talking again," she says, and despite the song drowning out half her words, they sound genuine. Her expression tightens, and she glances around. "No Jayson?"

It's an awkward but unavoidable topic. The massive rock on my finger is a reminder of my fiancé.

"Travelling for work." I sip my beer and hope the conversation will end there. The beer is cheap, and I nearly choke on it—blame it on all the champagne I drank with Arabella—but it's cold and does the trick.

"Congrats." Dee nods to my ring.

I pause a moment. "Uh, thanks."

Her eyebrow raises, a look I know well. She isn't about to let the conversation go. "You don't sound too excited about it."

"It's a long story." I shrug.

"Hopefully one you'll decide to share with me." She grins, and it feels like old times.

"Definitely." I laugh and knock my plastic cup against hers in an attempt to toast. I want to ask her about Nathan, to learn more about him in this life. I have yet to cross his path, but I am not sure how to bring it up, and after the discussion about Jayson, it seems out of place.

Then someone catches my eye. Tall, dark-skinned, and as beautiful as I remember her. It's Naomi. My brother's supposed-to-be girlfriend. Her delicate hands are wrapped around a plastic cup and she stands next to a group of other girls, smiling at the conversation but not saying much. Her hair is tightly braided, and she's dressed casually in khakis and a white tank top. I imagine she's returned from a trip abroad or some other adventure that she's always been known for.

"Earth to Maaaaaddie." Dee grabs my arm and shakes it.

I shift my gaze back to her, still in awe of the fact that my brother's girlfriend is standing only a few feet away from me. As if she was put in my path for a purpose.

"Sorry." I keep an eye on Naomi but do my best to focus on Dee. "What were you saying?"

Dee smiles, another knowing grin. "Just saying that maybe not all hope is lost." She winks, then moves away without another glance back. I watch her go for only a moment before shifting my gaze back to Naomi. There isn't a ring on her finger or a boy wrapped around her. I can only hope that this girl is still waiting to meet Declan, and maybe I can arrange it.

Thirty-Four

NOW

I'm at a loss. I know we have to break up, but this time feels much worse than my memories. When we split the first time, I was glad about it. I was moving on, enjoying university, and finding myself on a new course. This time, however, I worry about what will come. I'm in the same job, still unsettled in my personal relationships. I have doubts about my choices. But as I sit in the living room, waiting for Jayson to get home, I know I can't continue with this charade.

I expected Jayson almost an hour ago, but he's late and he hasn't called. When he finally walks through the front door, he drops his bags on the floor with a heavy clunk, then calls out for me.

"In here," I respond from my seat in the living room. My feet feel like bricks of cement.

Jayson shuffles into the living room with a steady frown. "Something wrong?"

The concern is written on his face as it's imprinted on mine. He can tell something isn't right. He knows me in this life better than anyone, better than I know myself.

I pat the couch beside me. "We have to talk." The action feels condescending but appropriate.

His shoulders stiffen. He crosses his arms. He doesn't sit next to me; he stands his ground, and his eyes fix on the ring that lies in my palm. The one I took off the night before. It feels wrong to continue wearing it. It isn't mine to keep.

"You hate it?" There's a hope in his voice that makes me hesitate. He wants me to hate the ring, not our relationship. But behind the hope is doubt.

"Will you sit?" I try again.

"No." The hope vanishes. Only hardness remains. "Spit it out."

I bite my lip and place the ring on the coffee table that rests between us. "I can't marry you."

My confession is met with silence. The long, unnerving silence that seems to last a lifetime. One that dares me to meet his angry gaze.

When I gain the courage to look up, I'm surprised to find passiveness behind Jayson's eyes as he bends down and reaches for the ring. His hand closes around it, and he retreats from the room with an exasperated sigh. No words. Nothing.

I move to follow him. He enters the front hall and gathers his things. He's still packed from his business trip and clearly doesn't plan to stay in my house any longer.

"Don't you have anything to say?" I'm surprised he isn't putting up a fight. Does he feel the same about this relationship as I do?

"No." He slips on his shoes. "I won't pretend I deserve you." He hesitates and looks at me with sad eyes. "I don't know why you forgave me after what happened with Dee."

The guilt rises up inside me like impending vomit. He takes the blame for every aspect of our relationship ending. Yet, whatever he's done, I've done worse. A part of me doesn't want him to feel the guilt for the end of this relationship. But the other part knows it's easier to let him go.

"It's not that—"

"I don't need you to lie to me," Jayson says, sadness still penetrating his once hopeful face. "It's never been right, not after Dee. I knew it too. I just couldn't admit it. I guess I couldn't let you go when you were still willing to have me."

"Jayson—" I have nothing more to say. The truth will only hurt him more. He doesn't need to know of my indiscretions any more than I need to admit them. So, I say nothing. We share one last hurtful look, and he picks up his bags.

"I'll come back for the rest of my things before the end of the week."

I nod, not able to say goodbye, then watch him leave. I've allowed him to walk away when a very different me desperately clung to whatever we had. I have given up the life I so recklessly ran to. All for nothing.

Thirty-Five

NOW

In the week that followed our breakup, my house felt bigger. Even though Declan had moved in, I found that as Jayson's things slowly disappeared, my life became wide and open again. We barely spoke while he packed and left our once-happy home behind. There was nothing to say, that part had ended, and Jayson had decided it wasn't worth trying. I was most grateful for that. I didn't need the guilt of reliving our ending.

"All good, Dec?" I ask when I find him staring at the blank TV screen in my living room. He clutches his phone in his hand, and his glasses have slipped down his nose. I choose to ignore the bottle of whiskey on the table in front of him, half gone, and the fact that it's only four in the afternoon.

He tilts his head to acknowledge me. His eyes are half-closed and glossed over. I don't need the bottle to tell me he's drunk.

"Dec?" I ask when he still doesn't answer me.

He blinks, and his words come out as a slurred mess. "Madsss I'm fiiiine."

This is the worst I've seen him. He usually can form coherent sentences when he's been drinking, but today getting a word out of him is a struggle. I lower myself to the couch next to him and reach for the bottle.

He's faster and snatches it off the table, dropping his phone in the process. That's when I see it, his call history featuring several outgoing calls to Arabella.

When he realizes where my gaze has landed, he tries to grab for his phone, spilling the whiskey as he reaches down—all over me.

"Aw, Declan!" I jump up, sending the bottle crashing to the now-soaked carpet.

He groans but clutches his phone to his chest. "Wha'd you ssssee?"

"Something I wish I hadn't." I scrunch my nose. All I can smell is whiskey.

"You dint see an-thin." He turns his gaze away.

"Arabella?" I cross my arms, unable to stop the disapproval in my tone. "I thought you'd stopped calling her."

"I did." He tries to stand to meet me but sways on drunken legs and falls back to the couch. He huffs then sighs. His brow scrunches together, and his eyes water. "I din't." He lifts his phone then drops it. "She dosn't answer an'way."

"Of course not, Dec." My voice softens with the pity that wells in my chest. "It's over."

"I know." He lets out another groan as he rubs his blood-shot eyes, then lets his glasses fall back into place. "But I'm not ov'r it."

I understand his pain, but it doesn't change anything. Things with Arabella have to be finished.

"Do you think 'bout 'im?" Declan hiccups. "Are you bothered by 'ow it turned out?"

The question catches me by surprise. He's asking about Jack, of course, not Jayson. We rarely discuss either of them.

"No." Whoever I was when I started sleeping with Jack, I'm not that person anymore. There were feelings when it came to Jack, feelings that I don't truly understand. But it doesn't matter. None of it does.

"It's different, though." His expression falls as if he hoped I was as hung up as he was. "There was nothing between Jack and me but sex and anger. It was never a relationship that was meant to be anything more than it was. He's married, and she's married. It's time we both let them go."

This realization is followed by another heavy sigh from Declan. He slowly attempts to stand and steadies himself on the arm of the couch before moving slowly towards the hallway with his shoulders slumped.

"Where are you going?" I follow his steps. "I thought we'd have dinner."

"No, Maddie." His tone is defeated. He tosses his cell phone on the couch where he was sitting moments before. "Can't t'night. Tired. Wanna sleep." He doesn't wait for me to answer as he trudges towards the stairs and leaves me alone.

I was thankful for the space Jayson leaving made in my life, but it didn't stop the house from feeling empty. Jayson's absence seemed to haunt the bedroom while a lifeless Declan roamed the halls. There's only one fix that will heal my younger brother. He needs his alternate life back as much as I need mine. He needs Naomi. He has to meet her before the darkness takes over, and he sinks somewhere that I can't save him. I look at the spilled bottle on the carpet and scoop it up, managing to keep only a bit of the amber liquid. I hope it's not too late.

That night I can't sleep. I listen to the gentle rumble of Declan's drunken snores and know I can't lie in bed any longer. I need to speak to Dee. She's the only person I can think of to turn to about Declan. I glance at the clock, which reads 11:30. I consider calling Dee to make sure she's still up. If she's the girl I used to know in university, she will be.

When I arrive at her condo, it's surprising how quickly Dee buzzes me in. However, my shock dissipates when I reach her floor and hear the music coming from behind her closed door. She greets me with a crooked smile and grabs my arm.

"Isn't this a surprise?" Her eyes are half-closed and blood-shot as she pulls me into the smoky condo.

Her circular coffee table is littered with beer bottles, playing cards, poker chips, and cigarette ash. Dee's famous bong—Dimitri—rests against her couch. A faint wisp of smoke leaks from the top, likely from a recent toke.

"Bad time?" I ask, taking a seat on the couch.

"Nah, the party just left." Dee goes to the kitchen and returns with two fresh beers. She flops back on the couch beside me.

"So, what's up?" she asks after a long swig. "Must be something big for you to show up like this. Is it Brian?"

Until she mentioned his name, I'd forgotten all about his parole hearing on Monday. I push thoughts of him aside; that isn't what I came here for.

"No." My fingers peel at the label of the bottle as I look down at my hands. "It's Declan."

"Ah." Her voice echoes as her teeth are clamped around the mouth of the beer bottle.

"And me, I guess."

Dee nods.

"I guess I realize all the bad I've done over the past few

years." The paper label breaks away in my hands, and I flick it onto the table. I feel exposed under her gaze. The irony isn't lost on me. She was once my most trusted confidante, and now I worry about her judgement above all else. When I risk a glance, there's no insult or criticism in her face, only the understanding that is so familiar.

"I've taken a path that has affected all the lives of people around me. I've lost friendships and love that I was supposed to thrive on." I draw a breath. "And worse, I've left Declan with a life that should never have been his. He had an affair that wouldn't have happened if I'd been there for him. I need to fix it."

"Mads, you can't blame yourself for anyone's actions," Dee says. "We all have a part in making our lives the way they are. You can't say you made Declan's choices for him."

"You're right." Only that isn't what I'm saying. I affected the outcome through my own decisions. He hasn't met Naomi because of me. He hated me for my cruelty in university, and he ended up with the life I pushed him toward.

"Declan will work things out. You can't rush him."

Again, I agree.

"Now, what about you?"

Another sigh, and I tell her about how I left Jayson. No look of satisfaction crosses her face. The sympathy remains in her eyes.

"You're doing the right thing." Her voice lowers. "Both of your recent relationships were soul-sucking. You have to cut the bad out of your life."

"And bring in the good."

Dee clinks her bottle against mine.

"Speaking of which," I say after we drink in silence. "I want Declan to meet Naomi."

Dee frowns. "Naomi Blake? What do you know about

her?" Then Dee grins. "Actually, they'd kind of be perfect for each other."

"Yeah, and I'm hoping she'll help right his path. I'll need your help, Dee. A party or something to bring them together."

"Call me Matchmaker Dee!"

We laugh as our bottles clink again.

"And hey," Dee adds after another swig. "Maybe I'll find someone special for you too."

"Maybe." Another round of laughter and cheers, but I only think of Nathan.

Thirty-Six

NOW

I wake up with a screaming headache before realizing part of it might be from my phone ringing. A glance at the time confirms that it's midafternoon on Monday. After staying with Dee most of the weekend, last night in particular, and plotting to correct my brother's crooked life, I slept most of the day away.

"Hello?" I answer without looking at the screen.

The greeting is met with sobs. "Maddie. He won."

It takes me a moment to register. I pull the phone away from my ear and see Gina's name.

"He won?" I repeat, trying to understand the words. Then it clicks. Brian. The hearing. It happened this morning.

My comment is met with more sobbing. "They're going release him. He'll be free."

"How do you know?" And what does that mean? Is he on the streets now? Is he outside my door? The questions make my stomach turn.

"My lawyer called me." Her voice cracks. "He'll be out in two weeks."

"Gina, I'm so sorry."

Brian said he'd use my visit to him in prison to his advantage. Did it work? I have to tell her the truth. "I need to tell you something."

"Come meet me and tell me then." She gasps and chokes on a sob that follows.

"Okay." I scramble out of bed. "Tell me where."

"Sherwood Park. I'll be there in an hour." The phone clicks, and I'm left alone with the silent buzz of my throbbing head.

The fog rests heavily on the ground like the growing pit in my stomach. I walk through the park towards the bench. I don't know what to expect but feel uncomfortable in the eerie setting. I should have just told her on the phone. The air is damp with the stench of wet grass and mud. One false step and I'm sure to fall.

Gina's already there when I arrive. She stands to meet me, her greeting as stiff as her posture.

I kick the mud. "So, what I wanted to sa—"

"What were you thinking?" Gina demands, cutting me off. Her face scrunches with anger, and her cheeks puff out like an agitated blowfish. "You ruined everything!"

"Gina, I—"

"He was released on parole because of you!" She starts pacing the ground in front of me.

I wrap my arms around myself, feeling the chill of her anger. "That wasn't my plan."

She stops and plants her hands on her hips, now regarding me like a disappointed parent. "My statement was a waste of time. The lawyer used your visitation as proof he was making amends with the people he harmed. I argued that I was the one he tried to kill, but he gave a statement apologizing for wronging me as well." She shakes her head, disbelief in her gaze. "The whole hearing went to shit! With his apparent good behaviour and rehabilitation, they sided with him. How could you not realize the damage that visit would cause?"

"I don't know." My gaze drops to the ground. Visiting Brian seemed like a good idea; it never even crossed my mind it could make things worse.

"Well, he's out. And it's because of you!"

I look at her, lost for words. I hoped Brian would clear up what had happened and make sense of my chaotic life. But he didn't. He laughed in my face. He told me I got what I deserved, that he'd make me pay for putting him there.

"I'm sorry, Gina. It was a huge mistake. I didn't think. I only acted."

Her lips purse. It isn't the answer she wants.

"You're right. It was a mistake. Huge. Now the man who tried to kill me and swore revenge on you is going to walk free thanks to your reckless actions." She takes a step away from me. "We're done, Maddie. You're on your own. I have my restraining order, but I know it won't keep him away. I'm leaving the country as soon as I can. At least then I know I'll be safe." Gina turns on her heel and storms out of the park, leaving me alone in the cool mist.

I listen in the silence for the sound of her car and the screech of tires. Then there's nothing.

The snap of a branch behind me makes me hesitate and glance around, but only the whiteness of the fog is visible. I draw a sharp breath. There's a sound of footsteps. But do they approach or leave? Squinting, I think I see the outline of a figure.

"Who's there?" My voice shakes. "Hello?"

Silence answers my call.

I glance around again, but the figure is gone. Maybe I imagined the whole thing. Shaking off the discomfort, I hurry to where I left my car, my feet sliding across the damp grass. Once inside, I lock the doors and drive home, keeping a steady eye on the rear-view mirror. The eerie feeling reminds me of when I was sure someone was tracking my every move, when I got the threatening letter, and when I approached Jayson about the contents. It seems to be happening all over again.

I don't breathe easy until I'm in my driveway, sure that I am alone.

Thirty-Seven

THEN

With the anonymous letter buried in my pocket, I pushed through the entrance doors at Jayson's condo and made for the front desk. The concierge was someone different from my last visit, though I hadn't focused on him. This one was young, perhaps early twenties, fresh out of university, maybe. His hair was buzzed, and the facial hair that speckled his chin looked incomplete as if he wasn't quite capable of growing it all in.

"I'm here to see Jayson Knoll in 1022."

"May I ask who is visiting?" the concierge asked as he reached for the phone.

"It's Maddie."

He nodded as he held the phone to his year. "Yes, Mr. Knoll? Maddie is here to see you."

There was a pause.

"Okay, thank you." The concierge hung up the phone then motioned to the door that led to the elevator. "You're free to go up."

"Thank you." I headed for the elevators. I was showing up

unannounced, but this was too important to leave for a bar meeting.

"Jesus, Maddie." Jayson threw open the door. "What is going on? Are you okay?"

I didn't answer. Instead, I pulled out the envelope and shoved it into his hand as I entered the three-bedroom condo.

"What is this?" Jayson looked from me to the letter, perplexed.

"Read it."

Frown lines crowded his face as he slowly opened the envelope and slid out the concealed letter. "Where did you get this?"

"Someone mailed it to my mom's house. Someone who has apparently seen us together."

"If someone has seen that much, Maddie, then you're being followed." Jayson's confusion switched to worry. "What does this person want?"

"Want?" I scoffed. "Nothing, or at least they've asked for nothing."

Jayson's mouth formed a hard line. "People don't send threats without terms. And this"—he waved the letter in front of me—"is a threat."

I lowered myself to the leather couch in front of his TV. "I guess I can expect another letter."

"Who would send this?" Jayson moved to sit on the couch next to me.

"I don't know." I had a good idea who it might be. Only one person ever made a habit of calling me Madison Jayne, but the reasoning wasn't there despite our past.

"Maddie," Jayson said in a low voice that told me he didn't trust what I was saying.

"Look, I may have an idea, but it doesn't matter. I can't

take this to the police. That exposes the secret. Either way, they win."

"We can confront them," Jayson said. "We can do something about this."

A shiver rolled down my spine as I considered the implications of confronting a blackmailer, especially one as violent as Brian. The last time had been uncomfortable, and I still wasn't convinced Gina's death had been an accident.

"No," I said, my voice firm. "I don't want to do that. We have to wait and see if there are going to be any consequences. Maybe he's trying to scare me."

"It seems like it's working."

I pursed my lips but didn't respond. I moved to stand. "You had a right to know since you're mentioned."

"You're not worried about it?" Jayson stood to meet me.

"Of course I'm worried about it," I said, gritting my teeth so as not to raise my voice. "But there is nothing I can do. I have to go." I turned for the door but stopped when Jayson spoke again.

"There is."

I turned towards him. "What's that supposed to mean?"

"You could tell him." Jayson's expression was neutral. I couldn't be sure if he was serious or joking. Would he actually suggest telling Nathan the truth?

I raised an eyebrow, shocked by his forwardness. "Tell who what?"

"Nathan."

The way he said his name made my stomach sink.

Jayson stepped closer to me. "About us, about this."

"Why would I do that?"

"What would be worse?" Jayson retorted. "This mysterious letter spilling the beans, or you being honest with yourself?"

I narrowed my gaze. How dare he imply something he knows nothing about.

"You have no right." I turned for the door, but Jayson caught my arm and whirled me around to face him again.

"I have every right," Jayson said. "This may be your mistake, but it's my life too."

I pulled my arm out of his grip, now seething with anger.

"Don't call me."

I turned and left his condo without another word and stormed towards the elevator. My chest rose and fell with heavy breaths. I had overreacted, but his suggestion made me worry. I wasn't ready to share my mistake with Nathan; what if it cost me everything? My girls? My life? I couldn't do that. I needed to deal with this blackmail and look forward. Jayson had been a distraction, a mistake, I knew that, but I also knew I couldn't take it back.

My anger wasn't at Jayson but at myself. I was frightened by the consequences and angry that I had let myself fall so far. I leaned against the wall of the elevator as it descended the building. A part of me hoped Jayson would call, but the other part knew it would be easier if he stayed away.

Thirty-Eight

NOW

A text from Dee detailed the party to bring Naomi and Declan together. This Saturday, at her parents' house. "Romance in Venice" was the theme. Naomi has already confirmed, and it's on me to convince Declan.

I'm sure it'll be easy until I hear the front door open and slam with a heavy thud vibrating through the house.

I exit the kitchen to find Declan kicking off his shoes and running his hands through his gelled hair, messing it. He wears a pressed suit, though he promptly loosens the tie and discards the jacket. He chews on the side of his cheek, and his eyes are half-closed, tired or sad or both.

"Everything okay, Dec?"

He jumps when he notices me, almost tripping over his newly discarded shoes. "Uh, Maddie. Didn't see you there. Didn't you say you were out today?"

I frown. "Not today. What's going on?"

"Nothing. I went to an interview and got denied."

"I'm sorry." I didn't know Declan was applying for jobs. "But it's great you got the interview."

"Apparently my degree only gets me that far." His hands thread together, and he keeps his eyes on the ground. He means his Master's in Archaeology. He was always book smart, my brother, and he graduated early, but after school finished, he wasn't motivated to do anything with his degree until Naomi came into the picture. Unfortunately, in this life, he doesn't have her to push him into success.

"What are they looking for?"

"Experience. I've done nothing but travel since I left school. My grades say one thing, but my history says another." He groans. "If I'm going to stick around and work, I'm going to have to take something below my pay grade and education. I don't see another way. I need experience to get anywhere."

He heads for the stairs, grumbling under his breath about his failures and inadequacies.

"Declan!" I call after him, now more determined than ever to get him and Naomi together. "You have any more interviews this week?"

He shakes his head.

"Let's let loose on Saturday." I try to suggest this nonchalantly. "Dee's having another party and insists you come."

He rubs his eyes, pushing his glasses up his face. "Not really feeling a party, but good that you and Dee are mending fences."

"Please, Dec," I beg, putting on my best your-big-sister-needs-you voice. "It will be so fun, and she'll be so bummed if I show up alone. Plus, I want to have a date go with me."

He doesn't look as if he's going to budge.

"Puhhh-leeeeeassssse." I clap my hands together in prayer.

He rolls his eyes. "Fine. I'll come for a bit. But don't expect me to be all happy-go-lucky about it."

"Coming is all I ask for!"

He trudges up the remainder of the stairs and disappears into his room. I shoot Dee a quick text letting her know Declan is in. Although I don't blame him for being upset, I hope his attitude will improve.

Thirty-Nine

NOW

A knock sounds at my front door, taking me away from my computer. I'm not expecting anyone, and it's the middle of the day. Who could it be?

My surprise isn't placated when I open the door to Jayson. He's suited up like he came from work, his hair flat and his face shaven. The faint hint of his cologne wafts through my door with the soft spring wind. The scent brings back many memories that I push from my mind.

"What are you doing here?" The question comes out as a demand, though I hadn't intended the nasty tone.

He shuffles his feet on my faded welcome mat. "Can I come in?"

"Okay." I step back and let him enter my home, glad that Declan stepped out for the afternoon. I shut the door behind him and lean against the wall, arms folded and back stiff.

He doesn't speak for several seconds, which feels like an eternity. Maybe I missed his company momentarily, but I've been out of this relationship since I woke up in this life.

"I wanted to talk," he says, his eyes still on the floor. "I've missed you. I've missed us. Nothing feels right anymore." He risks a glance at me. Sadness clouds his gaze. "I don't get where we went wrong. When it stopped being right."

"It was never right, Jayson." It's the only honest answer I can think of. "You and I should have never continued after you slept with Dee. The trust was broken; we can't ever get it back. We both made bad choices throughout our time together. We can't change that. We can only move on."

"Come have lunch with me. Or coffee. So we can talk. I think we can bring back that spark. I think it's still there."

"It's gone, Jayson. All of it. I can't be in your life anymore. I can't be in Arabella's. I need to find the things that make me happy and discover the person I want to be. I know you can too."

"Maddie, please." His pleading voice pulls at my heart but letting him back in isn't the right answer. My heart aches for my girls, for my husband, for the life I took for granted. The only way for my life to go the way it should is to fix everything I've done and recommit myself to my marriage— to Nathan.

My phone rings in the other room, and we both glance towards it. It's probably work.

"I can't." It's the simple answer. "If I came with you now, it would only offer a possibility that isn't there. You need to move on, Jayson. I need you to move on."

"I never will." His sadness, though still present, starts to fade with his words. Anger threatens to surface, but I don't think it's directed towards me. "If I could go back, I would have never done it. With Dee, with any of it. I would have been with you. Treated you right."

I close my eyes, knowing it wouldn't have changed anything no matter his past actions. With Dee or without Dee, there is nothing he can do now.

"I didn't want you. I picked Brian." My confession comes so softly I'm not sure he heard it, but when I glance at his pained expression, I know he did.

"What are you talking about?"

I draw a breath. "That night I found out about you and Dee, I was with Brian. I'd been with him a lot. It wasn't the first time. But it was the last."

"You can't be serious." He shakes his head in disbelief. "That was the night—" He doesn't need to finish his sentence.

"The night he almost killed Gina. I was there because I caused the fight."

"No," Jayson protests. "It was Dee's fault. You and Arabella always said it was Dee that had been seeing Brian and started everything between them. Gina knew it was Dee."

"It wasn't." I look at the floor. I didn't want to confess this to Jayson but I feel it's the only way he'll let me go. "So, you see, it wasn't meant to be. I took you back because Arabella threatened to tell everyone about Brian and me and what happened that night. She made me forgive you so that you'd never know the truth."

"Arrie wouldn't do that." Jayson's eyes narrow.

"Are you sure?" I challenge. "Arabella would do whatever she could to get what she wanted. You wanted me, and she wanted you happy."

"But you guys were friends."

"We were what we needed to be to keep up the charade. But it's over now. All of it."

His fists clench and release almost immediately. "You lied to me for years? Arabella lied too?"

I nod. "I never wanted you to know the truth, but you deserve at least that."

"You were never going to marry me." His heart is crushed

as if I'd taken it in my palm and squeezed until it burst. "There was never a chance for us."

"I was going to," I admit. "But I woke up from this cruel façade and knew I couldn't put you through anything more."

"You're not who I thought you were." Jayson frowns. "You never were."

"I know, and a part of me hates that. But now you have to let it go. Because you deserve more than Arabella and I ever allowed you to have. You deserve to be happy and free. Now you can be."

He turns to leave but hesitates as his hand reaches for the doorknob. His eyes droop, and I see a glisten of tears as he glances back at where I stand. "Was any of it real between you and me?"

I smile with sadness and pity. "Of course, it was real. But it didn't make it right."

He nods in agreement and says nothing more before leaving me standing alone in my front hall. I watch him from the window as he climbs into his car and drives slowly down the street, away from my house and out of my life. I hope I haven't broken him beyond repair.

My throat is dry from the confrontation, and my head is starting to pound, but I make my way into my office, curious about my missed call. Work has been up my ass all week about the article I'm writing. It isn't due for another five days, but they want to see draft after draft. I figure this time it's no different.

However, my luck only continues. First a visit from Jayson and now—of course—a phone call from Jack. There's a voice-mail, and I consider deleting it without listening to it but figure after my confrontation with Jayson, why not deal with Jack too?

"Maddie," Jack's voice comes through, sounding thin and

frantic. "I know I'm not who you want to hear from right now, but I need to talk. The last thing any of us want revealed is what happened between you and me. But someone knows. Call me, okay? It's serious."

The message ends, and I delete it. I stare at my phone for a minute before conceding and calling. The phone rings only once before he answers. His voice is low as if he's somewhere where people might be listening in.

"Maddie, thank God you called."

"What's going on? What did your message mean, someone knows?"

"I came home last night, and there was a strange email from an unfamiliar email address in my inbox."

I frown. "So what? Someone's talking shit."

"There are pictures." His voice lowers further. "From Texas."

I swallow the lump in my throat. Our famed trip to Texas where Jack was accused of sleeping with a waitress; that was me. An event I have little memory of but took part in.

"What did they want?"

"I don't know! There wasn't any demand. Just a threat that this information could be made public at any time."

My stomach twists with a sinking realization. It's the same as the threat from Brian before. No demand for anything, but it'll come.

"You'll get another email soon."

"How do you know?"

"I just do." The situation is all too familiar.

He releases a long breath, and the sound sends a chill down my spine. "You haven't heard or seen anything?"

I think back to the person I thought I saw in the park with Gina and letters I got from Brian. But how could any of that have to do with Jack? How would Brian know something so intimate or have that kind of dirt on me when he'd been locked in prison for the last four years? No, it was someone else, someone who wants something from Jack. Unless, of course, Brian had help.

"No," I say. "Nothing. But you'll call me if you get anything else?"

"Yeah, right away."

"And, in the meantime, get rid of that email and those pictures."

"Already done."

"Good."

There's silence for a moment before Jack speaks again. "Maddie, why would someone do this now?"

"I don't know, but I don't want to find out either. Whatever they want, give it to them, understand?"

"Yeah."

"Okay, I have to go." I end the call before he can answer, and I lower myself to my chair, heart pounding. Someone is following me and plotting against me. Whoever it is, I hope Jack can sort it out. With Brian's impending release, and my attempts to right my life, this will only complicate things further.

Forty

NOW

The party is packed when Declan and I arrive, with more people present than I expected. It seems as if Dee has invited everyone she knew.

Her elaborate decorations are striking. If there's one person who could pull together a bash in a few days, it's Dee; her parents' endless money and constant travelling gave her that ability. The walls are covered with large pictures of Venice, and on the opposite side of the front room, there's a photo booth with Venetian canals as the background. Couples gather to take pictures, smooching or joking around. The whole thing feels very prom-like.

I find Dee in the kitchen, surrounded by friends I don't know. She excuses herself as soon as she sees me.

"Hey, girl." She does a small twirl. "What do you think?" Her purple hair is pulled back into a tight updo, with a few curled strands framing her round face. Her eyes are painted with dark eyeshadow, and her lips are a deep mauve. The dress she wears reaches only her midthigh and hugs tightly to her hips. The bright red colour stands out amongst the other guests. She looks fabulous.

"Amazing, as always." I glance around. "And this party, wow."

Dee laughs. "I know, I've outdone myself, right?"

"You always do."

She passes me a glass of champagne and taps hers against mine before we sip.

"Oh, Declan." She moves around me and embraces my brother. "Don't you look like quite the heartthrob? Bubbly?"

He shakes his head. "Beer, if you have it."

Dee winks and nods towards the keg at the other end of the kitchen. Declan excuses himself and goes right for it.

"He cleaned up good today," Dee says, watching as he fills his cup.

"He's nervous."

Dee frowns. "He doesn't know, does he?"

"No. But he hasn't been out with a lot of people since everything went down with Arabella."

Dee's face scrunches with annoyance at the mention of my former socialite best friend. "Whatever. He's here now, and Naomi will be here any second."

"What's your plan?" Now that I'm here, I have no idea how to get Declan together with his wife-to-be.

"My usual subtleness, of course." Dee winks. "Speaking of —" She glances over my head and waves her hand. "Naaoomiiiiii! Get your fine ass over here."

The slender girl moves through the crowded kitchen towards us and gently kisses Dee's cheeks. "Hey, gorgeous."

"So glad you're home." Dee motions to me. "This is my friend, Maddie."

"Pleasure." Naomi offers me her hand.

"Same here." The formal greeting feels weird since my brain still sees us as close. But she's as beautiful as I remember her, looking the same as she did at Dee's last party. Typical simple clothing, tight braided hair that reaches halfway down her back, and the perfect complexion with little makeup to distract from it.

"How was Prague?" Dee asks as Declan returns to our sides.

"You were in Prague?" he intervenes. "That's one of my favourite cities."

Naomi smiles. "And who are you?"

"Declan," I say. "My brother."

"A big traveller then?" Naomi asks him, amusement written on her face.

"I wish I had travelled more." Declan adjusts his glasses. "I backpacked a lot when I first graduated. Haven't been anywhere great in a while. What were you doing in Prague?"

"Hey, Dee. Got more of this champagne?" I ask. We lit the match, and now they need to find the spark.

"Right this way." She brushes Naomi's arm. "We'll chat later."

"Definitely." Naomi turns back to Declan and continues discussing her research, which Declan is enthralled by.

"That was easier than expected." I continue to watch as Dee leads me away.

"I told you I'm a stellar matchmaker." Dee refills my glass. "Now, what about you?" She scans the guests. "You're looking fine tonight. Any hotties you want me to hook you up with?"

"Tonight isn't about me. It's about them. Besides, I'm not ready yet."

"Whatever, Maddie," Dee scoffs. "You had a relationship full of turmoil with Jayson, a steamy affair with Jack, and who knows what you had with Brian before all of that. You need some sort of normalcy in your life. A guy you can enjoy."

"I know." I can't argue with her logic. She's right about my relationships. But I want Nathan and no one else. Without him, I'm as lost as I am now.

"So?" Dee raises an eyebrow.

"Soon," I promise. "Just not tonight."

A brunette across the room calls out to Dee and waves a bottle of tequila in the air.

"Care to join in?" she asks.

I shake my head, knowing that tequila won't be a good idea if I hope to stay in control. "I'll sit out this round. But go ahead."

"Suit yourself," Dee says. "I'll find you later."

She pushes through the kitchen to the girls shooting tequila, and I turn the opposite way. Declan and Naomi are still speaking closely with animation. His smile is genuine and the best one I've seen in weeks. Pride bubbles up inside me as I watch them together—only a matter of time before Declan is back to the Declan I know best. I'm sure of it.

Sudden light-headedness overwhelms me, and I make for the front door. Dee's parents' house is filling up quickly, and the heat coupled with the champagne is getting to me. A bit of fresh air is my best option. Outside, I feel the dizziness subside, and I sit on the bench under the front awning. From where I am, I can easily see Dee's guests coming and going, so it's no surprise a certain one catches my eye. My heart slows as I take in twenty-seven-year-old Nathan. He's tall with a strong angular jaw and crew-cut black hair. Memories of our love, our marriage, and Ava and Haley come flooding back, knocking into me and taking the wind out of my lungs. For the first time since my reality changed, I set eyes on my husband. Handsome, perfect, my everything. *My Nathan.*

Except he isn't mine, and that is made clear by the tall, raven-haired bombshell that stumbles out of the cab and clutches his arm.

Heat creeps up my neck; my heart pounds in my chest. I hate her already, the way she sways and giggles. Her perfect makeup covers her prominent cheekbones and huge lips. Her tight dress hugs her slim body. I want nothing more than to hide, to get away from the party, and pretend I never saw a thing.

I watch him as they walk up the front steps and into the party. He doesn't glance my way. Of course he doesn't. He doesn't know me.

My body tightens with longing, and I stumble towards the stairs, missing the first step and nearly falling on my face. I cannot forgive myself for my choices, for my mistakes, for everything. Hurrying down the street, I hail a cab then send Declan and Dee a text explaining I felt unwell and had to leave.

In the cab, I breathe a sigh of relief. Seeing Nathan with another woman tore my heart apart. I'm single now, and I guess I expected our lives to fall together as easily as Declan's and Naomi's. But maybe the choices I made ruined any shot we had.

I wipe away a tear as a thought pushes to the surface, one I've tried to ignore for some time. *What if there is no going back?* Maybe Nathan and I don't have a future anymore. I ruined that life for myself. As more tears form and begin to slide down my cheeks, my heart mourns my marriage and my daughters. Ava and Haley are lost to me, possibly forever.

Forty-One

S everal days after we last spoke, Jack finally calls me with the news I had been dreading. He's received another email—this time demanding something.

"They want information on me?" I choke. The blackmailer isn't looking for money. They want dirt, evidence, anything that can tie me to Brian and Gina's incident. "What did you tell them?"

"Honestly, Maddie, I haven't replied," Jack says. "I don't know what to tell them. I don't know anything about your past with this Brian guy. Arabella might, but there's no way I'm taking this issue to her."

Of course, Arabella knows. She has all the dirt. It's the basis of her blackmail. Who knows what else she might have.

"No," I agree. "Don't take it to her."

There's silence between us then. Neither of us knows how to respond. On the one hand, we're being threatened with exposure, something that will cause a rift in our lives, and on the other hand, there seems to be nothing we can do to mend the issue. Jack doesn't have the information, and I'm unwilling to have it passed on. Or am I?

"How will you answer?" I ask after the silence draws on too long.

"I'll figure something out. I can't give them what I don't have." His voice is flat.

"And the pictures they have?"

"I guess we're risking their release." No emotion in his voice, only cold logic.

I imagine the shitstorm the press will stir up. *Truth Revealed: Maid of Honour Really Maid of Whoring* or *Best Friend Turned Slut: How Socialite's Closest Friend Ruined Everything.* It will be the gossip-worthy story of the year. Every entertainment news outlet in the city will want it, and everyone will read it. We'll be faced with judging stares, the girls who'll hate me, and the guys who'll think they can get some. Jayson would learn the truth, and it would hurt him more than I already have. This isn't what I want, but what can I do?

I release a long breath. "Tell them you'll give them something: pictures, information whatever. But they have to meet you somewhere."

I'm not sure what I'm willing to give up to these strangers. I hope I can at least figure out who would want to follow my life so closely and only want information on Brian in return. Who would care?

"Okay, I'll see what I can do." He hesitates. "But what happens when we don't have anything to give them?"

"I'm hoping we figure out who it is before it comes to that."

"That's a lot to hope for."

"Got a better idea?"

Jack remains silent.

"Didn't think so. Let me know what you come up with."

"Talk soon."

The call ends, and I sit back in my chair. My head starts to pound, feeling like my brain has swollen to twice its size and is pushing against my skull. The pain is unbearable. Stress-related. I have too much to deal with around Brian's release and trying to right my life to focus on this strange blackmail.

I have to shake it off, push it aside, and forget about it for now. There's nothing I can do until I hear from Jack. He's the point of contact, and I am left to wait.

I close the article I was working on and climb the stairs to my room. Declan's out again, which has been common over the past few days. I need to lie down and let the pounding in my head subside. Maybe once I can think, everything will start to make sense.

I must have fallen asleep because I wake up from a wonderful dream. I was happy, life was simple, and I was with Nathan. My daughters were alive and well. I was a proud mom, watching Ava and Haley grow into smart, beautiful young women. It was bliss. Waking up has ruined it all, reminding me I'm not with Nathan and that my daughters don't exist. Instead, I'm stuck in a strange limbo of affairs and blackmail.

Back at my computer, I try to focus on the work at hand. It's fruitless, of course, because although life seems to be pushing me away from Nathan, I can't get him off my mind. The way he touched me in my dreams, his steady smile, his sincere gaze, our perfect babies … all of it made me only want to try harder. I'm not ready to give up our rightful future together, no matter how much I screwed up. Ava and Haley deserve their lives. We deserve to have them. I need a chance to appreciate everything I was given and everything that was ripped away. I will do it right this time.

My email chimes, pulling me away from my thoughts and plotting. It's from my agent, with good news about a contract we negotiated weeks before. One I remember from my career but didn't get. Now I'm given the opportunity—a book deal with Black and Diggs, a major publisher. They like my manuscript. I am going to be a published author.

My heart races. It was years, and several ideas, before any of my books gained interest. Despite my wrongdoings during this timeline, at least I progressed quickly in my work. I grab my phone, ready to message the one person who always supported my writing dreams: Dee.

Got time to meet? Good news.

My phone chimes almost immediately.

Diner in ten.

See you then.

I scurry up the stairs to put on something more presentable than my sweats and ratty T-shirt. My stomach gurgles with hunger as I pull on a pair of jeans and a cute blouse and rush off to meet her.

Once seated, Dee orders us a bunch of greasy but delicious appetizers to share, each one bringing me back to our university days. Mozzarella sticks the size of my first two fingers, deep-fried mac-and-cheese balls, an order of crispy garlic fries, and three pounds of honey barbeque chicken wings, complete with two pints of beer. This girl knows the way to my heart. And my thighs. But the aroma is mouth-watering. Probably not the best brain food in the world, but it makes my stomach growl. I dig right in as the first plate comes to the table.

"Okay, spill." Dee chomps on a giant chicken wing, sauce getting all over her lips.

"They're publishing the Armalla novel." I try to keep my voice low, but the excitement breaks through. "They loved it."

Dee squeals. "Get out!"

"I'm serious. They loved the pitch. I need to get editing immediately. They want a draft before the end of the month."

"Amazing! Last time you told me about the Armalla novel, it was still in development. Where are you at with it now?"

"It's completely written now." I reach for the garlic fries and pop one into my mouth. The grease sizzles on my tongue, but the taste of salt and garlic makes me crave more. "And all the guilt I had about the story is gone."

Dee cracks a smile. "Still basing it off Arabella?"

"Parts of it, for sure." I match Dee's grin. "I mean, her life is a story, all I had to do was add a little more colour, and there's definitely something there. I'll have to work on the love story portion a bit more after editing. Neither Jayson nor Jack are great examples."

Dee's smile shifts from amusement to coy. "There's always Nathan?"

"What now?" My heart thumps, skipping a beat at the mere mention of his name. Cliché, I know.

"Yeah, you missed the blowout at my party since you left so early. He's single now. Maybe I could hook you up."

"Huh?"

"You two, dummy." Dee touches her two index fingers together with a playful grin.

"Do you think he would go for it?"

Dee puffs out her chest. "Matchmaker extraordinaire to the rescue!" She shoves a mozzarella stick in her mouth. "Ever hear anything about Naomi and Declan? They spoke most of the night, but I haven't had a chance to ask her about it."

"Me neither with Declan." I shrug. "I've barely seen the guy. Somehow in the last week, he's gotten a lot more popular than I ever was." I'm stuck on the idea that Nathan is single. Is it possible my chance isn't lost? Are my daughters still on the horizon? "If they talked all night, maybe they need another push. Another party to bring them together again."

"And we're talking about Declan and Naomi here, right?" Dee looks at me pointedly, though her grin reveals amusement.

"Of course, who else would it be about?" I try my best innocent look, but Dee sees right through it.

"I'm sure Nathan would be down for another party." She reaches for her beer. "As long as you don't leave early again."

I don't answer, only reach for my beer and contemplate the idea. Nathan is single and I am single. My daughters are finally within reach.

S ean calls me the moment Brian is released. Hearing he is back out in the world puts me on edge. Sean advised a restraining order in the weeks prior, and I complied. As far as I know, Gina did the same, and there's no way Brian can contact either of us. Still, something tells me a signed piece of paper will not be enough to stop him.

"You worried?" Declan asks as he enters the kitchen, likely having overheard my call with Sean.

I look up from my phone. "I'll be fine."

Declan grimaces as he reaches into the fridge and pulls out an apple. "You don't look fine."

"I am," I insist. "I've got the restraining order against him. He won't come near me unless he wants to go back to prison."

Declan is about to say something but turns without speaking.

"C'mon, Dec." I stand to follow his movements. "I know you better than that. Say whatever you're thinking."

"Maybe I should stick around today."

I plant my hands on my hips. "I don't need a babysitter."

"I didn't mean it like that." He adjusts his glasses.

"I'm fine." And I am, despite the way my skin prickles. "Don't change your plans for me. It's my life, and he's free to live his. I'll have to get used to it on my own."

His expression shows he disagrees.

"You can't bail on this interview," I say. "It's too important. Plus, I'm going to run to the grocery store and then I'll be here working all day. Nothing to fret over." I don't want him to derail his life again to watch over me.

"I won't be long," Declan promises.

I wave him off. "Take as much time as you need. I'll call you if anything comes up."

He hesitates at the door.

"Go. I'm a big girl. I can handle it."

Declan frowns but concedes before dashing out the door.

"Good luck!" I call after him as he climbs into his green sedan. I say a silent prayer, hoping this time the job will pan out for him.

When he's gone, I head to the store to pick up the ingredients for his favourite meal, Dad's famous burgers, hoping that a special dinner might bring him a little extra luck with his interview.

The bright sun on the warm day helps to ease my worry, and by the time I'm finished at the store, I feel better.

That is until I arrive home and see something stuck to my front door—a folded letter.

My steps are slow and cautious as I approach the front door and snatch the letter. I glance around once more before testing the door. Still locked and no sign of attempted entry. Whoever came by left only the note.

I clutch the envelope tightly as I fumble with my keys. My hand shakes, and the key rattles against the lock, but I manage to push it open, locking it behind me.

I lean against the door, trying to slow my rapid heartbeat, clutching the letter to my chest. I slide my back down the door and sit on the floor before risking a glance at the words written inside.

Life has a funny way of turning around. I'd be careful where you turn. I'm always watching, and I'm about to get exactly what I want. Don't forget, Maddie, payback's a bitch, and I'll make sure she hurts.

I shiver as I read the words again, sure that Brian wrote them, though something about the writing seems off. The strokes are smooth and connected, and there's a slight waft of rose water on the paper.

I have the sensation of being watched. Before pushing the door open, I steal a glance around the street through the door's glass. Nothing seems out of place. There's a car parked further down the road, but it doesn't look occupied. I shake my head, certain the feeling I have is one my mind has fabricated. I think back to the foggy day in the park with Gina. I felt watched then, was certain I heard footsteps, and swear that someone had been following us. Brian hadn't been released from prison at that point, but did he have someone on the outside keeping tabs on me? How else would he know details about my life? Could this be the same person who has dirt on me and Jack?

I run up the stairs to my bedroom, where I shred the note and dispose of it in the trash. I don't need Declan finding it and getting more worried about me.

A million questions race through my mind about Brian and my potential stalker. My body shakes with fear. My empty house isn't inviting or comforting, and this time I can't wait until Declan comes home.

The phone rings several times before I get Gina's voicemail. It's my third time trying to get through without any luck, and I'm starting to worry that something's wrong with her.

"Hey Gina, I wanted to check in with everything going on. I know we left things a bit tense when we last spoke, but something happened, and I could use some insight and guidance. Anyway, call me."

I click end on the call and shoot her a quick text for good measure.

This time, I get a quick response and my phone springs to life with Gina's name on the screen.

"Hey, Gina. Thanks for calling me back."

"What do you want, Maddie?" Her tone is emotionless.

I hesitate, a bit surprised by her coolness. I get she was angry at me for visiting Brian, but that doesn't change what we've been through together. I swallow the lump in my throat and pretend otherwise.

"I wanted to check-in. I haven't heard from you for a while."

"I didn't feel like talking to you."

I start pacing the room, my anxiety building. "I'm sorry for what happened. I didn't mean to be the cause of his release. I wanted some answers."

"Well, I hope you got them."

I didn't.

"Look, Gina, I wouldn't be calling if it wasn't important." I pause. "Someone left me a threatening letter, and I think it might be from Brian."

Gina scoffs. "Are you surprised? He swore he'd have his revenge. You're the idiot who didn't take him seriously."

Again, I'm thrown by her response. "Has he tried contacting you?"

"No," she says. "I haven't heard a word." There's a commotion on her end. "Look, Maddie. I have to go. Good luck with climbing out of the hole you've dug." The line goes dead before I can answer.

I must have really upset her with my visit for her to be so cold. Her literal disinterest in Brian's threats says as much.

Defeated, I lie on the couch, flick on the TV to a mindless talk show, and try to focus, but I can't tell you what it's about. My mind is buzzing from the phone call with Gina and the strange letter. I don't know where to turn next.

My phone rings again, pulling me out of my zombie-like state. I sit up and see Declan's number across the screen.

"Dec?" I answer, unable to keep the panic from my tone. "Everything all right?"

"Everything is fine." His voice is rushed. "Still planning on dinner tonight?"

My panic doesn't subside. "Yeah, of course. How was the interview?"

"It was good," he says nonchalantly. "Uh, for dinner, uh, just make a bit extra, okay? I'm super hungry."

"Happy to." I laugh, then hesitate. "You're sure nothing's wrong?"

"Positive." Then he adds, "I gotta go, Mads. But I'll tell you about the interview later." The call ends before I can respond. At least making dinner for my brother will prove to be some sort of distraction.

I pour a glass of wine and set the table as I wait for Declan's return home. For a moment, I think he may have forgotten about me until the creak of the front door halts that thought. I release a breath of relief.

Declan saunters into the kitchen. "Hey, Mads."

"Declan." I give him a quick squeeze. "So glad you made it home."

"Yeah. I actually didn't come alone."

I cock my head to the side as someone emerges from the hallway and steps into the kitchen. My heartbeat quickens. Naomi.

He introduces her. "Naomi, you remember Maddie."

"Of course." Naomi takes my hand in a gentle shake. I try not to be in awe of her delicate fingers and smooth skin. "Lovely to see you again. Declan talks nonstop about his sister."

I offer them both a drink; Naomi takes the wine, and Declan goes for a beer. As they settle around the counter, I ask something that just occurred to me. "So, Naomi, have you and Declan been spending much time together?"

Naomi smiles and looks down at the glass clutched gently in her dainty hands. "Almost every day."

"Really?" I sip my wine in an attempt to hide my smile.

Dee certainly is a matchmaker extraordinaire. "You haven't said anything, Declan."

He adjusts his glasses. "Nothing to say, I guess."

"Are you guys dating?"

Declan's cheeks flush, and Naomi forces an awkward giggle.

"It's not like that," Declan mumbles, though his reaction says he hopes it is.

Naomi nudges him. "Why don't you tell her?"

He glances at Naomi before looking back at me, then clears his throat. "I got a job."

"Oh, Dec, that's amazing!" I squeal. "What for?"

"It's a research position with the university. Archeology department."

I can't contain my excitement. Declan's path is finally going right. This is the perfect job for him. "Fabulous. Just fabulous!"

"Thanks, Maddie." He adjusts his glasses again. There's more, and he's nervous about telling me.

"What is it?"

He grins sheepishly as he shoots a glance towards Naomi. "I'm thankful for you letting me crash here. It was—no, is—a lifesaver. But this new job, well, in a week, I'm being sent on an expedition down to Argentina with Naomi and her team. It was a huge opportunity, and Naomi managed to get my name added to the list. But it means I'll be leaving, and I'm not sure for how long."

I smile, trying to hide the fact that my heart is sinking and anxiety is setting in once more. I'll be alone again in my empty house with a stranger who seems to be watching my every move. But I have to let him go. Declan is finally getting the life he deserves.

"I'm so proud, Dec. So proud."

He shifts under my gaze, hands on his glasses, fiddling.

"If you need to treat your room like storage, that's fine too." I place my hand on his shoulder. "I'll be here. It will all be here whenever you come home."

A broad smile spreads across his face, and he grabs Naomi's hand with a gentle squeeze. The look they share warms my heart. She cares about him, and she is making sure he follows her. He will have the life he's supposed to, his wife, his unborn child, and their adventures. I'm sure of it now.

When I've finished the tray of toppings, I place it on the table and pull the finished burgers from the oven where they'd been staying warm. I invite them to sit around my kitchen table.

I raise my glass to the group. "To Declan and Naomi's new adventure."

Declan stands and raises his drink. "And to you, Maddie. For bringing us together."

"Here, here!" Naomi agrees, and we all clink our glasses together then drink in unison before helping ourselves to the food.

To me, it's the perfect sight: my brother and his soon-to-be girlfriend. The only thing missing is Nathan, but their happiness and Declan's kind words will tide me over until I fix that part of my life.

Forty-Four

NOW

My email pings while I'm in the middle of a crucial paragraph, but seeing it's from Jack makes me hesitate. I click off the document and switch over to my email. The subject line reads Fwd., which means the message isn't from him but from someone else. The blackmailer.

Meet today at 9:10 King and Brant. Come alone.

At the bottom of the message is the short text from Jack.

Call me. Office number.

I pick up my cell and click the work number under Jack's contact, unable to quit the nervous drumming of my fingers as the phone rings.

"Mr. Davenport's office." The receptionist's tone is bored and, somehow, I can imagine how she's greeting me. She's definitely leaning back in her chair, filing her long, manicured nails, or twirling her straight blond hair. Jack keeps her around for the distraction, not the work. He likes to look down her busty shirt or at her round behind when she bends over. I remember him denying the accusation of sleeping with her. However, I'm not sure if the memory is real or fabricated.

"Jack asked that I call."

There's a moment of silence on the other side of the phone. "Ms. Butler?"

"Yes. Can you pass on the call?"

"One moment, please."

The hold music comes on, and I continue to drum my fingers until I hear Jack's smooth voice through the receiver.

"Got my email, I guess?"

"I did." I lean back in my chair. "What's the plan?"

"I'll pick you up."

"That's stupid," I say, imagining the consequences of having a limo drive up to meet a blackmailer. "The meeting place is around the corner from your office. Just walk."

"And you?" There's skepticism in his voice.

"I'll watch from a distance. I'll take Declan's car." If this person knows who I am, then going in a different car will help hide my identity.

"Then what?" He's worried. "What do I say to them? What do I give them?"

I frown. I found some pictures of Brian and me in my old school albums. It would have to be enough to appease the blackmailer because I'm not about to part with the video. "I have a picture, one that you can take. Give it to whoever this person is if you need to. I'm hoping I figure out who it is before it comes to that."

"And if that doesn't work?" Jack asks, voicing my next concern.

"We'll cross that bridge when we get there." I glance back at my computer screen. "I'll drop the picture off at your office this afternoon."

"Okay."

"Then I'll see you tonight."

"Yup." The line cuts out and Jack is gone.

After that, I try to focus on my writing for twenty minutes more before giving up entirely and calling Declan with an excuse to borrow his car.

Declan's sedan is dirty and smells like rotten cheese. Hopefully, I won't start to smell the same way after sitting in here. I tried looking under the seats to find the source of the awful stench, but it's no use.

I drum my fingers on the steering wheel as I glance at the time, five to nine. Whoever is coming to meet Jack will be here soon, and Jack as well.

The street corner where the blackmailer asked to meet is in plain view from my stakeout spot. It's a populated street, surrounded by offices, boutique restaurants with tinted or shuttered windows, and the occasional bar—plenty of places for quiet, private dining. Two doors down from Brant Street is a familiar oyster house. I must have been there before, likely with Jack.

I found the more I adapted to my new life, parts of this past life became clearer, and places and people were more familiar. It's as if the longer I'm stuck in this alternate reality, the more it becomes my truth. I have memories I can't explain, let alone be certain are real, but they're there; they inhabit the back of my mind as if I really lived them.

I have to accept this is my life now. People would kill to get to redo their twenties, to get a chance to rewind and fix their mistakes; one would think I would be grateful. But in this reality, I made the mistakes, not corrected them. When I wished to be with Jayson, I never considered the damage it would do and that I'd spend my life trying to undo all the wrong.

My thoughts are interrupted when I see Jack's limo pull up, and he climbs out. Then he waves Vincent away. Of course, he wouldn't walk. What did I expect?

He's dressed in a black suit with his typical slicked-back hairstyle. He holds a briefcase in one hand and his cell phone in the other. Jack leans against the wall of an Italian restaurant at the intersection and glances around. He may have been looking for me, but I doubt he knows what Declan's car looks like. Jack glances down at his phone, then mine pings.

The text from Jack reads: *Here.*

Me too, I respond.

Again, Jack looks up and glances around; still, he can't see me. It's encouraging, to say the least. If he can't see me and he expects me, then the blackmailer will likely be oblivious as well. Hopefully, it isn't too obvious with him glancing around like a fool.

After his response, he puts his phone away and places the briefcase at his feet. Another glance around, though this time it looks as if he's looking for his meeting.

There are few others on the street. Most are couples heading into one of the joints along the strip, and there are solo travellers in long coats and looking very prim, likely finishing their busy day at the office, even at this late hour, or going to meet friends.

Jack runs a hand through his hair, then goes for his tie and pulls it down, opening his collar. He's nervous. The habits are familiar, and a part of me yearns to comfort him. I grip the steering wheel tighter, determined to stay where I am, no matter what my heart tells me.

He pushes himself off the wall when he appears to notice something down King Street. The person that steps to meet him at the corner has their face shielded from my view, a hood drawn.

My phone rings, and I jump at the sound. Jack's name flashes across the screen.

I answer but don't speak.

"What did you bring?" The voice that speaks is female and sounds far away. This catches me off guard.

"I have a photo that I found in Arabella's things," Jack says. It's the picture I gave him earlier.

"Only one?" She's disappointed, whoever she is. There's a familiar twang in the voice—an accent—one I've heard before but can't place.

"It's all there was." There's noise on the other side of the phone—the unclipping of the briefcase and a rustling of paper.

The woman snorts. "You expect this to be enough?" The picture isn't anything incriminating. It shows Brian and me leaning very close, about to kiss, I assume. We have drinks in our hands, and the lights above us are red. I can't remember where the picture was taken or who the photographer was, but it's all I have without sacrificing the video.

"It's all I have," Jack says. "Without telling Maddie about this or getting my wife involved. I don't have anything else."

"Where did you find it?"

I hold my breath. We discussed this, but is it believable?

Jack sighs. "I had to go through my wife's old condo. It wasn't an easy find. It was in one of her old school albums."

The woman glances at the photo in hand. "I want more."

"I don't have anything else," Jack repeats with a flat tone.

"I could ruin you," the woman says. "And you'll do nothing?"

"I'm trying." He sounds desperate, and it worries me. He grabs her arm. "I don't know anything about Maddie and her relationship with this guy. I didn't know the guy existed until a year ago when Arabella started talking about it."

"What did she say?" There's interest in her tone as she shakes him off.

"I don't remember. Maddie had been involved with him and some girl. Her life before was never of interest to me."

"What did she say about them?" The woman's voice lowers.

"Nothing important," Jack says. "Maddie had screwed some girl over in university, and now she was going to pay for it. Arabella likes to blackmail."

"That sounds like her." The woman gives a short laugh.

"Do you know my wife?" Jack asks.

"Uh, no," the woman stutters. "But I've read about her. Both of you. This is why I know the pictures I have would be detrimental to your lives."

"I can't do anything else for you," Jack says, defeat in his tone. "I've given you all I have and all I know."

"Fine. It'll work, for now." She steps back from Jack. "I'll be in touch." Then she turns away and heads down King Street.

I want to follow her but don't want to be conspicuous, so I wait to get a comfortable distance.

When the woman is gone and Jack is alone, he brings his phone to his ear. "Did you hear all that?"

"Yeah, but I didn't see who it was. Did you?"

"She wore sunglasses," Jack says. "Looked familiar. Maybe I've seen her before. Can't be sure, though. Where are you?" He glances around.

"Down Brant, green sedan."

His eyes fall on the car. "Be right there." The call ends before I can tell him not to. Jack glances around before heading over to where I'm parked. He hops into the passenger's side then scrunches his nose. "Your brother keeps his things clean, doesn't he?"

I shrug. I'm used to the smell by now, plus a flowery scent wafts towards me when he gets in. "New cologne?"

"No." He raises an eyebrow.

"So, you think you've seen her before?"

"I don't know, maybe." Jack tilts the passenger seat back and reaches for his seat belt. "It seemed like she knew Arabella. Maybe they're old friends."

"Or enemies." I doubt a friend would use us as blackmail.

Jack nods. "Probably more likely."

"What now?" Do we look through Arabella's photos until he finds one that might have been the girl he just met? Or do we try to track the blackmailer's email? Both seem like dead ends.

Jack seems unfazed, however, and wears a devious smile as he holds up his iPhone 4. "We follow her."

On his phone is a picture of a map and a small blue dot flashing as it moves—a tracking device.

"How?"

"When I grabbed her," Jack says. "I slipped it into the pocket of her coat. Now let's get going before she figures out it's there."

I don't answer him, only driving the car the way he directs, thankful he was one step ahead of me on this.

Jack reaches across the car and places his hand on my knee with a gentle squeeze.

I risk a glance at him as we pull up to a stoplight. His smile is familiar, comforting. The feeling of warmth he gave me weeks before is still there. There was depth to our affair. That much is clear, even if I'm not sure what it was or if I feel it anymore.

"What?"

"It's a bit exciting, isn't it?" Jack asks, his warm smile

shifting to devious. "Playing stakeout together. Following someone. Having secrets again."

Although part of me doesn't want to, I remove his hand from my knee. "It's not like that anymore. This is business."

His shoulders stiffen. "I miss it."

"I know." I can't tell him that part of me feels the same; it's another memory I'm not positive is real.

"You don't?"

My eyes shift to the road when the light turns green. "I honestly can't think about it, Jack. It's not something we can have, either of us."

"What if these pictures do come out?" he presses. "And Arabella and I are done?"

What if? He asked that before. He had the opportunity to choose me over Arabella when the truth came out. I might have walked away, but he didn't fight for me. He didn't pick me. He didn't leave her.

I shake my head. "You aren't leaving your wife, and I won't be with you." My fingers grip the steering wheel harder. "I won't deny that what we had was something, but it's also over. It has to be. I need it to be." I risk another glance. "After all this is done, I need to let you and Arabella go. I need to find my life and find myself."

Jack looks down at his lap. "I get it."

"Thank you." There's nothing else to say, so silence drifts between us, and the only words are when Jack gives me directions.

"We're close now." He points to his phone. "The dot stopped moving."

"Close, or she figured out we were following her."

"Left here," Jack directs. "Then it's just down the road." His eyes are glued to the dot. "Slow down." He glances up. "Right here."

I stop a few houses down from where the icon indicates the blackmailer is, and together we watch as someone climbs out of the red car in the driveway. It's clear she's the woman who met Jack because she still wears the same long coat, although the hood is no longer drawn. Instead, the streetlight reveals a raven-haired woman with an amber complexion. The sunglasses aren't present. I squint in the short distance, almost sure my eyes are lying.

But they aren't. She turns and clicks the lock of her car with two short beeps, and that's all I need to confirm my suspicions.

Our blackmailer is Gina.

Forty-Five

THEN

A week after the first one arrived, another letter appeared, this time at home but still addressed to the same person, *Madison Jayne.*

I snatched it away from the mail and tucked it away when I saw the familiar scrawl across the envelope. Nathan wouldn't open my mail, but he'd certainly ask about it.

"I'm going to have a bath, hon," I called to Nathan, who was busy working in his home office. "Mind keeping an eye on the girls?"

He poked his head out the door and nodded. "Sure thing, enjoy."

"Thanks."

In the bathroom, I ran the bath and tore into the envelope, suppressing the gasp trapped in my throat. This time there was evidence. Photos. Me and Jayson together at the bar, multiple bars, entering Jayson's condo building, and, weirder, a shot through the window. As I glanced over the picture, I wondered how the shot could have been taken. A neighbouring condo building? Or was it an office across from

Jayson's place? I couldn't be sure. Only one thing was clear from the photos: different outfits and different nights. Jayson was right. I was being followed.

The note explained it. Twenty thousand dollars, cash, in one week, at Cheltenham Park, or the next letter would be going directly to Nathan.

I let out a long breath as I turned off the tap and climbed into the steaming water. Closing my eyes, I leaned my head back against the wall and tried to reason why Brian would be so intent on ruining my life. I'd barely seen him over the years, except for that spontaneous run-in at the bookstore, which I was now realizing may not have been as coincidental as I'd thought. Had he been keeping tabs on me?

I thought back to the last time we spoke—the day of Gina's funeral—when the service was over, and everyone had left but him.

The rain poured down in heavy sheets for most of the burial. I couldn't help but think the drab funeral in the grave-yard was cliché and depressing. It all felt so surreal, like a TV show, with the awful weather, the rain mixing with tears, and the lone man standing at the back, close enough to the crowd to belong but far enough away that he stood out.

He didn't carry an umbrella or wear any fancy clothing. He simply watched, with his hands tucked inside his black sweatshirt, the hood pulled over his head so that I could barely see his face, but his stance alone was unnerving.

Dee and Arabella were there, of course; all of us were best friends. Arabella was sobbing, pressing her face into her latest conquest, who looked bored even if he was trying to hide it. I didn't know his name, so it was likely he'd never met Gina. Just like Arabella to drag a random guy to the funeral. She could never go anywhere alone.

Dee, however, looked stoic. She'd cried enough over the

past few days; this was the end to all the hardship of Gina's passing.

Neither girl seemed to have noticed the man like I did. But neither knew him like I did either.

When the casket was lowered and the earth cast on top, the soaked crowd began to disperse. I hesitated. The man leaned against a nearby tree, and, although not seeing it, I felt his gaze on me.

"Are you coming?" Dee called.

"I'll meet you guys there. I need a minute."

Dee nodded and followed the crowd to the waiting cars.

I stared at the gravesite until the majority of the guests were gone, and then I turned to look at the waiting man. Drawing in a deep breath, I moved towards him.

"Madison Jayne." His sly voice broke through the steady rhythm of the falling rain. He pushed his hood back, revealing his shaven head and a wicked grin. "Mourning looks good on you. Black always did favour you. It was the only way you let your darkness show."

"What are you doing here?" My voice came out more forceful than intended, but it revealed my true thoughts. Things hadn't ended well between Brian and Gina, and I wasn't convinced he didn't have anything to do with her accident.

"Paying my respects." Brian crossed his arms, but his grin and tone belied his words. "I'm entitled to say goodbye."

"You had that chance," I said. "Before you made her leave the party."

"I have no idea what you mean."

I wanted to smack the knowing smirk right off his face. He knew exactly what I was talking about. Nathan and I had witnessed an argument between Gina and Brian before Gina stormed off, taking the car and never coming home. They didn't find the car or her body until the next day, but from what we heard, there was evidence of foul play—though nothing concrete. It was finally ruled an accident; the toxicity reports were positive, and she may have been speeding. According to reports, she wasn't wearing her seat belt, and after the car crash the injuries left her barely recognizable. It had been the worst days of my life, after my father's death, of course.

I'd told the police about the argument prompting Gina's disappearance from the party. Brian had been investigated but never charged. He had a solid alibi. He continued with his life, but Gina was dead. Lucky for me, he never knew I was the one who implicated him.

"What happened that night?" I asked. "Why did you two fight?"

Brian's grin faltered and he reached up, scratching at the stubble on his chin. There were dark circles under his eyes. It looked like he hadn't slept in days—on a bender, or perhaps haunted.

"Over you," he said it simply like it should be fact. "I didn't want Gina. I wanted you. But I couldn't have you. Instead, I got stuck with Gina's fat ass."

I cringed at his words. Only Brian would speak ill of the dead while standing above their gravesite. I shuddered with superstition and clutched my umbrella tighter.

"Stop it."

Brian laughed.

"Can't stomach the truth, MJ?" He shook his head, cocky grin back in place. "You were always weak, even when you tried not to be. I knew it was all an act."

"You don't know anything about me," I snapped. "We didn't really date."

"It doesn't take long to get to know someone when they

are so desperate for attention. Does Nathan notice that about you?"

"Notice what?"

"That you can't survive on your own," Brian said. "That you thrive under attention and that the only way he'll keep you is if he keeps you entertained." He touched my cheek with his cold, damp fingers.

I sucked in a sharp breath, the touch causing me to recoil with disgust. Brian only laughed again.

"Whatever you think now doesn't matter. I know how I kept you amused."

"Why exactly did she leave the party?"

"Because Gina was dumb." Brian shoved his hands back into his pockets. They were starting to rip at the seams as if he shoved his hands in them regularly and forcefully. A nervous habit I was familiar with. "She was insanely jealous of my interest in you, claiming you weren't worth my time. She'd tried everything to hold me to her except anger. I guess storming off drunk was her way of doing it." Brian shrugged. His expression was disinterested. "That only proved to me what I already knew: she had a few screws loose."

"Stop it."

"What do you want from me, MJ?"

"Nothing."

"That's not true, or you wouldn't have bothered to talk to me right now." Brian waved towards the cars that would soon be leaving the cemetery lot. "You would have gone with Dee when she asked you. But you had to come see me." His voice lowered. "You couldn't help yourself." He grabbed my arms, pinning them to my sides and causing me to drop the umbrella on the soft grass. The pouring rain soaked my hair. Brian pulled me closer to him. I held my breath, watching small droplets of rain roll over his cheeks and drip off his chin. He spoke in a low, dangerous tone.

"I know what you tried to do to me, and you will pay for it." He leaned closer and breathed deep. His breath against my neck sent chills down my back. "This isn't over." With a shove, he released me, turned on his heel, and walked further into the graveyard.

I stood, unable to move as if my feet were cemented to the muddy earth, watching him walk away. He never looked back, and when he was gone I allowed myself a breath of relief before picking up my umbrella and walking to my car.

That was the last time I'd seen Brian until a few weeks ago. After Gina's funeral, he disappeared from school and didn't go to graduation. He simply vanished.

And now he was back.

I opened my eyes and looked at the threatening photos, wondering what my next move should be.

It seemed, this time, he would make good on his promise. He would get his revenge.

Forty-Six

NOW

The car feels cramped and hot. My eyes blur and my chest feels heavy. I can't breathe. I'm having a panic attack.

"Maddie, what's wrong?" Jack's voice sounds slow and distant.

But I don't answer him.

"Maddie." Jack grabs my shoulder.

"That was Gina." I choke on the words as if they have a bad taste.

"Gina?" Jack asks, disbelief evident in his tone. "Are you sure?"

I nod. Of course, I'm sure. Her look is etched in my brain. I spent the last weeks feeling insane guilt over our past and what I had done to cause her grief, and now she's blackmailing me? My chest tightens, and I gasp for breath.

"Maddie." Jack's voice softens. He strokes my hair. "Relax. Breathe."

My eyes close, and I tilt my chin forward, feeling my slow breaths against my chest.

After a minute, I grab Jack's hand, saying, "I'm okay." My panic attack has subsided for now.

"You sure?"

"Yeah." I release a long breath between my teeth. "Let's get out of here." I shift the car into drive and leave Gina's neighbourhood, heading out the way we came. I keep my eyes on the road and my mouth shut. Yet Jack's concerned gaze stays on me the entire way back to his house. I stop around the corner from his mansion.

"You should get out here."

"Maddie, please talk to me."

"I can't." What can I say?

"What does Gina have against us?" Jack asks. "I've never met her. Weren't you friends with her?"

"Seriously, Jack?" I gape at him. "She was in your wedding party." He'd met her at least a handful of times.

The accusation doesn't faze Jack, who simply shrugs his indifference. Obviously, Arabella's friends were of no value to him unless they gave him something in return.

I shake my head, reminded why our affair was such a joke, and consider his question.

"I thought Gina and I were friends." But I don't know anything about this life. Maybe it's all another act I convinced myself to believe. Another lie.

"There has to be a reason for all of this." Maybe his obvious disinterest in Gina was enough to tie him into her sick games.

I shake my head. I can't do this with him right now. "Please go, Jack."

"This is about me too. I want to help."

"You need to go." I look away from him. "When I've figured things out, I'll call you."

Jack reaches for the handle but hesitates. "You promise?"

"Yeah." I mean it, at least I think I do.

"Okay." He opens the door and climbs out without looking back.

I watch him go, his stride quick, but his shoulders are slumped. The discomfort between us is clear. Does he hope our secrets will be revealed and that we'll have a future together? Or does he worry about the consequences like I do?

How can I do anything when I don't even know why Gina's coming after me? I need to find out more. My mind immediately goes to Dee. She helped solve all my problems in my old life; she seems like the logical choice now.

I dial her number.

"Maddie, darling! So good to hear from you."

"Glad you're around."

"I've been dying to talk." Dee laughs. "You've been holding out on me. Naomi tells me your brother is going on an adventure with her. You must give me all the dirt about it."

"I will." My mind has other topics that take priority. "Okay if I come by?"

"Do it up, girl. I'm at the condo."

"Perfect. Be there soon."

The weight on my shoulders lifts slightly as I follow the familiar roads to Dee's condo. If there's one person who can help me see things in a better light, it's Dee.

She answers her buzzer right away, and I'm at her door in minutes. I don't bother knocking; this time, I walk right in.

The strong aroma of marijuana greets me. I steady myself on the wall as my head spins and adjusts to the hazy room. This is the Dee I remember.

"Hey, girl!" Dee calls to me from her living room. I round the corner to see her bong between her knees and a lit smile on her face. She's high as all hell. But at least high Dee can still be insightful, or she was in my previous life.

"Flying high?" I nod to Dimitri, the bong.

"You know it!" She holds the multicoloured device up to me. "Want a hit?"

"I'm good, thanks." My anxiety is way too high to think about indulging in drugs.

"Suit yourself." She takes another toke, then places Dimitri aside and blows out the smoke.

I crinkle my nose.

"So, Declan and Naomi." She wears a cocky smile. "Didn't I say I was the matchmaking queen?"

"Can we talk about them later?"

Dee's smile disappears. "What's wrong? Is it Brian?"

"No, well, yeah. Sort of." I sigh and sit down on the couch next to her. "It's actually Gina."

"Is she okay?"

"Better than okay, it seems." My fingers thread together in my lap. "She's been helping Brian, I think."

Dee's eyebrows fold together. "What makes you think that?"

"I guess I don't know for sure. But she's doing something." I explain the blackmail and the strange letter at my door, about how Jack and I followed her home and the truth revealed itself.

"Have you tried talking to her?" Dee asks. "Did something happen?"

I pause, wondering if I should confess everything I learned from Brian. I hadn't spoken the idea out loud because I didn't want to believe it was true.

She must have read my discomfort because she reaches out and places her hand on mine. "Hey. It's okay. Whatever it is, we'll fix it."

I suck in a sharp breath. "I went to see Brian in jail a few weeks ago. It was a mistake, but I was so confused that I needed answers. I believed he could give them to me."

Dee doesn't respond.

"And he told me something." I draw another breath. "Something I'm afraid might be true."

"What?"

"When I asked why he hurt Gina, he told me it was because I asked him to. That I asked him to kill her."

Dee starts to laugh.

"Dee, it's not funny."

"I'm sorry, Mads," she sputters, then draws a breath to compose herself. "I don't mean to laugh. It's just not true."

"How do you know?" I doubt anyone can be totally sure what was discussed between Brian and me during our time together.

"Maddie, you were my closest friend. You told me everything." Dee shakes her head. "Just because Brian is a psycho who interprets everything wrong doesn't make you a bad person. Look, I never agreed with it, but you liked Brian, and the asshole was sleeping with both of you. You didn't ask him to kill her. You asked him to be rid of her. Only a crazy person thinks you're asking for someone to get murdered."

Her words trigger a memory.

We sit alone in his car, overlooking the lake. We've been here for almost an hour. He's barely spoken.

"Bri?" I try again. "I don't think I'm being unreasonable."

He sneers. "So what, MJ? We're going steady?" Even his tone mocks my request.

"I don't want to share." I cross my arms. "Get rid of her."

"What am I supposed to do?" His fingers tighten on the steering wheel. He's never been good at the emotional side of our relationship. He understands sex and drugs. Why do I think I can get him to give me more?

"Just end it," I say, reaching for the car door. "Or we're done."
As soon as I'm out of the car, he screeches off. I don't know if he'll
take me seriously and stop sleeping with Gina, but I hope he will. I
grab my phone and call Dee. She's the only person I want to tell this
story to.

"That's what I meant," I say under my breath. "Not like this."

"What?"

I lock eyes with Dee. "Arabella has—or had—a video of what happened. A poor quality one. When Brian tries to attack Gina, I'm yelling at him. Telling him that I didn't mean it like this."

"And that's what she's blackmailing you with. Keep the secret, or she will show the video and let everyone know what really happened. Or what it looks like happened." Dee reaches up and rubs her eyes. "Look, Maddie. Arabella never wanted the truth of what happened to come out, so she convinced everyone that you and she had nothing to do with the whole thing. That it was entirely my fault. Obviously, she held that video over your head, so you'd agree. Without that video, you looked like the hero, selflessly rescuing Gina from the clutches of Brian."

She shakes her head. "I honestly never got how Arabella convinced everyone that it was all me or why. I guess she's more influential than I ever gave her credit for." Dee grimaces. "I always thought you'd have my back but not after you found out about Jayson."

"I'm sorry," I say. "I wish I could change things."

"Me too," Dee agrees. "So, what are you going to do now?"

"I don't know." Which is the truth. I need to know more; the curiosity is eating my insides and making my stomach churn. It isn't like I can walk up to Gina and ask her why she's helping Brian. Who knows what she's capable of? I don't want to find out.

"What about your lawyer? He would have some answers about Gina, or at least Brian." Dee leans back on the couch and stares up at the ceiling. "She said she got a restraining order, right? I'm sure he could find out if that's actually true."

Of course. Sean would know what happened at the hearing I'd forgone, and he'd be able to find out about Gina's actions after Brian's release. It would be one way to figure out where she stood in terms of Brian without confronting either of them.

"You're a genius, Dee."

"And don't forget it." She tilts her head towards me and winks.

"I won't." I smile. "At least, not again."

"Good." Dee pushes herself back to an upright position. "Now, spill about Declan."

Forty-Seven

NOW

I experience a moment of relief when I sit beside Sean at the small table in his office. His comforting smile seems to tell me all my worries will vanish, that he will make it right. It's how Dad used to make me feel.

"Why does this case have you so frantic? It wrapped up quite nicely. The restraining order is holding up, correct?" Sean crosses his left ankle over his right knee, drawing his pant leg up slightly, revealing his colourful striped socks.

"Didn't Mom get you those?" I ask with a smile, nodding at his socks.

He nods, but his expression doesn't change. "Madison, don't deflect. Tell me what's wrong."

I release a long breath. "I think someone is watching me."

"A stalker?" His eyes narrow, and he leans forward. "Have you told the police?"

"I'm not ready to go there yet. I'm not totally sure what's going on, plus I think I know who it is."

"Who?"

"I think it's Gina."

Sean frowns. "That's why you asked for information on her and her involvement in Mr. Cordes's trial?"

"Yeah." I look down at my hands. "I don't know if they're working together, but she's been angry ever since I went to visit him."

"Which was a terrible thing to do," Sean states, as he had when he found out about my unorthodox visit.

"I know." I don't need him reminding me of my mistakes. "What's done is done."

Sean shakes his head. "That aside, I'm not certain why this visitation would upset Ms. Rojas when she visited him shortly after you did."

"What?" I meet his gaze, unable to believe what he said. Gina only told me she saw him at the hearing, that it was my fault he was released. My fears that they have reconciled are being confirmed. "Did she speak at his hearing? Did she get a restraining order?"

"No." Sean stands and moves back to his desk. He flips open the manila file folder that rests on top. "There was never a restraining order placed against Mr. Cordes on Ms. Rojas's behalf. Further, Ms. Rojas didn't appear at his hearing. She never spoke against his release. In fact, Mr. Cordes is on record that he and Ms. Rojas have mended their relationship. There are letters between them to back up his claim."

Letters, what letters?

My head begins to spin. "No, that's not possible. Why would she risk it?"

"Risk what?"

I meet Sean's eyes again. "She told me she'd been there and got the order. She said I was the reason he was released. Why would she risk keeping herself open to him?" I know the answer—she lied.

"I can't answer that for you, Madison." Sean's eyes fill

with pity. "It seems only Ms. Rojas can provide reasons for her actions."

"Do you think I should contact her?"

Sean grimaces. "Not if you believe she is stalking you and means to cause you harm. In fact, I would advise against it."

"She wouldn't actually hurt me." I sound more confident about it than I feel.

"Madison, I would call the police," Sean says. "Get them involved if you are fearful for your safety."

"Thank you. I know what to do." I stand and turn to leave, but not before hesitating and glancing back at him. "I appreciate your help. You'll call me if you hear from Mom?"

Sean nods. "And you'll call me if you need anything else?"

"Of course."

He rounds his desk and embraces me as my father once did. He whispers into my hair, "Don't do anything stupid, Madison." And for a moment, I see my dad saying those exact words to me when I was a teenager. I close my eyes, enjoying the moment with the man who'd become a father figure in my life.

"I won't." We separate, and I leave the office without another word.

Despite Sean's warning, I have to call Gina and figure out why she lied. I need to meet with her and sort it out. I don't have evidence to pull the police into this. The letters are destroyed, and all I have is Jack's word and my own. I don't know what else to do.

Back in my car, that feeling of being watched returns. I ignore it and reach for my phone, dialing Gina's number. It rings five times before directing me to voicemail. I consider going by her house, but if she's screening my calls and hoping to do me harm, as Sean suggests, it probably isn't a good idea.

Reluctantly, I try Arabella. Together she and Gina have a mutual hatred for me. She's the last person I want to deal with, but I hope for the best.

Forty-Eight

NOW

A rabella didn't answer, so I left a voicemail, vague about why I wanted to meet. It starts to rain after I leave Sean's office, and my drive home is slow. The idea of Gina and Brian working together still burns in my mind.

Covering my head from the cool drops, I dash from my car to the front door, only to find another note stuck to the handle. It's folded with my name scratched across the front, and the paper is still dry. Whoever came by had done so recently. When I unfold the note, two pieces of paper flutter out. Photographs.

Lying whores belong deep in the ground. Watch your back, bitch!

The pictures are of me—one with Jack and one with Brian. Jack and I are at a restaurant, which I presume is the one in Texas, and the other is the photo I allowed him to give to Gina, so it's clear who sent this threat to me. Maybe Sean is right; maybe she is planning to hurt me.

I jam my key into the lock and get out of the rain as fast as I can. Gina probably isn't far away, considering the state of the letter, and the last thing I want is a confrontation in this awful weather.

Inside my house, I consider discarding the letter and photographs but decide against it. I destroyed all the evidence I was being threatened with last time. This letter threatens to bury me, put me in the ground. The photos are proof that someone has a motive. Gina and Arabella look like prime suspects. I have to keep this one intact and away from Declan's eyes. The last thing I want is my brother to use these threats against me as a reason not to leave.

My phone chimes with a new message. A text from Arabella.

What do you want, Maddie?

I answer to request a face-to-face with her. She doesn't respond for several minutes, and as I wait, I listen to the patter of the rain on my windows and the faint thunder in the distance. I didn't expect a storm. Then again, I didn't expect a lot of things that happened lately.

Fine. Come over.

I grab my purse before heading back out to my car. *Be right there.*

As I climb in, Declan's sedan pulls into the driveway. He rolls his window down.

"Where are you going now?" he calls over the sound of the growing rain.

I keep my head shielded with my jacket. "To a friend's place. I'll be home soon."

"Okay. See you in a bit." He rolls up his window.

At least Declan will be home when I return. There'll be someone around to make sure no more weird letters show up.

When I arrive, Arabella answers after a quick knock and allows me to enter. I move to take off my shoes and discard my coat, but she stops me.

"You're not staying," she says, glancing over her shoulder. "Jack's upstairs, and we're expecting company."

I almost groan but push it back. "I need to talk. If we can't have a bit of privacy here, then how about a coffee?"

"I'm not going anywhere with you." She crosses her arms. "But fine, come in. We can talk in the office." She waves to a room off the front hall.

"Okay." I leave my shoes and coat at the front door and make my way into the room she mentions. She follows close behind.

"What do you want?" Arabella crosses her arms. "Shouldn't you be out ruining more lives? You've already done your damage here."

"I have to ask you about Gina."

"Why don't you ask her?" Arabella snaps. "You're the one fraternizing with her enemy."

"How do you know about that?"

Arabella purses her lips. "I don't know anything."

"I don't believe you." I grab her arm, making her look at me. "What do you know about Gina? Why is she doing this to me?"

"I don't know what you're talking about." She tries moving her arm out of my hold, but I only grip her tighter.

"Why is she doing this to me? Why is she threatening my life?" I raise my voice. My nails dig into her forearm.

"Because you wanted her dead!" Arabella cries, pulling her arm out of my grip with force and putting space between us. Small spots of blood appear where my nails were ripped from her arm. I step back. I hadn't meant to hurt her in my anger.

"No, I didn't want that. Brian made it up." I hesitate. Brian accused me of wishing for Gina's death. A story I now know is false, thanks to Dee. He convinced himself that was what I wanted. But it was a conversation between us, so how would Arabella know?

I take a short step closer to her. She stiffens but doesn't move. With a low voice, I ask. "How did you hear that?"

Arabella purses her lips, standing her ground, but the way her hands shake reveals her fear. "It's common knowledge."

"It's not. Brian told you. You've seen him?"

"I would never. I know what that bastard is capable of."

"Then it was Gina." It's true. She is working with Brian. She saw him, and they are working together to destroy me.

"No!" Arabella replies.

"When did she see him?" I demand. "You know she's left threatening letters."

"She hasn't."

I pull out the letter from earlier that day and thrust it into her hands along with the photos.

Arabella shakes her head as she looks over them. "It's not true. She didn't do this. She promised."

"Tell me. Right now, or I'll report you at the same time I report them." I take the letter and photos back. "I have the evidence now. I have a lawyer who has already told me to call the police. How long has Gina been writing Brian letters?"

"What are you talking about?" The perplexed expression on Arabella's face seems too real to be fabricated.

"My lawyer told me that she and Brian have been in communication via letters since before the parole hearing. How long?"

Arabella shakes her head. "I don't know about any letters. But I know they've been talking since she returned to Canada and seeing each other since he got out."

"Sleeping together," I correct.

"She was angry, Maddie. She wasn't herself. She wanted revenge. I told her to stop. She wouldn't listen. She wanted to scare you. After everything, I thought you could use a bit of intimidation. But I wasn't helping. I wouldn't."

I scoff. "Yet you keep a video of me for years, blackmailing me into silence?"

Arabella looks down at the floor. "I had to. You wanted to tell the truth. I couldn't get caught."

"What are you talking about?"

"It was the drugs," Arabella said. "I was dealing, helping Lance. It was a mess." Tears form in her eyes. For a moment, I pity her before remembering she's been blackmailing me and controlling me for years.

"That isn't what nearly killed her," I say. "You could have been honest, and nothing would have mattered. Brian was the problem."

"I told her to follow you," Arabella says. "It's my fault she was there."

I shake my head in disbelief. "Why?"

"Brian was trash," Arabella cries. "You were making a mistake. I didn't know he was going to attack her. I didn't know he was that unhinged. But after everything went down, I couldn't have anyone finding out about the drugs or what I'd done. I have a reputation."

"And Dee?"

"She was no saint," Arabella says. "She slept with Jayson when you were supposed to be her best friend. She deserved what she got."

"You had no right."

"You went right along with me." Arabella sneers. "And Gina, she's gullible enough to believe anything."

"She's not your little puppet now that she's threatening to

expose everything between Jack and me. And now I have to do something about it." I turn to leave Arabella standing alone in the office.

"Wait, Maddie! Where are you going?" Arabella follows me into the front hallway, where I grab my shoes and coat.

"To end this." I throw open the door and walk out into the rain. This time, Arabella doesn't call after me, and I don't look back. I'm going to find Gina, and I'm going to put a stop to the torture by whatever means necessary.

Forty-Nine

NOW

The adrenaline makes my heart race as I drive through the city faster than I should. My foot feels like a cinderblock on the gas pedal. I only press harder, desperate to confront Gina while my anger is still running at full tilt. Who cares if she plans to hurt me? With this anger flowing through me, I'm prepared to injure her first.

My tires squeal as I turn the corner into the subdivision Jack and I visited the day before. I pull right up to her house and storm up her front walk. Her car is in the driveway, and despite the drawn blinds, lights are on inside the house. I don't put on my coat or shield myself from the rain. I am soaked in seconds but too focused to care.

I bang on her front door as another clap of thunder sounds. For being early in the evening, the sky is dark as night, and the clouds overhead swirl in threatening patterns. A crack of lightning lights the sky as I bang on her door again.

"Gina!" I yell, uncaring if the neighbours may be watching or people might hear. "Gina, open the door!" I bang harder now, another clap of thunder sounding, but still, there's no answer.

I try to calm my rapid breathing as I glance around. The street is empty; this crazy storm would drive most people inside. The water rushes down the street towards the large metal storm drains. The rain pounds harder, heavier. The wind blows, sending the rain flying sideways and forcing an involuntary shiver down my back.

"Gina, open up!" I yell, banging again. Still, there's no answer. Without another thought, I reach for the door handle. It's unlocked and slams open with a gust of wind. I take a deep breath, trying to slow my heartbeat. Intruding in Gina's rental home feels wrong. But another angry clap of thunder has me inside and closing the door behind me.

Her front hall is brightly lit with an ornate chandelier, making me squint. The carpet underfoot is scrunched, as if someone slipped on it trying to enter or leave. There's a faint sound of gentle music coming from the room close by. I follow the noise. The storm still brews outside, but the sound-proofing from the house silences much of the clatter. Only the gentle tap of rain against the covered window and the low vibration of rumbling thunder can be heard.

She isn't in the sitting room, but the stereo in the corner is on, allowing the soft classical music to drift towards me. Where is she? The place feels empty, but why is music playing?

Another clap of thunder and the lights flicker. The storm is getting worse. The low whistle from the wind grows louder. I approach the front window and peer around the curtain. The street lights have flicked on from the darkness, and the surrounding trees are bending, bracing with their sturdy trucks against the wicked weather.

A flash of lightning forks across the sky, lighting the street.

The lights go out. The stereo silences, and I'm immersed in darkness with only the sound of the storm for company. My heart races as I suppress a scream and reach for my phone, finding the light. I can't stay here in the dark. The house puts me on edge with the strange music, the dead TV, and no sign of life.

I turn to leave when another sound makes me pause. It isn't the rain, but running water. There's a tap on somewhere in the house. My gut tells me to leave, but my curiosity holds me steady.

"Gina?" I try calling again, but I'm met with silence. What if she's hurt?

I run out of the sitting room and back into the front hall. The sound is faint, coming from further down the hallway, past the stairs leading up to her top level. I step carefully with only my small cell phone light to guide me. There's a soft splash underfoot. I look down, shining the light on the floor. Water. The door in front of me is closed, but the light shows water is flowing from underneath. I draw a sharp breath and push it open.

It's the kitchen. My light shines on the opposite wall; a tap is running. The sink overflows. I dash to turn it off but trip halfway through and stumble, catching myself on the counter. I look back to see what tripped me. A scream bubbles up in my throat, coming out silent.

"Gina?" I choke out. "Gina?" I shine my phone over the floor. It's Gina. Her amber skin looks pale and sickly under my flashlight. Her black hair is messy and soaking wet as she lies on the floor in the slowly flooding kitchen. But worst of all are her wrists, limp and slit open.

"Gina!" I kneel at her side, placing my fingers to her neck. No pulse. "Gina?" I touch her cheek, turning her face towards me. I fall back. Her eyes are wide open, glossed over, and lifeless. She's dead. This time I do scream. I stand on shaking legs and look at my phone. I have to call someone, the cops. Anything. I move to the kitchen counter, finding a seat on one of the stools. I dial 9-1-1. It rings twice.

"Emergency Response."

"Help," I squeak, my voice coming out breathlessly. "She's dead."

"Ma'am, relax." The voice on the other end is male. He speaks slowly, trying to calm me. "Who is dead?"

"Gina. She's dead. Slit wrists. Someone has to come."

"Where are you?" he asks, his voice remaining level and calm. "What's the address? We'll send help."

"Forty-four Terrance Avenue." I close my eyes, my elbow on the counter. "She's in the kitchen. The power's out."

"Are you in the house?" he asks.

"Yes."

"What's your name?"

"Maddie." I swallow hard.

"Maddie, I'm Jim." He still speaks slowly. "There is a unit heading to your location. I will stay on the phone with you until they arrive. Are you alone?"

"I think so." Though I don't know. Maybe someone's here. Did Gina do this to herself? Did Brian?

"Are you okay?"

"Yeah."

"Not hurt?"

"No."

"Good. Maddie, I suggest you get out of the house and wait for the unit outside," Jim advises. "But stay on the line."

"Okay." I push myself to my feet and return the way I came. The hallway is dark with my phone to my ear, but I'm in a daze as I head to the front door.

"How did you find her?"

"I came over. The door was open. She was on the floor." I push out the front door. The rain is still heavy and cold on my cheeks. It wakes me from my dazed shock.

"Are you a friend?"

"Yeah." What else can I say?

"Okay, Maddie. I understand this has been very traumatic for you. But help is around the corner."

"Okay." The sirens sound in the distance. "I think I hear them."

"Good," Jim says. "Are you safe? Do you feel comfortable?"

"It's raining." The comment is dumb, but I am too dazed to think of anything else.

"Is there somewhere you can wait where you'll stay dry?"

"I'm okay." The sirens sound louder, close now.

"You should be seeing some help arriving now."

"Not yet, but I hear them." A low crash of thunder followed by a distant flash of lightning lights the area and I freeze. There's someone across the street—a shadowed person, standing there, watching me. I open my mouth to say something to Jim when an ambulance and a police car come wailing around the corner, lights flashing. "They're here."

"Good, Maddie."

"Thank you."

"You're welcome." The call ends as the emergency vehicles pull up to the side of the road, and help starts piling out. I try to glance around them to see the person standing on the street, but there's no one there. Did I imagine it? If I did, this is quite the nightmare.

Fifty

NOW

It's all a blur after I hang up. The blue uniforms rush towards me and usher me away from the house's front door to the awning over the garage. One wraps a blanket over my damp shoulders and tries speaking with me. Their questions are fuzzy, and my answers are slow. They tell me to sit. I rest my back against the garage door, my head between my knees. My stomach twists and threatens to release, but I hold it back. Gina's dead. *Again*. Getting a chance to redo everything wasn't enough to save her. Words like *suspected suicide* and *paring knife* ring clear from the police discussion, but the rain still patters on the ground, and I might have misheard. Does that mean Brian didn't kill her? Has the guilt I've lived with my whole life been a product of my feelings and not something I deserved?

I hear one man say I'm in shock; a woman is told to stay with me.

"Can you tell me your name?" the officer asks. She's young, possibly younger than me, in uniform, and soaked by the rain. She's pretty, I think. My eyes seem to blur her features together. Are her eyes blue or green? Is she blonde or brunette? It isn't clear. Nothing is.

"It's Maddie."

"And what happened here?" She crouches down before me.

"I, uh, don't know." What did happen? I showed up, and Gina was dead.

"Power's out!" someone calls from the direction of the house.

"Yeah," I say. "The storm."

"You've been inside?" the woman in front of me asks.

"I called 911." Do they think I'm some random walking by?

"Officer Burke, get her to the station," a man's voice directs.

"Maddie," the woman, whom I now assume to be Burke, wraps her hand around my arm. "We want to get you away from the scene and out of this weather. Will you come back to the station with me?"

"Why?" I want to go home; my car is here. I can leave.

She helps me to my feet, and my shaking legs reveal that I probably won't be able to drive. "We think it will be safer that way."

Too weak and dazed to resist, I let her lead me to a waiting cruiser. She helps me into the front seat and then leaves without a word to the other officers. Burke tries to speak with me on the way to the station, but I don't respond. The whole scene still runs through my head. The eerie house, the sudden power outage, Gina's dead eyes. The fact that I didn't save her again. All of it. I shudder.

"Maddie, are you okay?" Burke asks when she pulls the car up to a stoplight.

"Fine." It's an automatic answer, the one you give your

boyfriend when you're mad at him and don't want to talk. Easy to say and meant to keep the conversation short. I mean, who can argue that you aren't fine?

My phone chimes with a message from Declan, asking when I'm coming home.

My reply is brief.

Car at Gina's. Headed to the police station. Am fine.

"We're here," Burke says.

I glance up and see the police station in front of us. The rain is hitting the window with loud splats, and the road is wet, lit up by the headlights of her car.

"What now?"

"We'll go inside if you think you can walk. You were pretty unsteady before."

"I can walk."

She nods. "Follow me."

I squint as she pushes through the front doors, my eyes bothered by the bright lights. Burke directs me to the chairs by the front desk and asks me to wait. She brings me water, though I refuse it. I'm not thirsty. I don't think I'm traumatized; I just don't know how to process what I saw.

Was it a suicide? It sure looked that way. But why would Gina slice her wrists with a kitchen knife? Brian has to tie into it somehow. Had he done it himself? Had that been him I thought I saw on the street?

My phone beeps with a barrage of questions from Declan, but I can't focus enough to answer them.

I place my head in my hands, my elbows on my knees, and take long, slow breaths. My heart rate calms, but the blood still pounds in my ears. I will my body to relax, but it won't silence the frightening thoughts rolling through my mind.

I'm not sure how long I sit in that position before someone approaches me. "Ms. Butler?"

"Maddie's fine." I raise my head to see a burly officer standing before me. He wears only a button-down shirt, though his pants looked splashed with water. He likely came from the crime scene. Have I been sitting here that long?

"Maddie." He says my name like he's testing it on his tongue. He then offers a tight smile, one that isn't sincere but seems like an attempt to calm me. It doesn't work. "Mind accompanying me into my office? There's a bit more privacy there."

"Sure." I'm not sure why I need privacy, as there doesn't seem to be many people in the station.

In his office, he offers me a seat, then introduces himself. "Detective Bruno." He motions to a younger man standing behind him. "Officer Fraser."

The latter is in full uniform and looks like he's young enough to be in training. He has smooth features, not a speck of facial hair; in fact, it seems like he can't even grow it. Probably fresh out of college. Bruno, however, is a thick man with a full beard to match. There's nothing on top of his head. Baldness isn't something I usually notice, but it looks rather intimidating with his dark beard. His dark brown eyes peer at me like I've done something wrong, despite his forced smile. Fraser is the more approachable of the two. Maybe that's their tactic. Is that how good cop/bad cop works?

"How can I help you?" Sitting in the enclosed room makes me feel claustrophobic.

"We have a few questions to ask," Fraser says, pulling up a chair in front of me.

"Sure, go ahead." I don't have anything to hide.

"How do you know the deceased?" Fraser asks.

"Uh, we've been friends since university. I've known her for years."

"And what were you doing at her house tonight?" He glances down at a paper in his hand as if reading from a script.

"I'd gone to see her because I had to ask her about a friend of ours. She wasn't answering her phone." I decide to keep the real reason I was there to myself. "The door was unlocked when I arrived. I went in to see if everything was okay, the power went out, and I found her in the kitchen."

"Dead?"

"Yeah."

"What do you think happened?" Bruno cuts in.

"I don't know." My hands twist in my lap. I don't like being at the police station, but at least it isn't an interrogation. My mind floods with memories of the precinct and questions that followed Gina's death the first time. I never expected to relive those feelings, but this life has a different plan for me. "I saw someone right before the police arrived. They were standing across the street, then they were gone. Maybe I imagined it. A man, Brian Cordes, was just released from prison. We have a history with him. I wouldn't be surprised if he was involved."

"It wasn't clear if someone had been there," Fraser says.

"Only Maddie here." Bruno sneers. He leans closer to me. "You saved her before. What happened this time?"

"What?" I ask, unable to believe what he'd just implied.

"Did she say something you didn't like?" Bruno presses. "Or maybe you lied all those years ago, and your lies have caught up to you?"

"Ahem, Officers." There, in the doorway to Bruno's office, stands Sean, briefcase in hand, only looking a little damaged by the rainy weather. "I do hope you aren't questioning my client without me present." How strange; I didn't call him.

"There are no charges laid, sir." Bruno crosses his arms over his hulking chest. "We're just having a conversation with Maddie."

"No charges?" Sean places his briefcase down and offers his hand to both interrogating officers. "Then you've no reason to be questioning her, especially not without my consent."

"She agreed," Fraser says.

"Was she not found trying to visit her friend, only to discover her dead?" Sean challenges. How did he know that? "That is questioning under severe duress, Officer. My client is not capable of giving consent at this time, as I'm sure you're aware."

"I'm fine." I try to intervene, but Sean only steps between the police officers and me.

"We will be going now." He looks over his shoulder at me. "Meet me by the front door, Madison."

I leave the office as I'm told and wait until Sean joins me. He stands in Bruno's office for a few more minutes. Bruno's hands fly wildly, making it look like they are having a heated conversation, though I can't hear their words. Then Sean fetches his briefcase from the floor and joins me at the door.

"Where's my car?" I ask.

"I dropped Declan off to pick it up. He called me after he got your message." Sean ushers me out into the night. "Come along. I'll get you home."

The cool evening air strikes my face and makes me hesitate. Since my arrival at the station, the rain stopped, but the parking lot is still wet and dark. The clouds hang in the sky, shielding the stars and moon. Everything feels distorted.

I climb into the passenger side of Sean's car, and he drives away from the station.

"Are you all right?" He casts a sideways glance at me while keeping his eyes fixed on the road.

"Fine." My stock response.

"What happened?"

I recite the events of the afternoon for him. My visit to Arabella, my arrival at Gina's, the storm causing an outage, the flooded kitchen, her lifeless body, and finally, the figure on the street. The entire time he watches the road. His grip tightens on the steering wheel with each addition to my story until his knuckles begin to go white.

"Madison, I told you not to get involved with this. I told you to go to the police." He grits his teeth and loosens his hold. He's trying hard to keep calm.

"I know, I'm sorry." I look down at my hands. "I thought I could fix this."

"You could have been killed." He hits the steering wheel.

I flinch. "I'm sorry." I didn't realize the real dangers before. I do now. At least I think I do. "I won't do it again."

"It's too late." Sean shakes his head as he pulls up outside my house. As promised, my car is in the driveway as if I'd never left. "They found something in Gina's house. They think you were involved in her death."

"But it was a suicide." And I'm not involved.

"Suicide was the initial claim. The cuts on her wrists aren't consistent with a typical suicide."

"What did they find?"

"A letter in her bedroom." Sean turns his body towards me. "Threatening Gina for stalking you. Finding you at the house gives credence to the message."

"I didn't write any letter. How could they have that?" I shake my head. "An officer said something about a knife."

Sean nods. "They found a knife, and they're looking for prints. They think you did it. I need you to come by the office tomorrow. I need to know everything you said to them today."

"We can go now. I didn't do this. We can sort it out."

"You need to go home," Sean says. "Rest. It's been a hard day for you."

"Then what?"

"Then we figure it all out. Until then, stay out of trouble, don't panic."

"Okay." I reach for the door.

"Madison," Sean calls me back to him. "It will be fine. I know you didn't do this."

"I'm being framed."

"It's possible, but we'll sort it out in the morning. For now, rest."

"Thanks." I climb out of his car. He waits until I'm inside my house before leaving.

Declan comes from the kitchen when he hears me. "Are you okay?"

"It's a long story." I move to go around him but hesitate. I'm hungry, but the thought of entering my kitchen puts me on edge. Visions of dead women lying in the centre of the room make me wobble.

Declan catches me. "Maddie."

"I'm fine." I try to steady myself, but my knees buckle.

He lifts me off the floor and carries me to the couch in my living room. He sets me down and stands in front of me.

I lean back against the couch, my hand over my eyes. There it is again, the image of the person watching me from the opposite side of the street, the flash of lightning that sent the lights flickering then off, and finally Gina's cold, lifeless eyes. I shiver.

"Maddie, talk to me."

"She's dead, Declan," I huff out. "Gina is dead."

"What happened?" He lowers himself to sit beside me on the couch.

"I found her." I stare at the opposite wall, blank, but to me, it looks damp, like dripping water—rain, maybe, or flooding. I shake my head. Sean was right; I need to sleep.

"Holy shit." Declan grabs my hand. "What did the police say?"

The wall changes colours. The dripping water darkens, becoming red, opaque. Blood. I drop my gaze to the carpet, shaking. "They think I did it."

"Maddie, what?" Declan grabs my shoulder and shakes me.

I look up at him, my eyes droop. My head spins. "I didn't do it."

"Why do they think you did?"

I slump against his shoulder, feeling very tired. My eyes barely stay open. "I don't know."

"Maddie?" He shakes me again. This time his voice sounds very far away. "Maddie, wake up."

I can't. I let my eyes close, and my head falls forward until there's nothing but darkness.

Fifty-One

THEN

S tanding in front of Arabella Davenport's mansion was the last place I wanted to be. I wouldn't be here now if I had another option. After being invited in by the comm system at the gate, I took the long, winding driveway up to the sheltered house away from prying eyes. Of course, the paparazzi would always find a way to meddle, especially into the lives of socialites like Arabella and Jack Davenport.

The red brick house had more black-framed windows than I could count, and it sprawled across much of the property, casting me and my car in a dark shadow. Even the yard was expansive, in sharp contrast to most Rosedale mansions, which tended to have smaller properties. Several manicured gardens surrounded the house, likely requiring a full-time gardener to maintain them in the spring and summer. Stone steps led to a white marble archway encasing the jet-black front door.

"Are you going to come in or stand there gawking?" A blonde, Barbie-like woman stood in the doorway waving at me. I hadn't seen her in years other than during the evening news or in the odd tabloid yet, somehow, it was as if we had never parted ways after university.

"Sorry." I hurried up the steps to the open door. "I didn't think you'd be waiting on me."

Arabella pursed her pink-toned lips and regarded me with disdain. "You didn't give me a choice."

I didn't answer because that was true. I had contacted Arabella with a cryptic text, simply calling in an old favour.

"I know, I'm sorry."

Arabella led me further into the large house. The entrance hall was bright, with white paint and white marble tiles. To the right was a large sitting room with three white couches on top of a rectangular paisley carpet covering much of the dark hardwood floor. To the left of the foyer was an office, likely Arabella's husband's, with a large, antique oak desk, stone fireplace, and a bookshelf so tall that a ladder leaned against it to access the top shelf.

The hall expanded forward, passing the kitchen and the dining room as well as a winding, spiral staircase that disappeared into the depths of the upper floor. Arabella turned right into a solarium near the end of the entrance area that overlooked a bright, blooming garden and a perfectly manicured lawn, complete with patio stones and an intricate wicker patio set. The latter looked aged compared to the rest of the modern design.

In the solarium, Arabella motioned for me to sit in one of the white cushioned chairs surrounding the round glass table. She sat opposite, all the while watching me with narrowed eyes. Her walls were up; she was skeptical but concerned.

"I need a favour," I said as an older woman emerged from the house carrying a tray with two glasses and a pitcher filled with a pink liquid. Lemonade.

"As you said." Arabella reached for the glasses and filled one, offering it to me.

I took the glass to my lips and knew before taking a sip it wasn't just lemonade. The vodka was potent. Of course Arabella would serve hard lemonade in the middle of the day. Maybe some things hadn't changed from our university days.

"What's going on?"

"I need to be sure you'll be discreet," I said, though it was a risk even asking.

"Discretion is my game, honey." Arabella placed her glass down and waved around. "Do you think we could keep all this if the paparazzi were always spilling our secrets?"

"This one could ruin my life," I urged. "And possibly, your brother's."

Arabella's hard expression softened for the first time since I had arrived, and for a moment, she reminded me of our close friendship before everything fell apart. Before the betrayal, before Nathan, and before Gina's death.

"Tell me."

I took another swig of the strong drink. "We had an affair."

"You and Jay?"

"Yes." A lump formed in my throat as I admitted it. This was the first time I'd spoken the truth out loud.

"I'm not surprised." Arabella leaned back in her seat with a smug expression.

"What?" This wasn't the reaction I expected.

"I always told you that you shouldn't have broken up with him for Brian." Arabella shook her head. "I never got what drew you to that psychopath in the first place."

"Yeah, that's the other problem."

Arabella frowned. "Brian? You're sleeping with him too?"

"God, no." I gasped. "And I'm not sleeping with your brother. We had one night. One drunken night."

"Then what's the problem?"

I slid the photos across the table, followed by the note.

"You're being blackmailed," Arabella said.

I nodded.

"Has Jayson seen these?"

"He saw the first letter." I fidgeted. "I haven't shown him this. I don't want to involve him any more than he has been. I want this to go away so both of us can move on."

Arabella didn't answer. Instead, she glanced over the pictures again. I remained silent as she did so. Arabella would help. She had to. If anyone would want to protect Jayson, it was her. Besides, she owed me for what happened to Gina. When I finally did talk to the cops about my suspicions over Brian, I never once mentioned the drugs that Arabella and her boyfriend had sold to him. I didn't reveal that Gina hadn't drank or done drugs for over a year. As friends, we made a pact to keep each other's involvement quiet. Gina died in an unfortunate accident; who cared if she haunted us for the rest of our lives.

"You think Brian did this?" Arabella placed the photos down. "Have you seen him? I assumed he'd died, the idiot he is."

"He hasn't," I said. "And apparently, he's been keeping tabs on me. I ran into him a couple of weeks ago at the bookstore. I thought it was a coincidence, and then this started, and it made me rethink that point."

"So, your crazy ex-fling is stalking you in hopes to blackmail you for a few thousand dollars over your affair with an ex-boyfriend, or he'll tell your lawyer husband all about it?" Arabella cracked a smile. "Damn, Maddie, and I thought my life was the soap opera."

"Twenty grand isn't a few thousand dollars."

Arabella shrugged. "Knowing your history, I'm surprised he didn't ask for more."

"He was never the brightest."

"What do you need me for?" Arabella asked.

"The money."

"You've got twenty grand," Arabella scoffed.

"Not that I can access in cash without Nathan noticing." Nathan managed most of the finances, and twenty thousand dollars would show up on his radar. The whole cover-up would be for nothing.

"And you think I can?"

"I know you can." I crossed my arms. "Besides, you owe me."

Arabella looked like she was about to disagree.

"We both know that what happened with Gina wasn't an accident. And I left you out of it."

"I don't know what you're talking about." The concern that crosses her features said something different.

"How you and Lance found the car before the police did?" I said. "Or that Lance was Brian's alibi when we both know it wasn't true."

"We don't know that," Arabella snapped. "For all we know he never left the party."

"That's what you've been telling yourself all this time, haven't you?" I looked down at the table and pushed the half-full glass of lemonade away. "What about the drugs? We may not have killed her, but because of us, her killer still walks free. Maybe helping me will clear your conscience."

Arabella pursed her lips but didn't reply.

"Fine." I stood. "This was a mistake. Thanks for nothing." I turned to leave, but when I was outside of the solarium, Arabella called me back.

"Maddie, wait. I'll do it."

A weight lifted off my constrained chest as I turned back to acknowledge my once close friend.

"But," Arabella said. "After this, we are done. I don't owe you anything and you'll leave my brother alone. We all made choices, and now we have to live with them. Don't go dragging Jayson into something that isn't about him."

I nodded.

"Wait here." Arabella turned for the spiral staircase. "Jack has always kept some money in the safe."

She was only gone a few minutes before descending the stairs with a bag over her shoulder. She shoved it into my hands.

"Two hundred Borden's," Arabella said. "Count them if you want."

"I'll pay you back when I can."

Arabella waved her off. "Don't. This isn't a contract; it's a goodbye present. I don't expect to see you at my door ever again."

"You won't."

"Good luck, Maddie." Arabella stepped aside to let me pass. "And have a nice life."

"You too." I slipped out of the house without another word and found my way to my waiting car. There I opened the bag to find a box of neatly stacked bills. I'd count it at home but had no doubt Arabella came through for me. She wanted to forget the past as much as I did.

Fifty-Two

NOW

When I wake up the next day, I'm drenched in sweat and gasping for air. I saw Gina again, this time in my dream. I'd stumbled over her limp body. But she wasn't only cut open at the wrists. She'd been maimed, slit through her gut; she was naked. Then I saw him. Brian. Laughing in the corner, pointing at me. He spoke. "You did this." I tried to protest it, but he didn't listen. "It's your fault. This is what you wanted."

It's all so real. The stench of her rotting body, the fear pumping through my veins, the hatred I had for Brian's stupid face. All of it. She's gone, but she taunts me as much now in death as she had in life. When is it going to end?

It's midafternoon, and Sean Onyx expected me in his office for a debriefing. When I finally drag my exhausted butt out of bed and get ready, Declan meets me at the door with a travel mug of coffee.

"You okay?" His face is creased with lines of worry. His glasses have slipped down his nose, but he doesn't reach up to adjust them, only gazes at me with genuine concern.

"Yeah. Yeah, I'm okay; I slept late."

"You don't seem it." He finally fixes his glasses.

I only shrug. "What are you doing?"

"Taking you to see Sean." He jingles his keys as he says it.

"I can drive myself."

He doesn't respond to my comment. "Dee dropped by. I tried to wake you earlier, but you wouldn't budge. You kept calling Gina's name. It seemed like you were in a trance."

The previous day was traumatic. I can admit that now. Yesterday I'd been too shaken by what I'd found to process what had happened.

"What did you tell Dee?"

Declan shakes his head. "I didn't need to tell her anything, not at first. She heard you."

Embarrassing.

"She's going to call later," Declan says. "Let's get moving."

I follow him to the waiting sedan.

"Now tell me what's going on," he says as he shifts his car into gear.

I draw a deep breath and tell him everything, starting from the beginning. He gasps at hearing about how Arabella and I blamed Dee for Brian and how Gina accused me of being the cause of Brian's release. It's cathartic in a way, getting all of this out and telling him about the feeling of being watched, finding Gina, and being suspected of her murder.

"I'm going to call Naomi," he says when I finish. "There's no way I'm leaving while this is going on."

"Declan, no!" I'm not about to let him throw his life away for me. I refuse to screw him up even more than I already have.

"Maddie, I'm not leaving."

"Yes, you are. And I don't care what happens to me; you're going on this trip with Naomi. This is the opportunity of a lifetime. I won't let you pass it up."

"Maddie, you're in trouble." His voice is low, serious. He's right, but I don't want him to have any part of it.

"Sean will get me out of it. Like he did when you blew over the legal limit in university and got busted with pot in high school. He will fix this. It's what he does." I release a calming breath. "But I wouldn't be able to live with myself if you don't take this opportunity because of a mess I caused."

"This isn't your fault."

"It doesn't matter where the fault lies. Only that you will not suffer the consequences. Promise me you'll go as scheduled. You won't look back." If my life is beyond saving, so be it. My brother's isn't.

"Maddie—"

"Just pretend we aren't talking again." It hurt to say this, but I need him to leave. "Go. Forget about all of this and become the Declan you were always meant to be."

He releases a long breath. "Fine. I'll go."

"Good. Declan, I—"

He cuts me off. "I'll go, but I'm not going to forget about you and your problems. You'll call me and make sure I have all the details. This isn't going back to how it was. You're my best friend, Maddie. Without you, there would be no trip or adventures for me. I'll go because you're basically forcing me. But if anything happens, I'm on the first flight back."

I open my mouth to protest, but he silences me.

"Those are my terms. Accept them, or I'm staying."

He leaves me no choice. "As long as you go."

"I will," he says. "Now, Sean better fix this for you. Dad's probably rolling around in his grave."

I laugh, only because we cremated our father.

"And you'll let me know how it goes."

"Of course."

I'm seated in front of Sean, and it's clear things aren't good. He wears his reading glasses on the tip of his nose while he scans the documents in front of him. His forehead is wrinkled with concern, and he's barely glanced at me since I arrived, speaking only a few words as I told him the full story of my questioning with the police.

"I can't take the silence anymore." I tap his desk, hoping to draw his attention. "I need you to tell me what's going on."

Sean sighs, takes off his glasses, and rubs his tired eyes. "It's not good, Madison."

"They're investigating me for murder?" My tone is flat. I'm not sure what I expected. I can't give an explanation as to why I was at Gina's house that doesn't incriminate me and, other than my denial that the letter isn't mine, things point in the opposite direction.

Sean nods. "The letter works against us, but a handwriting analysis will confirm it's not yours. However, a woman has come forward, claiming you and Gina had some bad blood, and you threatened her."

"And they believe her?" That seems so flimsy.

"They're taking it very seriously." Sean lowers his voice. "They don't have a lot of leads right now, so they will work this angle until we can prove otherwise."

"Who is speaking against me?"

"Hmm." Sean flips up a page. "Arabella Davenport."

Of course. She's the last person who saw me before I

stormed off to see Gina. Not to mention she's still angry about the Jack situation.

"She says you left her house claiming you were going to end things with Gina. Is that true?"

I nod.

"Madison, you need to tell me everything. Leave nothing out." Sean's shoulders tense. He doesn't typically handle murder cases, but I don't want another lawyer. There's no one I trust as much as Sean.

"What about Brian? He seems like a more plausible suspect than me."

Sean grimaces but agrees. "His lawyer is claiming he has an alibi. Until that is disproven, they will set their sights on you—the person inside the house."

I clench my jaw. Someone always seems to cover for Brian.

"I've told you everything. I'm innocent. Wrong place at the wrong time. What can I do now?"

Sean sighs. "You go home since you aren't under arrest as of right now. Don't get into any trouble, and don't leave the city. They're doing an autopsy, and we'll have some more answers once that is done." Sean stands. "I'll call you for a handwriting sample and there will be more information with the fingerprints on the knife. Until we have all of that, don't panic."

"Okay." Of course I'm going to panic. I'm the centre of a murder investigation. It takes all I have not to begin hyper-ventilating. I stand to meet Sean as he rounds the desk.

"And have faith, Madison." He takes my shoulders. "We both know you didn't do this. The law is on our side."

He pulls me into a strong, fatherly embrace. It sure doesn't feel like the law is working with me.

"I'll call you tomorrow."

I nod, then leave his office and hurry back to where

Declan is parked. Seeing the distress on my face, he steps out of the car and catches me in a hug. The stress of my situation, the memory of Gina's death, and the knowledge that my life has become completely fucked are too much to handle. Unable to keep up my strength any longer, I rest my head against my brother's chest and let myself sob.

Fifty-Three

NOW

Declan answers the door when they come for me two days later, but I'm already on my way down the stairs. In my doorway stands Detective Bruno and Officer Fraser, the latter in full uniform and each wearing stern looks. Behind them are two other officers. Their police cruisers wait on the street.

"Madison Butler." Bruno's cold gaze finds me. He lifts his handcuffs from his waistline and motions me towards him.

Declan steps between us. "What is the meaning of this?" His shoulders are square and stiff as he keeps me defensively behind him.

Bruno ignores him, leaning around my brother to keep his gaze on me. "It would be easiest if you came quietly."

"Declan, I'll be fine." My words are flat as I gently push my brother's shoulder, moving him aside. I swallow hard, attempting to keep the vomit from sliding up my throat.

"Maddie." Declan's fists clench.

"It's fine." I turn my back so Bruno can cuff me. "Call Sean."

"Madison Butler, you are under arrest for the murder of Regina Rojas," Bruno says, reciting the words required by law. "You do not have to say anything unless you wish to do so. Speaking will not offer you favour or threat; however, anything you say may be used as evidence."

I wince as the handcuffs tighten around my wrists.

"You have the right to retain and instruct counsel of your choice in private and without delay. Before you decide to answer any questions concerning this investigation, you may call a lawyer of your choice or get free advice from duty counsel. If you wish to contact Legal Aid duty counsel, I can provide you with a telephone number and a telephone will be made available to you."

I meet my brother's horrified gaze but continue to remain silent. Sean will meet me as soon as he can.

Bruno continues. "If you have spoken to any other police officer or persons in authority, or if any such persons have spoken to you relating to this matter, I want it clearly understood that I do not want it to influence you in making any statement."

I suppress a cough, worried the churning bile will come spewing out.

"Do you understand these rights?"

"Yes." I clamp my mouth shut, partly to remind me to keep quiet, partly to hold back the threatening vomit.

I meet my brother's gaze again, this time to silently tell him I'll be fine. His worry remains as they direct me from the house to the waiting cars. My neighbours are on their front steps and stare out their windows, watching me be taken away in handcuffs. Bruno opens the door and protects my head as he forces me into the back seat.

There's no way to get comfortable in the barred vehicle with my hands behind me. So, I angle myself awkwardly and look down, away from the stares and accusing eyes. To them, I'll be guilty until proven innocent. To these people I've known for years, I am a murderer.

The motions that follow feel like a bad crime show. Bruno directs me into the police station where I'm processed. He asks me basic questions that I answer automatically, like my full name, my address, and my birthday. Not that he needs any of it. They take all of my possessions, including my cell phone and wallet.

He leads me to a smaller room where I'm positioned against the wall and told to turn as they shoot pictures from the front and side. My first mugshot. Followed by fingerprinting. They offer a phone call that I refuse, knowing Sean will already be on his way to help me. Then, cuffed again, they direct me out to the police car, indicating that I will be taken to the remand centre to await trial.

The car ride is a blur, and once my butt hits the hard mattress on the bench of my small cell, reality starts to set in. I am being charged with murder. I will be spending who knows how long in jail. I am going to trial.

The cell itself is nothing special, with beige walls, a barred front, and a stainless steel toilet and sink, both devoid of water. I guess I'm a suicide risk. I've heard that can happen with the accused. My father never sugar coated his trials.

Other than the thin mattress provided, they gave me a small blanket, and I shiver in the dank coldness of it all. One isn't expected to sleep well here.

Every part of me wants to break down, let the vomit inside me release and splatter across the cell floor. But I'm not alone. I'm being watched by the police around the centre and by the other criminals in the holding cells. I have to keep holding on. I fold my hands and stare at my lap, slowly, silently, counting to one hundred and then back again.

"Madison?" A gentle voice draws me from my counting. I release a breath of relief when I meet his concerned gaze. Sean.

"Thank God." I stand and walk to the front of my cell, where I grip the bars.

He touches my hand. "Are you okay?"

"As okay as I can be given the situation."

"We'll get you out of here." Sean drops his hand. "I've already set a bail hearing for the morning."

My stomach flips. I'll be stuck here overnight.

"I know it's not ideal," Sean says, reading my fallen expression. "But one night is better than many."

"I'm accused of murder." The words sound so foreign coming from my lips. "What if they don't set bail?" The question is moot as I know what will happen if there is no bail. I will go to prison and await my trial.

"There will be bail." The determination in his eyes makes me want to trust him. But I've followed enough trials. Murderers rarely get bail.

I don't bother to argue with his words because there's no point. Sean will try his best and if he can't, they'll lock me away until they decide my fate. I can only imagine how Brian is enjoying this. Now, after four long years, I'm stuck in his place. Will he be brave enough to speak against me? The irony almost makes me laugh.

"You'll be okay." Sean offers a weak smile. "It's just one night."

"One night." I force a smile and drop my hands from the bars. "One night," I repeat quietly to myself as I retreat, returning to my seat.

"They'll be by with a meal." Sean's voice holds hope, though I've let most of mine slip away.

"Good." I resume my position, hands folded and gaze lowered. One night here. One night sleeping in a barred room. One night where all my privacy is removed. One night locked away without freedoms.

Sean stands before me for a few moments longer before the click of his shoes echoes his departure.

One night, I remind myself. But the twisting in my stomach, the shiver that courses down my spine, tells me that it isn't going to be one night. One night is asking too much. One night is already too many.

Fifty~Four

NOW

W hen Sean comes to get me the next morning, I feel like a train has run me over. The mattress I had to sleep on was hard and unforgiving. I wouldn't have slept even if that had been the only obstacle, but worse was the sounds of the other prisoners in holding. Though I couldn't see them, I could hear them: drunken groans, retching, and mumbling. The lack of sleep makes me feel like I'm going slightly insane.

"Are you all right?" Sean asks as the accompanying officer opens my cell then fixes me with handcuffs. The motion of having my wrists bound is getting old fast.

I don't answer him, only giving him a tired look. I haven't slept, I've barely eaten, I'm a suspected killer. So, no, I'm not all right.

Despite this, Sean chuckles. "Enough said."

The officers direct me from holding, and I get my first glance at some of my cellmates. Most look how I expected— hungover, haggard, and probably worse than I do.

Sean and I don't exchange any words as they lead me into an interrogation room. They remove the cuffs and leave Sean and me alone, locking the door behind them.

I rub my wrists. "So, what, I'm not a threat to you?"

"I'm the one trying to get you out, remember?" He places the bag he's carrying on the table in front of me. He nods towards it. "A change of clothes and a few things Declan put together for you." Then he glances over me. "Did you sleep at all?"

I shake my head as I reach for the bag. My purple sundress, a lightweight black sweater, and a pair of wedges. My brother has terrible fashion sense, but it's better than what I'm wearing. He even tossed my makeup bag in. I glance around.

"When you want to change, an officer will escort you to the bathroom," Sean says.

I nod that I'm ready, and Sean knocks at the door. A woman officer enters and leads me to the bathroom, where they allow me a moment of privacy to get changed. When I am finished, we return to the interrogation room where Sean still waits.

"We'll go before the judge in an hour. I'll plead your case, and they'll set your bail," he says when I've returned to my seat across from him.

"And if they don't?"

"They will." Sean's response is firm. "The charges have been lessened to second-degree murder. Handwriting analysis confirmed the letter to be fake. The judge will let you off on bail, though it may be high."

"If the letter was fake, why aren't they assuming I was set up?"

"They still have a witness statement that implies intent."

I frown. *What could Arabella have told them?*

"You said you were going to end this." Sean glances at me with a cocked eyebrow to answer my silent inquiry. "And they currently have no other suspects."

"What about Brian? Did his alibi check out?"

"They're still investigating it. But there's word his lawyer can prove he was at an event with plenty of witnesses during the hours of Gina's death."

Convenient. I only hope this can be disproved.

"Right. Hopefully it isn't too expensive. I can probably sell the car if I need to, or remortgage the house—"

Sean cuts me off. "We'll cross that bridge when we get there. For now, you should prepare yourself for whatever outcome possible."

"Okay…" I look away. "What if I don't make bail?"

He looks down at the floor. He doesn't want to think about it, but I need an answer.

"Madison—"

"Sean, tell me."

"If you don't make bail, you'll be taken into custody and put into general population." He still doesn't look at me as he speaks. "I will push for your trial to be escalated, but I can't be sure how long they will keep you locked up until then."

I swallow the hard lump that forms in my throat. I hold back the tears that want to fall. As Sean said, I need to prepare myself for whatever outcome. Crying won't get me through prison. I have to learn to hold it in and force myself to deal with it.

"But you will." Sean touches my hand, offering a sincere smile. "There is no reason for them to deny you on a second-degree charge."

I nod, unsure what else to do.

Sean continues, "Once in the courtroom, remain quiet. I will do all the talking." He lowers to the chair across from me. "I will argue your good standing in society, how you've contributed to the community, and your clean record."

He pauses for a moment. "There will be terms set, like a promise to appear in court, to keep the peace, no leaving the province, or possession of weapons."

"I don't own any weapons."

Sean gives me a look that tells me to be quiet. "We can't have any outbursts in the courtroom."

"Right."

"You'll be barred from contacting witnesses," Sean advises. "Which may include people you've considered friends."

He means Arabella, whom I have zero interest in speaking with.

"You'll have to let your lawyers handle all those communications."

"You've been good at that." I glance over at him, and that concerning grimace returns.

"I won't be your trial lawyer for this."

"What?"

"Madison, I don't have the experience. You need a lawyer who's argued these types of cases."

I purse my lips. "You mean a lawyer who probably thinks I'm guilty but is good at setting the guilty free?"

"That's not what I'm saying."

"I don't trust anyone like I trust you." My voice starts to rise. I can't stop it. "You promised you would help me fight this. You're going to abandon me when it gets tough?"

"Madison, calm down." Sean stares me down with a stern gaze, his voice hard and firm, reminding me of my father. "I didn't say I was going to abandon you, only that I'd bring another lawyer into the case. I will still be there every step of the way. I am not letting you go to prison for something you did not do. Are we clear?"

I swallow, leaning back in the chair, letting my rapid breathing calm. "Yes."

"Now, you need to relax. You can't go into the courtroom too emotional. The judge will not respond to that." He reaches out and places a hand on my shoulder. "We can do this. It will be okay."

I suck in a long breath before releasing it between my teeth. Despite my attempts to calm down, my heartbeat won't slow.

He meets my gaze and we stare at each other for a moment before he asks, "Are you ready?"

I nod.

He walks to the door and knocks. An officer enters, cuffs me, and leads me out to the waiting police car that will escort Sean to the courthouse. I've never wished so hard for my previous life, knowing I will happily take all the bad I thought I had to kiss my girls again and escape this hell.

They don't remove my cuffs until we are set to enter the courtroom; even then, they follow us in and sit in the first row, awaiting my verdict. If allowed bail, I'll be free to retrieve my things and leave with Sean. If not, they'll cuff me again and return me to police custody.

My case is brought before one man. He's middle-aged, with dark hair speckled with white. He wears his judge's robes well, and his face is lined with wrinkles, but his eyes hold a steady gaze. He doesn't seem angry or particularly happy. His presence, though intimidating, doesn't frighten me.

After the bailiff tells us to be seated, Sean stands and addresses the judge, "Your Honour—"

I glance away from the judge to the opposing bench where a woman is seated. She wears a pressed pantsuit, expensive, possibly Gucci, and doesn't look in my direction. The prosecutor, the one that wants me in prison and the one that will fight the Crown's battle.

That prompts me to look around more. Bruno sits in the seats behind the prosecutor's desk. He stares at me with a hard gaze, his face telling me only one thing: I'm guilty of murder, and I deserve to pay for it. His unblinking glare sends a shiver down my spine as I remember his invasive questioning and accusing tones. I tear my eyes away as Sean finishes his speech.

The prosecution speaks next, arguing against Sean's points, but their claim is weak. I have a clean record, not even a speeding ticket. I've been living in my community my whole life and have a history of charity work. On paper, I'm not a threat.

When the prosecution rests, the judge looks directly at me, and I return his gaze. I won't look away like a guilty person. I won't shy away like someone ashamed. I deserve my freedom.

"After considering your arguments," he says, his voice deep and clear, "bail is set at $100,000, no cash, on the promise to appear. The defendant is expected to check in with weekly reports, is not allowed to leave the province, or disturb the peace."

The weight lifts from my chest. I'm free, at least until we go to court. I don't hear what follows as they still have to set a court date for me. It could be months, even a year, but at least I won't be rotting in a cell until then.

The prosecutor packs up her things and leaves. Bruno follows closely behind her.

Sean pulls me into a side hug. "Let's get you home."

Those words are a balm to my soul.

Fifty-Five

NOW

It's another two days before Sean calls me into his office for a meeting regarding my case. In the meantime, Declan flutters around me like a worried father the whole time, and I can't seem to shake him. He even threatened to call off his trip again, which I vehemently refused to allow him to do.

A trip to the office is a welcome relief, even if we are discussing my impending trial.

Sean meets me with his usual rigid posture, but this time he seems a bit different. Like something is bothering him.

"Madison." He waves to the seat across from him, not standing to meet me but only keeping his eyes on the computer in front of him. "Thank you for coming."

"I should thank *you*." I take the oversize armchair. "You are organizing my defence, after all."

He nods with a tight-lipped smile then looks back to his screen, typing furiously and not speaking another word.

When his fingers stop moving across the keyboard, and he

still doesn't look up at me, I ask, "Is everything okay? You seem—stressed."

He folds his hands on the desk before him. "The prosecution is moving forward with the second-degree charges, and I've found someone who I think would best handle it. I intend to bring in Caroline Briggs from Briggs, Daniels, and Associates. She's diplomatic, approachable, and has a lot of experience with those wrongly accused." He adds with a smile, "And a killer record for winning."

"Sounds promising."

"It is," Sean agrees. "She and one of her associates will be joining us shortly for a quick introduction and to go over some of the details of your case. Do you have any questions before then?"

"One." I glance at the table before finding my strength to look him in the eye. "Do you think I can get off?"

"Yes." Sean doesn't miss a beat. "I think the prosecution's case is weak and that we will be able to find enough credible witnesses to back you and secure your freedom. You are not a murderer, Madison."

Though I know it's true, it feels better to hear him say it out loud.

"Anything else?"

But before I can ask anything, his com buzzes. "Ms. Briggs has arrived."

"Send her in." Sean stands, and I do the same.

The door opens to reveal a slender woman with mahogany skin and sleek dark hair that reaches the middle of her back. She wears a fitted grey pantsuit and minimal makeup save for the red lipstick adorning her full lips. She presses them into a hard smile and approaches Sean.

"Sean." She shakes his hand.

"Caroline, thank you for coming on such short notice." He waves to me when he releases her hand. "This is Madison."

"Ms. Butler." Caroline turns towards me with a firm handshake. "A pleasure."

I nod my response.

"Please sit." Sean motions to the chairs, of which there are three. "I was expecting an associate."

Caroline nods, taking a vacant chair. "He'll be along. Parking the car."

I follow her movements, take the seat next to her, and leave the third one for the unknown associate.

They begin discussing my case, covering aspects I've already considered, the likelihood of my acquittal, and possible witnesses who can aid in my case.

I am so distracted by my thoughts I don't realize when Caroline's associate arrives until they are standing to greet him.

"And this is our new client, Ms. Butler." I turn as Caroline introduces me, only to be stopped in my tracks. My breath catches. There before me stands Nathan, dressed in an expensive black suit and carrying a shiny leather briefcase. He looks different from when I saw him at Dee's party, but how I remember him from my other life. Serious, professional, and a killer lawyer. I nearly forgot he'd considered criminal law before I convinced him to switch to corporate law.

He greets me like the stranger I am. "Hello, Ms. Butler, Mr. Onyx." He catches my hand, sending electric currents through it. "Nathan is fine."

"Uh, thanks." I shake his hand, my hold loose and motionless, like my confused mind. "Maddie is fine."

Nathan offers a taut smile, then takes the remaining seat before we return to ours. "Sorry for the delay. Please proceed."

They continue to talk about my case, and I try not to look at Nathan, though he's in my peripheral vision. He never tries to catch my eye and only nods along with their assessments of my trial and makes minor suggestions when prompted.

He's my attorney for a grisly murder case. I can't even imagine what he's thinking, but I know it's not romantic.

His expression doesn't reveal a thing. I'm possibly going away for murder.

Fifty-Six

NOW

Two days following our first meeting, Caroline Briggs schedules a follow-up at their downtown office. To my dismay, Sean calls early in the day to confirm his inability to join, leaving me at the mercy of Nathan and Caroline. Not having him at the meeting disorients me.

Their law office rivals Sean's in size and number of staff. The building is three times larger, with multiple named partners and countless associates. Though he wasn't working for this firm in our past life, in this one, my luck somehow placed Nathan on my case.

I tap the armrest of my chair impatiently as I wait in the boardroom for Nathan and Caroline. It's nearly ten minutes before Nathan pokes his head in, apologizing for the delay. I stand to meet him, smoothing my skirt in an attempt to dry my clammy palms. This is the first time we've been alone together since he took my case.

"Coffee?" he asks. "I just need to grab one."

"Uh, sure," I say. "With two creams, please."

He smiles but doesn't speak as he leaves me alone again.

When he returns a few minutes later, he has two cups and hands one to me.

"I'm sorry, Maddie." He sits across the table from me. "Caroline is unable to join us for another twenty minutes. She apologizes for making you wait."

"It's fine."

Nathan flips open the file folder he withdrew from his briefcase and dives right into the trial. "First, we'll have to formulate a list of witnesses we intend to question in the pretrial. The prosecution will get a chance to review our list, as we will theirs."

I nod along, understanding the process of the system. After the pretrial will come my actual trial, though it could be another year following. The judicial system isn't quick with these things.

"This is the preliminary list of witnesses that Sean drew up." He slides a piece of paper across the table to me, careful not to make any contact.

I pretend to read over the names, but I can't focus. I'm too thrown by our newfound relationship. Lawyer and accused murderer. What a romance.

"Looks fine." I slide the paper back to him. I barely glanced over the names, too distracted by the thought of our children. The ones he doesn't know once existed.

Nathan frowns. "Did you even read it?"

I nod, embarrassed I've let my distraction get the best of me.

"Tell me two names on this list."

"Uh." I run a few witnesses through my mind. "Arabella."

Nathan sighs. "Mrs. Davenport will be on the prosecutor's witness list as she is speaking against you." He slides the paper back. "You have to take this seriously, Maddie."

"I'm sorry." I lift the paper again. "I can't focus."

"What's on your mind?" There's concern in his question, but it's professional and not affectionate.

"Nothing." What's on my mind—our beautiful daughters, our years of romance, our once perfect home—isn't something to bring up now.

"Maddie, if the case is causing duress, you can share that with me." Nathan folds his hands on the table. "Why don't you tell me more about the victim?"

What can I say about Gina? I dated the guy she liked and did too many drugs to know what happened? Lawyer or not, Nathan is the man I want to be with, and the last thing I want to do is share my dark secrets with him in this setting.

"There's nothing to tell. They're looking in the wrong place. I'm not the guilty one. Brian Cordes is."

"Should we put him on the witness stand?" Nathan asks.

I almost choke at the suggestion, and that awful feeling of irony comes rushing back. "No, that would be a mistake. He'd lie."

"We could catch him in a lie."

"I have a restraining order against him. I don't want him anywhere near me."

Nathan grimaces and looks down at the paperwork. "Very well. One thing I can assure you is that the prosecution's case isn't strong. It's very possible the whole thing will be dismissed during the pretrial."

This information isn't new. The letter was forged. My prints aren't on the murder weapon. The only thing the police have going for them are my fingerprints at the scene, and Arabella's statement, which I hope will soon be proved inadmissible.

"Tell me more about Brian Cordes."

My stomach lurches. "No."

"If you think he's guilty, we need to know more. Who is he?"

I draw a long breath. "A guy I knew in university. A bad guy." Talking about Brian makes me feel shame. Whether for this life or my past one, I don't know.

"A guy you were close with?" Nathan's voice softens. Like he knows he's treading on a sensitive topic.

"We were close once." There's no reason to lie. "But that was a mistake I regret."

"You know, Maddie, I have a saying."

I smile because before he even speaks, I know exactly what he's going to say.

"Never regret what happens in your life because the universe has a way of righting itself."

He used to tell me that all the time. He told our daughters the same thing, like on the morning Ava twisted her ankle and couldn't participate in her dance competition.

But right now, I'm having a hard time appreciating it.

"I can't say I feel like I'm where I'm supposed to be."

Nathan chuckles. "No, but I'm sure it will work out."

Just as our conversation starts to feel easy, we're interrupted by Caroline, who enters the room.

"Ms. Butler." She offers her hand. "Forgive me for the delay. Let's get started." She sits next to Nathan and dives into the casework. Again, I nod along, put out that she ruined our moment, and hopeful that Nathan's words of advice prove to be true.

Fifty-Seven

THEN

After three days with the blackmail money hidden in the house, I decided I couldn't do the drop alone, and I didn't trust anyone as much as I trusted Dee. It had been hell lying to her these past weeks, and the only way I was going to rid myself of my demons was to lay it all on the line and come clean. I told Dee about the affair and Brian's threats. After a moment of silence to comprehend, Dee agreed to accompany me.

Cheltenham Park was empty given the fact that it was Monday afternoon. Most kids were in school and most adults at work. The park was small compared to others in the Toronto community. Although it featured two baseball diamonds, they were run-down and poorly kept. Even some of the benches on the walking path were cracked and broken.

A lone hooded figure sat on a bench near the furthest ball diamond, a distance from the road.

"Wait here, okay?"

"No," Dee protested. "I want to come too."

"I think I should do this part alone." I didn't wait for her to argue further and got out of the car, clutching the briefcase.

The walk towards him seemed slow and agonizing. I didn't know what to expect; I was taking a gamble.

Brian stood as I approached and pushed back his hood.

"I guess you got my message, MJ." He wore a playful grin, but it unnerved me. That grin was too familiar, and the things Brian found playful weren't fun for anyone else.

"I got it." I dropped the briefcase on the ground in front of him. "That's all of it. Now you'll leave me the hell alone."

"So feisty." He chuckled as he reached for it and snapped open the clasps. "But you've done good."

"Now you'll leave me alone?"

Brian ran a hand over his buzzed hair. "As long as it suits me."

"That wasn't the deal."

"It's blackmail, MJ. There is no deal." Brian smirked. "You've paid me for this secret. I have no doubt there will be others." He stepped closer, causing me to jolt backwards. The last thing I wanted was for him to touch me.

"Leave me alone." I turned on my heel. "If you don't, then I'll be forced to report you."

Brian laughed. "You do that, and Nathan will know your precious little secret. Don't forget, I've got nothing to lose, unlike you."

I didn't answer because what he said was true. Without a witty response, I returned to where Dee waited.

"Are you okay?" Dee asked. "It looks like you've seen a ghost."

"No, I'm fine."

"So it's done?" Dee shifted the car into drive.

"It's done." But it wasn't. Brian said it all. He would continue to watch and threaten me.

Fifty-Eight

NOW

I return home in time to find Declan packing up his little sedan.

"Stop that." I grab one of the bags that Declan had loaded into his trunk. "At least let your big sister drive you to the airport."

"It's fine," Declan protests, taking his bag from my hands. "I don't want to put any more pressure on you. You have enough on your mind."

I take the bag again, moving it out of his reach. "I am driving you no matter what is going on. I'm your big sister, and you're leaving the country. I'm at least taking you to the airport."

"Maddie—" Declan frowns and adjusts his glasses.

"I'll be fine, Dec." I place his suitcase in the back seat of my car. "You can fly off to Neverland without any worries, Lost Boy." I wink as I reference Declan's favourite childhood story. He always felt like a lost boy growing up with an older sister and, eventually, no father.

"The Lost Boys were never worried." Declan chuckles, helping me finish loading up the car.

"Except when it came to Captain Hook."

Declan puts up his dukes in a mock fight stance. "I could take him."

"Of course, you could." I glance at my full car. "We're not leaving already, are we?"

"I was hoping to."

"But the flight isn't until nine."

"Yeah, but an hour to get there in rush hour, arrive three hours before."

"That still puts you two hours ahead of schedule." I smile. "I thought you were the smart kid."

He shifts and looks down at the driveway.

"What's happening before the flight, Dec?"

"I'm going to meet Naomi," Declan mumbles. "Have an early dinner, then meet the rest of the crew."

"Ah."

"You're not upset, are you?" Declan asks. "I mean, I wasn't even sure I'd see you before I left."

"I'm not upset." I give his hand a gentle squeeze. "I can tell she's important to you. You should meet her. I'm not going anywhere, and I'm going to bet you don't want to let that one get away."

Declan smiles. "I don't."

Saying goodbye to Declan is hard, but as soon as I see him embrace Naomi, I know it's the right thing to do. In a few hours, he'll be on his way to South America to do what he was supposed to be doing all along. It may have taken longer than expected, but his path is set. He's going the right way.

I hope my path is moving the right way, too, even though

things with Nathan are complicated. I try to avoid focusing on it.

By the time I arrive back in North York, the sun has started to set, and I stop by the grocery store for a few choice items before heading home to spend my first night alone in a long time. First, there was Jayson, then Declan. I don't know the last time I lived on my own. Despite the possibility of a murderer being on my tail, I am excited about it. I was planning on a night with Ben and Jerry's and countless cheesy rom-com movies—the ones that star Drew Barrymore.

Once I'm out of the grocery store and back in my car, the eerie feeling returns. The one that tells me I'm not alone. The parking lot surrounding the grocery store is huge, larger than it needs to be for the small family-run business. It has only a few cars parked. It's late enough that most people will be sitting down to dinner with their families; it's only people like me, the singles and the alone, that are still out right now. The ones who have no one to go home to.

I lock the car doors for good measure and drive out of the parking lot and, as I do, I notice a black SUV do the same thing, following my right-hand turn, although keeping a slight distance. It seems to mimic my every move.

When I end up on my street, and the car is still behind me, I drive right past my house without stopping. If this person is following me, I'm not about to put myself in danger by getting out by myself.

I dial Dee as I drive.

"Hey, girl," her cheery voice answers.

"Dee, are you home?"

Her tone immediately drops. "Maddie, what's wrong?"

"I think someone is following me, and I don't want to be home alone. Are you at the condo?"

"Yeah, of course. Come here now."

"On my way." I hesitate. "Dee…"

"Yeah?"

"Mind meeting me out front?"

"No problem." There's movement on the other end of the phone. "I'll be waiting in the lobby until you arrive."

"You're a lifesaver." I glance in the rear-view mirror. The SUV is still in sight, so I press on the accelerator and try to put some more distance between us.

Whoever's behind me flashes their high beams, forcing me to glance away from the mirror. I only drive faster as my heart pounds in my chest. It has to be Brian. Who else would be doing this to me?

I turn into Dee's condo complex, and the SUV drives by, going around me. The windows are too dark to see who could be inside. I squint at the license plate as it rushes by—LEKM 665. I've never seen it before, but I type it into my phone along with a brief description of the car to give to Sean next time we speak. If it is Brian, the police will know, and Sean can find out.

Dee is standing outside her building when I pull into the closest visitor spot. I grab the few groceries then rush to her side.

"You okay?" She wraps an arm around my shaking shoulders and directs me inside.

"Yeah." I glance back at the road. "Whoever it was drove by once I turned in here."

"You think it was Brian?" Once inside the building, Dee grabs the one of the bags and we go to the elevator.

"I don't know, but who else could it be?"

Dee shrugs her response. "Stay here tonight, girl. I've got

clothes you can wear. And from the looks of this"—she peers into my shopping bags—"we've got an awesome chill night ahead of us."

"Too bad the wine is in my fridge." I groan.

Dee winks. "I got us covered."

"You are a lifesaver."

"You know it."

Fifty~Nine

NOW

I invited Dee to come stay with me until this whole trial and Brian situation is figured out. She jumped at the opportunity, claiming it would be like a permanent sleepover from our high school days. I didn't comment on the fact that there is a possible murderer after me. She's been with me almost five days now.

This morning I find Dee sprawled on the couch, watching the morning news. My heart stops when I look at the screen. There, in the corner, is Brian's mugshot, and below it indicates there's a red alert out on him.

"What's going on?"

Dee glances towards me. "Oh, hey." She sits up on the couch, making room for me beside her. "Did I wake you?"

I crack a smile. "Always listen to the TV this loud?"

"I think I'm partially deaf."

I take a seat beside her. "Yeah, it's probably because you talk so loud."

"Gee, thanks." Dee rolls her eyes with a hint of a smile then looks back at the screen.

The reporter on-screen moves to the next piece of news as Brian's picture fades away and another item comes up. Dee grabs the remote and turns down the volume.

I nod towards the TV. "What were they saying about him?"

"That he's missing." Dee straightens and turns towards me. "His parole officer and lawyer don't know where he is, and he's been away from his safe house for several days. That probably confirms what you were thinking about him following you. Did Sean ever find anything on the license plate?"

"If he did, he hasn't mentioned it." I've barely spoken to my lawyer since he passed my case off to Nathan. I haven't heard from any of them, in fact. Sean only called to make sure I wasn't staying alone. He was happy to hear I had a temporary roommate.

"Probably for the best."

"Yeah." I don't want to talk about it anymore. I've focused too much on it over the past few days. "Is there coffee?" I glance to the kitchen door, and my heart picks up speed. I'm still having trouble going in there. Each time I remember finding Gina her kitchen, I feel light-headed and ill.

"Yeah." Dee moves to stand. "I'll get it for you. Stay here."

"Thanks." It is a blessing having Dee around.

She comes back with a steaming mug of coffee, then sits next to me on the couch. "Have you seen him lately?"

"Who?"

"Brian," she says. "Or whoever was following you."

"Not since that night at your place." I sip my coffee; the warm liquid is creamy. Perfectly made, thanks Dee. "Maybe I imagined the whole thing."

"I doubt it." She leans back on the couch, then grabs the remote and switches off the news entirely.

"Why's that?" I give her a gentle nudge. "We both know I have a flair for the dramatic."

"That you do." Dee laughs. "But this is too much of a coincidence. You literally have your first night alone and a random car starts following you, past your house, and all the way over to my place. Nope, definitely sounds like a psycho."

She has a point.

"I guess so." I wish I had imagined it all.

"Maybe Brian's gone now," Dee says, that hopeful tone in her voice. "I mean, you haven't seen him, and the cops have no leads. Maybe he did leave town."

"Maybe." My gut says he hasn't. Brian's still out there, waiting to exact the revenge he's been plotting on me for four years. He'll be back, even if there's no sign of him right now.

"Gotten any work done?" She glances to the corner of the living room where my computer and desk are set up. The computer is off and has been untouched for days.

"Not in a while." I haven't even told my editor I'm behind. "I can't think about it right now. Too much going on."

"You should tell them. I bet they'll extend your deadline."

I look away. "Or they'll cancel the contract."

"Maddie, you found a dead girl, are suspected of murder, and now you're being stalked by a potential killer. I think they'll give you a break for that."

"You might be onto something." I crack a small smile.

"Okay, if you aren't going to get any work done today, let's at least go to brunch." Dee stands.

"Don't you have a job to go to?" Dee hasn't been to work in several days now.

"Not today, I don't." She smiles. "Besides, I told them there were some personal issues and that my best friend might be a murderer. They were pretty willing to let me take a couple of days." She lowers her voice. "I mean, God forbid,

I send my murderous best friend after them and their families."

"Oh, Dee, you didn't!" I grab her hand. and she pulls me to my feet.

"Of course I didn't," she chuckles. "I had some vacation time saved up. I told them I needed a mental health break."

I open my mouth to retort, to tell her I don't want her wasting her vacation on me, but she doesn't give me a chance to speak.

"Now, go get dressed." Dee shoos me from the room. "I've got a great brunch place in mind and it's my treat."

"How can I say no?"

"Obviously, you can't. Now go!"

"Thanks, Dee." I give her one last smile before heading up to my room to get changed.

The place Dee takes me to is one I've never seen before, not even in my old life, but I certainly wish I had. It's one of those restaurants with all the tacky decorations, which you know have a story. It reminds me of Dee's cluttered condo, which was probably why she likes it so much. The hostess greets Dee by name with a warm smile and directs us to a waiting table, her "usual" as the young woman calls it.

The square table is made of wood, sanded and varnished, but looks as if it has been through a few family meals as there are scratches in the seal and indications of markers scribbled across the table. My thoughts are confirmed when I glance around and see children seated nearby with pieces of paper in front of them and several markers to colour with. A family-friendly place, another reason Dee probably enjoys it, as she loves kids.

"It's cute here." I reach for the menu and am greeted with a large selection of breakfast and lunch items, most accompanied by a picture of the food.

"I knew you'd like it." Dee smiles with admiration as she glances around, then waves at one of the chefs behind the back counter. "I've been coming here for years."

"You've never brought me here."

Dee shrugs. "You and I haven't been this close in a long time, Maddie. But that's changed now."

The waitress comes by, and we place our orders. Dee begins fidgeting, looking like she wants to say something.

"Spill it," I say.

"There's this party tonight …" Dee offers a sheepish grin.

I raise an eyebrow. "The last place I need to be is at a party." I can only imagine how that would go. My guard down, alcohol, drugs.

"I think it's the best place to be."

The waitress returns with our drinks and first courses.

"Are you kidding me?" I bite into my appetizer. French toast bites. The sweet, cinnamon goodness is what I crave.

"You don't have to drink."

I only continue to look at her with skepticism.

"C'mon, Maddie, puh-lease." I hate when her whiny tone comes out. "It'll be fun."

"I don't think so." I glance out the window to the busy street. "I'm not feeling a party."

"But it's at Rich's house. So Nathan will be there." She adds the last part with a singsong tone. Ever since she discovered Nathan was acting as my trial lawyer, she couldn't let the topic fall.

Rich. That's a familiar name. "Rich Cooke?"

"Yeah." Dee frowns. "How'd you know?"

I know because Rich Cooke was the best man at my

wedding. He's been Nathan's best friend since university. They were inseparable, and I was close with his wife, Cheryl. We had dinner parties together, then kids around the same time. Rich had been one of my best friends.

"I know him." I shrug. "From another life."

Dee rolls her eyes. "Oh right, you're from the future." She laughs off her joke. "I think a party would be fun."

"I don't. Besides, the last place I want to go is somewhere that Nathan will be. I mean, he's my lawyer because, you know, I'm a suspected murderer. I'm sure there is no interest."

When we met in my old life, he called me the next day. Then the one after that, and the one after that. It was a whirlwind and wonderful. This time it's slow and painful, verging on torture. His life must be so different without me in it. I worry it's different enough that we'll never be together.

"Whatever." Dee waves off my worry. "He's a guy. They don't know what they want. And you're not an actual murderer, so it's fine."

"I still don't think Nathan is interested."

Dee laughs. "I know for a fact he's looking to get a slice of the Maddie pie."

I almost spit out my drink as I laugh. "Ew, Dee, that's gross." Though it only makes me wonder what she's been saying to him.

"Really?" Her devious smile remains. "Look who's had a bite of it—Jayson, Jack, Bri—"

"Okay, now I'm going to vomit."

Dee cackles. "Come with me, and I'll never mention your dirty pie again."

I give her a stern look but can't stop the creeping smile.

"Fine."

"Yes!" She pumps her fist up in the air in mock celebration. "Finally." She lowers her voice with a playful smile. "I'm glad you agreed because I would have felt pretty awful about leaving you alone tonight."

"Oh, so you were going even if I had disagreed?"

"Well, duh." Dee laughs. "It's a party, Maddie."

Sixty

NOW

A s Dee advised, I reached out to my editor and agent. I wasn't brave enough to call, only to craft an email that I read six times before hitting send. Even as I did so, the knot in my stomach didn't subside. I explained how my life had fallen to pieces and requested an extension on my delivery date. I didn't mention the party I was convinced to attend, only my inability to write with the turmoil in my life. However, while waiting for their reply, I couldn't determine if I was more nervous they would terminate the contract for my not holding up my end of the bargain or scared about seeing Nathan. Maybe it was both. Maybe neither. With all the changes and drama in my life, there was no way to be sure.

Still, when the day ends and I find myself dressed in one of Dee's skimpy party dresses and wearing way too much makeup, I begin to think it's Nathan causing the real nerves. Everything else in my life is so unknown, but when I think of Nathan he's still shrouded in that cloud of hope. The idea of losing that makes me hesitate in the bathroom when Dee calls my name.

"Anytime now, Maddie!" Her voice echoes from down-stairs—she's likely waiting by the front door. "You've been in the bathroom for almost twenty minutes, and I know you're not taking a poop!" Dee laughs at her own joke. "And if you are, make sure you spray something."

I exit the bathroom and head to the stairs. I look down at her.

"Finally!" She grins. "And don't you look lovely. How was the poop?"

"For your information, I was nervous and struggling to breathe." I descend the stairs.

Dee's face scrunches. "That bad, eh? Please say you at least put some perfume on."

"Oh my God, Dee!" I gently slap her arm. "That's not what I meant."

"No?" Dee raises an eyebrow in mock interest. "What else could possibly have you holed up in the bathroom?"

"Maybe the fact that you're making me attend a party with a guy who is my lawyer and who may or may not be interested in me." I place a hand on my chest. "I think I might be hyperventilating."

"Maddie, relax." Dee hands me my shoes. "I wouldn't put you in a situation that would go badly, I promise."

I take the shoes but remain skeptical.

"Trust me, will you?" Dee offers a sincere smile. "I know I like to joke, but with everything that's happened I wouldn't do anything to make it worse."

"I know," I concede. "I do trust you."

"Okay, good." Her upbeat voice returns. "Because Nathan is probably going to be looking fine tonight, and you totally are, so it's going to be great!"

Nathan always looks good, so tonight won't be any differ-ent. I don't feel great about this, but do my best to hide it from Dee. She's excited, and I've been enough of a downer as it is.

I put on a smile. "Can't wait!" My excitement sounds forced.

Dee points at me with gun fingers. "I know that was so fake, but I appreciate the effort." She winks. "Let's do this!"

This time I smile for real. I follow her from the house to the waiting cab.

Rich's place is only a few minutes from my own, but this isn't anything like attending a party at Dee's. There aren't any decorations, no theme. Simply a whole bunch of people, sitting or standing, dressed to impress with drinks in their hands. A few play card games like poker or kings. But most hang around the house, listening to music and chatting amongst themselves. I recognize most of them from Dee's parties. She says hi to a few people as we make our way to the kitchen, where I find myself hesitating.

"Oh, right," Dee says. "Stupid me, totally forgot. Wait by the stairs. I'll grab you a drink."

I smile my thanks and wait where she indicated, glad I'm not going to have a panic attack in front of these strangers.

"Maddie." A smooth voice speaks behind me.

I almost melt at the sound and turn around to be met with a beautiful sight: Nathan, in a button-down shirt and dark jeans. Damn. I wish my memory of his good looks had faded with time, but he's as *hot* as always. I notice a small scar missing from his jawline. He'd cut it open, jumping off a cliff on our honeymoon. I smile at the memory. He'd been so stubborn when I'd told him not to do it. But always the adventurer, he was set in his decision.

"Oh, hey, Nathan." I offer my hand, but he moves closer, giving me a one-arm squeeze. It's less intimate than a kiss on the cheek, which I would have liked, but better than our last awkward meeting as client and lawyer. It's still wildly inappropriate; I wonder how many beers he's had.

"Good to see you."

But is it? Is seeing me now really what he wants?

"Yeah, you too."

"I had no idea you were Dee's friend," he says, reaching up and scratching the back of his neck. "The famous Maddie."

"Famous?" I stifle a laugh. "Famous how?" The comment has me wondering how much Dee has told him about me.

"You're the girl who never showed." He gently pokes my shoulder.

I suddenly feel stupid. I'd forgotten that I'd stood him up in this life when Dee had first tried to make us meet. The stubborn, angry me picked Brian over a chance meeting with Nathan. What a fool I was.

"Oh, right. Sorry about that. I was dumb and young. My loss." Though he has no idea how much of a loss it is. But I do —two missing girls and one life I now realize I took for granted.

Nathan waves off my response. "Old news. You doing okay, with everything?"

I force a steady smile. "Yeah, taking it in stride. Thanks again for your help. I never did get the chance to say that."

"It's my job." He sips his drink. "But I'm glad we can work together. This is a wrong that needs to be corrected."

Before I can respond, Dee bounces to my side and shoves a beer into my hand. "Oh, hey Nate."

His nose wrinkles. "You know I hate the short forms, Dee."

"I get special privilege." She sips her beer.

"Nathan, how about an introduction to these lovely ladies?" a guy says as he comes up behind Nathan and drapes his arm over his shoulder.

I used to see that face almost every day. It's Rich Cooke, Nathan's best friend. His blond hair is the same spiked style he wore in university, and even when he married and the kids came, he never bothered to change it. His nose is still as crooked as it was when we first met. He claimed it was from a bad hockey fight in high school.

"Sorry, Rich," Nathan says with mock sincerity. "Where are my manners?" He waves to Dee. "You already know the lovely Dee-Anne." Nathan earns an annoyed look from her with the full name.

"Well, yes, Ms. Dee." Rich takes her hand and gently kisses the back. "Don't you look ravishing."

"Charmed." Dee bats her eyelashes, then laughs.

"But this other lovely specimen is a mystery to me." Rich looks right at me now.

"Rich, my boy, I wish I could explain this one to you," Nathan says, reaching up and tapping his chin. "Because Ms. Maddie here is a true enigma to me as well."

"But at least the beautiful conundrum has a name." Rich throws his hands up in celebration. "Huzzah!"

"Richard!" The loud squeal sounds from the opposite side of the party and makes Rich drop his hands.

"Oh, I should go." He flashes a perfect smile at me. "Nice to meet you, Maddie. Always a pleasure, Dee. Take care of my boy here." He pats Nathan on the chest, then turns and hurries away from us to the petite, raven-haired beauty in the corner. I smile. It's Cheryl, his future wife.

I jump when a slight vibration from my purse jiggles my arm. My phone. I grab it, but the call is from an unknown number. Declan has been trying to get in touch with me for days, so my mind jumps to my younger brother. I lift my phone for Dee and Nathan to see.

"I have to take this." Then I point to the front door. "I'll be outside."

"Don't be too long, girl," Dee calls after me as I retreat. "You're here to have fun."

I step out into the night air; it's cooler than it was when we arrived. I bring my phone to my ear, stepping down from the front porch and away from the thumping music of the party.

"Hello?"

My phone buzzes with dead air, but there's no one on the other end.

"Hello?" I try again, continuing my distance from the party. "Declan, is that you?"

Still nothing but dead air. I pull my phone away and glance at it. The call is still going, but there's no one there. My bars are full so it can't be from my service.

Determined to get a response, I try again. "Hello? Is anyone there?"

Still nothing. I end the call. Declan's reception must be terrible. I hope he'll call back. Maybe I should have let it go to voicemail.

I hear footsteps on the driveway behind me, and I turn to face the person when something heavy collides with the side of my face and sends me crashing to the pavement.

"Hey!" I try to yell out as my arm hits the asphalt. Searing pain shoots through my body. My vision blurs, but I see someone standing over me with a clenched fist. "Hey—" My eyes flutter as they reach down. I try to move away but can't. Then dizziness overcomes my senses, and darkness consumes me.

Sixty-One

NOW

A low buzzing noise increases the growing pain in my head. My arms are heavy and sore, and I realize it's because they are pulled back behind me, tied. I'm on my side, something soft beneath my head. My eyes flutter open. It's dark, mostly, but I can see streetlights through the windows. The buzzing is the gentle purr of an engine and wheels moving along the asphalt. I'm in a car.

I groan as I try to straighten, struggling with my unmoveable hands, and my head feels twice the normal weight. What happened? The last thing I remember is being at the party, and then someone attacked me in the driveway. My heart races. Where am I?

From the texture and feel, my hands are bound around my back with a rope. Tight, but not impossible to undo. My head rests in the centre seat, my feet near the door. A figure sits upfront, only a foot from me. I move to reach for the door handle when I notice the driver is only clutching the wheel with one hand, the other is gripping a handgun. A flick of his wrist and that gun will be pointed at me.

I draw a quick breath and glance up. Our eyes meet in the rearview mirror.

"I wondered when you'd wake up." Brian chuckles with cruel laughter. "I thought I might have hit you too hard."

My head throbs. Everything hurts.

"Where are you taking me?" And what exactly is he planning? Will he shoot me? My imagination goes wild with the possibilities.

"Back to where it all started," Brian says. "And where it should have ended."

"You already ended it. You killed Gina."

His passive, amused expression vanishes and his face scrunches with anger. "Gina was weak. She needed to die." He spits the words at me as if they were venom on his tongue.

"But she was helping you."

"For a time."

I wriggle my hands, hoping to free the binds around my wrists. "Why? You always wanted her dead." I think back to our conversation in prison.

"I tell a good story, don't I?" That amused smile appears again. "Made you think that Gina was on your side. Your friend, when she'd been writing to me for years."

My clouded head tries to understand his words. Sean had mentioned the letters. Arabella had denied them. Why had Gina written to him after everything that happened?

"It was amusing at first," Brian says. "Gina was still so desperate for my attention. Desperate for me. You and Arabella thought she was so gullible that she'd just go along with your lies. Gina always intended to make you pay for what you did to her."

"I didn't do anything. You did," I say firmly. "You were the one who hurt her."

"And yet she still obsessed over me." Brian chuckles. "It's funny how attraction works."

"Why did she write to you?" I press. If I can distract him long enough I might be able to get free.

"Because she missed me," Brian says. "She told me everything. How she envied you and Arabella from afar. Until she found out the truth. Both of you lived such lies. Fake friendship, false love. But when she found out you wanted her dead…"

"That's not true."

"It is, and Gina believed it. That's why she helped me with this." Brian shakes his head, still wearing a wicked grin. "That's why she came back for my parole hearing. For years we'd been talking about my release. For years she'd been promising to help me get out and get my revenge. You know she always hated you for everything that happened with me."

"But you never liked her. Why would you want her help now?"

"That's true," Brian agrees. "So I just toyed with her, welcomed her letters. Welcomed her help to get me out. But when she came home and came to see me … I remember how fat her ass was, but Maddie, that ass got tight. She wanted revenge for what you'd done. All your lies. And I would have done anything to stick my dick in that."

My stomach lurches, but I feel the binds loosening.

His displeasure returns. "But it wasn't enough. She was happy to torture you and have a few goes with me. She was good at the threats. Better at sucking dick. But when I told her what I wanted to do, and how I'd end you, she panicked." He shakes his head, disgust written on his face. "She hated you, but she didn't want you dead. She didn't have it in her."

"Maybe she was scared." I keep moving my hands, using

my nails to pull at the rope, feeling some give. "Maybe she didn't want to get caught."

"If she'd stuck to the plan, we wouldn't have." His grip on the wheel tightens. "We would have been free of you. She was a coward. Weak. She couldn't do what had to be done."

"Then why kill her?"

"I had to finish what I'd failed to do before." His fingers twitch on the gun, feeling for the trigger. "I guess I always knew I'd have to put her down eventually. She wasn't supposed to be here. You changed that when you saved her. Women, you're weak when it comes to what needs to be done."

"Maybe you're the weak one?" I challenge him as I continue to loosen the bonds. I can loop my finger beneath one of the knots. "Maybe your weakness is in the need to destroy instead of endure."

Brian laughs, turning the car down a quiet, empty road. "Strong words from a person about to face their death."

"They'll know it was you." I hope that will be enough to deter him. "You'll go back to jail."

Brian doesn't look at me this time. "I've already sent off the pictures of you and Jack to the best editors in town. With a note that says that you couldn't keep the secret any longer, and you couldn't suffer the consequences of betraying your friend, so you killed yourself." He shoots a glance over his shoulder, wearing a sick grin. "Kind of a poetic suicide note."

Memories flash in my mind as I take in the darkened surroundings. I've been here before. It's the road we'd found Gina's car on. It's the same place I almost watched her die.

I have to think fast. "This won't work, you know. There are too many flaws in your plan. They'll know it wasn't suicide. They aren't stupid. It'll be just like Gina. They'll know someone did it, and you won't have me to take the fall."

"So what if they do?" Brian says. "I'll be long gone by then."

I can feel my hands slipping free. Almost there.

"And now for the grand finale." He continues to creep down the road, looking for the perfect spot.

Finally, I'm able to pry my right hand free. I try to keep my movements minimal so as not to arouse suspicion. When I'm able to loosen my other hand, I carefully unravel the rope. If I'm fast enough, I can get away.

The car slows to a stop and I act, throwing the loose rope over the driver's seat and wrapping it around his neck, pulling it tight. He struggles against me, dropping the gun and grabbing for the rope. In his surprise, I'm able to secure it with a quick knot before dashing out of the car.

I sprint away from the car; my heart thumps against my chest, and my lungs start to burn. My head spins, pounding from being hit. I don't look behind me to see if he follows; I keep running.

I risk a look when I hear the sound of tires and headlights light up the road from behind me. The car races towards me and I dive to the side, narrowly avoiding it, sliding across the shoulder of the road and rolling into the muddy ditch, surrounded by tall reeds. Brian slams on the brakes, but before he can turn around, another car turns down the road, causing Brian to speed off. I try to stand, to wave to the oncoming car, but my ankle gives way when I attempt to move.

"Help!" I call, waving my arms from where I'm stuck. The car only drives by.

Tears well in my eyes as I attempt to move again. The pain in my head grows too strong to ignore, and dizziness forces me to sit. I want to lie down and sleep. Instead, I lean back against the grass, certain no one will find me now, and Brian will be back to finish the job. I stare up at the night sky. It's clear, starry. As my eyelids grow heavy, headlights light up the road once more.

Sixty-Two

NOW

I bolt upright, gasping for air. I'm vaguely aware of something tugging at my forearm. Brian hasn't succeeded in killing me. I'm still alive.

"Maddie, are you okay?"

The voice catches me off guard, and I nearly tumble out of bed, realizing I'm not alone. I'm not at home either. The room is white, pristine. The bed is small, a cot, and surrounded by a curtain. There is a gentle beep of a heart monitor. In my right arm is a needle, attached to an IV. I am in the hospital.

"Maddie?" The voice comes again, and I force myself to look at the person at my side. Relief washes over me as I'm met with kind eyes, the very ones I fell in love with. Brian's cruel features are gone and are now replaced with Nathan's genuine concern. I can't believe my luck. Why he's here escapes me. We aren't close, as much as I wish we were.

"I…" The confusion must be written on my face because Nathan's brow crinkles, and he quickly tries to explain.

"You didn't return from your phone call at Rich's party, and I got a bit worried," Nathan says, looking down at his lap and not meeting my eyes. "And there's a murderer on the loose."

Right, I was doing something stupid.

Wearing a sheepish grin, he scratches the back of his neck. "Actually, I was hoping to get a moment to talk to you alone. Seeing you at Rich's party was my first chance. I shouldn't have followed you outside, but Dee insisted. I saw you being hauled into the back seat of an SUV, so I ran to my car and followed."

I draw a sharp breath, pain coursing through my body.

"I stayed on his tail. When I turned down the empty road, I saw the SUV speed away. It took a few minutes until I found you in the ditch. And, Maddie, you weren't moving. I was worried I was too late, that I'd found your body." Nathan shakes his head. "I checked your pulse and had you at the hospital in less than twenty minutes."

"How long has it been?"

"Almost twenty hours. You've been in and out of consciousness. They gave you morphine to ease the pain." Nathan gives me another sheepish smile. "I, uh, had to tell the nurse we were dating so she would let me stick around. Hope that's okay."

He has no idea how okay that really is.

"Thanks," I agree with a weak smile, the best I can muster in my exhaustion.

He takes my hand with a gentle squeeze. "Glad you understand my predicament."

"I do." We maintain eye contact, in silence, for some time, neither of us sure what to say. If he hadn't followed me, would I be dead? As much as I am enjoying this time with him, there's something important on my mind.

"Uh, Nathan."

"Yeah, Maddie?"

"About that guy you saw taking me away." I remove my hand from his grasp and look away. "What happened to him? Did the police find him?"

"I told the police about him, gave a description as best I could. I managed to get his license plate number, and they're on the lookout for him." I meet his eyes when he reaches over and takes hold of my hand again. "I'm right in thinking that he was Brian Cordes?"

"You are," I confirm.

"And you thought to wander off on your own in the dead of night?" Nathan is scolding me like a child. And a part of me loves it.

"I didn't wander off!" I pull my hand from his grip. "I was attacked from behind when I tried to answer my phone. Besides, Dee knew what was going on. She shouldn't have let me off on my own." That's mature, Maddie. Deflect onto your best friend.

"On the bright side, I've got some good news for you. The police searched Brian's house after the attempt on your life and found evidence linking him to Gina's death. They cleared you of all charges this morning. You are innocent."

"Oh, thank God!"

"But—they do have a few questions. I told them they would have to wait until I signed off on your bill of health." Nathan puffs out his chest, acting like a protective guardian.

"And they agreed to that?"

Nathan scratches the back of his neck, a sheepish grin in place. "Well, no, but the nurse said she'd call them when she felt you were ready to handle their presence. I thought my story sounded better."

"It did." I laugh. "Thanks. I figured I'd have to speak to them about him eventually. God, I wish I never got involved with him in the first place."

"It'll work out for the best." Nathan smiles. "Never regret what happens in life—"

I cut him off. " ... because the universe has a way of righting itself."

As I speak the words he shared when I was a suspected murderer, and words we lived by in our past life, my previous worries feel far from my mind. Despite everything, he's here, by my side, making sure I heal. I helped Declan and encouraged him to go off where he belonged, and I'd righted things with Dee, coming clean about my many mistakes. Maybe, despite it all, I can do better. Maybe the universe will take my mistakes and turn them into lessons. I learned from them after all; I aspire to be better. I want to change.

"Good memory."

I return his smile. "Not really. Someone special to me once told me those exact words. I didn't believe him then, but I do now."

Nathan chuckles. "Sounds like a brilliant guy."

"He is." So brilliant and sitting right beside me.

Sixty-Three

NOW

Nathan left the hospital room to get coffee. He wanted to get me one, but the nurse refused me the joy of a warm, rich caffeinated beverage while I was connected to an IV.

"How did you react when you found out I was the girl that Dee tried to set you up with?" I ask in a joking tone.

Nathan chuckles. "Surprised at first, but then intrigued. I didn't think you were guilty, but I also didn't think I should compromise our lawyer-client relationship. It was hard though. You were as beautiful as she described." He doesn't mention that compromising that relationship could get him disbarred. I wonder how much he risked even being here, despite my case being thrown out.

I snort a laugh. "Was it scary that you almost went out with a suspected murderer?"

Nathan grins. "Why no, Maddie. I think you made my life a bit more exciting."

"I'm glad my trauma can spice up your life." I almost roll my eyes.

He jiggles his shoulders, as if dancing in his seat and starts humming the Spice Girls' "Spice Up Your Life."

Now I do roll my eyes. "Don't start."

"What? Not a Spice Girls fan?" Nathan wiggles his shoulders again. "La, la, laaah."

"Yeah, in grade school." I shake my head. "I'm surprised you were a fan."

"C'mon Maddie. Every respectable gentleman loved Sexy Spice."

"I'm pretty sure it was Ginger Spice."

"Details." Nathan waves off my comment.

"Important ones, I think." I smile. Our playful banter is at its best, and I enjoy every second of it.

"Ahem."

I glance towards the door seeing someone familiar blocking the entrance. It's Detective Bruno, your unfriendly neighbourhood police officer.

"Maddie," he says, clearly remembering my invitation to call me such in our last meeting. "We hoped to discuss what happened to you the other night." He glances towards Nathan then adds, "Alone."

Nathan crosses his arms. "I'll be staying."

"I don't think that would be appropriate." Bruno frowns, making his bald-headed, bearded face more intimidating. But he doesn't scare me.

"He's staying."

Bruno switches his stern gaze to me.

"Since you guys had no problem questioning me without a lawyer when you thought I was guilty, I don't think having a lawyer privy to our conversation will be much of an issue."

Bruno's expression softens. "You aren't under investigation."

"He'll be staying."

Bruno grits his teeth and moves into the room, Officer Fraser following at his heels. The young officer offers me an apologetic smile. Great, good cop, bad cop once again.

"It's your call, Maddie." Fraser pulls out a pen and paper.

I tell them everything that happened from Gina to visiting Brian in prison to being kidnapped at Dee's party. It all feels like some terrible dream that I've finally woken up from.

"Well, Maddie," Bruno says, somewhat reluctantly. "We are on the lookout for Mr. Cordes. We'll pool all our resources to make sure we find him. There will be an officer stationed at your door. No one will be getting in or out without your consent."

"Oh. Thank you."

"We want to catch him as soon as possible, before there's another casualty." Bruno strokes his thick beard. "We were lucky with you. We may not be so lucky again."

Before anything else can be said, the nurse hurries into the room. She's a petite woman with dark hair pulled back into a tight bun. From the cold expression on her face I bet she's a force to be reckoned with. Hands on her hips, she looks pointedly at the officers. "You're still here? My patient has been through a traumatic experience. She needs to rest." She points to the door. "Out with you. All of you."

Bruno and Fraser leave without a word but Nathan doesn't move.

"You too, Mr. Page."

Nathan protests, "You said I could stay."

"Only until she woke up. Now she's up, and you need to go."

"But—"

"I'll be okay." I release Nathan's hand. "Do what she wants. But come back in the morning."

"I'll be here first thing." He leans down and lightly kisses my forehead. "Keep well, Maddie."

I smile as he leaves, then I look over at the nurse.

Her stern expression has shifted, and her bedside manner improves. She regards me with a warm, motherly smile and lets a long sigh. "I'm glad you've woken and am so sorry for the interruption from the police. I hope it wasn't too much."

"It was fine."

The woman nods. "I tried to keep them away, but after what happened, they insisted."

"I understand."

She rounds my bed and taps my IV. "How are you feeling?"

"Fine, honestly."

"Good." She smiles again. "We'd like to keep you for a little longer to monitor things."

"I'm in no rush." Especially with my attempted murderer still on the loose.

"I'm sure your handsome fellow will be back in the morning."

"I hope so." I lean back against the pillows after she adjusts them.

"He never left your bedside after we brought you in. He's a fine gentleman."

"He is." I know Nathan better than anyone. He's one of a kind. I let out a yawn, more tired than I realized. It's been a trying week and, for once, I finally feel safe.

"I'll let you rest." She motions to a button near my bed. "If you need anything, buzz me. And, as the officers probably told you, there is an officer stationed outside your room for your safety."

"They did."

"Good." She offers another warm smile then motions to the button again. "If you need anything."

"Thank you."

I'm left alone in the silence of my room with only my thoughts to keep me company. For the first time in as long as I can remember, they aren't dark but optimistic. I'm hopeful about a few things: all bad things will pass, I'll remain safe, and Nathan will be here when I wake with the morning light.

Sixty-Four

NOW

The following morning, I wake to find I am not alone. The attached bathroom door is closed, but I can see the light beneath it. My heart flutters. Nathan came back.

However, when the door opens and reveals my visitor, it's a man, but it isn't Nathan. Instead, I'm met with a steady smile, square-rimmed glasses and a hipster haircut. My baby brother.

"Aren't you supposed to be in South America?" I can't believe he's here. I dropped him off at the airport only a week ago. Why is he back?

"Nice to see you too, Mads." He rolls his eyes and comes to my bedside.

"That's not what I meant, Dec." I frown. "You aren't supposed to be here."

"I'm here because you almost died." He takes the seat that is meant for Nathan. "How the hell am I supposed to ignore a call like that? Put yourself in my shoes."

He's right, but that sort of logic isn't what matters here. "But I'm fine. Whoever called you must have told you I was fine. Yet you hopped a flight anyway! Did you even think about your job? What you were giving up? What if they don't take you back? Think of the money you wasted!" I'm nearly shouting now, frustration boiling up inside me. Declan worked so hard to change his life, he finally met the girl of his dreams, and got the trip of a lifetime, and he threw it all away, again, for me.

"Of course I thought about those things," Declan says, his voice rising as well. "But I was more concerned about the sister I left behind."

"But I'm fine!" I grit my teeth, trying to breathe to calm myself down. "I bet Naomi thought leaving was dumb."

"For your information, she actually encouraged me to go." Declan crosses his arms. "Family is important to her."

"It was still stupid to leave your life behind when I'm fine."

"Maddie, that's enough!" Declan's voice rises to meet my own, but our confrontation is soon cut off.

"Now, now, Declan." A voice comes from the doorway. "Don't get your sister riled up after everything she's been through." In all her glory, there stands my mother with her tanned skin, tightly styled grey hair, and a bright pink sundress.

"Mom?" She's supposed to be halfway around the world. "You're here?"

She sashays to my bedside and plants a warm kiss on my forehead. "I'm here, sweetie."

"What about Bali?" She's only been gone a few weeks. Normally, she left for months.

"I flew out the moment I heard," Mom says. "I've been travelling for what feels like days. I must look like an absolute mess." She doesn't, of course, as my mother never goes out in public without looking her best.

"No, Mom. You look great."

She gives me a sad smile. "I wish I could say the same about you, baby." She rests a hand on my forehead. "You look like you've had a rough time. How are you feeling?"

"Fine, honestly."

Her eyes well with tears. "Look at your bruises." She begins to sob. "I almost lost you."

"Mom." But her sobbing doesn't stop. "Mom," I try softer. "I'm okay, Mom."

She pulls up a chair and rests her head against my arm, sobbing quietly. I look to Declan, begging him to handle the situation. He rolls his eyes and comes to Mom's side, gently patting her back.

"Mom," he says. "Pull yourself together. You're going to ruin your makeup."

That works. My mom straightens and sniffs, wiping the tears away from her eyes. She blinks at Declan. "Do I look okay?"

"Always," Declan replies.

"Okay, no more tears." I pat her hand. "Why not tell me about Bali instead."

Mom's face lights up with a wide smile. "It was amazing, dear. The weather couldn't be beat." She stretches out her arms, having me admire her tan. "It's a bit of culture shock being back, honestly. I was sad to leave."

"You didn't have to come." Now I feel doubly guilty. Not only did I ruin my brother's job, but my mom bailed on her vacation for me.

"Oh no, honey." Pity crosses her face. "That's not what I meant. Rodrigo understands why I had to go."

"Rodrigo?" Declan groans. "Really, Mom, another one?"

"He's my personal trainer, sweetie," Mom coos. "Not my future husband."

Declan makes a face that matches my own. We both know what *personal trainer* is code for, and it isn't something we want to think about in terms of our mother.

"Am I interrupting?"

I close my eyes and smile at the sound of his voice. Nathan returned as he said he would.

"Who are you?" Declan asks, giving him a once-over.

"I'm, uh—"

I cut him off. "This is Nathan. He's the one who rescued me. Brought me to the hospital."

"Then you must join us." Mom grins. She always loves a handsome young man.

Nathan looks to me, waiting for my approval, and I nod.

He enters the room, though his steps are hesitant. "I didn't know you'd have company." He'd been the only one at my bedside for the past day. Sean called, and a few others stopped by briefly, but no one stayed while Nathan was here. Definitely not Dee. She only offered me a knowing smile, expressed her happiness that I was still alive, and claimed she'd meet me at home. I guess she decided, even while I was in the hospital, she was staying in my house. I hadn't thought her staying in my house was the best idea with Brian still roaming around, but Dee has always been fearless. Besides, it isn't her he wants.

"Neither did I. They surprised me as much as you did yesterday."

Nathan smiles and squeezes my hand. "How are you feeling today?"

"Better, a bit tired." A few things hurt, but no permanent damage. The IV was pulled from my arm in the middle of the night when my nurse came by to check-in. Now I'm being kept under watch for an additional day to make sure my condition doesn't worsen. "On that note, I need you to excuse me." It's been almost all night since I used the bathroom. I push myself out of bed, and Nathan is quick to grab my arm and help me. After spending a couple of days in bed, my body is weak. Still, once I'm upright on albeit wobbly legs, I pull my arm from Nathan's hold and limp on my good ankle to the bathroom.

After I close the door behind me, I give a sigh of relief. Being surrounded by my family is always a lot to handle and now tossing Nathan into the mix, I'm overwhelmed.

Looking in the mirror, I understand the real reason my mom panicked upon seeing me. My cheek is still swollen from where I collided with the concrete, and my eyes have fading purple bruises. An awful goose egg protrudes from the side of my head. Probably from when Brian hit me. My arms and wrists are cut and bruised, so it looks like I'm wearing strange matching bracelets. I look like an accident victim. I'm lucky I don't have any broken bones because it sure appeared like I took a beating. No wonder no one listens whenever I say I'm okay. I shouldn't have snapped at Declan. If I saw him like this, I'd lock him up and never let him leave the house again.

Tears form as I think about how close I was to losing my life. How close I was to letting my past destroy me. How one choice had cost a woman her life and affected so many around me. I'll never question my influence on others again.

As much as it frightens me, it fascinates me too. Is it possible that someone I don't know affected my own life and made it what it is? My mistakes are my own, but a domino effect changed so much around me.

Breathing slowly, I regain my composure before heading back out to face my family. It wouldn't have mattered if I hadn't, as no one even glances my way as I return except Nathan. Instead, my mom is practically leaning on Nathan's arm, listening to his every word. Declan is disinterested until Nathan asks him about his trip and Naomi, then he looks up from his phone and makes a comment about returning once I'm released from the hospital. At least that answers my concerns.

I crawl into bed before anyone acknowledges my return.

"Oh, Maddie," Mom coos, still looking at Nathan. "Nathan here was going to step out and get us some coffee. Would you like anything, honey?"

Oh, sweet Jesus! Coffee! "Yes, yes, yes!" I can't contain my excitement. "I'll have—"

"I know what you'll have." Nathan winks and leaves the room.

Mom doesn't hesitate before jumping on the Nathan bandwagon. "Oh, I adore him, honey. Just adore him. What a sweet, attentive boy. Where did you meet him? Are you dating?"

"He's a friend of Dee's." I leave out the fact that he was my trial lawyer.

"I'm glad you're speaking with Dee again, honey." Mom pats my hand. "Maybe some good came out of all this after all."

I only smile. Maybe it did.

Sixty-Five

NOW

The next morning the doctors sign my release papers, and while I'm excited by the prospect of freedom, it also means I'm not going to have a police officer outside my room anymore keeping an eye out for Brian. They still have no trace of him, though they aren't keeping me in the loop about the investigation.

My mom decided she was sticking around for a bit and would be staying at my house, along with Dee. That way I will have a constant babysitter.

"All set?" Nathan lifts my bag off the ground and motions to the waiting wheelchair.

I don't want to be wheeled out of the hospital like a sick patient.

Nathan grimaces as if reading my thoughts. "I was told it was protocol. Just until we leave the building. Your mom is waiting with your car at the front."

I climb into the wheelchair and let Nathan slowly wheel me out. The hallway is worse than my room. It smells of sterilizer. While this is the trauma ward for injuries and not disease, the idea that it reeks of sick people sticks with me. I'm glad to be leaving these white brick walls behind and have no intention of returning.

Gentle wind brushes my face as Nathan pushes me through the front doors. He stops and lets me climb out of the chair. I gingerly test my ankle before putting weight on it. At least the swelling has gone down.

"See, that wasn't so bad," Nathan says. "Sorry I had to make you do that."

"Protocol, right?"

"Exactly."

Mom waits with my car in the pickup area, and we head towards it, but before we get too far, someone calls my name.

"Maddie." I turn to see Jack, the last person I expect to see, standing next to his limo. "I tried to come in yesterday but the cop wouldn't let me through."

Nathan frowns and in a low voice asks, "Isn't that Jack Davenport?" Of course, Nathan knows Jack Davenport. The entire city knows who Jack is.

"Yeah. We were friends once. Or I was friends with his wife before the murder investigation." I motion to my mom and the car. "I'll just be a minute. Wait for me?"

"I will."

I make my way over to Jack, unsure what to expect. "What are you doing here?"

He kicks at the pavement, though there's nothing underfoot. "I got a call. Some photos leaked."

"I know." The ones Brian sent. I'd barely given a thought to them since I spoke to the cops. The damage is done.

"They said you sent them." His words are accusatory.

"I know." What else can I say? I don't need to argue that I didn't do it. The pictures are out there now. So is our secret.

"Why?"

"If you think I did this, Jack, then you're not as smart as you pretend to be."

"They said you were going to kill yourself." His sad eyes lock on the pavement. "You ended this, not me."

"I was never going to kill myself. Do you really believe that I would?" I shake my head. "It was a ploy by a very sick man. One who wanted me humiliated and dead. It wasn't even about you."

"But it involved me."

"Yeah." I glance over my shoulder where Nathan waits, leaning against my car. His arms are crossed, and he keeps a steady eye on us. From here, I can't read his expression or gauge what he thinks about our interaction.

"I guess it's done," Jack says.

I shift my gaze back to him. "There's nothing to be done about the pictures."

"No," Jack says. "I mean, they're gone. I paid off the tabloids who got the email. They signed an NDA. The information can't be leaked. And if it is, I become an even richer man."

"That's good for you." I had accepted that my secrets were out in public for all to know. The fact that they aren't doesn't matter anymore. Locked up or open to criticism, they are my mistakes.

"Good for you too, Maddie. Our secrets are safe."

"No secret is ever really safe." I shrug. "But I appreciate what you've done." I turn to go, but he catches my hand.

"We're finished now," he says. "All of it. No more talking, no more plotting. Done."

"We've been done for a long time, Jack."

He frowns. "This time, I mean it. We can't see each other again, ever."

"Okay," I agree as I have nothing more to say.

"Have a good life, Maddie." Jack turns and climbs into his waiting car.

I stare for a moment as he drives off before heading back to where Nathan stands waiting.

"All good?" Nathan asks.

"Perfect."

He smiles and opens the door. "Now get in so we can take you home."

"Gladly."

I've never sat in the back seat of my own car, but I could get used to being driven around, especially after all I've been through. The ride to my house is peaceful. Mom and Nathan speak mostly between themselves while I rest my head against the window, watching the city pass by, and when we arrive Nathan climbs out and opens my door for me.

"Home sweet home." He offers a smile.

Mom's already on her way up the front steps, and Dee throws the door open in greeting.

"They've arrived!" She hurries down the steps and catches me in her arms. "Damn, girl. Other than a few bruises, you look fine. They must have been lying about all that trauma."

"Okay, Dee. Can't breathe."

She loosens her hold on me. "Sorry." Then she looks to Nathan. "And if it isn't Superman. Won't let Lois Lane out of your sight, eh?"

"Just making sure she gets home safe." He glances in my direction. "Should your bag go upstairs?"

"Yeah, second door to the left."

He nods and disappears inside, leaving me with Dee.

"So?" Dee gently wraps her arm around my shoulders and leads me into the house, but her grin is saucy.

"So what?" I raise my eyebrow. I know what she wants, but I won't give it up without coercion.

"So, you and Nathan, obviously!" She squeezes me, and I flinch. "Spill."

"Honestly, I'm not sure."

"Figure it out, girl!" Dee releases me, but gives me a gentle hip bump. "Because you don't want to let a guy like Nathan get away." She winks. "Again."

That much I know.

Footsteps sound down the stairs, and we're joined by Nathan in my living room.

"Sorry to interrupt, ladies." Lines of worry crease his face. "I got an urgent message from work and I need to head out for a few hours."

"You'll come back later?" I worry my voice sounds too hopeful.

Nathan scratches the back of his neck. "Maddie, mind if I have a minute?"

"I'll be in the kitchen," Dee says, then takes her leave. Guaranteed she'll be listening through the door to our every word.

"Everything okay?" Maybe I was too hopeful.

"Yeah." He offers a steady smile.

"About the hospital ..." I trail off, for a moment unsure what to say. "Thank you for saving me, for staying. I know we never got a chance to get to know each other, but having you with me ... I don't know. It was comforting, and I appreciate it."

"Maddie." He keeps his eyes on the floor. "When I saw you were in trouble and got you to the hospital, I couldn't leave you. I didn't want to leave you, but I also don't want to put any pressure on you now."

I hesitate, then reach out and take his hand. "What if we start slow and see where life takes us?"

"I like the idea of a bit of spontaneity." Nathan gives my

hand a gentle squeeze.

"So you'll come back later?"

"As soon as I can." He releases my hand and turns towards the door. But before he reaches it, he stops and looks back at me.

"Oh, and Maddie?"

I look up at him. "Yeah?"

"One more thing." He's in front of me in two short strides. He gently caresses my cheek, gazes into my eyes, and lowers his lips onto mine. I pull him close as he kisses me. His soft, warm lips send my mind spinning, as I imagine the whirlwind life we have ahead of us. Our relationship, our wedding, our daughters, our love. Each one so wonderful and perfect in its own way. We'll vow to never stop appreciating each other. Brian may still be out there but I am safe with Nathan.

I hold on to these feelings as tears of joy slip through, finally realizing I've done it. I've made it back. I am going home.

The End

Acknowledgments

First I have to thank Alexandria Brown and Tina Beier at Rising Action Publishing Collective. Without your belief in me and this book, we would not be here. Your insights, talents and patience helped bring this book alive and make it the story it is today.

Thank you to Ashley Santoro for the beautiful cover design, Hailey Alcaraz for doing a thorough sensitivity read and Beth Attwood for your meticulous proofreading skills.

The Things We Lost began as a story about what if. It started when I too had my own what if questions about the turns my life had taken and how I had ended up where I was. What started as a therapeutic project, turned into a relatable story that has a woman wondering if the grass is truly greener.

I must thank my family.

Mom and Dad, without your continued support, love and encouragement, I would not have been able to start writing this book in your basement all those years ago. You have been nothing but positive in the face of all the ups and downs I have experienced, and your guidance when making the tough decisions will never be forgotten. Thank you for being early readers, the comforting hugs and the unending patience when I was feeling just a bit dramatic.

To my ever supportive sisters, Lindsey and Katie, thank you for always cheering me on and sharing my social media posts. I could not ask for better siblings to see their baby sister through all the trials and tribulations.

To the members of the Women's Fiction Writers Association, words cannot describe what you and this organization have done for my writing, my community and my appreciation of the arts. It has been an honour to enter the query trenches together and follow alongside all your journeys. In particular I want to mention Orly Konig, for jumping at the chance to offer early feedback on a rough draft, Laura Drake and Kelly Duran for helping me hone a messy query letter and Tiffany Yates Martin, who I was lucky to be paired with in the WFWA mentorship program and forced me (somewhat reluctantly) to change the order of some of my chapters for the better.

To the ladies of Same Story Different Year, a sub-group of WFWA, thank you for supporting me on my journey each step of the way and asking me excited questions about how it was going. Thank you, Kathy Dodson for starting the weekly write-ins that keep me accountable and productive (My editor also thanks you!)

To my friend, Luke Lichty for answering so many questions without complaint!

To my Scribophile friends, Stuart Turnbull and Eric Hubbard who started this writing journey with me and helped me hone my craft into something that is legible.

To the Ubergroup, thank you for the countless rounds of beta readers. To Polly Brown, Laura Creedle, Susan C. Boesger and K. Rina, for helping me cut unnecessary words and merge similar characters.

To Taher Safavi for being an amazing friend, mentor, uberlord, cheerleader and "boyfriend" from the cross the border. Without you and your acceptance of me, my craft would not be what it is today.

I want to thank Emily Montfort for encouraging my journey and constantly sharing her favourite novels with me. And Jillian Westbrook for being an early reader and falling head over heels in love with Jack.

To my Collingwood girl-gang and book club, thank you for keeping me reading and encouraging my writing time. I know you are all anxious to see this final project and I cannot wait to be part of the discussion around it.

To Mike Singh, thank you for your patience with my many writing ventures and meetings over the last year and for the times when I blew you off because I had to write.

Thank you to all my wonderful readers who took the chance on a new author and followed along Maddie's turbulent journey. I hope you enjoyed it and I hope it helps bring peace to those ever nagging what if questions.

And finally, to my bestie Celeste Rattray, without whom there would be no writing. If not for our wild backpacking trip and the casual pass off of a notebook, writing a novel professionally would have never crossed my mind. Thank you for being a steady reader, support system and always having my back. You are my person and this one is for you.

The Things We Lost

MAGGIE GILES

Questions for discussion

1. At the beginning Maddie is very unhappy in love and life. She struggles to find a reason to feel joy daily and the only thing holding her to this world is the love she feels for her daughters. She tries to pinpoint where she and Nathan went wrong and seems to put a lot of blame on Nathan. How fair, in your opinion, is her assessment of their relationship and how does it change throughout the book?

2. When Maddie learns more about her new life, she realizes all the mistakes she has made in the present and past. Do you have any big regrets that you believe would have greatly impacted the route your life took? In what ways do you think you would be different now?

3. Maddie's biggest fear is never seeing her children again. How would you feel if you woke up tomorrow with a completely different life and those most precious to you were gone?

4. What do you think happened to Maddie at the end of the book?

5. Knowing Gina's fate in both timelines, do you think Maddie was in any way responsible or if she could have done anything different to help?

6. Maddie became a very different person when she let her life take a different path. Do you have any past relationships that may have changed you as a person if you had continued to hold on to them?

7. Having met Brian in both the past and the present, how did his obsession with Maddie affect her choices and influence the path she took?

8. The title "The Things We Lost" explores the idea that Maddie maybe lost more than she gained by going back in time. Do you think she will be happier in this new timeline, grateful for what she has than she would have been if she had never been given a second chance?

9. When Maddie discovers the truth about her relationship with Jack, she has mixed feelings of dread and excitement. What does this say about her character when it comes to her relationship with Arabella and Jayson?

10. Maddie wants nothing more than to return home and right her mistakes. When she is not given a chance to, she works towards mending her relationships and finding a way to connect with Nathan. Given where she was in life, do you think she could have been more aggressive in her pursuit of Nathan and attempt to right her story?

11. Throughout the novel, Maddie has flashes of memories and a personality that she didn't' realize was a part of her. Do you believe that by entering

this alternative timeline her previous life effectively no longer existed, or do you think there are multiple lives out there where different choices were made and they co-exist along side each other?

12. Jayson is a prominent character in both parts of Maddie's life. She attributes a lot of changes to him and how he re-entered her life. Do you think it's fair for Maddie to put so much intention on Jayson when he too was just living his life and making his own choices?

13. Dee and Maddie had been best friends for ages. A couple big mistakes caused them to drift apart, something Maddie truly regretted. Do you feel they both equally caused the relationship to flounder? How do you feel about Dee giving Maddie a second chance despite everything they had been through? Do you believe their friendship will be as strong as it was in the past?

14. When Maddie begins to take responsibility for her actions, she starts to realize she is the product of her own unhappiness. As humans, we put a lot of pressure on happiness and finding it wherever we can. How much do you think our happiness relies directly on our choices and how likely is it that we can find happiness despite the scenarios we put ourselves in?

About the Author

Photo credit: Captured by Kirsten

Maggie Giles is a Canadian author who is usually daydreaming about fictional characters. Always looking for a new creative outlet, Maggie dove into writing a novel head-first. She has been a member of the Women's Fiction Writers Association since 2014 where she works as their Social Media Director. She lives in Collingwood, Ontario with her Bullmastiff Cross. *The Things We Lost* is her first novel. To learn more visit maggiegiles.com